THE
GAME
YOU PLAYED

ANNI TAYLOR

THE GAME YOU PLAYED

First Edition July 2016
ISBN-13: 978-1534888821
ISBN-10: 1534888829

PROLOGUE

THERE ARE TWO TYPES OF PEOPLE in this world. People who steal other people and people who don't.

There are lots of ways of stealing a person.

Grabbing a small child and running away with them is one of the worst ways of all.

Six months ago, you did that.

In the last days of December, the city of Sydney is shot with the blistering heat of summer, buzzing with festivals and exhibitions. The voices of Chinese, Japanese, British, American and other international tourists mingle with those of Australian couples and families.

At Darling Harbour, people dart in and out of the zoo, museums, and the IMAX, while diners people-watch from the open-air upmarket cafés and restaurants that hug the square-shaped harbour. In the middle of all this, a playground captures the children's attention. The children grow shouty as they race from the water park to the giant slide to the climbing frames, their hands and faces sticky with ice-cream.

Luke and I were there then with our two-year-old son, Tommy.

You were there, too. Watching.

Waiting for your chance to snatch him.

Already, you had the letters prepared—the letters about Tommy you'd start sending us six months later.

The game was about to start. Only I didn't know it.

He gave a toddlerish shout of approval, his small face creasing then as he turned his attention to the complications of managing the ebb and flow of water through the canals.

Luke's phone rang—it was his mother. I could tell by the sudden change in his tone. Even though she was staying with us, she called him several times a day.

"Tommy, do you want an ice-cream?" Luke said as soon as he'd finished the call.

Tommy thought for a second, his chubby fist tightening on the boat, then shook his head.

"Okay, well, I'm going to get one." Luke dropped the phone back into his shirt pocket.

I shielded my eyes from the sun. "Just get one scoop in Tommy's."

"He just said he didn't want one."

"He thinks he'll have to leave the water to get ice-cream. Of course he wants one."

Luke laughed his booming laugh, shaking his head at Tommy's toddler logic. His voice carried, and people glanced at us, smiling. Luke always laughed easily. It was one of the things I loved about him, about *us*. His easy-going nature had become so intertwined with me, I could take credit for it and bask in it.

A couple of mothers nearby gave their children grabby hugs and kisses on their foreheads. Luke's feel-good nature was infectious. As he strolled away, the mothers watched him, but I watched them. They wore long cargo shorts and long pastel T-shirts and pastel hats. Their husbands were dressed in the same outfits as their tiny sons. They were nothing like Luke and I, in their pastel tutti-frutti. We were the café set in our greys and blacks and neutrals.

But as I watched the tutti-fruttis, something was wrong. A sadness crept inside me that I didn't understand, draining the saturation from the day and giving a leaden quality to the air. Like something had just been snatched away from me.

No, that's not right. I imagined I felt that way.

I was a trained actor, and actors sometimes slipped into roles without realising what they were doing. (Okay, so I'd only sometimes been a *paid* actor, but it had still been my profession.)

I blinked as I turned back to the water canals, adjusting my eyes to the sun's sudden glare as the day turned from grey to yellow again.

Tommy wasn't in the same spot.

My stomach dropped, as it had a hundred times before when I'd momentarily lost sight of him. He moved like his feet were on wheels. But he was never too far away.

I raked my gaze along the snaking paths of the canals.

He wasn't *anywhere*.

Jumping to my feet, I padded around the edges of the water park, searching. Having no idea which direction to head in, I looked for clues as to what had caused him to wander off. It'd have to be something pretty damned compelling to tear him away from the water. Some other kid's toy? A puppy?

"Tommy," I called.

There must have been a worried edge to my voice—one of the T-shirted mothers looked my way with sympathetic eyes.

"Tommy! Daddy's got your ice-cream!" If he was accidentally-on-purpose ignoring me, that would make him come running.

But Tommy didn't produce himself. How could he be so far away that he was out of earshot? I only looked away from him for a moment. Didn't I? *Didn't I?*

I calmed myself. He must be absorbed in something. That's all. Too busy in his own little world. But a wave of panic careened into my island of calm.

Tommy! Tommy! Tommy!

I was running now, calling out frantically. No longer caring about looking like a crazy woman who couldn't keep watch over one small boy while other women were happily herding tribes of kids about.

A pale, red-haired woman with a baby on her hip touched my arm—one of the T-shirt women. "I'll help you look. He's about two, right? What's he wearing?"

"He was wearing blue," I said, both relieved and shocked. The fact that someone was worried enough to offer help meant that things had gone a step further. Tommy was lost.

"All blue? A hat?"

I nodded. "Blue shorts and T-shirt. Yes, a hat." *Which hat?* The one I'd bought from a fair last month. "It's blue as well. With a giraffe on the front."

"What's his name?"

"Tommy. It's Tommy."

She hurried across to the T-shirt brigade, most of them with young children and babies. "We'll see if we can spot him," she called back. Three sets of pram-wielding persons moved off in different directions.

My heart sank. There were hundreds of little boys here that looked just like Tommy, unless you were close enough and low enough to look under his hat. How were strangers going to find him when I couldn't spot him myself?

A thought jumped into my mind, and I grabbed hold of it. Maybe Tommy tried to follow his father. Yes, that was the only explanation.

I headed towards the cafés. Luke was ambling back to the water park, laden with ice-cream and drinks. *Without Tommy.*

Luke stiffened like a pole at the sight of my anxious face and the sight of people moving about in unexpected patterns behind me, gently calling Tommy's name. It was instantly clear what the problem was.

"Where's Tommy?" he asked reflexively.

"Luke! Tommy just wandered off!" Everything was okay now. Luke would find Tommy.

"What do you mean he just wandered off?" He stared down at his cardboard tray of ice-cream for a moment, as though he didn't know what to do with it. "Where was the last place you saw him?"

The way Luke was staring at me in fear and disbelief caused a stabbing feeling in my stomach that reached all the way to my throat. "Exactly where he was when you left."

"He's probably still there somewhere." Luke made his way back to the water canals. I followed, glad to have some sort of direction.

Luke stopped and stared at the spot where we'd last seen Tommy, like it should have an arrow pointing to where Tommy had gone. He hurried around the canals, searching. His eyes filled with a hazy panic. "*Fuck.* What if he headed for the harbour? To sail his boat?" Dumping the cardboard tray of ice-cream and drinks in the trash, he bounded away.

My breath stilled. I didn't think of the harbour. It didn't even enter my head that he could get that far. What if the whole time I'd been looking for him, he'd been heading in a beeline for the water?

I trailed after Luke—Luke already far ahead of me.

But there was no tufty-haired Tommy anywhere along the long line of concrete steps that edged the harbour. I scanned the surface of the water alongside Luke.

"Call the police," Luke called to me. "I'm going to keep looking."

I fumbled in my pockets, searching for my phone. Neither my fingers nor my mind was working. I couldn't find the damned phone. Terror roared inside me.

The red-haired woman moved in front of my face again. "Excuse me, I just called the police for you. I hope that's okay."

Something in the way she said that and the guarded look in her eyes made me think it was *me* she was concerned about. But I was imagining that, surely. I was a responsible parent. As responsible as *she* was for the red-haired baby on her hip.

"Thank you," I breathed, although I wanted her to go away—her and her doppelgänger baby who was staring at me reproachfully.

It seemed wrong that a stranger had taken it into their hands to call the police before I did. Tommy was *my* child. And the more that strangers pushed their way in, the farther away Tommy got from me.

By the time the police arrived, a frantic half hour had gone by.

Luke and I met up again. He handed me his phone. "It's Saskia." He hadn't answered it yet—there was just her name flashing on the screen.

My mind grabbed onto yet another desperate possibility. Had Saskia found him just wandering around and she was calling to tell me?

"Phoebe," she said in an excited voice. "I couldn't get you on your phone, so I tried Luke's. There's an art exhibition you *have* to see with me!"

"Sass, I—"

"What's wrong?" she interrupted.

"Tommy."

"My God, what? What happened?"

"He's missing, Sass. He's just *gone*. We're at the playground at Darling Harbour."

"I'm there."

Fifteen minutes later, Tommy was still missing.

Less than a minute after that point, not only Saskia— but Pria and Kate—were rushing up to me. The whole gang. I had no idea how Sass had been able to rally them and herself so quickly.

My friends' faces were blanched with worry. They all loved Tommy. Sass, with her strawberry-blond waves spilling over her red city jacket. Kate, with her impossibly straight brown hair and gym clothing form-fitting her angular model's body. Pria, with her warm dark eyes and shoulder-length blond hair and soft green dress. Sass worked for a company a couple of blocks from here, organising home renovation shows. Kate did brochure modelling but was mostly at home with her three-year-old twins. Pria, a single mother with a daughter, worked from a home office as a counsellor.

I was too numb to feel their sympathetic hugs, oblivious even to the December heat that had me complaining earlier.

Pria held my arms, her brown eyes crinkled and anxious beneath her thick fringe. "Honey, what can we do to help?"

"Pray," I said, my voice cracking.

"We'll spread out." Kate tied her hair into a messy knot. "Maybe he's scared and hiding." She nodded firmly. "That's what my twins used to do at that age."

Sass whipped out her phone. "I'm calling the media."

"The what?" I frowned. "What would—"

"It's my job to know this stuff," Saskia told me, her tone brisk and efficient. "If you need help in a hurry, call the media. Every minute counts, right? Well, we're going to blast this across Sydney. Everyone in this city is going to know there's a little boy missing, and they're going to be on the lookout." She stopped for a breath. "Trust me."

While Saskia called up her media contacts, Pria and Kate raced away. I noticed then that Luke's business partner—Rob Lynch—was talking with Luke.

Somehow, it panicked me that everyone was rushing down here. No one was treating this casually. No one was saying, *never mind, Phoebe, he'll turn up in a little bit.* This was serious. And everyone knew it was serious.

Fifteen minutes later, Tommy was still missing. He'd been missing an entire hour. An army of people had joined the search, moving in swarms. The voices of strangers, male and female, called Tommy's name. My son's name. Until I wanted to scream at them: *You're going to frighten him. Stop yelling his name. Just . . . find him.*

But they couldn't find him.

Because he was no longer here to be found.

2. PHOEBE

FOUR DAYS LATER
January 2

I DIDN'T KNOW WHAT CLOTHES TO put on my body. What did one wear to a press conference to talk about her missing child? What would people make of me, watching from their TV screens, bleary and hungover from New Year's Eve celebrations?

It was one of the few occasions in my life that I wasn't thinking about how an outfit would suit me or not. I just wanted something that would shield me and would make me look like someone who was capable of watching their child—a responsible parent.

"Time to go." Luke paused at the bedroom door. He had his sensible suit on, the one he wore when meeting older clients at his real estate agency.

"How does this look?" My voice was stiff and unnatural. The fifth outfit I'd tried on was a deep-green jacket and skirt that I'd barely worn. It had fitted me much better last time I'd worn it—that was before I was even pregnant with Tommy. Now, it fitted too snugly. It was stupid, worrying about my weight today, but people would be judging me. If I couldn't look perfect, I had to *be* perfect. I had my dark hair scraped back into a severe ponytail and had swapped my usual red lipstick for a subdued shade. I felt like an imposter, trying too hard to look like something I wasn't.

"You look just right, Phoebe."

I knew that he'd say that no matter what. But his words gave me the courage to walk out of the house.

We drove to the police station, and the police drove us to the media conference from there.

Luke gave my hand a few pumping squeezes as we were guided to two seats behind a set of narrow tables, alongside the detective in charge of the case—Detective Trent Gilroy.

The press were already assembled. So many of them, their faces eager, their cameras ready. Fixed microphones were set up on the table in front of us.

The detective leaned close to Luke and me. "Remember what I said yesterday? They'll fire all kinds of questions. You don't have to answer them all. It's okay to say you're not prepared to answer a particular question."

My throat was too dry to talk. How was I going to face answering questions?

"Hell." Even Luke—unflappable Luke—was nervous. "They're not going to interrogate us, are they?"

"No," the detective answered. "Well, a few might try. But I'll stop them if they go too far."

Luke sat back, nodding obediently.

We were out of our depth. We shouldn't be here. It was Tuesday today. Luke was supposed to be at work. I was supposed to be at home, wiping sticky custard from Tommy's hands and face.

It was only when I heard Detective Gilroy speak my son's name that I realised the conference had begun. He was saying:

". . . and in the four days that have passed since Tommy Basko went missing, the police and rescue teams have mounted massive operations in order to locate him. Police divers and other experts in retrieval of bodies from water have searched what they can of the harbour. All footage from Sydney council cameras in the area has been painstakingly analysed. We've also had teams going through hours of video shot by visitors to the harbour area at the time of Tommy's disappearance.

We're confident but cautious in saying that we believe that Tommy didn't wander down to the water that day. He didn't get that far. The most likely scenario is that Tommy was taken or led away from the area in which his parents last saw him. We're following a number of leads and also investigating information given to us by persons who were in the area that day. At this point in time, we're hopeful that Tommy is alive. And our focus is on his safe return to his family."

Detective Gilroy glanced at us, giving us an encouraging nod of his head. "Tommy's parents would like to give a statement to the press now."

Beneath the table, Luke still had my hand. He lowered his head to the microphone. "My wife and I have suffered every day, every hour, and every minute since our son went missing. We need to know where he is. He only just had his second birthday on the fifth of December. He needs us. And we need him. Anyone who was in the area taking photos or video that day, who hasn't already come forward, please contact the police. It doesn't matter if they were taken before or after our son disappeared—they still might hold a vital clue."

Luke's eyelashes were wet when he looked at me. He tightened his hold on my hand as I prepared myself to speak.

"Please," I began, "we just need Tommy back. Someone out there knows exactly where he is. Just give him back. Give him back to us. *Please.*"

My carefully worded speech had fallen apart at the seams. I was begging, pleading, trying to appeal to people who didn't care. Because whoever had taken Tommy didn't care about us. They'd stolen him from us. I felt raw, sounded raw. Like I'd been split open and my insides were on display. Cameras flashed in my eyes.

It'll be over soon, I told myself.

Saskia had told me I needed to do this. It was my second appeal to the public. She'd set up the first one—an impromptu interview at the playground—an hour and a half after Tommy vanished. She'd told me that holding it as soon as possible was best, and at the place where Tommy went missing (the playground), and that to have the mother appeal directly to the public was better still. People operated on emotion, and a mother desperate to find her child would have everyone's sympathies. She'd quickly schooled me on how to act. No matter how much I wanted to run off and keep searching, I had to give the camera my full attention. Forget everything else. I had to be exactly what the public wanted to see. I had to cry, even if I was too much in shock to cry yet.

After the interview with the reporter had started, and after I'd ended up freezing and faltering, Sass had taken over, filling the reporters in on all the details. She'd even supplied them with photographs and short video clips that she had of Tommy on her phone.

She'd been completely right that the media would pick up the story and run hard with it. Within an hour, all of Australia knew Tommy's name and what he looked like. They knew what colour his eyes were and what his giggles sounded like.

She'd coached me before the press conference, too. It was important to show a united front together with Luke. In the eyes of the public, we had to be model parents. Luke and I must never so much as squabble in public.

Detective Gilroy shot me a reassuring glance. He cleared his throat and told the press they could ask questions now.

I stiffened like a deer in headlights. I was the parent who was with Tommy when he disappeared. Not Luke. The questions would be for me.

At first, there came a flurry of questions about how we'd been coping, if we'd sought counselling, and if we were offering a reward for the safe return of Tommy.

Detective Gilroy pointed to a skinny, bearded man in the front row who had his hand up.

The bearded man stood. He was tall, his shoulders looking as if they were permanently lopsided from the weight of the camera equipment he wore on his right side. "Mrs Basko, what was Tommy doing the last time you saw him?"

"He had a little plastic yacht, and he was sailing it in the canals at the water park." I'd already answered this one many times in the past four days.

He thumbed his beard. "You were talking with someone at the time Tommy disappeared. Who was that?"

I stared at him, confused. "I wasn't with anyone at that time. Just Tommy."

"Sorry," he said, "I meant to say you were on the phone to someone. On your mobile."

"No, I wasn't on the phone," I told him. "I actually didn't have my phone with me at all. I lost it sometime before going to the playground that day."

He blinked his eyes tiredly, but there was a glazed glint in his eyes. He wasn't going to let this one go. "I was one of the first reporters on the scene. I spent quite a bit of time going around talking to the people who were searching. I found a woman who was at the water park at the same time as you and Tommy. She said she'd seen you on the phone, with your son playing next to you."

I frowned, startled, twisting my head around to Detective Gilroy. He shrugged slightly, a vague look of confusion tempering the annoyance in his eyes.

I turned back to the man. "She's mistaken, whoever she is. She must be thinking of my husband. He took a call, from his mother. It was right after that point that Tommy went missing."

Detective Gilroy inclined his head towards the microphone. "We'll leave it there."

The bearded journalist didn't sit down. "Her name is Elizabeth Farrell. A redhead. She also said that you and your husband had some kind of tense argument just before the kid—your son—went missing."

The detective nodded. "We've spoken with Elizabeth. There was nothing mentioned about a phone call. Or an argument. There was a slight disagreement about ice-cream. Completely normal talk between a husband and wife. I'd advise everyone here not to report this as fact, because it's not in the official statement from the person in question. The last set of questions needs to be edited out of the footage. Please, no more questions down this line."

The man reluctantly seated himself.

I exhaled a tightly held breath as the next question came. This one was for Luke. Relieved, I sat back in my chair.

A woman with sharp eyes and dyed black hair stood. "Luke—Mr Basko—you left the water park to get ice-creams. Is it possible that Tommy followed you?"

Luke hunched his shoulders—a protective mechanism. "It's possible."

"Did you go directly to get ice-creams?" she asked him.

"Yes. Straight there."

"I'm asking because it seems there was a bit of a disagreement between your wife and yourself at the time. Maybe you went to grab yourself a beer first and cool down? Maybe you went somewhere that Tommy couldn't follow?"

"No, I didn't go get a beer." Luke sounded annoyed. "And that was hardly a disagreement. Tommy said he didn't want an ice-cream and Phoebe insisted that he did. He thought getting ice-cream meant leaving the water park. I just don't understand toddler talk like my wife does."

"Mr Basko," said the woman, "I understand. I have a four-year-old at home. I was just framing a likely scenario. I know that when you turn around and your child is gone, often they've followed a family member or friend of the family. The child thinks they're safe, because they're with a trusted person. Only, they're not safe, because the person has no idea they've got a kid following behind."

Detective Gilroy adjusted his microphone. "We agree that it's the most likely scenario. That Tommy followed his father. But we can't say that for sure, and we have to remain open to any possibility. We've studied all video footage between the water park and the ice-creamery that we've had available to us so far, and we haven't found anything conclusive. We're following up on a number of avenues of investigation. In short, the person who took Tommy will be in a number of the videos taken that day. It's just a question of time before we discover their identity."

The reporter nodded, seeming satisfied with that, and she sat down again.

Trent Gilroy breathed deeply and spoke into the microphone again. "The person who has Tommy Basko needs to either present themselves at a police station or release Tommy to a safe place—a school or a hospital. Because we *will* find out who you are, and the safe return of Tommy will go in your favour."

The detective ended the conference there. It was over.

3.   PHOEBE

SIX MONTHS LATER
Late June, Tuesday night

I GLANCED AT THE TIME AND panicked. Almost 6:00 p.m.

Luke would be home from work any minute. And I looked like I'd slept the day away and had barely been up out of bed. Which was true.

I changed my clothes, ran a brush through my hair, and applied a minimal amount of makeup. Then dashed out to the courtyard to spray the plants with water. As long as they were wet, the plants gave the appearance of being looked after. Cucumbers were actually growing on the trellis, against all odds. Maybe I could make a show of picking them and putting them in a salad tonight. Wait, no, it was Tuesday. Luke always bought Thai on Tuesdays. My head was fuzzy—so fuzzy. I forgot things.

Next, I did a tour of the house, moving a few cushions around, switching the TV on, opening a magazine, placing a couple of plates by the sink. Enough to look like I'd been down here during the day. Enough to look like I'd eaten.

Then I rushed upstairs. The last stop on the tour was for my sake, not for Luke's. I headed into my bedroom and pulled out the shoebox in my wardrobe. Six packets of sleeping tablets left. I counted the number of tablets in each packet. It was a ritual I performed every day. Maybe I was more like my mother than I thought. She'd had undiagnosed OCD tendencies.

I needed those tablets. There was no guarantee my psychiatrist would prescribe me more of them.

In the drawer in my bedside table, I kept two packets of the sleeping pills and three of the antidepressants. The pills in the drawer were the only ones Luke knew about.

I never took any of the antidepressants. I flushed two of those tablets down the toilet every day. I only wanted the sleeping tablets. I took one of those from the packet in my bedside table every night, and two from the secret stash in the shoebox.

Luke would never understand why I was taking so many of the pills. These were a new type of sleeping tablet that Dr Moran—my psychiatrist—had switched me to a couple of months back. I'd begged her for something stronger. The pills I'd had weren't working. I wasn't sleeping.

The new pills had had unexpected side effects. They'd given me extraordinarily vivid dreams. Dreams that were of Tommy. Always of Tommy. I couldn't see him anymore in real life, but I could visit him in dreams. I could see him and smell him and touch him. I could even direct the dreams to some extent.

I'd asked my psych about the episodes, and she'd mentioned *lucid dreams*. In a lucid dream, you were conscious that you were dreaming and you could make things happen within the dream. Everything was sharp and real and intense. I could be in the middle of a field of wildflowers, with Tommy in my lap, listening to him try to sing a song (he'd hum most of the words). I could walk with him down a city street, his tiny hand in mine, just walking and experiencing the world together. I could put him to sleep in his bed and brush his streaky blond hair back from his forehead. I'd never realised how precious those small things were when Tommy was here.

The worst times were when I'd wake from a dream of Tommy. My heart would tear in two all over again. I'd curl myself up tightly and bawl (being careful not to wake Luke).

I'd become an addict to my dream world.

Last Saturday had marked a whole six months of Tommy being gone. *Six months.* My dreams were my only path back to him.

I must have alarmed Dr Moran in some way when I'd spoken to her about the dreams because she'd said that it might be an idea to switch back to the old sleeping pills.

A week ago, the pills stopped having the same effect. I'd sleep dreamless sleeps. I was in darkness, searching, but finding nothing.

In desperation, I took an extra tablet.

That night, I'd woken outside in our courtyard. In the moonlit darkness. I'd been watching Tommy play with his set of trucks. He'd loaded the pebbles from the garden into the dump truck and giggled hysterically as he tipped the pebbles out again (everything was hysterically funny to toddlers).

Even inside the dream, it'd seemed wrong that I was allowing him out here at night. Bad mothering. But he was so happy, I didn't have the heart to tell him to come in. When I tried to pick him up, he somehow slipped through my fingers.

Then I'd woken fully. Alone in the courtyard.

It was the first time my dreams had physically taken me to another location.

I should have stopped the pills then.

But I couldn't stop.

I'd woken in different rooms of the house every night of the past week.

Once at the front gate of the house.

But I had Tommy back again.

I lived for the nights. I'd spend all day in a depression so deep, I was buried in it.

Every week since Tommy had gone missing, the news websites seemed to have some new snippet of information about what might have happened to Tommy. But none of it led to anything. My hopes would be raised and crushed. Raised and crushed.

Speculation. So much speculation. Maybe it was the mother. Maybe it was the father. Maybe he fell into the harbour, after all, and became entangled in the ropes of a boat and then had been taken so far into the heart of Sydney Harbour that no one would ever find him. And the media reminded people that the harbour was full of sharks.

The police talked of lonely, desperate women who took other people's children sometimes. They talked of people who were prepared to pay a kidnapping ring to snatch the child they want and pretend to themselves it was a type of adoption. The other endings for Tommy were worse. Being murdered by a paedophile or psychopath.

It was all talk. I was bone weary of the talk. No one knew anything. It was all *what if* and *what could be*. It was all *continuing investigations* and *leads*. In the end, it was just all goose chases and finger pointing and gossip.

All I remembered of the minutes before Tommy went missing was a strange sense of dread and the stop of transmission in my mind. But was that because of what was about to happen to Tommy or something else?

4. LUKE

Tuesday night

I GAVE PHOEBE A CALL AT six, to remind her about the dinner tonight.

As I predicted, she'd forgotten.

There was never any guarantee she'd remember what we had scheduled on any day. And even if she did remember, she might have worked herself up into too much of a state to do anything but to sit and stare into space.

She answered the phone and told me she'd been planting lettuce seedlings out in the garden. I breathed out relief. That meant it was one of her better days. We only had the tiniest courtyard, but I'd paid for a wall garden to be installed a couple of months back. Cost me a packet. It had a mix of flowers, herbs, and vegetables. Phoebe seemed to like it. She watered it and fiddled about, planting things. Before the garden, I'd bought her a puppy—one of those poodle-mix fluff balls that the breeder told me you need to keep inside. I thought it could be company for her. Phoebe promptly gave it back. *I can't take care of anything,* she'd told me.

"Phoebe," I said, "I'll be home at six thirty, and we'll head out to the restaurant at seven, okay?"

Silence for a few moments. "Isn't this the night we have Thai?"

"Yeah. But tonight we were going out for dinner. Remember?"

"Oh. That's right. I haven't got much of an appetite. Is it okay if I skip it?"

"No, babe, it's not okay. These dinners are not about dinner. It's networking. You know that."

"Yeah, I know . . ."

"So, you'll go?"

"I'm really kind of tired."

"Feeb, it's really important to me. You're my wife. I'd like you by my side sometimes."

"It's business, Luke. Not a social occasion."

"But it's all couples who'll be there. It's that kind of thing. And you have to eat anyway, even if you're not that hungry. You need to eat. The doctor said so."

I heard her softly sigh.

"All right, I'll go," she told me.

"You will?"

"Yes."

It could have easily gone the other way. She almost always refused to leave the house.

I drove home at exactly 6:15. Any earlier, and Phoebe might say I was rushing her. Any later, and she might say she thought that the plan had been changed and that dinner was off.

She was wearing all pale grey—a thin wrap top and wrap skirt that both tied at the back. Her long hair was in a sleek knot, and she had a bit of colour in her face for a change. She looked incredible. Bemused by the expression I must have had plastered on my face, she asked me to fix the ties of her outfit.

Somehow, the outfit was exactly Phoebe. Like her, it looked fragile.

She didn't say much on the drive to the restaurant. But she was with me and making an effort, and I hadn't been able to ask for more than that for months.

The restaurant was new and expensive. It had a no-children policy, and I'd chosen it deliberately for that alone. I hated to watch Phoebe staring forlornly at the toddler of some other couple. Also, it made the parents uncomfortable when she stared. Sometimes, it was me staring at lookalike Tommys. If people didn't like Phoebe staring at their kid, they even less liked some strange guy staring.

My business partner Rob and his wife Ellie were already there with the two couples who were among our best clients: Cindy and Grant Clofield and Mirima and Orlando Suez. The clients were in their midthirties, with a multitude of properties in Sydney, Queensland, and the US. I aspired to be like them. As did Rob and Ellie.

It was important to surround yourself with those at a higher level than yourself. The Clofields and the Suezes had a lifestyle I wanted. They afforded Rob and me lucrative sales commissions, and they also supplied our agency with contacts we couldn't have accessed on our own. By the time I was thirty-five, which was a little over five years away, I planned to be at the top of my game. And then Phoebe and I could combine months of overseas travel with business acquisitions and networking, just like the Clofields and Suezes did.

I didn't know where any future children fitted into the dream. The Clofields had no kids. The Suezes had two young ones that they took with them on the overseas trips, paying for nannies and tutors along the way. Whether Phoebe would ever want to have another kid was uncertain. She hadn't brought the subject up. She'd loved Tommy to bits, but she'd struggled with motherhood. Motherhood had been a foreign land to her.

The party of six sitting at our table waved as we stepped over. I had my hand lightly on the small of Phoebe's back, steering her in. I knew she'd prefer to run back to the car and drive home. I could feel her apprehension through her skin. But she somehow switched modes when everyone greeted her. She became the old Phoebe who easily charmed people. She took a sip of the white wine that Mirima poured for her and told her it was wonderful.

I knew exactly what Phoebe was doing. She'd slipped into a role. She was playing the part of my wife, a supporting role. And she could play a part better than anyone I knew. When she used to perform in theatre, she took the limelight whenever she walked on stage. Not deliberately, but there was something about her that just captured people. A fragility that had an undercurrent of strength. It was the thing about Phoebe that had terrified me the most in those days. That some director would swoop on her and carry her away and make her a star and then she'd become inaccessible to me. When she agreed to marry me, she was already pregnant with Tommy. At the back of my mind, I always wondered if she would have said yes to me if her belly hadn't been swelling by the day.

Everyone clinked glasses. It was a good start.

"So what's new with you both?" Phoebe asked Mirima. "It's been a while since I last saw you."

"Lots of little things," answered Mirima in her faintly Chilean accent. "I'm taking Asian cooking classes. And Ollie got the idea that he can play drums, and so he bought a drum kit. I think I need to buy ear plugs."

It was typical Mirima. She downplayed their wealth and acquisitions, and she chatted about the everyday stuff. She hadn't talked about her kids in front of Phoebe ever since Tommy vanished, except in passing. I was grateful for that.

"Hey," Orlando protested. "I'm no Dave Lombardo, but I can bash out a bit of a set."

"*Bash* being the operative word," said Mirima dryly.

Phoebe laughed. I rarely heard her laugh anymore.

"And what's new with you, Phoebe?" Cindy Clofield turned her sleek blonde head and bright-blue eyes towards Phoebe. I was nervous as I noticed Phoebe hesitating to answer. Cindy was smart as a whip when it came to business dealings, but I knew she had little understanding of Phoebe's situation. She was the kind of woman who was always on the go and didn't let anything hold her back. She lost her father in a car accident last year, and she picked herself up the week after and negotiated the purchase of a two-million-dollar apartment.

If I had to choose a wife from the table, other than Phoebe, it would be Mirima. Cindy was too much like me. And Ellie was too much like Rob—pushy and over-critical. Mirima had a warmth that even Phoebe lacked.

It seemed to me that all couples ran on different types of fuel. The Clofields were fuelled by the cold closing of the deal—life for them was all about the relentless churn of wealth for its own sake. Rob and Ellie Lynch were fuelled by nothing ever being good enough, and so they needed the next big thing that was going to make them happy. The Suezes were fuelled by the poor background they grew up in—they were constantly outrunning it, trying to ramp up their wealth so that things couldn't ever come crashing down on them. The Suezes kept telling me it was all for the kids, and I knew they believed that, but their kids already had far more than they could ever want or need. But I guessed there was always that next level. No matter how rich you were, there was always someone on a higher level than you.

What was it that Phoebe and I were fuelled by? There was a time I would have said that we were fuelled by the same thing. We were both adrenalin junkies. We liked doing things that terrified the living daylights out of us, like deep sea diving in a remote part of the world where we didn't even know the language. Phoebe once backpacked China on her own. Building up my real estate business from scratch seemed like a natural extension of that. Anyone looking at Phoebe now would say she was fuelled by the search for Tommy. Anyone looking at me now would say I was fuelled by my business. But I wasn't. I was fuelled by Phoebe. Everything I did was for her.

Everyone was still waiting for Phoebe to answer Cindy's question. Phoebe eyed Cindy in that direct gaze of hers that took no prisoners.

"What's new?" Phoebe finally said, repeating Cindy's question. "Not enough."

It caused a stall in the conversation. I knew exactly what Phoebe meant. There was nothing new and of note in the search for Tommy. I didn't blame her for answering in the way she did. Socialising was hard for her these days.

Everyone was too uncomfortable to jump in and say anything. It was up to me.

"Hey, people," I said. "Phoebe and I were wondering if you'd all like to head out on the yacht after dinner. Sail around the harbour for a bit. For winter, it's a nice night."

Phoebe nodded, and everyone visibly relaxed.

I hadn't taken the yacht out for over a month. I had a few bottles of a nice red stored on there—I could break out a couple of those. The wine should be maturing nicely—faster than on land due to the sway of the boat.

Most of all, I hoped Phoebe would enjoy a trip around the harbour. She didn't do anything with her days, didn't find joy in anything.

I'd do anything to change that.

5.   PHOEBE

DREAMING

IT WAS A STRANGE MIST, FOR summer.

Sydney in December should be smothered in summer humidity, inescapable and suffocating on the hottest of the days.

But the night was cold. The mist curled around the chipped edges of corner buildings and massed in alleyways. My mind was cloudy and confused. I needed to focus.

I caught a blur of Tommy's T-shirt as he headed into one of those foggy alleys. I didn't understand why he was out here in the darkness, but I needed to catch him.

He was too fast for me. Even though Tommy was just two, his little legs were quick. He stalled every now and again and peered back at me, making me think I could catch him. But it was just a ploy.

Stopping yet again, he stared at me solemnly from beneath his messy dark-blond mop, knowing he was out of reach.

I ached to touch him, to encircle him in my arms, have him *koala* onto my side like he used to. He'd been gone far, far too long. How long? I couldn't remember. Had it just been a day? A week?

Tommy shook his head. "You'll never find me, Mummy, if you don't know where to look for me."

Tommy couldn't speak quite that well before he went away. How did he learn to talk like that?

"But I already found you, Tommy. I can see you. I can hear you."

He just eyed me blankly.

I clenched my fists as old homeless men stirred in their blankets in the alleyway, like bundles of rags come to life. I hadn't noticed them before. Every one of them looked the same. Long, greyish hair and tangled beards, like wizards.

They knew everything, saw everything, but told nothing.

I was sure of it.

Tommy seemed to have grown bored of the game because he was already running away. I chased him down street after street. All the way to the playground. The playground in which he went missing. He'd never taken me this far before.

Worry wound around and around me like a rope, tightening and suffocating me. There were too many places in which to lose him again. Even when it was the middle of the night and the playground was empty.

Instinctively, I headed for his favourite part of the water park. Where the water streamed through little canals.

He was there, already huddled over a canal, zooming his plastic sailboat backwards and forwards.

Someone shuffled behind me. A bone-chilling mix of crisp, rattling sounds.

When I edged my head around, I saw one of the homeless wizards gazing at me. I hadn't heard him coming. He must have descended from the night sky itself.

He stretched out his hand towards mine, pressing something into the palm of my hand. At first, I thought it was a coin. As if the old man was a gypsy and he was crossing my palm with a gold coin. For luck. But it wasn't a coin. I stared down at my palm to find a moth. A fluttering, half-dead moth with ruined wings.

Why would he give me such a thing?

When I turned back to the water canals, Tommy was gone.

Panic squeezed my heart with an iron fist, punching up into my throat.

Tommy wasn't anywhere. There was just his toy boat lying on its side in the water. But as I ran to it, the boat upended and disappeared completely. Even though the water was only ankle-deep.

I raced back to the wizard man, grabbing his shoulder with my left hand. "Where's my son? Where is he? Where did he go?" My voice rose to a scream, echoing everywhere.

The man gazed back at me with pale, sagging eyes that were hollow underneath. Moisture appeared in his eyes, the wetness tracking into vertical crevices in his cheeks. I was committing a grave sin, harming one of the wise wizard men. But I couldn't stop. He needed to tell me what he knew.

I snapped awake.

Fully awake.

My arms dropped to my sides in horror.

I was here. *At the playground.* Panic buzzed through me.

How did I get all the way to the playground?

Oh God. Oh God. I'd been dreaming.

Sleepwalking.

There was no toy boat.

No moth in my fist.

No Tommy.

It wasn't summer.

It was June.

Winter.

That was the reason for the fog.

Tommy had been missing for six months. Not a day. Not a week. *Six months.*

Jumping back, I held up the palms of my hands in an apologetic gesture. "I'm sorry. So sorry. Please believe me. I didn't mean—"

But I was waving my arms around so much I was frightening him.

No, not frightening him.

Worse.

He wore a defeated expression, as if he was used to people yelling at him and shaking him, while all he was trying to do was survive another night.

I backed away completely.
And ran.

6.   PHOEBE

Wednesday morning

BY THE GREYISH QUALITY OF THE LIGHT, it had to be close to seven in the morning. A chorus of traffic from the streets rumbled to life, as though a button had been pressed to unmute the noise. As I neared the harbour, the first pale light of dawn washed through the sky. Everywhere, the fog sat heavily, pressing on the city.

People sparsely dotted the streets. Drivers delivering loads and early-bird business owners stared openly at me. I was clothed in pyjamas. Barefooted. My steps clumsy.

I was a strange sight for them. Did I need help? Was I drunk? A drug addict? They didn't know, their eyes cautious.

The walk back home seemed to stretch out infinitely.

Hell. I'd come all this way inside a dream.

Anything could have happened to me.

I couldn't take the sleeping pills again.

They'd become dangerous.

The moist, salty air of the ocean clung to my skin as I finally reached Southern Sails Street. My street ran vertically to the docks, rising crookedly up a hill.

The street didn't welcome me. The terrace houses stood with dour expressions. All the houses here were the same inside and out. Tall, narrow, and joined together like skeletal ribs. My family had lived on this street for ten generations. But the houses had older, more distant thoughts than those of a little boy lost and a woman on the edge of losing her mind.

Built by the government over a century ago to house its lowly-paid maritime workers, the terrace houses had stayed the same all this time. Back then, fashionable Sydneysiders didn't want to live in this rat-infested area. No one had cared about the harbour view or the proximity to Circular Quay and the ferries or the history (the first fleet landed here from England in the 1700s). The rats brought the bubonic plague, which swept through Sydney in the two decades from 1900. One of my ancestors had made a fine living as a rat-catcher in those days, until he succumbed to the plague himself. A massive pylon rose behind my street—one end of the Sydney Harbour Bridge. The descendants of the maritime workers, squeezed in the middle of a modern, burgeoning city, had been hanging on by their fingernails. None of them owned their houses. But now, investors were circling like sharks, eyeing this street greedily. The government was selling it off, piece by piece, to the rich. The houses on one side of the street (the lower, less moneyed end) had been knocked down months ago—the flattened side of the street a constant reminder to the residents living on the other side that their time was running out. They'd all soon be gone, too.

My head was woozy. I could still hear the boats knocking against the docks as I headed up the slope of the street. The sounds seemed to scatter and echo everywhere.

Knocking. Knocking. Knocking.

Grabbing a fence, I steadied myself.

I had to get home.

Luke woke at seven every morning, like clockwork. I couldn't let him know I'd been out wandering the city in a dream. I hoped no one else was awake and peering through their windows.

I passed Nan's house at number 25. She was an early riser, but she'd be busy with her housework. Next door to Nan's at number 27 was the Wick house—old Mrs Wick and her thirty-two-year-old daughter

Bernice, who rarely left the house. Both of them slept in until way past ten.

Next was number 29. The abandoned house.

Did a curtain just shift as I passed by? I craned my head to gain a better view. The living room curtain was as it had been for years—hanging on the same crooked slope, undisturbed. Still, I *thought* I'd seen it move. Maybe squatters had moved in. Or maybe it was my memories of that house playing tricks on me. The terrible thing that had happened at that house threatened to push its way into my mind. But I pushed back, as I always did. I'd learned how to shove that memory deep and stop it from surfacing.

I shivered, wishing that of all the houses on this street that were due to be demolished, this one would be next.

Luke's parents' house was next, at number 31. At least I knew that they were away at their holiday house and weren't there to see me walk past in my pyjamas. Their front yard was the most perfect in the street. Tiny, like all the yards—but perfect. They had a gardener looking after it at the moment. Inside and out, their townhouse was pristine.

I envied the kind of home life that the Baskos had given Luke when he was growing up. They hadn't been rich (they'd had more than most on this street), but they'd doted on him. I'd never even heard them argue. Hell, I'd never heard them say an unkind word about anyone. Luke's mother even found compliments for people behaving badly.

I continued up the steep hill that led to the gate of my house. Number 88. The gate was hanging open when I got there. God, I must have blundered through there an hour or so ago, in a dreaming haze.

A stiff blue envelope stuck out of the mailbox. I pulled it out as I stepped past. There was no name or address on the outside. Probably one of those *To The Householder* campaigns that promoted sticky labels for little Sally's school lunchbox and *fat exploder* pills for her mother (because women apparently were in constant need of having their fat exploded).

A faint coffee scent wafted from the envelope. I imagined the letter deliverer gulping a quick cup of coffee in his or her car before running out to stuff mailboxes. I knew the scent, the exact type of coffee. My eyesight wasn't the sharpest for someone my age, but I had the keenest sense of smell of anyone I knew. I could tell what someone had last eaten when they walked near me. At school, I'd always won the blindfold contests where you had to name a scent.

The envelope smelled of the caramel mochaccino that was sold at the Southern Sails Café—the coffee shop down at the harbour end of my street. They roasted their own coffee beans there.

Continuing down the front path, I turned the handle on the front door as slowly and cautiously as if I were trying to crack a safe. Stepping inside, I caught sight of myself in the hall mirror. I could see what everyone had seen on my way here. My hair hung long, dark, and limp around my face and shoulders. A faint dusting of freckles sat on top of chalky skin. My eyes dull and stony. My body clothed in wrinkled pyjamas (I barely ironed anything, let alone pyjamas).

Dropping the envelope on the hall stand, I continued on, stealing up the stairs and along the cushioned hallway that led to the bedroom. With the blinds completely drawn, it was like the world was still in the deep of night.

Luke faced away from me, quietly snoring. I slipped in beside him, taking care that I didn't disturb him. If he woke, I could say I'd just been to the bathroom. But that wouldn't explain my cold skin or the smell of the docks in my hair. I should have gone straight into the shower. But I was exhausted.

He had that same spicy scent of perspiration and musky aftershave he always had before his morning shower. Manoeuvring closer, I let his scent become mine. His body against mine felt good. I needed shelter, sanctuary.

He murmured something I couldn't quite understand. Talking in his sleep was what he did. He talked in his sleep, and I walked in my sleep. Both of us trying to figure things out in our minds during the sleeping hours. The insanity of having a child vanish into thin air never left either of us, night or day.

A minute later, I felt him stirring.

He made grumbling, protesting noises before waking fully and rising. But I knew that once he'd showered, he'd snap fully awake. He'd start mentally planning out his meetings with colleagues and clients. He'd be rehearsing his spiel for later, when he was leading fussy home buyers and Chinese investors through outrageously expensive Sydney real estate. As the man who built one of the top agencies in the city, he knew exactly what to say. He prided himself on being honest, and he was. He often disarmed buyers with a completely unexpected comment about the dated look of a bathroom or the crack in a wall. It made him sound open and gregarious. Then he'd follow up with a burst of positives that made the negatives sound either inconsequential or easily fixable.

Luke picked up his suit from the bedroom chair when he returned from the shower. His eyes looked intensely blue beneath his wet hair. I liked him like that. All his layers peeled off. Once the shirt and jacket went on, it was like he was wearing an armour, and he became *business Luke*. *Business Luke* was someone much more distant.

"I'll bring home some dinner tonight." He buttoned his shirt. "That okay?"

"Of course."

"Feel like anything specific?"

I shook my head. "Anything."

"Give me a call if there's anything else you want me to get." He kissed my forehead, and with a quick *love you* he was out of the room.

The house felt empty even before I heard the slam of the front door downstairs.

I sat on the bed, trying to psych myself to move from the bedroom.

Some days, I didn't move from here. Each day consisted of dead hours: twenty-four hours with all the minutes ticking too fast and too slow at the same time.

I lived for the nights and my dreams of Tommy. I'd totally lost enthusiasm for everything else. But I couldn't have the dreams anymore and risk wandering outside at night.

Somehow, Luke had managed to pick himself up and carry on. Less than a month after Tommy went missing, Luke had been back at the office. My career (if you could call it that) had been in acting. My two recent attempts to perform in a local amateur theatre production—just to get myself back on track—had failed miserably. Luke had come along and watched and clapped harder and longer than anyone else, but it'd been obvious to everyone that my acting was as hollow and putrid as an old gym shoe.

An injured moth fluttered in circles inside my head.

Tommy's voice repeated itself over and over.

You'll never find me, Mummy, if you don't know where to look for me.

7.   LUKE

Wednesday morning

FROM MY OFFICE WINDOW, THE CITY was a swirl of wintry fog and
tall towers of Lego bricks. It looked like it could all tumble down and
disappear into the harbour. Sometimes, I wished it would.

The first time I walked into this office and saw that view, I thought I
had the whole world in my fist.

I'd already secured *the girl*, and now my life was complete. Later,
when Tommy came along, I even managed to replicate myself.

That life was gone.

Six months without Tommy. No real leads. Just dead ends.

And guilt.

When Tommy first went missing, I never thought a day could go
past ever again where he didn't consume every second of my thoughts.
But I was wrong. Someone had to go back to work, and after months,
slowly, a day did slip by where I was so flat-out busy that I didn't think
of him—until I came home and saw the reminders and photos of him
everywhere.

Sometimes, there was a reminder that hit me in the face so hard that it took my breath away. Like one of his old baby rattles that I found lying in the bottom of an office drawer, long forgotten.

How did a couple move on after their child went missing? Short answer: they didn't. You just kind of moved sideways, trying not to lose sight of that point where you last saw your kid.

But if I had to pinpoint the exact moment that things went wrong in my life, I couldn't say it was the day Tommy went missing.

When it came to real estate graphs, I could chart the swings of the market—the busts and the booms. If I were to try and graph my own failures and successes, I wouldn't know where to start. No, it wasn't Tommy's disappearance where the line began trending down. The trend started before that, but it was hazy.

I still couldn't let go of what it was supposed to be: my perfect life with Phoebe.

When I was growing up, other girls were other girls. But Phoebe was always *the girl*. Even when I kissed other girls. Even the year I lived with Kate.

Phoebe was the least accessible person I knew. Every part of her mind was held in compartments. Some compartments were securely locked. Some compartments were open, but only sometimes. You could knock on a door and maybe, just maybe, Phoebe would let you in.

It was no different when she was eight years old. Phoebe, Saskia and I grew up rough and determined on the city streets. The three of us lived on the low end of a street of neglected townhouses that were desperately buying time: Southern Sails Street. All soon to be knocked down to make way for those who *deserved* to be there (those who could afford it). At the high end of Southern Sails, huge old mansions graced the street. No one was threatening to knock those down. The government had never owned them. Kate and Pria had lived up that end—still did—in their parents' expensive houses. They'd attended private girls' schools and used to walk primly down the footpath in their straw school hats.

When we were all around age nine, Saskia commandeered Kate and Pria into our unruly gang. The five of us made a force to be reckoned with, even if most of us were girls. Bernice Wick had come in last, but she was never one of the gang. Not because she was a couple of years older but because she just didn't fit with us. She was too damned strange.

Phoebe didn't try at all. She didn't have to. She had an aura about her even back then. Her name had been Phoebe Vance. She was fiercer than anyone, but she'd drop everything and climb a tree or drainpipe in a flash if someone's mangy kitten had got itself stuck. She entranced me with large brown eyes that seemed like they could shoot lasers if she chose them to.

All of us were in and out of each other's houses on the weekends. Except for Phoebe's house. Her father, Morris, dominated the Vance family home. His moods controlled the atmosphere. Stormy day, winter or roasting summer, it was all under Morris's sky. Phoebe's mother reminded me of a sapling, struggling to find its way above the forest canopy to find its own sunlight, but ending up aging and withering where it stood. It was obvious to me that Phoebe had learned to put up a protective barrier. If her father was raging, she pretended to understand and she sidestepped him. If he was drunk and bitter, she'd get him coffee and cake. If he was in one of his rare sunny moods, she'd laugh along with him.

But I watched her. I saw her fingers twisting around each other as she laughed. I saw her smile drop like a stone when she left a room in which her father was. I heard the false tone in her voice when she asked if he was okay and if she could get anything for him.

Phoebe was always acting. Pretending that her life was better than it was. You could hear her father roaring at her mother, and Phoebe would come out of the house with her head up and a smile. No wonder she became an actor as a career choice. She'd had plenty of practice.

I wanted to save her and give her a different life.

I worked hard, and it was all for her. I built up a real estate agency that was one of the best in the city—and the most profitable. I wanted her to be proud of the man I'd become. I'd be her port in the storm, always. I'd never *be* the storm.

I knew that Phoebe loved her mother, but she never respected her. Roberta Vance had poured all her energies into the house. It had to look exactly right at all times. Especially during Morris's meanest bouts. Her dinners were legendary. She pored over recipe books and came up with meals that made me secretly wish she'd teach them to Phoebe. It seemed that the worse Morris got, the more effort Roberta put into dusting and arranging every item in the house. As though putting the house into order somehow neutralised Morris's tantrums. She could clean and mop and sterilise Morris's existence in the house. At times, I caught her counting and recounting things. And dusting imaginary dust.

When cancer got Phoebe's mother, it seemed to me like the house itself had crawled inside her. All of the caustic cleaning chemicals and Morris's rage mixed together into one toxic brew.

Phoebe was just sixteen then. She was left living with her father and Nan—her maternal grandmother. How Nan had produced a daughter like Phoebe's mother, I'll never figure. When I was growing up, I always saw Nan as a scowling, embittered but stoic presence. She was still there, the old battle-axe, firmly wedged into the wood of the house. Nothing—not the government or anyone else—was ever going to dislodge her.

Morris drank himself into an early death a decade after Phoebe's mother died. In those years, he'd had a continuous startled look on his face, as though he couldn't accept that she was really gone. As though at any moment, she was going to come back through the door, put his shoes away, and make him dinner.

Phoebe was living in London then. I'd been on an extended holiday, staying with her. And she was pregnant with Tommy. We returned to Sydney for her father's funeral, and we never went back to London. I got stuck back into the real estate agency that I'd created with my old school friend and fellow shyster, Rob Lynch. It happened just at the right time. In the months before a real estate boom, Rob and I rode the crazy wave.

When Tommy was nineteen months old, I paid a bomb for one of the new townhouses that had been built near the upper end of Southern Sails Street.

I thought Phoebe would love that. So many people she knew were there. Her grandmother and my parents still lived there. Pria still lived in her childhood home with her nine-year-old daughter, Jessie. Kate lived with her husband and twin boy and girl (in the newly renovated upper level of her parents' house). Saskia was on the next block, in a swish apartment that overlooked her old street. So we were all still there—the Southern Sails gang.

Stepping over to my desk, I tapped a few keys on my keyboard and had a florist send Phoebe some flowers. I needed to give her some kind of reward for coming out to dinner last night.

I knew Phoebe wouldn't really appreciate the flowers, but I didn't know what else to give her. Nothing impressed her. Before, I'd given her the world. But there was nothing I could give her to fix her life now. I couldn't give her Tommy back, no matter how much I wished I could.

8.   PHOEBE

Wednesday morning

YELLOW LIGHT PEERED IN THROUGH THE blinds, investigating me, querying why I still occupied my bed. The grey fog had been replaced by sunshine.

Two hours had passed while I dozed. I'd barely had any sleep last night. That wasn't unusual. On most days, I didn't have more than five hours' sleep, in scattered patches.

My outfit from the restaurant dinner last night was lying in a tangle on the floor. I'd made an effort to get through the dinner for Luke, but it'd been a strain. Those people all existed in such a different world to me. I didn't care about the things they and Luke cared about.

Dragging myself from the bed, I dressed in my usual—jeans, T-shirt, and a hoodie. My daily clothing selection consisted of two pairs of jeans, five T-shirts, three jackets, and the hoodie. That was all I'd worn in months and months. I hadn't bought a single piece of clothing since Tommy went missing. I'd dropped three dress sizes, and I'd had to dig into the boxes of clothing I'd worn before I'd been pregnant.

Heading downstairs, I made myself a lemon juice. I never used to like lemons all that much. Now, I liked the sharpness of them.

Taking the drink, I went out to the living room. Before I realised what I was doing, I was pacing. Up and down the hallway.

Stopping before the hallstand, I gripped it, putting the drink down.

Crazy people paced.

I couldn't say it was the first time, either. Some days, I paced endlessly, trying to shake the darkness inside my mind.

Picking up one of the hair elastics I kept in the keys bowl, I tied my lank hair up into a ponytail. I stared at my face in the hallstand mirror, as I found myself doing every day. I'd come to hate the face I saw reflected there.

The envelope I'd taken from the mailbox was still lying there where I'd left it. Normally Luke opened all the mail, but he'd missed seeing this. Which was a good thing, because if he had, he'd have wondered how it got there between last night and this morning.

I picked up the envelope. The paper was of a thicker quality than that normally used for mass mail outs. Maybe it was a letter from a neighbour. An invitation to a housewarming party or something. Only, no one new had moved to the lower end of the street in a long time. The rich people buying up the new properties on the street were mostly investors.

Hooking my finger inside the envelope, I tore it along the top. There was a piece of paper that looked a little yellowed but was a similar blue to the envelope.

I unfolded the letter. There were just a few lines in the middle of the page:

Little Boy Blue
Alone and forlorn.
From the meadow led.
From your mother torn.

At first, my mind saw the Mother Goose rhyme. When I finally understood that the words had changed, my fingers started to tremble.

Who'd sent this to me? Anyone who knew about Tommy would know how I'd react to those words. Tommy had been dubbed *Little Boy Blue* by the media. He'd been wearing all blue when he vanished.

Someone sent this to us deliberately.

Someone who wanted to hurt us.

Then another, more desperate thought: *Whoever sent this was the person who took Tommy.*

My lungs were airless rooms closing in on each other as I picked up the phone on the hallstand.

Luke didn't pick up. He'd probably gone straight into a meeting. Leaving him a message to call me, I hung up and called Detective Trent Gilroy. It'd been a month since I'd last spoken to him, and that had only been a brief conversation. He'd called *just to check in with me*. As if that had become his job now. He couldn't find Tommy, so he'd keep checking in with me, to make sure that I still existed, that I hadn't vanished, too.

"Trent," I breathed. "I got a letter. About Tommy."

Silence on the other end of the phone. Then, "What kind of letter?"

"It's a children's rhyme, but they've changed the words. It was in our letterbox."

I read out the rhyme.

His tone became dead serious. "Drop the letter. *Now.* Use tweezers to place it into a plastic bag and bring it down to the station. The envelope too, if there was one."

I opened my fist and let the letter flutter to the floor. "I shouldn't have touched it, should I?"

"You weren't to know. Well, it's likely to be someone playing a very stupid prank. Still, we'll certainly investigate it. Can you come down now?"

"Yes, I'll be there."

I dropped the letter and envelope into a zip lock plastic bag using eyebrow tweezers. Then rushed upstairs to find my mobile phone. It was almost out of charge. I switched it off and pushed it into my pocket.

Breaking into a run, I headed out the front door. I didn't drive anymore—the sleeping medications I'd been on meant that I was too drowsy during the day to be on the road, especially in the hectic rush of inner-city traffic. I'd let my car's registration lapse, much to Luke's chagrin.

I raced to the tall brick fence at the end of my garden path and through the gate. And smacked straight into someone.

Pria's daughter Jessie stood there in her calf-length private school uniform and straw hat. The zip lock bag flew up in the air, landing near the drain. Jessie rushed across the path, but before she could get to the bag, I snatched it up.

"I could have lost it!" I cried.

Her expression immediately crumbled. "I'm sorry, Phoebe."

I wanted to smack myself for snapping at the kid. "No, I'm sorry. It was my fault. I shouldn't have barrelled out of my gate like that."

"What is it?" She screwed up her forehead in that gaping, wrinkled-nose way kids did when they were puzzling over something. She was so like Pria, with her almond eyes and high forehead, except that her hair (unlike Pria's) was dark.

"Just a letter. But an important one. Are you okay? Hope I didn't hurt you." I rubbed her arm.

"Yeah. I'm okay." She paused, glancing down at the pavement. "Phoebe, how come you don't come around and see us anymore?"

"I will. I've just been . . . caught up."

"Mum says she misses you. I miss you, too. And maybe when you come over, you can convince Mum to let me walk our puppy sometimes. She says he's already too big and strong and might get away from me. She walks him when I'm at school."

It was so like Jessie to ask me over. She'd always been like a small adult, organising and worrying about everyone. The other side of that was a hint of anxiety. She often seemed to be analysing her own words. She'd tell you something that happened at school and then pick the whole thing apart, scene by scene.

"I'll do my best to convince your mum about the pup," I assured her.

Jessie cut a lonely figure as I said good-bye and headed away. But I couldn't stop and chat. Not now.

I rushed along the hard pavements to the end of my street, turning right at the Southern Sails Café and then jogging the two blocks to the police station.

The station was big and busy and intimidating. It had become my second home in the months after Tommy vanished. The kind of home you wished you could run away from and never see again.

I was shown into Detective Gilroy's office. He looked up briefly from a phone conversation. "Please, take a seat. I'll just be a moment." His tone was neutral. I knew already that he didn't hold out much hope for this letter to lead to anything.

I sat and waited, impatience spinning through me. I wanted him to move on this. Get things happening.

So many times in the past six months, I'd sat here like this, impatient like this. Those times had become less and less frequent. There'd been no leads to follow, nothing to discuss. Until this morning.

The detective kept talking on the phone. From his end of the conversation, it sounded like it was about a domestic violence court order. A husband taking an order out on his wife, worried that she was going to hurt the kids.

I studied Trent Gilroy's face. He was the man who I'd once seen as holding the fate of Tommy in his hands. That was in the early days, when he all but promised me he'd find Tommy (before hope of finding Tommy had faded to nothing). He was in his early forties I guessed, his hair a mix of black and silver. He wasn't bad looking. He had a single deep line running across his forehead that looked like a statistical line graph, with a blip to the right of it.

I handed him the plastic bag as soon as he ended his call, before he had a chance to ask for it.

Frowning hard, he turned the blip on his forehead into a statistical anomaly, tugging the letter from the envelope with his own special detective set of tweezers.

"Hmmm. . . ." He sounded noncommittal as he read it. He looked up at me with a faint look of surprise. "This has been written with a typewriter."

"Are you sure?" I'd never seen something typewritten before. Typewriters were relics of an era before my time. I knew that you could get fonts on the internet that matched the old typewritten look.

"Yeah." He held it up to the light, examining it closely. "I'm sure."

"What do you think about the rhyme?"

"Well, it's hard to determine what the person wanted to achieve in sending this. It doesn't say very much. I mean, we don't know for certain that it's not well intended."

"Well intended?" I raised my eyebrows incredulously.

He scratched his temple. "Maybe. But if it is, it's very misguided. We'll run tests on it anyway. Just leave it with us. We already have your fingerprints and Luke's on file, so we'll be able to distinguish different prints on the letter and envelope."

The police had taken our fingerprints after Tommy had gone missing, so that if they found anything belonging to Tommy, they could quickly tell which prints were ours and which were those of a stranger. They had Tommy's fingerprints, too, from the ornaments of Nan's that he touched on the day he disappeared. They even had items of his clothing from my dirty laundry basket (for the sniffer dogs), including one of his T-shirts that had a tiny patch of blood from when he'd fallen and grazed his knee the day before.

"Could it," I began, "I mean, is it possible that the person who took Tommy wrote this? Maybe they're feeling bad about what they did."

He exhaled a drawn-out sigh. "Unlikely. In the realm of possibilities, no."

"Why not?" I asked bluntly.

He took a moment before answering. "Because people who take children don't want anything to do with the police. They don't make contact with the parents of the child, unless it's a ransom demand. And ransom demands would normally come in close to the time of abduction."

I'd sat here in this office with Luke six months ago, our hands grasping each other's as Luke asked the detective for cold facts. Gilroy had admitted that children who were abducted by strangers had a high chance of being murdered. And of those children who were murdered, three-quarters of them were murdered within three hours.

Three hours.

If that statistic included Tommy, then he'd already been dead when Luke and I were still searching the playground and surrounds for him with the police and others who'd joined in.

Did Detective Gilroy believe that Tommy was dead, despite him claiming that he didn't?

Dead, dead, dead. Such a flat, final word. There was no light or hope in that word. There was no Tommy in that word. There was only the possibility of a body. After all these months, if Tommy was dead, there wasn't even any possibility of a body: there was only the possibility of Tommy's skeletal *remains*.

Suddenly, I couldn't breathe. There wasn't enough oxygen in this tiny office. I couldn't stay here in Trent's office any longer, with his abduction statistics and his neutral voice and the graph line on his forehead.

"Are you okay, Phoebe?" His eyes flicked over me in concern. I knew the laundry list of what I looked like: dark circles under my eyes, no makeup, untidy hair spilling out of a ponytail. I didn't look *okay*.

Nodding, I got up too quickly. The room tilted and spun.

"Phoebe?"

"I'm just tired. Please let me know if you have any news."

I hurried out, my head still swimming, trying to look normal. Out on the street, the wintry air stung my cheeks, but at least I could breathe again.

I'd know if Tommy were dead. *Wouldn't I?*

The answer came to me instantly. I wouldn't know. A stranger had taken him from under my nose, and I hadn't even known that was happening. In those moments that I thought he was playing near my feet, he was being led or carried away from me.

When I looked back, I imagined I had a sense of dread right at that time. But the dread had to be in retrospect. If I'd known what was about to happen to Tommy, I would have stopped it.

9.   LUKE

Wednesday morning

"MATE, WE CLOSED THE MONAHAN DEAL." Rob grinned. At six and a half million dollars, we were going to get a tidy commission out of that. Sitting back in his chair, he crossed his feet on the desk.

Every morning, Rob and I had a brief catch-up. We'd been caught a few times telling clients different things, and now we made sure we had our stories straight. Selling real estate was an art. You tried to funnel buyers towards the top of what they could afford, sometimes to the properties that weren't selling, or to the deals if you thought they'd be a good repeat customer. You had to know when a buyer was worth going the extra mile for and when a buyer was a time-waster.

Behind Rob lay the same view I had from my office window. But for some reason I couldn't determine, the scene looked different from Rob's window. Maybe it was because I felt myself moving inside Rob's frame here in his office. He lived for the thrill of the big sales and saw everything as an opportunity.

"Gonna call Ellie." With his feet still on the desk, he grabbed the phone.

Ellie was one of our best salespeople—the best actually. I'd been wanting to put her onto handling the auctions. Almost all of our sales were via auctions. And Ellie had a sense of drama and theatrics that Rob and I lacked. But Rob kept holding out. I couldn't be sure, but I thought maybe that he just couldn't cope with the idea of his wife being on the same level as him. Maybe I understood that, in a way. The auctions were a male bastion. I only knew of a handful of female auctioneers in the whole city. If Ellie proved to be better than Rob, that could be a bitter pill for Rob to swallow.

The Monahan sales commission would help Rob and Ellie hang onto their ritzy house and Italian cars a bit longer. I'd known for a while that Rob and Ellie spent more than they earned, but that was something Rob would never admit.

There was a time when I would have called Phoebe and whooped like a little kid and told her we were dining out at the most expensive restaurant. And she'd have gotten excited with me. But those days were gone. Now, I would barely get a glimmer of acknowledgment.

"I'll go give Feeb a call." Pulling myself to my feet, I exited Rob's office. I was lying. I wasn't going to call her.

I had a stack of paperwork sitting on my desk. A stack of bills to pay. The mortgage on my house and the lease on my office were crippling. I needed to put my head down and keep working.

I dug out the folder of photos taken of the properties belonging to my newest client. He had an apartment with a million-dollar view of the harbour, and he wanted me to sell it. I needed to give him my attention right now. The Monahan deal was good news, but we had to keep the mill churning.

First I'd check my phone messages. During our morning meet ups, Rob and I had a no-phone-calls policy. Otherwise all we'd do was answer calls.

I frowned. There was a message from Phoebe to call her and a message from Detective Trent Gilroy.

My stomach clenched. Phoebe never called me. And when Gilroy called me, it was always about a lead in Tommy's case that I was going to hear about in the news, and he wanted Phoebe and me to know first. (Not one of those leads had turned up anything.) Gilroy usually called Phoebe to reassure her that they were still working hard on the case, and he called me to tell me about the news items. Almost like he were running a PR company rather than a police division.

Still, there was always the sword of Damocles hanging over my head, waiting to drop the news that the police had actually found Tommy. To tell me that Tommy was dead.

I had to suck down a deep breath before I returned the calls. I didn't know which to return first. I decided to return Gilroy's.

"Detective Gilroy," he answered.

"Hello, this is Luke Basko. Returning your call?"

"Luke, yes. Have you spoken to your wife?"

"Not since I left for work. What's happening? Is she okay?"

"She's fine. She brought in a letter earlier—"

"What letter?"

"She found an unaddressed envelope in the mailbox. The letter inside has no name on it. It's just a children's rhyme."

"I don't get it."

"Well, neither do we. It's just a piece of paper with a rhyme printed on it. It's the Mother Goose rhyme, Little Boy Blue. Only, the words are changed. Now, we're not certain, but it does sound like it's about Tommy. Phoebe's convinced that it is."

"What does it say?"

He read the rhyme out to me.

Dumbstruck, I stared at a space on the wall that seemed to dissolve into a memory, reaching all the way back to the nursery rhyme book I used to read to Tommy at night. I knew the rhyme and what the person had changed. How could he say it *might* be about Tommy? Of course it was.

I expelled a hard stream of air. "Phoebe doesn't need this. She isn't coping as it is."

"I thought so. She was very distressed. I'd like to ask if there's anyone at all you can think of who might do something like this. Someone with a grudge?"

"I don't know. I mean, that's a pretty strange letter."

"Agreed. Well, could you let Phoebe know that we've had someone look at it and we couldn't find any fingerprints, apart from her own? We'll keep looking into this. I wasn't able to get her on the phone."

As I ended the phone call I reflected that it was unusual for Phoebe not to be contactable. She always had her mobile phone with her, like a security blanket, waiting for a call. Waiting for *the call*.

I dialled her number.

10. PHOEBE

Wednesday morning

I TOYED WITH THE THOUGHT OF dropping in to Nan's townhouse as I passed by. To tell her about the letter. She'd want to know.

But it was hard to even speak about Tommy with her. She still couldn't understand how someone was able to snatch Tommy away on my watch. She fixed me with that vaguely unforgiving look whenever I mentioned his name. I couldn't shoulder that right now. I'd wait a couple of days, until I was stronger.

I kept walking.

Next door to Nan's, Mrs Wick trod down her garden path, her cat winding itself around her frail, stick-like legs. She and Nan had been friends ever since they were children themselves, growing up in the same houses they lived in now. To me, it seemed their friendship was based on their mutual disapproval for just about everything in existence. Most of their conversation circled around cuts to pensioner benefits, how useless doctors were, and the general downfall of society.

Mrs Wick sped up a little, which was unusual for her. Especially with the cat threatening to trip her up at any step. She reached her mailbox just as I was about to walk past.

"Is everything all right?" Her eyes were bright beneath her glasses.

"Everything's . . . yes, fine, thank you."

"It isn't your nan is it, that had you running down the street earlier? I saw you from the living room."

Yes, you old busybody. Of course you saw me. Well, I'm not going to hand you the latest tasty morsel of gossip on our street.

"No, it wasn't Nan. I was just late for an appointment."

"Oh. I guess you have lots of appointments, you people from the high end of the street."

Luke and I had become *you people* ever since we'd bought the very expensive high-end-of-the-street property. Before then, she'd called us *you young people.*

Mrs Wick's daughter—Bernice—peered through the blinds, her eyes squinty in her pudgy face.

Bernice broke off her engagement to a man twelve years ago and had come back home to stay with her mother. Since then, she'd never been out with another man (as far as I knew.) And she'd barely worked. She'd studied at a technical college to become a safety officer, and she'd worked as a combined yacht hand/safety officer in the yacht races for less than two years before throwing it in.

I had no idea what Bernice did with her time now. I remembered her as a kid, hanging on the fringes of the Southern Sails Street gang—Sass, Pria, Kate, Luke, and me. She was skinny then and awkward. She'd been at least two years older than Sass and three years older than the rest of us. From the time she was thirteen, she started ditching school— she'd hang around the streets and talk to the boys when they got out of class. She'd been anxious for a boyfriend and anxiously trying to hide the fact that she wanted one.

When Luke was twelve and she fifteen, he made up a terrible rhyme about her:

> *Bernice Wick*
> *Sittin' in a tree*
> *Waitin' for the boys*

'Til half past three
Couldn't catch a dick
'Cos she made 'em all sick
'Cos she got hit
By the ugly stick

A couple of times, I knew she overheard him chanting that. I'd like to say that Kate, Pria, and I didn't giggle at it. But we did.

Luke made up stuff like that about everyone, only usually not quite so insulting. Despite his rhyme, Bernice was never ugly. She was gangly, but lots of kids that age were. She'd kept her blonde hair long and half-hiding her face.

But there *was* something about Bernice that was ugly. It was Bernice that had carried out the terrible thing next door at number 29, back when she was a teenager. It was one of those things that you couldn't explain, no matter which way you tried to look at it. In the darkest moments of Luke and me, our suspicions about the abduction of our son had turned to her. We'd told Detective Gilroy of our uncertainty about her, and he'd done his best to check her out. But every painstaking study of the videos that day showed no trace of Bernice Wick. She was a tall woman and beefy. There was no hiding her.

Mrs Wick had given birth to Bernice when she was forty-six—a surprise child seeing as Bernice was her first (and only, as it turned out).

Bernice's father had died when she was ten, of a heart attack in the yard where Mrs Wick was standing. He died five days after he retired from his job as a government clerk, the job he said he'd been waiting all his adult life to leave.

Bernice backed away when she saw me looking her way.

"Well, I'd better get home," I told Mrs Wick. "I have a lot to do today."

"Oh yes, it never ends. I have to deadhead the roses today. They're not looking their best."

Giving her a tight smile, I walked away as quickly as I could without being impolite. I wished I did have a long list of things to do today. But I had nothing with which to occupy myself. I'd sit in the too-quiet house counting the hours until Detective Gilroy called me. Or I'd pace again.

No curtain shifted at the next house—number 29—as I stepped past it. Had I just imagined it before?

I kept walking.

As I reached my own house, my gaze fell squarely on the mailbox, half-expecting there to be another letter.

I remembered then the aroma of coffee that the envelope had carried when I'd first taken it out. That smell had disappeared later in the morning.

Coffee.

The person who delivered the letter had been drinking coffee just beforehand. The coffee scent had come from the café at the end of my street. I'd been certain of it. I'd forgotten to tell Detective Gilroy about the coffee. I needed to go inside and call him, now. I didn't know how much battery power I had left on my mobile phone—I knew it was low—so I'd switched it off.

I opened the gate then stopped, reconsidering. Trent had seemed dubious that the letter even meant anything. Even though the letter was the first and only tangible thing in relation to Tommy that had come our way. I made the decision to go down to the café myself.

I retraced my steps to the harbour end of the street. Mrs Wick seemed to have forgotten all about deadheading her roses because she was nowhere in sight. Her roses stood like rotting zombies in her garden.

The café was busy when I arrived there. Stepping into the warm interior and over to the counter, I ordered a caramel mochaccino.

"I've never had one of these," I told the girl behind the serving counter. "But someone walked past me in the street early this morning, and it just smelled wonderful. I knew the coffee had to be from here."

The girl—in her late teens with a freshly scrubbed look—smiled, looking pleased I'd started a conversation with her. "They don't get ordered as much as the others, but they're great."

"Do you get regulars in here who only order the caramel?"

"Not often. People usually have them just for a change. It's good to try something new, and we have so many varieties that I mean, well, why wouldn't you?"

Her enthusiasm and company spiel made me guess that this was her first job. I hadn't seen her here before.

I wanted to ask every detail of every person who'd ordered a caramel mochaccino between four and five in the morning. I wanted to pull out a notepad and pencil from thin air and ask her to draw each person in intricate detail.

Instead, I nodded as if my questions were done.

Moving to a seat that gave me the best view of the patrons, I tasted the coffee, allowing its aroma to saturate my sinuses. It was too overly sweet for my taste buds, but it carried the same scent as from the envelope. Unmistakeable.

People sat reading newspapers, tapping and swiping at electronic devices. Older women sipped their milky coffees and teas and looked out at the harbour from the broad window.

Taking out my phone, I navigated to today's news. I had to pretend to be engrossed in my tiny screen, too. Reports of terrorism and counter-terrorism and various wars dominated the headlines. In my darkest moments, I used to comfort myself that if Tommy was really dead, then he'd never have to know the ongoing horrors of the world. All the labels these horrors carried seemed meaningless. It was just all people hurting people. Every day brought another feast of headlines, like seven-course meals, neatly styled on plates. We were all fat on the suffering of others.

I stole furtive glances around the café in between screen swipes, briefly scanning and studying each person who was within my view.

If the person was here, they could be watching me right now.

Who'd sent the note? They were sure to be a key tapper or screen swiper, too. Except the note had been written on a typewriter. Could it be an elderly person? The words were centred on the page, both vertically and horizontally. Someone who cared about presentation. No spelling mistakes either, though the words used were so simple they'd be hard to misspell. It had be someone who lived close—close enough to walk to my house.

My screen went dead.

A momentary sense of panic raced through me. I never let my phone run out of charge. If the police ever found the tiniest piece of evidence in relation to Tommy's disappearance, I wanted to know in that instant.

I calmed myself. I was just a fifteen-minute walk away from my house. I'd call Trent Gilroy when I returned home and see if there was any news.

Pretending to keep reading my blank phone screen, I looked up every few seconds.

Was anyone else only pretending to look at their device, like I was? Was the person a man or a woman? Then another thought: did they work here?

My coffee went lukewarm, and I headed across the café to order a plain coffee. I studied the faces of the staff behind the counter. Was anyone purposely looking away from me? No, the letter-writer couldn't be someone who worked here because none of them could have left behind the scent of only one type of coffee.

Not knowing what else to do, I headed back through the café.

A three-quarter wall divided the café in two, running about a third of the length of the cafe, covered in framed paintings. A large noticeboard occupied the middle of one side of the wall, littered with flyers and handwritten notes.

The noticeboard caught my eye. Large lettering on one of the notes asked, WHERE IS HE?

My throat tightened at the question. Probably a missing dog. But still, I stepped towards the board like a moth towards a flame.

My eyes swept the notices and pamphlets about lost pets, book club meetings, mother-and-baby groups, vaginas-as-flowers painting classes, men-after-divorce groups, and psychic readings. (Something for everyone.)

I sipped the coffee, making a show of looking interested in the notices. Again, my gaze was drawn to the question that asked, *where is he*? There was nothing to explain the message. The note it was written on was too small to say anything more. Was it someone just putting a message out to the universe? A lament for a husband who'd run off with a work colleague maybe?

The message was typewritten, on an envelope-sized note. Blue.

A chill sped along my back.

Setting my coffee down on a nearby table, I stripped the note from the board. It *was* an envelope. The same kind of envelope as the one from my mailbox. I no longer cared if anyone was watching me. I was going to open this.

Now.

My heart felt as though it were locking up as I tore the envelope open and took out the letter:

> *Little Boy Blue*
> *Why don't you grieve*
> *for the mother you leave*
> *and the life you knew?*

I couldn't control the tremors that passed through my arms.

A second letter.

Another cryptic message.

This person was trying to turn my mind inside out.

How did they know I'd find this letter here?

What were they trying to do to me?

Other, deeper thoughts slipped through: *Tommy didn't cry for me after he was taken? He didn't grieve me like I grieved him? Did he forget me straight away?*

Pain speared deep inside my chest.

Wait . . .

The only person who could possibly know that Tommy didn't remember me was the person who took him. This was proof that the letters were from the abductor.

Wait . . .

This was proof that Tommy was alive. The letter was written as though it was something that was happening *now*. Not at the time of the abduction. Tommy was starting to forget me and his old life *now*.

I whirled around.

The abductor wanted to see my suffering first hand.

Well, here I am. See my suffering.

People caught my eye and quickly looked away. My breaths were shallow, too quick.

Who are you?

Who are you?

Who are you?

I pushed the envelope and letter into my pocket, remembering too late I wasn't meant to touch the stationery.

Ten minutes later, I was walking into Detective Gilroy's office for the second time that morning.

His dark eyes showed a faint look of bewilderment as he looked up from his paperwork. "I'm afraid I don't have anything much to tell you. We didn't get any fingerprints. I called your husband and told him as much."

"That's not why I'm here."

"It isn't?"

"I found another letter. At the Southern Sails Café."

"You found a second letter? *There? How*—?"

"It was pinned to the noticeboard, with a message on the front of the envelope. They wanted to get my attention . . . and it worked."

"So, you stopped off for a coffee after leaving here?"

"Not exactly. I got all the way home, and then I remembered something. The letter I gave you had the scent of coffee on it. Caramel mochaccino. I knew where that smell had come from. So I went there."

"I know the café. Where's the letter? Is it still there?"

"It's here." Carefully, I slid the crumpled letter and envelope from my jeans pocket and smoothed them both out.

"You've already held them, so just put them down on the desk," he instructed. "I won't touch them." I sensed a reprimanding tone in his voice.

He moved from his desk to walk around to the letter, expelling a long breath of air as he read the message on the envelope and the letter. "It certainly seems to be from the same person."

My hands curled into fists on my lap. "If they're saying that Tommy doesn't remember me, then that means that he's alive . . . right?"

The words that had sounded feasible inside my head sounded like a fairy tale when they left my lips. Like I was asking if an evil wizard might be keeping Tommy in a tower. And by the cloud that entered the detective's eyes, I knew he wasn't buying into the fairy tale.

"We still can't say for sure that this is the person who took Tommy," he told me noncommittally.

"But you can't say that it isn't."

"No. But I'll be honest, Phoebe." Leaning his hip against the desk, he folded his arms. "The odds of the actual kidnapper contacting you are very, very low. After you left, I spent some time looking up child kidnapping cases. Just to see if there's something I'm missing. I didn't find any instance of this happening before. Look, we'll certainly cover all bases. How about we start with the most likely scenario? There could be someone who wants to cause you emotional pain. Is there anyone in your life at the moment that you're having issues with?"

"No. I barely see anyone. Apart from Nan. And Luke's parents on occasion."

"What about in the past few years? These could be small issues that seem tiny to you . . ." He trailed off, looking at me expectantly, like I was going to produce some obscure person from out of my hat. "Hang on, didn't you have a problem with a neighbour at some point? Bernice, wasn't it?"

"Bernice Wick, yes."

"Okay. It might help if you tell me what the grudge was all about."

I twisted my fingers together. I couldn't tell him what happened back then. He was the police. *I couldn't tell the police. I couldn't tell them what Bernice Wick had done at house number 29, not even after all this time.* "It doesn't matter now."

"Could give us some insight."

"It was just kids' stuff. I don't really remember what it was all about."

"Okay, well, remember that these letters could be from someone you don't expect. Think on it overnight. Someone's name might come to you. Just write their name down so you don't forget."

"I will." I took a breath. "But I just need to know . . . that you'll be treating this seriously."

"Absolutely. I assure you it has priority. The first thing we'll do is put your house and the café under surveillance. If this person is planning any more of these notes, we'll catch them. If not, we still might notice some unusual activity. We'll also contact the shop owners to see if they have any surveillance footage, to see if we can find out who pinned the envelope. And I'll send this note off to the lab." He paused. "You say the original letter smelled of caramel macchiato?"

"Mochaccino. Yes."

"Okay, I didn't notice any scent. I'll check that with the lab."

"Thank you." I nodded, closing my eyes briefly, relieved that he was going to investigate this properly. Things were going to happen.

He was staring at me fixedly when I opened my eyes again. "Phoebe, if you don't mind me saying so, you look really beat."

"I feel like I've been put through the wringer."

"Are you okay to drive? It's been quite a day for you."

"I haven't driven for three months now."

"Okay, I didn't realise you didn't have a car. Well, I'll take you home."

"Are you sure? I don't want to take up your time."

"It's no trouble at all." He grabbed a notebook and pen from his desk. "Forgot to ask. What time did you find the note at the shop? I need to know that for when I talk to the owners."

"Around ten 'o'clock. I came straight here after I found it."

He checked his watch and scribbled down the time. "Okay, we'll see what we can come up with."

11.　LUKE

Wednesday midday

A WORM OF WORRY BURROWED ITSELF into my gut. I still couldn't get Phoebe on her mobile or the home phone.

She'd been different lately in a way I couldn't put a finger on.

In the months directly after Tommy vanished, Phoebe had obsessed over what the police were doing to find him. She would be up until three or four in the morning, poring over missing child cases, taking notes on mistakes that were made by investigators and writing down if the child was ever found or not. At times she'd shrink back from the computer in horror, after finding out about a particularly bad case.

I didn't see the point in knowing things like that. I'd told Phoebe to stop, for her sake as well as mine. It was bad enough that Tommy was gone, without trying to imagine every possible horrific scenario.

And she *had* stopped. But then she'd gone the opposite way, drifting along like an unanchored helium balloon.

Until maybe two months ago. Sometimes it seemed like there was nothing left inside her, other times like she was hiding something from me. Sometimes I got the impression that she was trying to placate me.

It scared me. I didn't know if my wife was drawing close to the point of suicide. I didn't know what people who were close to committing suicide acted like. Phoebe had packets of sleeping pills in her drawer. I knew people offed themselves using those.

I kept meaning to go and see her psych and ask about that, but I'd been so caught up with work I hadn't made the appointment.

And now, someone had sent us a damned stupid letter. Something like that could be enough to tip Phoebe over the edge again. Maybe back to her OCD-like research of child abduction cases or maybe to something worse.

I had to get home and see for myself what was happening and put my mind at rest.

Telling Rob I was leaving for the day, I packed up and headed out of the office.

As I drove up our street, I spotted a police car sitting in our driveway. Phoebe and Detective Gilroy were just getting out of his car. I'd no idea why she was with him. She'd left the police station quite a while ago, hadn't she?

I parked on the street and headed over to them, enveloping Phoebe in a hug. It killed me that she'd had to deal with this alone.

Gilroy shook my hand. "It's good that you're here, Luke. We've got some things to talk over."

Gilroy and Phoebe sat on the stools at the kitchen bench while I made the three of us coffee. Phoebe was looking kind of dishevelled. No, actually really dishevelled. Phoebe didn't make much effort with herself anymore, but she didn't normally look quite that messy.

"Did something change?" I asked Gilroy. "You found out something about the letter after all?"

He raised his eyebrows. "Yes and no. We didn't find out anything different about the letter from this morning, but Phoebe found a second letter later today."

I turned to Phoebe, gaping.

She nodded. "At the coffee shop. Southern Sails."

I set the three cups of coffee down on the bench. "I don't get how—"

"It was pinned to the noticeboard," she told me.

"Where anyone could see it?"

"Yes." She explained why she'd gone there and about the message on the front of the envelope.

"The message wouldn't have stood out that much among all the missing pet messages," Gilroy added, taking his cup in hand. "But the person who wrote it knew what it would mean to Phoebe. Someone's targeting her for some reason."

Nudging a stool out with my foot, I sat down heavily. "Fucking insane. What did the letter say?"

My wife turned to the detective, prompting him to tell me. I guessed that the content of the letter was bad. Gilroy cleared his throat and recited a rhyme. A crazy rhyme that didn't say a lot, but I knew it would have hurt Phoebe.

I swallowed a mouthful of burning coffee. "But why now? It's been six months since our son went missing."

"Hard to say," said Gilroy. "If there's one thing I've learned on the job, it's that there's a lot of very strange people out there. They just don't think like you and me."

"That's two notes now," I said. "Doesn't that give you something to go on?"

"It gives us a bit more," he agreed. "But it's not easy to track down a person who's leaving notes around. Especially if they don't leave them in the same place twice."

"Will there be more?" My tone was almost demanding, but I failed to hold back. I was asking questions he couldn't answer.

Gilroy frowned deeply. "I can't predict that. The notes don't follow any usual pattern. They're not asking for money. Which is why my best guess is that this is some individual with a grudge against one or both of you, and it's not the kidnapper. It could be someone who has something against you, Luke, and they're trying to get back at you through Phoebe. We're open to possibilities at this point."

A cold hope rose in my chest. "But you don't know for sure that this isn't the person who's got Tommy. I mean, could these letters be leading up to a ransom note?"

"I've never seen anything like that," he answered. "I've never personally dealt with a ransom note, but in all the cases I know about, the first note will be the one with the ransom demands in it. Ransom notes are very to the point. Give us what we want or else. But these letters aren't like that. And they're arriving a long time after the fact."

I reached for Phoebe's hand when I noticed her face crumpling. I could almost physically witness the wounds opening inside her, both fresh and old.

"What do you think it means that these notes are coming now?" I didn't want to ask that in front of Phoebe, but the words rushed out. "If it turns out that it's just someone who wants to hurt us, why did they wait? I mean, why didn't they send them straight away?"

"Well, one possibility is that they didn't feel secure enough to do so. There was a heavy police presence in the early months. Maybe now they feel bold enough to send the letters."

Phoebe pulled her mouth in. "Makes me feel sick to think that someone might have been out there planning this all along."

I caught her eye. There was something fierce in her eyes, something I hadn't seen for many months.

"It's all speculation at this point," Gilroy said, glancing at both of us. "For all we know, this person might have seen a story on the internet about Tommy, and for some reason, it provoked them into doing this. Some people would do it for the attention alone. Even if it landed them with criminal charges. For that reason, I'm not going to make this public. Not yet anyway. I'd ask you both not to go to the media either. Keeping it quiet might draw this person out."

"So what now?" I said. "Could this person be dangerous?"

He took a moment to answer, as if weighing up his words. "I don't think so. But take the normal precautions you'd take, living in the city as you do. Ensure all windows and doors are secure, even when you're at home."

Gilroy stayed a while longer, even though there was nothing more to be said. A bit of small talk, something to bring us back to normality. But from the distant expression on my wife's face, there was no going back from this, not even back to how things were yesterday.

*

I jolted awake. Someone was knocking.

The clock's illuminated display on my bedside table had the time at ten past two in the morning. Maybe I'd dreamed the sounds.

Rolling over, I turned to Phoebe, to check if she'd heard it too.

There was no Phoebe in the bed.

She wasn't in the ensuite either. The door to our bathroom was open, the room empty.

The knocking sounds rattled through the house again.

Throwing off the covers, I jumped out and rushed down the hall. Did we have an intruder? *Fuck,* I should have run out and bought an alarm system last night.

Whoever the person was, they were in Tommy's room. Banging things—maybe going through his set of drawers. I should have a baseball bat or something—*why didn't I own a baseball bat?*—and where the hell was Phoebe? If they've hurt her—

From the doorframe of Tommy's room, I got the answer to my last question. My wife was kneeling on the rug in the middle of the floor, rolling Tommy's trains along his wooden train tracks. The carriages rolled down the hill, whacking into the carriages at the bottom, the magnet connectors making a loud metallic clatter. I hadn't heard that sound in six months.

She was fully dressed, in jeans and a jacket and shoes.

"Feeb, what are you—?" I stopped mid-sentence. The expression on her face was so strangely *content.*

She didn't turn around or even acknowledge my presence. I realised then that she couldn't hear me. She was in some weird state between being asleep and awake. Leaning against the doorframe, I watched her, not wanting to disturb her.

Sleepwalking?

Was it possible for someone to dress themselves and then drag out a whole train set and put it together while they were sleepwalking? It seemed that it was.

Tommy's toys had all been put away months ago. My mother had taken it upon herself to do the clean-up. She'd said that the way the toys had been left, all half set up and scattered on his floor, it looked like Tommy still occupied the room and was coming back any moment now. With a shake of her head, she'd called it morbid. She'd even washed Tommy's sheets and made his bed. That had killed Phoebe. After

Tommy vanished, Phoebe used to slip into Tommy's bed and sleep there, just to breathe in the scent of him. My mother had apologised profusely for what she'd done when she saw the effect on Phoebe, but there'd been no way of fixing it.

Phoebe started humming.

Pain corkscrewed up from my stomach. I hadn't seen Phoebe this happy, maybe ever. The back of my legs weakened, and I knelt to the floor. I couldn't hold back the tears.

She turned her head, confused, and then she stretched a hand out to me. At first I thought she was trying to comfort me. Leaning towards her I reached to hold her hand. But she immediately pulled hers away, closing it into a fist. Slowly, she opened her hand and studied her palm.

She thought I'd given her something.

Her brow furrowed, and she tilted her hand, as if to gain a better look at the mysterious object. Her fingers and lower lip trembled.

What was she seeing?

Whipping around, she looked at the train tracks again. Crying out, she stood and fled from the room, knocking hard into my shoulder.

I followed. She was heading for the stairs. Terrified that she'd stumble and fall down the staircase, I raced up behind her and grasped her arms. "Phoebe . . . Phoebe . . ."

At first, she struggled. Then the stiffness in her body gave way.

Gently, I turned her around. She was awake now. Still a little dazed, but her eyes were focused. She touched my wet face, running her fingers from my temple to my jaw.

She gripped my shoulders then and cried. As I held her close, she sounded so damned mournful, like those birds you heard in the small hours. But more than that, in the angles of her thin body, I felt a burning rage.

"Babe," I said softly, "are you okay? You were dreaming. I found you in Tommy's room, playing with his train set. Were you dreaming about Tommy?" For a moment, I was envious. If I'd ever had any dreams of Tommy, I didn't remember them.

"I must have been. I don't remember." Moving back, she smiled, but the smile seemed forced.

I led her back to our room and into bed. I wanted to protect her, to somehow make things better for her. Keeping her close, I rested my head on her chest. Maybe I needed comfort just as much as she did.

"I'm worried about you," I said gently. "When's your next appointment with Dr Moran? Maybe you can see her sooner. I'll take time off work to take you."

"I saw her just last week."

"You did?"

"Yeah."

"You didn't tell me."

In response, she wriggled down and kissed me. And she kept kissing me.

That was unusual. It'd been a long time since Phoebe kissed me like that.

She stopped kissing me to undress herself down to the skin.

My breathing and heart rate rose.

She kept kissing me, touching me.

I responded.

Sex had been very infrequent this year. I'd tried hard to understand, but sometimes it was difficult. I wasn't in control of what my body wanted and needed to do. The year before, it had been her wanting more from me, and me backing off. The long hours at the office had left me trying to fire on one cylinder.

Even in this strange, half-dazed state, Phoebe was beautiful.

As her arousal grew, she closed her eyes.

She was always totally removed from me when she reached that stage—it was never shared.

12. PHOEBE

Thursday morning

LUKE INSISTED ON STAYING HOME WITH me today. He didn't dress for work.

I didn't want him here. I needed time alone to think.

He brushed his teeth at the sink as I finished my shower. Tucking a towel around myself, I walked from the shower and kissed him on the cheek. "No, you need to go. I'm okay. I'll call you if anything else happens."

Looking at my reflection in the mirror, he shook his head then bent to rinse out the toothpaste. "I'm not going." He dabbed his mouth with a towel. "Phoebe, you really worried me when I found you like that in Tommy's room."

"It was just a dream."

"I know, but this whole thing with the letters is really getting to you."

"Yeah, it is, and I didn't sleep well. But I'll have a long nap today. I'll be fine."

"Look, I'm staying. I'm getting another alarm system. The one we have never worked properly."

"Okay," I said softly, and I hugged him from behind. Luke had his mind made up, and I knew I couldn't change it. We caught sight of each other again in the mirror. We smiled, but the smiles seemed *obligatory*. Did Luke see what I did? Sometimes, we were like strangers, just going through the motions of being a married couple. Were all couples like this? You realised that the person that had lit up your life was also the one throwing shadows on all your other possibilities.

I hated it when those thoughts slipped in. He was my husband, and he'd been my rock. I needed to remember that.

Luke stayed until the time was late enough for the hardware store to open, then he headed out. He'd insisted that he was going to buy an alarm system.

Alone in the house, I felt a shift inside myself, a recalibration.

Something important happened in my dream last night. What was it?

My head was so, so hazy. I had to remember.

I sat myself down on the edge of the sofa.

Yesterday, after Trent Gilroy left our house, I'd had the words to the second letter hanging in my mind like a dark cloud. Trent had spoken of different possibilities—of a random person wanting attention, of a grudge against Luke, of a stupid prank. It wasn't any of those things. The letters were for me. Only for me. The person, whoever they were, knew me. Those words, they were intended to wound. In the two years that I'd had Tommy, I'd never felt like a *good mother*. Sometimes, I hadn't even wanted to *be* a mother. I used to see the mothers in the street and at my mothers' group (with their doting voices and their full schedules of mother/baby activities) and think that Tommy would rather be with any one of those mothers than me. He'd run off and never look back.

Someone, somehow, knew all of that about me.

And if this person was someone who knew me, then I knew *them*.

Surely, some part of me must already know who they were.

I'd barely spoken to Bernice since I was sixteen. But Nan spoke about me to Bernice's mother all the time. Just like Mrs Wick spoke about Bernice to Nan and Nan passed that information onto me. Bernice could know more about me than anyone, besides Luke and Nan.

But I needed some proof. And I had none.

But the dreams—the dreams were sending me clues.

The night before last, Tommy had taken me all the way back to the exact place he'd gone missing. And the wizard man had given me a moth (injured).

There was a thread running through everything. I just had to grab hold of the end and unspool it.

Last night I'd taken the sleeping tablets. I'd promised myself that I wouldn't do that again, but the letters had changed everything. My dreams might show me what my conscious mind could not. Beforehand, I'd hidden the deadlock key to make sure I couldn't get out of the house. In case I wandered.

In my dream, Tommy visited his bedroom, and he'd wanted to play trains. He always used to ask me to play trains with him, but I rarely did. Last night, while we were playing, he was laughing, excited. Then, somehow, the old homeless wizard man had found his way up into Tommy's room. He'd handed me an object—an eyeball.

An eyeball.

I sat up straight on the sofa. That was what I'd forgotten. The eyeball. It had looked around wildly in the palm of my hand. Startled, I'd dropped it. It'd rolled away, disappearing through the floorboards. Tommy had run from the room then, and I'd desperately chased after him.

Why had the dream given me *that*? I wanted a clue—a real clue.

When I'd woken from the dream, I'd been in Luke's arms, at the top of the stairs. He'd looked at me like I was a strange thing, and he'd spoken about taking me to see Dr Moran. I'd lied that I'd seen her recently. I hadn't. I'd done my best to reassure him, to make love to him like a wife would. I didn't want him to call her.

I felt jittery. Exhausted and jittery at the same time.

Grabbing my jacket from the hall cupboard, I decided to head out. I'd go down to the café and check the noticeboard. Just in case.

Luke had made me promise to leave all that to the police. But I couldn't wait. I'd had six months of waiting and leaving things to the police.

I stood before the hallstand mirror, running my fingers through my hair.

My eyes came to rest upon the notebook that we kept on the stand for messages. *I should start taking a notebook with me everywhere. Train myself to notice everything and everyone. And take notes.*

When the phone pealed out from the hallstand, it seemed like the sound was clanging around inside my head. It was Nan. Wanting me to come and help her dust the house. Her *frozen shoulder* was preventing her from lifting her arms above her head.

I wanted to tell her no. But if I did, she'd bring it up in conversations for the next month. And dusting wouldn't take long. I'd told her I'd be straight down.

Slipping the notebook and a pen into my pocket, I headed out the door.

The fog was so thick this morning, I couldn't see the water at the end of the street.

I didn't even notice Bernice Wick in her front garden—deadheading the roses that her mother seemed to have decided she was never going to prune—until I was just a short distance away. Giving me a guarded look, Bernice rose heavily to her feet and plodded inside. In the dark hallway of number 27, she turned her head and watched me walk past.

With a glance back at her, I walked on into Nan's house. *I'm watching you, too, Bernice.*

Nan was batting at the dust on her shelves with a cloth, her thin body swaying unsteadily.

It was so like Nan to be up first thing in the morning doing her housework. But I didn't know why she bothered. It wasn't as though she ever had a full day of activities planned. After getting up at six and cleaning, she'd spend the rest of the day in her armchair, watching TV and doing puzzles.

"I need to get at the dirt on top of the picture rails and the bookshelves," she said in a stressed tone, as though it were a matter of critical urgency.

"Sure. What happened to your long-handled duster?"

"Broke it trying to get a damned spider web out of the fireplace."

The fireplace, clogged with soot and leaves, hadn't been used in decades. Nan used a small bar heater and a blanket for warmth during winter.

"Do you still have the duster?"

"Yes, it's in the broom cupboard."

"I'll see if I can fix it. There used to be lots of spare handles out in the shed." I started towards the hall that led to the courtyard.

"No, Phoebe," she called after me. "Don't worry yourself. I thought you were tall enough to reach with the cloth, that's all."

I stopped in the hallway. "I'm not six feet tall, Nan."

She hurried after me as I continued out to the courtyard, grabbing my elbow. "Don't worry about it, I told you. None of them would fit."

Twisting around, I shrugged at her. "I'll use some electrical tape or something."

"I've lost the key to the shed anyway."

Sighing, I returned down the hall and picked up a stool from the kitchen.

Nan seated herself in her armchair, casting stony looks at me while I cleaned the dust from the picture rails from the stool.

"Bernice hasn't been well," she said finally. "Intestinal trouble. Bit of pain and bringing up her food."

Her intestines are probably in knots from thinking sour thoughts all the time. Maybe even from sending me terrible letters. "Nan, too many details."

"Why don't you go see her? You two used to be friends."

"Not really, Nan. We were never good friends. And we haven't talked for ages."

"You could make an effort."

"I don't have a reason to make an effort."

She sank back into silence. The entire house sank into silence. I suddenly wanted to be away from here. Away from the musty quiet and old memories tightly locked away in rooms and photo boxes and bric-a-brac.

I turned around to Nan. "All done. Is there anything else?"

"No, that's all. I might do my crosswords now. And I won't want any banging around."

So, my cleaning your house is just me banging around?

I hesitated, wanting to tell her about the letters, but her mention of Bernice had put me on edge. Better not to mention them yet, in case she told Mrs Wick. "Okay, then I'll head home."

She just nodded her head without looking up, already engaged in her puzzle.

But I wasn't going home. I was going straight to the café to check the noticeboard and keep watch.

Outside Nan's house, Bernice Wick walked past, heading in the direction of the harbour.

13.   LUKE

Thursday morning

I HAD A FOLDER OF PHOTOS of Phoebe that she knew nothing about.

I kept the folder at the office, locked in a bottom drawer: all the pictures I took of her when we were growing up, at parties we went to, at trips we went on.

I'd dropped in at the office just after buying the home alarm system. Rob had called me about an issue with a client's sale. The buyer had pulled out of the sale, and the client was screaming bloody murder. It was Rob's sale, but I had a couple of possible alternative buyers on file—I just needed to look them up.

With the client now somewhat sedated by the thought of new buyers and a possible better price (Rob had undervalued the property) I'd headed into my office for a breather.

Not knowing why, I pulled out the photos from the bottom drawer and started flipping through them.

Maybe this folder represented my fantasy world. A lifetime of memories of Phoebe in a fictional life where she had always been mine and mine only.

Photos of Phoebe at Bondi Beach. Photos of Phoebe in nightclubs. Photos of Phoebe that she'd sent me when she backpacked China. I didn't keep the photos in which any of her dates or boyfriends had been in the frame. Because that would have destroyed the illusion.

I grinned at the picture of Phoebe at Pria's baby's first birthday party. Pria had only been twenty when she became pregnant with Jessie. The father of Jessie had run off to New Zealand before Jessie was even born. In the photo, Phoebe was balancing baby Jessie on her knees, but she looked damned awkward.

Phoebe was always awkward with small children, even years later, when we had Tommy. She didn't seem to quite know how to play with him. Neither did I, for that matter, but those things were supposed to come instinctively to women. Weren't they? I admit that I was too focused on my business, on securing the deal and making the sale. On ensuring that my family was going to have the good life. Often, I was too tired at night to sit on the floor and play mindless games with toy cars and plastic dinosaurs.

I pictured Phoebe in Tommy's room last night playing trains with him in her sleep. I didn't know which was more surprising: the fact that my wife was sleepwalking or the fact that she was playing toddler games with Tommy with an actual smile on her face.

At the time I married Phoebe, I thought I had everything in place. It wasn't perfect, but all the pieces were there. What I didn't understand about Phoebe was that she was a moving target. I never had her *in place*.

Everything about the harbour and this street reminded me of Phoebe. I first moved to this street when I was eight. My grandfather on my mother's side of the family had been ill, and my parents moved in to help care for him.

As soon as my parents had stopped the car outside the terrace house that was to become my home, I'd torn away and gone exploring.

Sass and Phoebe had been together in Sass's front yard, hammering together a billycart made of old pieces of wood. Sass was a cute blonde with an upturned nose. Phoebe, with her ponytail and serious eyes, wasn't beautiful yet, but something about her when she squinted up at me grabbed hold of me.

The two of them had been making the billycart all wrong.

I'd taken the hammer from Phoebe and tried to help them.

Phoebe stood up and pushed me, telling me that I just thought they were doing it wrong because they were girls and I was a boy. But that wasn't true. I could see that the wheels weren't going to turn properly on their axles. But Phoebe couldn't admit that. And then Sass stood beside Phoebe and told me to get lost.

I came back the next day with a new tactic—a can of red paint and paintbrush I'd stolen from my dad's shed. The girls didn't let me paint the billycart though. They grabbed the paint and did the job themselves. The thing actually rolled along just fine, in the end. It was just that the way I'd seen them putting it together didn't make sense to me.

I was on the outer of Sass and Phoebe for the first month. I'd turn up and hang around until they pushed me out. Eventually, they let me in.

About a year after that, Pria and Kate got free passes into the group. Because they were girls. And because they had money. Their families were rich. That meant tickets to the movies and buying stashes of food at the local cafés. Bernice got in by stealth. She just appeared whenever we were out in the street doing stuff. No one invited her. She barely spoke, which is probably what saved her.

Life went on like that for years. They were the best years.

Until I turned twelve and realised that my friends were five females. (Yes, so I'd already known that, but those five females hadn't been rapidly morphing into women before. And I hadn't rapidly been becoming a hormone-infused male.)

I wasn't proud that I'd tried kissing all of them at various times. It was Phoebe I wanted—it was always Phoebe—but if I couldn't have her, then one of the others would have to do. I got rejected by all of them, except Bernice, but after I kissed her I decided I didn't want to go in for round two. Trying to kiss the girls put me on the outer of the group again. I was Georgie Porgie.

With each year that passed, the girls made less sense to me. Just like the day when I watched Sass and Phoebe put the billycart together. The teenage Sass, Phoebe, Kate, and Pria were interested in boys that were not me. Even though I was the one that was there and available.

Things changed around the time I turned sixteen. I had a growth spurt that made me sprout taller than any of the girls. I grew stubble, and my voice deepened, and my legs developed a new swagger.

The girls started looking at me differently. They acted differently towards me. I became their collective boyfriend. One that they practiced with.

Sass and I were a thing for a while. The whole thing fizzled after two months—mostly because I didn't want to be what Sass wanted me to be. She wanted some kind of brooding, romantic figure. Then it was Pria— Pria and I hooked up at a party, drunk on bourbon. Six weeks later, she had a late period and two blue lines on a pregnancy test. A month after that, it was all over. A miscarriage. We were off the hook, both of us so relieved and ecstatic we were in tears. She didn't want much to do with me after that—too scared of another pregnancy. The next cab off the rank was Kate, when I was eighteen. We lasted a whole year, even living together. Kate was starting to get her first gigs as a model then. She made doubly sure that no pregnancy bump was going to distort her figure. Things went sour when she found a photo of Phoebe in my wallet and asked me straight out if I would be with Phoebe if I could. I'd taken too long to answer, and she'd guessed the answer for herself.

After that, the girls all took off to university. Not me. I stayed here, kicking around in a few dead-end jobs. My parents bailed me out of a few holes here and there.

Then I saw her again. Phoebe. I was at a mate's house. There was a group of us. Drinking. Thinking about women. Cursing about women. Bragging about women. The usual.

An Australian movie started on the TV. At the beginning, there was a scene of a girl out on a lake with her boyfriend, in a rowboat. The boat overturned when the man stood, and the girl fell in the water, drowning, caught up in reeds beneath the water. The girl was Phoebe. Watching her drown provoked a visceral reaction in me.

I called her up that night. She said she was mostly doing commercials and getting bit parts in movies here and there. She was seeing some actor slash musician guy, but her focus was on her studies. She was going to leave for London once her study at the Australian Film Institute finished.

I needed a plan.

First I borrowed a sizable amount of money from my parents and conjured up a small real estate business. I cleaned myself up, stopped drinking, and got myself a decent wardrobe of clothes. I took on a friend as a business partner—Rob—who'd been working as a junior real estate agent at the time. With his basic knowledge and my bravado, we faked having a wealth of expertise. We were hungry, and we worked harder and longer than anyone else. I packed money away like a squirrel packing nuts in its cheeks.

Eighteen months later, Phoebe had made the move to London. She said she was happy. She'd met a new man—another actor—aptly named Flynn. She and Flynn were doing stage performances together. They were dirt poor and sharing a tiny flat, but I could hear the undercurrent of excitement in her voice. They'd already been to France and Germany together. Life for her had become an adventure. I wasn't part of that adventure.

I hated Flynn instantly.

After that, I'd look up the performances that she told me Flynn would be in, and I'd call her when I knew he wouldn't be around. I wanted her all to myself.

Then came the day she didn't sound the same. I was too stupid at first to know that she was holding back the tears. Flynn had scored a small movie role in Ireland, and he was away on set. He'd called her and told her that he loved her but he needed some space. He'd asked if she wanted to explore an open relationship. He'd told her his feelings for her wouldn't change.

I knew what that meant. It was guy code for *I want you, but I want other girls too. But I'm probably not going to be able to handle seeing you with another man. So how about I leave you dangling on a string while you let me see other girls? In return, I promise not to leave you.*

I knew because I'd had the same thoughts myself, the year I was with Kate. Not that I'd actually gone ahead with verbalising the prospect of an open relationship to her. I didn't know if I'd really want to do it.

I caught a flight to London the next day.

Being in the real estate game had taught me one thing—to move on an opportunity the instant it presented itself.

On the pretext of me *being a friend* to Phoebe and needing her to show me around London, we dined out at night and caught art shows during the day. I went to every show she did. I bunked in with her, sleeping on the floor. Until the night I took Phoebe to a bar and bought her every cocktail known to mankind.

Flynn had called her at the start of that night, to apologise, saying he was flying back from Ireland especially to see her. He was coming tomorrow. She'd dissolved into tears, but I didn't give her time to think too long about him.

When Phoebe and I had returned to the apartment, I'd pretended to take a call on her apartment phone from a strange woman looking for Flynn, calling the phone from my mobile. I told Phoebe the woman had called herself Flynn's girlfriend.

Phoebe and I woke up in bed together the next morning.

When Flynn came to the door in the morning, it was me who answered it. I told him to *fuck off*, in those exact words.

I left Rob managing the real estate business for the next three months. I wasn't going to allow Flynn to weasel his way back in. I'd have risked everything not to let that happen. Even my business. Now, it was Phoebe and I who were doing Europe together, not Phoebe and Flynn.

That guy would have hurt her over and over again.

By the time Phoebe realised she was pregnant, she was already two and a half months in. She was terrified, but from my point of view, things couldn't have worked out better.

We married in England in the spring, in a little stone church in the countryside. My parents, Sass, Kate, and Pria flew over for the ceremony. I offered to pay for Phoebe's grandmother, but she said she'd only be persuaded to fly to the ends of the earth for a funeral.

14.   PHOEBE

Thursday morning

BRINE THICKENED IN THE AIR AS I made my way down to the docks.

The fog had barely eased, still hanging fast at nine in the morning. I didn't like the fog. It hid things from me. Pushing my hand into my coat pocket, I closed my fist around the notebook. After six whole months, today was my first day of pushing back. I'd keep notes on anyone who looked vaguely suspicious. Including Bernice.

A woman dressed in mismatched layers stepped inside the café, carrying an umbrella with a carved duck's head on the handle. Bernice. She always dressed herself strangely.

I crossed the road to the café, giving Bernice a minute first to order her tea. I knew what Bernice always ordered. Straight-down-the-middle tea with milk and three sugars.

There was an unusual amount of tables empty by the window this morning. As though no one wanted to stare out into the mist.

I made a beeline for the noticeboard.

There were just the usual notes and brochures. Nothing else.

I went to grab a coffee, wondering if any of the staff who were here today knew about the envelope that had been on the board yesterday. The police must have spoken to them by now. The young girl wasn't here today, nor the other two staff I'd seen.

A woman with brassy blonde hair served me a coffee and cake. I didn't want the cake, but I could pretend to pick at it. I seated myself at the same table as last time, where I had a good view of most of the patrons.

Bernice was sitting with her back to me. She had her umbrella looped over her chair, the wooden duck's head of the umbrella handle staring at me. She often had umbrellas with her, even if there was only the barest hint of rain. *Maybe she'd melt like a pillar of salt if she got wet,* I thought darkly.

Taking out my notepad and pen, I wrote down today's date. No one would question me writing in the book. There were often writers here — some of them pompous looking, some of them serious looking, either jotting things down with a pencil or tapping away at a keyboard.

I scanned the patrons, looking for someone to start with.

The person who'd written the letters could be anyone. I couldn't make judgments. I had to keep my eyes open for the *I-never-would-have suspected-them* person.

I noticed an angry-looking young girl stirring her coffee. I'd seen her in here before. She always looked that way. I'd start with her. I began writing:

Girl with dyed black hair and dove tattoo is looking especially fierce today. Sits close to the wall, like she's protecting herself from attack from behind. Stirs her coffee like she's mixing poison. No jacket or warm clothes despite the chill. She's either someone who doesn't feel the cold, or she's the typical young person who pretends not to feel it.

She was twirling the spoon in her fingers now, her lips set hard together. She drank the liquid down fast, with an expression of distaste in her eyes.

The girl left abruptly. I could hear Nan's voice in my head: *Boyfriend trouble.* According to Nan, all girls had *boyfriend trouble.* Boys never had *girlfriend trouble.* Boys and men held all the cards, in Nan's eyes.

I finished writing up my notes about the girl.

Sipping my coffee, I looked around for someone new to study, someone who looked a little out of place.

I noticed a man in a suit sitting two tables away from where the girl had been. I realised he'd been looking at me before I glanced his way. He turned his head before I did. Was that because I caught him looking or because he had something to hide?

I made a new page for the man.

Midforties man, in a suit that's seen better days. Probably working in low-level management. Full head of grey-brown hair—more grey than brown. Slouching in his seat. He doesn't want to be here.

I called him *Crumpled Suit Man*. To be fair, the suit was not really crumpled. It just looked like a suit that had been lounged around in a lot and was soft around the edges. I made a guess that the man came home from work each night, mixed himself a tonic of disappointment and dissatisfaction, and then fell asleep on his sofa. Later, he'd wake and call a takeaway place for dinner. He'd silently curse the declining quality of the food and then watch some reality TV show. He didn't live with a woman. At least, I didn't think so.

He turned his head as a woman entered the shop. With interest, he watched the woman in her tight black skirt, boots, and oversized jacket. He drummed his fingers on the table. I didn't see a ring on his hands. He was probably divorced, with an ex-wife and kids somewhere out in the 'burbs. Everyone was someone else's ex.

He kept his eyes on her until she had her coffee and doughnut in her hands and she was walking his way.

I wrote on his page: *Not a paedophile.*

Then shut the book quickly. The look and sound of that word made my stomach turn on itself. Allowing myself to think about what might be happening to Tommy if he was still alive was a type of insanity. No parent could bear to think on it.

People were shuffling in and out of the shop, disappearing into the mist.

I watched them all.

An elderly homeless man wandered past outside the window, deep in the fog. He glanced in momentarily. He seemed so *other*. It was not his life to be sitting on a comfortable chair in fresh clothing drinking coffee.

I lost sight of the man in the fog when a woman inside the shop drew my attention. She was positioned towards the back of the shop, sitting alone. She was past the age of being a city worker. She couldn't see me. I had a view straight through the potted fig tree that was next to me.

Flipping my notebook open again, I made a new page for her.

Woman, late seventies, red coat bunched around her. Hair whitish. Not blue.

Old ladies didn't have blue hair anymore. What had happened to the blue-rinse set? Who told them to stop dying their hair that powdery shade? Someone was replacing them. There weren't even as many little old ladies around anymore. In their place were sharply dressed, coiffed ladies who looked well travelled.

Would I be one of those well-dressed, poised ladies when I reached that age? Or would I turn into Nan—spending my days doing puzzles in my armchair, suspicious of everyone? I was suspicious of everyone now. The only difference was age. Or what if I became Bernice? Living a life away from everyone, never having children. God, why did that thought panic me so much? I hadn't wanted to have children. That was the life that Saskia had chosen. She'd adored Tommy, but said she intended never missing a night's sleep for a baby or having to deal with fingerprints on her walls.

My thoughts were running in all directions. I needed to refocus.

The woman in the red coat was sealing an envelope on her table.

An *envelope*.

It looked blue.

Was it blue? I couldn't tell from here for certain.

I needed to see. Standing, I slipped the notebook into the back pocket of my jeans. Taking my coffee, I wound my way through the tables. The crumpled-suit man looked hopeful as I walked in his direction. Maybe he thought I was going to ask if I could join his table. His face fell as I moved past.

I stopped a couple of tables away from the red-coat woman. She didn't have a view of me. She wouldn't see me looking over her shoulder.

A scent reached me, above all the punchy, rich scents of coffee and Black Forest cake. Caramel Mochaccino. That's what she was drinking.

The envelope sat on her table, resting against the sugar jar. She was finished with it. But there was no name, no address. The envelope was completely blank. Except for its colour. The colour wasn't blank. Because the colour was blue.

Blue.

I held my breath, looking away. The envelope looked similar to the ones I'd received before. Not *exactly* the same, but close enough.

I sensed eyes on me.

When I turned, I expected it to be the crumpled-suit man.

It was Bernice. I guessed I did look strange, just standing here in an odd spot instead of at my table.

Bernice had cake on her table. Banana cake with cream cheese frosting. Didn't look like she was having any trouble with food, as Nan had told me.

When I glanced back at the red-coat woman again, she was gone.

My eyes darted around the shop.

Outside, a flash of red punctuated the dull grey mist. Ignoring Bernice's stare, I headed out after the woman.

She'd had slow movements when she was seated at the table, but she was quick out in the fog. The fog inhaled her, its breath thick and damp. But she'd chosen to wear red, and that was her mistake. I followed her like a human missile, locked on, dogged. People in dark, wintry clothing bled past—like paint running from a watercolour picture. Guarding suitcases, clutching scarfs.

I only just managed to catch up with the red-coat woman in order to board the same bus that she did.

She got off the bus at Circular Quay. The noise of the city intensified here. Commuters running for ferries and trains, disturbed and annoyed by the mist obscuring their view. Ferries and boats slogged through an unseen ocean.

The red-coat woman practically ran up the ramp to the Cremorne ferry, her head bowed.

I hurried through the crowd. I was supposed to have a travel pass—an Opal pass—but I had no time for that. I squeezed through the turnstile together with a surprised child and then rushed up the ferry's ramp.

Businesspeople were sitting inside the ferry like proverbial sardines. But not the woman. Her shoes clattered on the metallic stairs to the top deck. I followed her.

Holding onto the railing out on the open deck, she stared out at the drifts of fog on the harbour. Hugging my arms close to my chest, I moved alongside her.

A corner of the envelope was visible from her handbag. I'd intended just to follow her. But what if she jumped into a taxi once we reached Cremorne (or another destination) and I lost her?

I could slip the envelope out and take a look without her noticing.

Could I really do that? Take something from a stranger's handbag?

Yes, I could. I could do the things that the police couldn't do. The things they weren't allowed to do and didn't have time for.

My fingers trembled as I tugged the envelope free.

She jolted and spun around like some kind of red-coated Whirling Dervish.

"What are you doing?" She tried to snatch the envelope back.

"I need—" I didn't know how to finish that sentence. My brain was fused to the thought that I needed to look inside it. But I couldn't tell her that.

She yanked the envelope again.

It tore. There was a card inside. And a red twenty-dollar bill. Half of the bill shot upwards in the wind, swirling out above the ocean and disappearing into the mist.

She stared with horror at the ripped money and envelope in her hand. "I saw you, in the coffee shop. You watched me put that money in there, didn't you? You stole it. My great-grandson's birthday money."

People on the ferry were eyeing us with confusion and disgust. *Stealing from an old lady! For twenty dollars!*

I backed away. "I didn't know. I'm sorry. I thought it was something else." I dug in my bag for my wallet. "I'll give you the twenty."

"Just leave me alone!" She was shrieking righteously now, spurred by the attention of the people who were gathering around her.

Someone had me by the shoulder. A man's voice came from behind me. "Get your drug money someplace else. Kings Cross, maybe."

The man kept hold of me until security arrived. Until the ferry docked and the police arrived.

I was led from the ferry with the mist saturating my hair and clothing.

15. PHOEBE

Friday morning

LUKE AND DETECTIVE GILROY BANNED ME from the Southern Sails Café. Trent called Luke down to the station, and the two of them had sat there with their arms crossed, telling me that I was to stay completely away from the café and its noticeboard. The only thing I was allowed to check was the letterbox. (I'd checked it twice today already.)

Trent managed to keep my name out of the media reports. The red-coat woman herself was simply told by the police that I'd been suffering an emotional disturbance, and she'd agreed not to press charges.

The medication and lack of sleep were leading me to make poor decisions. I had to be smarter than that.

For the second day in a row, Luke stayed home from work. This time to keep watch over me. He was fiddling with the arsenal of intruder alarm equipment that he'd bought yesterday, cursing loudly at the instructions. He knew a bit about alarms—he'd had to deal with enough of them at the properties that he'd sold over the years—but still, this one was causing him a bit of grief.

I stayed out of his way, busying myself with the wall garden, making curried egg sandwiches for us at lunchtime and making a batch of scones for afternoon tea. I needed to redeem myself somehow in his eyes, and making food was the (second) best way I knew how.

Luke liked me in this mode.

I wiped the bench free of flour from the scones I'd made, picturing myself in one of the TV ads I'd once made, in which I'd played a smug homemaker serving dinner to her family.

I'd made two commercials that day. One in which I was a happy-go-lucky girl enthused by her tampon brand choice, and that afternoon a homemaker magically transforming *an ordinary meal* into a gourmet meal (with the addition of a packet sauce).

Women were always the ones serving food in ads. Unless the ad was for pre-packaged diet food. Then the husband would serve the wife—showing prospective female customers how easy and sublime it was to lose weight (also sending the subliminal message that your husband wanted you to lose the chub).

The only real difference in my physical look between the tampon and sauce ads had been the clothing. Homemakers wore sensible shoes and neatly pressed pastel shirts over their pastel tank tops. The pastel layering was important. Homemakers layered their clothing.

Homemakers no longer found joy in the outside world. They weren't like tampon-girl out water-skiing and diving. They were fulfilled by the indoor environment. By the type of butter and washing powder and antibacterial spray they were clever enough to buy.

In every one of those kinds of ads, the female homemaker frowned as a problem presented itself. But after a brief moment of stress, she solved her dilemma with a brand-name product. Then she could relax and sit down with a coffee, assured in the knowledge that her offspring now had the right kind of butter on their sandwiches or that her husband had soil-free shirts or that her house was completely sanitised.

I didn't get chosen for the same kind of commercials that the male actors did. Men weren't happy in domesticity—the ads told everyone so.

Men were always trying to sneak away from their wives, to win some time drinking beer with their mates or watching the game. Wives and girlfriends were boring creatures who tried to hold men back from their fun. (Unless the women were walking past in a bikini. Then women turned on the fun like a tap.)

Luke and I had fallen into our respective roles even before Tommy was born. Luke had been absorbed by his work, and he used to go drinking after work with Rob, fulfilling his role of getting away from the wife and home. And I'd stayed in the house, becoming a thing I no longer recognised. I'd sanitised myself.

I didn't hear Luke step up behind until his arms were halfway around me.

He kissed my neck. "Alarm is in. No one's getting past that."

"Great." *What if I sleepwalked around the house while that thing was switched on? I'd set it off.* I put a smile on my face before I turned around to him.

He eyed the plate of scones on the bench. "Nice. Hey, did you even have any?"

"I had a couple." I hadn't. Luke wouldn't know that the scone tray made ten and that the four he'd already had were the only ones missing from the plate. Luke had never made scones or cupcakes in his life.

"Good. You have to start building yourself up again." He spread butter and jam on a scone and ate it in two bites.

Noticing the alarm remote control sticking out of his shirt pocket, I slipped it out. "You'll have to show me how to work that thing."

He took it back. "It's okay, Feeb. I'll set it every night and turn it off before I leave in the morning."

"But I still need to know how to use it. What if I want to set it during the day while I'm sleeping?"

"I didn't think of that. Okay, I'll take you through it in a bit. Might kick back with a beer first. Come and sit down with me."

"I was thinking of heading out for a walk." *If I couldn't go to the café, I'd planned on watching who went in and out.* I still had the notebook and pen in my pocket.

"Phoebe, you can't go anywhere near the—"

"I know. I wasn't planning on going that way. Just along the water."

"I'll come with you."

I pressed my lips in and gave him what I hoped was a reassuring expression. "You don't have to do that."

"I just don't think you should head out that far alone. Not until they catch the whacko who's sending the notes. We don't know what or who we're dealing with."

"It's daylight. *You* go out running by yourself. At night."

"Phoebe . . ." He eyed me intently, repeatedly flipping the remote over and back in his hand, almost as if he wished he could press a button on it and stop me from leaving.

I needed him to trust me again. At least, as much as he trusted me the day before yesterday. My shoulders went slack. "Okay, I'll stay at home."

Sitting with him, I watched TV instead of going on my walk, his arm safely around me. But I couldn't focus on the show that Luke had put on. I started planning for tonight.

I didn't have time to *leave everything to the police*. The letters were personal, sent to me. And I had to figure out who was sending them.

*

I watched Luke sleeping in our bed, waiting to make sure he was in a deep, unshakeable slumber. The muted horns and blasts of the distant boats in the harbour penetrated my mind. It was only in the early hours of the night that you could hear those sounds from way up here on the hill.

Luke was snoring rhythmically now. He wouldn't wake.

I stole from the bed and entered the guest bedroom. I locked the door and pushed a set of drawers firmly against it. My head was heavy and drowsy as I slipped into the bed.

I'd already taken the sleeping medication. And I'd disabled the alarm, just in case. But I intended not leaving this room tonight.

Now all I needed to do was to get to sleep. I tried a trick that Dr Moran had recommended. Imagining myself stepping down a staircase as high as a mountain, to my comfortable bed below, feeling myself growing wearier and heavier with each step.

I drifted along in a haze.

Someone was bouncing something outside the room. I tried to keep sleeping, but the noise wouldn't stop.

Thump, thump.

Thump, thump.

It sounded like a ball bouncing down the stairs.

I sat up like a springboard.

Thump, thump.

Thump, thump.

Yes, exactly like a ball on the stairs.

Tommy?

He could fall down the stairs in the dark.

In a panic, I rushed to the door. Something was blocking me. Who'd left a piece of furniture here? I set my shoulder against the set of drawers and nudged it out of the way.

I clicked the door lock open.

Out in the hallway, I looked for the stairs. They were in a different place to normal. I'd been sleeping in the wrong bedroom.

I forgot my confusion when I noticed Tommy's small frame crouching at the top of the staircase.

It *was* him. Holding a ball.

He let the ball go and watched it bounce down the stairs.

He was wearing the same T-shirt, shorts, and hat that he always wore, the plastic yacht under his arm. He covered his eyes like the wise monkey who could see no evil.

Turning his head in my direction, he snatched his hands away and cried, "Boo!"

"Tommy, it's dangerous to play here," I chided him.

He tilted his head as he looked up at me, his church-pew eyes luminous in the dark. Rising, he jumped onto the first stair.

"You'll fall!" I ran, trying to reach him, but the hallway spanned out like a tunnel and suddenly Tommy was so, so far away from me. I panted with the effort of trying to reach the end of the tunnel. My lungs ached.

Without warning, the stairs fell away, leaving a bottomless chasm.

Time seemed to speed up now as I raced forward.

I teetered at the edge of the gap, unable to jump it and get to Tommy. A moth fluttered in front of my face, blurring my vision. I swatted it away. It spiralled down into the hole, its wings broken.

Tommy was running for the front door.

Closing my eyes, I made the jump.

I landed at the bottom of the staircase.

Somehow, the ball was still bouncing down the last of the stairs. I held out my hands to catch it. The ball was Tommy's, and I had to give it back to him. But the ball transformed into something else. An eyeball. It rolled in my palm until I cried out and dropped it.

I turned sharply as I heard the squeaking sound of pedals behind me.

Tommy was sitting on my old tricycle from Nan's house. How had he managed to get that? He giggled, pedalling it towards the front door. How was he able to ride it? He wasn't quite big enough.

I didn't have time to think on that because the front door was open, and Tommy was passing through it. Even at this time of night there would be cars out there.

Wind made the door slam shut.

I rattled the handle, but it was firmly locked.

Key. I needed the key. Where was it?

I remembered. I hurried to the hallstand and yanked the drawer open. With the key in hand, I returned to unlock the door.

A blast of chilled air froze me instantly as I stepped outside. Where was Tommy? He wasn't wearing warm enough clothes for this kind of weather. I searched along the garden path and out into the street.

A hand grabbed me from the bushes of my neighbour's front yard.

Was it the wizard-man again? I couldn't see him properly. It was dark, and he was well concealed.

"Please help me," I begged him. "I'm looking for Tommy."

He nodded and gave me something.

It was a knife. A kitchen knife. A dark liquid gleamed on its blade. A coppery scent rose in the air. Blood. It was blood.

What was I supposed to do with the knife? Did the wizard want me to kill Tommy's abductor? *I would do it.* A cold rage flashed through me.

But I didn't know the identity of the abductor yet.

The shadowy wizard told me to hide the knife until it was time. Obeying, I took the knife to a safe place.

The sound of the tricycle echoed way down the hill. How did Tommy get down there so fast? He must have taken his feet off the ground and just let the bike go.

I raced after him, the wind rushing against me. I found him sitting on the tricycle in the middle of the footpath, with the wide darkness bearing down on him. Waiting for me.

He shuffled the bike around and tugged open a gate.

Nan's house. He was going into Nan's house.

Standing on the tricycle seat, he wriggled Nan's front door open and rode inside.

As I ran the rest of the way to Nan's house and along the path, the door swung shut. I tried to open it, as Tommy had done, but it was locked now. I knew that Nan kept spare keys nearby, inside the screw-top head of the fisherman statue. Luke had bought her the statue to stop her from leaving the keys under a pot plant. Two keys were needed to open Nan's door, but my fingers felt too fat and clumsy for the task. What was wrong with me? I persisted until I had the door open.

Tommy was inside, waiting for me again. He rode the tricycle through the narrow hallway that led directly to Nan's courtyard. Nan would be upset with him when she heard him riding the tricycle in here.

At least I'd be able to corner him out in the courtyard. There were six-foot-high brick walls and nowhere for him to go.

I dashed into the hallway and through to the courtyard. The familiar smell of damp, mouldy earth enveloped me.

Tommy had climbed onto the seat of his tricycle again, and he was banging on the toolshed door.

There must be something he wanted inside the shed. I had to get it for him.

I started helping him, shifting the pot plants out of the way. Why did Nan have so many of these damned pots jammed up against the shed door? Three of the pots shattered, dirt spilling on the paving.

When I turned around to Tommy, he was gone. And so was the tricycle.

I didn't get the shed open fast enough, and he'd grown impatient. I needed to do this thing for him, and then maybe I'd gain his trust. I couldn't figure what could be in Nan's old shed that he wanted. But then, I didn't know everything there was to know about Tommy. Even though I was his mother. After all, he'd gone with a stranger all those months ago, and he hadn't called out for me or screamed. No one had even reported seeing a crying child. Had he cried for me at all? The letter said he hadn't.

A mix of annoyance and anger burned through my veins.

Tommy hadn't grieved the loss of me.

But I had a job to do right now, and I had to get it done.

Encircling the largest pot with my arms, I puffed and grunted as I wrenched it out of the way. Then I returned to the shed.

A rusted bolt was lying horizontally across the doors. Padlocked.

Where was the key?

Nan said she'd lost it.

I rattled the doors repeatedly.

I needed to get inside. I needed to get to Tommy. Kicking at the door, I cried out in frustration.

Hands reached around my middle, forcing me back.

The hands spun me around.

Luke, dressed in nothing but sleep shorts, frowned at me. "*Phoebe!* For God's sake! What are you doing?"

I stared back at him in confusion. How did Luke suddenly get to Nan's toolshed? "Tommy was just here. We need to—"

"Tommy isn't here. Calm down, honey. You're dreaming. Just dreaming."

I wanted to hurt Luke for saying that. I wanted to—

But then the fog inside my mind lifted.

God, I was all the way down here, in Nan's yard. Not just dreaming. *Really here.* Somehow I'd gotten myself out of the house.

I remembered chasing Tommy outside into the street and down to Nan's house. I remembered him trying to get into the toolshed. But of course, I hadn't been chasing Tommy. I'd been chasing a dream. The familiar hollow feeling swept through me, as it always did after a Tommy dream.

Nan stepped out from behind Luke. "You scared the living daylights out of me. Out here carrying on. I tried to call you inside, but you wouldn't listen!"

The lights were on at Mrs Wick's house. She must have heard the pots smashing and me rattling doors and screaming like a lunatic. Bernice was staring down at me from her bedroom window, her fingers touched to the glass.

Ignoring Bernice, I eyed the damage I'd caused to the yard. Upset pots were strewn across the ground, gaping mouths with earth vomiting from them.

"I'm sorry," I told Nan remorsefully. "I didn't hear you."

"Didn't hear me? I think the whole neighbourhood heard me. I had to call your husband to come and restrain you!"

"I'm sorry, Nan. I thought I was following Tommy, and then—"

Her sharp eyes narrowed. "You're not taking drugs, are you?"

Luke slung an arm around me protectively. "Of course she's not. I told you she must be sleepwalking." His arm was cold on my neck. He must have run down here as soon as he got Nan's call and not bothered getting dressed.

"I haven't known anyone to travel this far in their sleep." Nan drew her dressing gown together under her neck. "Now, get back to your own house, the two of you. We'll see about this trouble in the morning."

"I'll come by in the morning to tidy the mess," Luke told her. "And pay for the broken stuff." He squeezed my shoulder. "Let's go."

I took a few steps then stopped, hesitating. "Nan, why do you keep the shed locked?"

"There's nothing in there anyone needs," she answered with irritation in her voice. "Just old things belonging to your grandfather. I locked it up when Tommy first started walking. I didn't want him getting into anything nasty."

I sucked my lips in tightly, trying to hold back my growing desperation. "Could I see inside, just for peace of mind? I dreamed that Tommy needed something in there."

She shook her head "I've misplaced the key. I told you that when you wanted the broom handles."

"Then Luke can open it. With a hammer or something."

"He'll do nothing of the sort." She waved her hand as if to shoo us away like bothersome insects.

"Phoebe, let it go." Luke said gently. "It's enough for one night."

My shoulders slumped inward. "Okay."

Like a contrite child, I let Luke lead me away and into Nan's house. I sensed Nan's gaze like sharp pins raining on my back. I'd forgotten about Bernice, but I knew she'd still be there, watching.

A light rain began to mist in the air as Luke and I walked the hill to our house. Me in pyjamas and Luke just in sleep shorts.

"Who's that?" Luke said suddenly. He pointed ahead, quickening his steps.

I peered into the night, trying to see what he did. Across the street and up a short distance, the tall shape of a man lingered near our front gate.

Luke broke into a run. *"Hey!"*

The man ran off. There was no way Luke was going to catch him, but he barrelled after the man anyway.

I continued on to our house, shivering in my damp clothes.

Luke returned, panting heavily, his hair plastered across his forehead. "Couldn't—catch—him."

He clutched the gate, catching his breath. He'd grown unfit over the past few months, despite his nightly jogs.

Frowning suddenly, he stepped past me to the mailbox.

Something had been shoved inside it.

Luke stared back at me. "It's an envelope."

I gasped. Even in the deep of night, I could see that it was blue.

The man we'd seen—*he was the person who'd written those letters*. He had to be. We'd almost had the guy in our grasp.

When I looked up at Luke, I saw that he'd had the same thought. "We're not letting him get away."

He charged into the house for the car keys and out again.

We jumped in the car.

Luke roared up our street and around onto the next block. And the next block, and the next after that and back again.

The man had vanished.

"Call the police," Luke instructed me.

I picked up his mobile phone from the car's console and made the call.

The police asked for a description. I couldn't tell them anything apart from the fact he was wearing a long jacket and cap. I could barely think. My head was hazy from the sleepwalk episode and too full of terror at what this next letter would say. I stared across at Luke, but he shook his head. He hadn't seen anything more than I had.

The police said they'd send two police cars to scout the streets to see if they could find the man. We were to head back home and give the police a statement about what we'd seen.

Luke pulled up outside our house and hit the steering wheel with both hands. "Hell, he was right there, Phoebe. He was right there."

"Maybe he wanted us to see him," I said darkly.

"What?"

"It fits with the letters. It's a game. He wanted us to see him. He already had a hiding place planned. That's why we couldn't find him."

"That's a stretch."

"Is it? Isn't sending these letters to grieving parents a bold move as it is?"

"Guess you're right. It's a risky thing to do."

The letter. We hadn't forgotten it, but in the race to grab hold of the man, we'd pushed all thought of what this letter would say aside.

"Feeb, go in and get dressed. I'll stay out here and wait for the police. I don't want to touch the letter, and I don't want to leave it unguarded either. Don't want to give him a chance to come back and grab it." His voice hardened. "Maybe this is going to tell us something."

"I'm not going inside. I'll stay with you."

We stood together, clutching hands, watching the envelope as though it were a bomb that was threatening to explode, each of us fighting an urge to yank it out and tear it open.

16.   LUKE

Saturday morning

FIRST THING IN THE MORNING, I cancelled all my appointments.

Long hours dragged by as I waited with Phoebe for Gilroy to arrive. It was already 11:15 a.m.

The police had taken the letter with them last night, at 3:40 in the morning. I didn't know why the hell it was taking them so damned long to look at the letter and get back to us. My fear was starting to turn to frustration and anger. I wanted things to happen, but everything was moving like it was stuck in sludge.

Phoebe and I spotted a couple of police cars moving up and down our street, still looking—we assumed—for the man from last night.

Gilroy finally showed up at 11:27.

He walked into our house with an expression that didn't give a lot away, which only added to my frustration. He had us sit down, and he pulled out a handwritten note from his pocket. "I copied this down from the letter," he started. "Like the others, the real letter was done on a typewriter. The same typewriter. The same paper."

"What . . . what does it say?" Phoebe's fingers closed tightly around mine.

Gilroy silently handed the letter to us. I murmured the words as I read the note:

Little Boy Blue
Why'd she let you go?
On red ships and yellow boats
'Round and 'round you row

"That gives us exactly nothing!" Phoebe cried.

The pain in her voice tore at me.

"We were hoping for more." Gilroy's shoulders rose and fell as he sighed heavily. "I think we're dealing with a person who just isn't well."

I shot a sideways glance at Phoebe, not wanting to voice what was on my mind in front of Phoebe but losing the battle to hold it back. "It sticks in my throat to say this," I said to Gilroy, "but could this person be wanting to tell us that Tommy drowned in the harbour, or that his body is being concealed on a boat there?"

Phoebe made a choked noise, taking the letter from me with stiff fingers and rereading it, as though it had some proof in it of what I'd said.

I shouldn't have said it.

Gilroy watched Phoebe then flicked his eyes to me. "We investigated both of those options in the weeks after Tommy went missing. We searched all the boats."

"I know," I said, rubbing my neck, "but I'm just trying to get some meaning out of that note."

Gilroy perched on the edge of the sofa opposite us. "I'll tell you that we're certainly going to follow this up to the best of our ability. But there just might not be any meaning to the rhymes."

"But the guy from last night has to have had something to do with Tommy's disappearance, right?" I nodded at him, expecting him to agree with me.

"We're running a few lines of investigation, and of course we'll take the man you saw into account."

"What about the lab tests on the letter?" I asked.

He finally nodded, watching Phoebe again as she let the note drop through her fingers onto the coffee table. "They'll take a while. We'll be going over the envelope and letter with a fine-tooth comb, trust me." He still had his eyes on my wife. "How are you today, Phoebe?"

She glanced across at him. "Fine, thank you. I think these notes must be stressing me out. I've never been a sleepwalker."

"Well, that was some extreme sleepwalking last night." He looked worried. "You're going to have to take precautions to make sure it can't happen again. Not safe to be out there wandering the streets at night."

Gilroy's phone buzzed, and he had a brief conversation with the person on the other end of the line.

"I've got to run," Gilroy told us. "But I'll let you know that we're throwing everything at this. Luke, we've got your statement about the height and body shape of the man, and we're following that up. We've got forensics analysing the letter and envelope. Rest assured we're keeping our minds open."

I stayed by Phoebe's side the rest of the day, waiting for more news. She read and reread and reread the note, as if trying to glean some meaning from between the lines.

The hours had weights attached to them. It seemed like things were moving like a freight train and stalled at the station at the same time. Three notes in as many days. What the hell did they mean? I imagined having my hands around the throat of that guy. My mind should be fixed on Tommy, but it wasn't. I wanted the cold release of choking this person until they had no air left in their lungs.

"Want me to make you something for lunch?" Phoebe stood before me, the sun that was coming in from the rear glass doors giving her hair an intense glint. Her eyes looked dull and tired, but you otherwise wouldn't know she'd been roaming the neighbourhood in her sleep last night. I could tell from her barely controlled posture that she was looking for something to do, somewhere to direct her energy.

"Are you eating, too?"

"I can't. . ."

I shook my head slowly. "I'll make it, and you're going to eat it with me."

"I'm sick in the stomach. I'll only throw it up."

"Feeb, you haven't been eating enough. Your hip bones are sticking out."

Straight away, I felt bad. She didn't need that. Not now. And I couldn't separate out how much of that comment was concern for her health and how much was my distaste at how angular she'd become.

Her expression changed to a mix of defensiveness and hurt. "I'll go make us coffee." She headed out to the kitchen before I could formulate something to soften what I'd just said.

I switched on the TV, wanting something to fill the silence that Phoebe had left behind.

There was an ad about life insurance: a smiling woman giving her family dinner while the husband looked on, thinking about happy-sunshiny dinner topics, such as his own mortality. He was worrying himself into the grave about the kind of dinners and lifestyle the family would have in the future if he wasn't around to provide it.

I flicked around the channels, hunting for something to catch my attention. But nothing did. I slumped on the sofa, watching part of a Star Wars movie.

The ad break cut to a news broadcast.

I saw Tommy's face. There on the screen.

No warning.

Cut to our street. My house. *My damned house.* A reporter outside talking about the notes. *Live.*

News had got out about the letters. In a big way.

I loped across the room and through the hall, to the small foyer that had the only downstairs window that looked out onto the street.

Cameras. Reporters. Neighbours peering from their front yards.

I turned as Phoebe walked up behind me with two cups of coffee. She stared out at the scene on the street with troubled eyes.

17.   PHOEBE

Saturday midday

I WATERED THE WALL GARDEN FURIOUSLY, drowning it.

Cameramen were camping out in our street. Reporters were interviewing neighbours so that they had something "new" to report each hour. Luke turned down all attempts by reporters to interview us.

I ended up in my room, curled on my bed, waiting for all of it to end.

The activity happening down there was going to scare the letter-writer underground and make it harder for the police to find him. It was the first real breakthrough we'd had. There was a real possibility that the kidnapper was coming to *us*. My heart alternatively squeezed and pounded. I didn't know how long a person could exist in this state. But I couldn't calm myself. Not until the moment the police had this man in their hands.

I heard Luke opening the door to someone downstairs. Surely he wasn't letting any of the reporters in?

"Phoebe," he called up the stairs, "the girls are here to see you."

I'd barely seen any of my friends since the day Tommy disappeared. I'd locked myself away, refusing to see people. The only thing I'd had energy for—mental or physical—was the search for Tommy.

Combing my fingers through my hair, I stepped out of my room to the top of the stairs.

Saskia, Kate, and Pria stood huddled together, staring up at me with anxious faces, the three of them dressed in smart jackets, scarfs, and jeans. Saskia led the charge—all of them rushing up the stairs to me.

They grabbed me in a hug.

"God, this can't be real," Sass exclaimed. "Letters about Tommy? Why didn't you call us?"

Pria swept her blond locks back, tucking her fringe beneath her knit cap. "I was in shock when I saw the news. I called everyone."

I bunched my eyes shut for a second, shaking my head. "It's been a whirlwind. Three notes in two days."

Kate's large blue eyes went watery. "The news said you saw a strange man just before you found the last note. I feel terrible . . ."

I frowned at her in confusion. "Why—"

Kate sucked her lips in, running her hand distractedly along the long dark plait that was draped on her shoulder like a rope. "Elliot and I have been noticing a man hanging about our block at night. We take turns to go for a run, after dinner when the twins are in bed. About nine o'clock. I mean, it's not unusual for there to be a stranger around here, but it's just that this guy seems to be hanging around night after night, not really going anywhere. I didn't think to tell the police. It wasn't like he was doing anything illegal. But what if—"

"Where do you see him?" I straightened, shivering.

"Along our street and down at the docks," Kate answered.

"What does he look like?" I asked straight after she'd finished, desperate for a clue about the man's identity.

She winced apologetically. "Can never see him all that well. It's dark, and it's been a foggy winter. He's about six foot. Wears a big jacket and a cap. And he's got a bit of a goatee. Or maybe a beard."

"So he's just always hanging around?" I pressed. "Could he be homeless?"

An awful picture flashed through my mind of Tommy being kept by a homeless man. I remembered from my research that a homeless man had abducted a toddler from a library in California. *A library of all places.* A sharp-eyed bus driver had recognised the man and child from a police bulletin when the man took the boy onto a bus. The boy was returned to his mother within hours.

Kate thought for a moment. "Could be homeless, but he's definitely not one of those dudes you normally see with the long beards and the dingy old clothes."

I took out my phone from my pocket. "Kate, would you mind, I mean, telling the police about him? They're looking for the man I saw now."

"Sure. Anything if it can help."

"Thanks." I breathed out a tight breath. "How about we go downstairs and get a bit more comfortable?"

I led them down into the kitchen. Luke was on the phone with an aunt, talking about the notes. The whole world was talking about the notes.

He nodded at them in acknowledgement and then headed upstairs, still on the phone.

I made the call to Detective Gilroy and then put Kate on. I listened with chills crawling down my spine as Kate told the detective what she'd seen.

Was she describing the same man? What was he doing in the street every night?

Sass busied herself around the kitchen, putting the jug on and getting cups ready. Pria helped her, finding the tea and coffee.

Kate finished her call and handed me the phone. "I hope it helps. I'm afraid I couldn't provide much information."

Sass distributed the cups of hot liquid. In an emergency, the person you'd always want to call was Sass. She was a born organiser.

Sliding back onto a stool, Pria eyed me with a worried expression. "I couldn't believe it when I heard what's been happening. You poor thing. Are you okay?"

"Yes, I'm okay. So far." Gratefully taking the coffee that Sass offered me, I told the girls about the letters, starting with finding the first one in my mailbox after an early-morning walk.

I left out the bit about my sleepwalking. I knew that Pria, as a psychologist, would switch to her professional mode. She'd ask awkward questions about my sleeping patterns and medications. I knew she'd try to get me to stop taking the sleeping pills. And I didn't know if I could stop.

"Crazy." Sass shook her head, stirring her coffee. "After all these months."

Pria reached for my hand and squeezed it. "I pray that it's leading somewhere."

"I hope so." I rubbed my forehead. A headache that had sprung to life in my temples a few minutes ago had migrated behind my eyes.

Kate picked through a box of varied herbal teas and delicately selected a tea bag. Since her late teens when she'd first started modelling, Kate had been a devotee of clean living. "The press had better pack up and leave soon. How're the police supposed to do their job with *them* hanging around?"

"Well," said Sass, "you never know what the broadcasts might dig up. Someone might know something. Maybe someone even drove past and saw the guy putting the letter in Phoebe's letterbox."

Kate lifted her chin in a half nod, still looking dubious.

She and Sass had had the same argument many times before—about the police versus the press and public. Kate was strong on law and order. Sass believed in the power of the people. Kate never used to be like that. But she'd changed after she married a cop.

Pria was usually the peacemaker in between. Me, I was none of those things. I'd slip randomly into any role or point of view. Loyal to no cause.

Sass tugged at the scarf around her neck, loosening it, a U-shaped frown settling in between her eyebrows. "Kate, was the guy you saw sort of wide across the shoulders?"

Kate twisted her mouth, thinking. "Yeah. But not in a muscly way. More in a *just big* kind of way."

"That half sounds like Justin," said Sass. "He was that guy I went on a couple of dates with about a month back. When I told him I didn't want to see him anymore, he became a huge pain in the butt. Turning up at work, loitering outside my apartment block. It's probably not him, though. Justin's a gym junkie. You know, with the guns and the shoulders and the abs."

Pria set her tea down on the bench. "That's stalking, Sass. Is he still doing it?"

"No," Sass replied. "He stopped after a couple of weeks. But Kate's mention of a guy hanging around made me wonder. Only, Justin doesn't have a goatee. He's clean shaven. All over." She paused. "But I guess he could have grown one. How long does it take a guy to grow a goatee?"

Kate gave a slight grin. "About as long as it takes you to grow back your map of Tasmania."

Smirking, Sass glanced down briefly at her lap. "Can't compare. I go in for deforestation every six weeks at the salon. But men don't wax. Usually. So a guy's beard would grow a lot faster." Sobering, she eyed me directly. "If your detective wants any details about Justin, just let me know. But I can't see there being any connection."

"Okay, thanks." I breathed in and out slowly. "Sorry that this Justin guy ended up having a screw loose."

A wry smile dimpled her cheek. "I'd rather be on my own anyway. No more men."

Pria raised her left eyebrow, angling it high. She was so expert at doing that that it was more effective than speaking.

"It's common in Japan," Sass studied her red, expertly painted fingernails.

"What is?" I asked.

"Living alone," Sass answered with an almost prim air. "Focusing on your career. When I went there last year I was blown away by the way many of the women live. It's a new era. You don't even need sex. What's it good for? Babies and STDs."

I shook my head, smiling. Sometimes, it was hard to know if Sass was serious or not.

Kate raised her eyes at Sass from above her cup of tea. "But what about, you know, fun?"

Sass shrugged. "My job's fun. All the travelling I do is fun. And when I want the other kind of fun, I've got my trusty rabbit."

"Except, men don't run out of batteries," teased Pria.

"Elliot does." Kate twisted her plait around her finger. "A lot. He's tired all the time. Stressful job I guess." She kept her eyes on Pria. "How about you? Didn't you meet someone new? The navy dude? How's his batteries?" She winked.

Pria nodded. "Yeah. Michael and I are still seeing each other. Believe it or not, we haven't done the deed yet."

"Makes me feel bad you've been seeing someone new and I didn't even know," I told Pria. "I ran into Jessie the other day—literally—and she made me promise to come and visit."

"You so should," Pria said.

"I will." In truth, I didn't know if I would. "How's Jessie and your new guy getting on?"

"Oh, the whole thing is so difficult. He's away a lot with the navy. I want him to have a relationship with her, but I can't see how that's ever going to happen."

Sipping her lemon camomile tea, Kate studied Pria's face sympathetically. "Shame he can't be there with you. I hate it when Elliot is away for even a night. And that's only happened twice. If I'd had a break-in, I'd be so nervous being on my own that I couldn't sleep."

I frowned at Pria. "Your house got broken into?"

She pulled her mouth tight. "Yes. Back in January. You had enough to worry about without me telling you my woes. It was nothing, really. Someone got in through one of the downstairs windows. They stole a bit of jewellery. Probably teenagers."

"Still, it would make you worry," I told her.

"It did unsettle me," Pria admitted. "Even more because they got in while I was sleeping. Thank God Jessie was away at a holiday camp. Anyway, I got us a dog. Nothing's happened since."

"God, I'm glad you're okay." I was relieved to hear that Jessie wasn't there. If she'd woken when the intruders were in the house, things could have gone badly.

"Anyway, enough of that," said Pria, brightening. "Have you been back to the local theatre group, Phoebe? Jessie and I have been waiting for your next performance. We really enjoyed the last play you were in."

"I gave the whole theatre thing away," I told her. "My heart's not in it anymore. Showed in my performance, too."

"No way, girlie." Saskia waggled a finger at me. "You were great in that play, and don't go telling yourself any different."

They'd all come to the play. Luke and Nan, too. Even—strangely—Bernice. But I'd let them all down.

If I'd ever been any good at acting, I wasn't now. There really wasn't anything that I *was* good at. I hadn't proved to be much of a wife or a mother. I wasn't good at supporting Luke with his business—I had no interest in it. There was only one thing left, and that was finding Tommy. And I was determined to be good at that.

"You were always making us act in your one-minute plays when we were kids." A wide smile dimpled Kate's face.

The conversation shifted to our old days together on this street. All our conversations led back there, and once they did, we knew we were in for the long haul.

Moving from the kitchen to the living room, we chatted about the homes that had been demolished and the people who were missing from the street, about Luke stealing flowers from people's gardens to give us all flowers, about how Saskia's bedroom was so messy you had to excavate it just to find her in it, how Pria used to rescue all the abandoned cats in the neighbourhood, how Kate used to switch the garden gnomes around in people's front yards and how I used to pretend to busk on city streets—randomly walking up while a real busker was taking a break and bursting into some song from a musical.

A wave of exhaustion hit me.

This day had left me so, so ragged.

I woke on the sofa, with a blanket over me. Sass, Kate, and Pria were gone. The wall clock had the time at four in the afternoon. I'd slept for hours—the longest stretch of sleep I'd had in weeks.

Padding over to the window at the front of the house, I peered out. One diehard reporter remained.

I couldn't take the sleeping pills tonight. I couldn't risk ending up out there on the streets again. First, I needed to find a way of securing myself so that there was no way of getting out.

God, I'm like an addict planning my next fix. Is this real—are my dreams really giving me clues? Or have I just become addicted to the dreams or to the sleeping pills or to avoiding life?

Behind me, the sudden peal of the home phone in our silent house made me jump.

18.   LUKE

Saturday afternoon

I GRABBED THE PHONE FROM THE kitchen wall before it woke Phoebe.

"Hello?" Crazily I was almost expecting it to be the letter-writer himself, reading out one of his rhymes over the phone.

It wasn't.

"Luke," said Gilroy, "we've got some new information." An edge cut into his voice.

I jumped to my feet. "What have you got?"

"I'd like for you both to come down to the station."

Phoebe came running into the kitchen, stopping and staring at me with wide eyes.

"Just tell me one thing," I asked Gilroy, trying to keep my teeth unclenched. "Do you have an idea which fucker is sending those notes to us?"

"We need to discuss this in person, and naturally it's going to be very upsetting for you both. But yes, we do have information."

"Hell. You *do* know. We'll be there." I ended the call, a million thoughts ramming my head.

There'd been something in Gilroy's tone that had flattened me. He should have sounded a bit more celebratory if they had their guy. What was wrong here that he wasn't saying? Did the police now know for certain that Tommy was dead? Was this the end of the journey that started with Tommy being abducted? Whatever the news was, it wasn't going to be good. I didn't know how to begin to prepare Phoebe.

"They know who it is?" Phoebe put a hand across her mouth, pinching her cheeks in.

"Sounds like it." My breath caught on the end of that sentence.

During the drive to the station, I could tell that Phoebe was like me, struggling to just *breathe*.

It wasn't just Gilroy in Gilroy's office when we got there either. When we walked in, there was a team of three detectives looking back at us. *Three*. I'd met the other two before but hadn't seen them in a while.

"Please have a seat." I couldn't read Gilroy's expression, nor the expressions of the other detectives.

I needed them to lay it down on the table. Tell us. But I sensed a hesitancy.

"Who is it? *Who?*" I held Phoebe's hand in mine as we sat.

It was Detective Ali Haleemi who spoke first. His thick eyebrows rose and made waves of creases all the way up to the shiny bald dome of his head. "Luke and Phoebe, so, it's been three months or so since we last spoke in person. But I'm still one of the detectives working on this case. Trying to solve it as best I can. I know you both want answers, and this has been a nightmare for you both. I need to say up front that at this stage, we don't have new information on where Tommy is. But we do have information on who was sending the letters."

Mentally, I recalibrated. They didn't know anything about Tommy. Didn't know whether he was dead or alive.

Phoebe gasped quietly. "The man from last night?"

"No," Haleemi said shortly. "No, we don't think he has any connection."

"Then. . . ?" She shook her head questioningly.

He exhaled, his eyes directly on her. "As far as I understand, Detective Gilroy informed you that we were going to install surveillance cameras on your street and in the café. Do you remember that conversation?"

She touched her head, her eyes growing large. "God, I'd forgotten. So you have this person on film? *Actually on film?*"

He nodded. "I was in charge of that operation, and the cameras were installed yesterday morning. This morning, I went through the footage together with Detective Yarris." He glanced at the female detective beside him. "And the footage clearly shows who placed the third letter in the mailbox."

I couldn't control the frustration simmering in my stomach, turning the toast and eggs I'd had for lunch into some kind of toxic sludge. Why didn't they just come out and tell us? "Who the fuck was it?"

Gilroy walked around the desk to sit on the edge of it, in front of us.

It was obvious that *he* was going to be the one to tell us.

19.   PHOEBE

Saturday afternoon

I HEARD A NAME.

A name that didn't fit Luke's question about who this person was.

A name that didn't fit anywhere. A name that suddenly turned as sharp as a knife, slicing everything I knew into tiny julienne pieces.

"I don't—" I started, unable to finish my sentence.

"Phoebe," said Detective Gilroy, his voice breaking through this new alternate reality. "It's you."

Luke's hands slipped away from mine and hovered mid-air, like he didn't know what to do with them anymore. "What the hell? Of course it's not Phoebe."

"This is difficult for us," Gilroy said in a careful but determined tone. "But the video leaves no doubt. Before we say anything more, we'd like you both to come with us now and see the footage for yourselves."

Luke and I followed the detectives like obedient children into what they called the interview room. The room was dead plain. White walls, a single table, chairs. We were instructed to sit.

Detective Annabelle Yarris loaded a micro card into a computer tower. A screen on the wall blinked and then showed a still. A still of my house. I'd completely forgotten that Trent Gilroy had said he'd install a camera. The last two days had been a rush, a whirlwind.

Annabelle turned and looked back over her shoulder at Luke and me. "I'll be starting the film at the point where you left the house that night." She pressed a brief smile against her teeth.

Luke had his arm around me, his hand on my shoulder—the pressure of it seeming more apprehensive than it was comforting.

As I watched, I saw myself. But not any self that I knew. This was a raw, stripped me, without societal pretensions. I walked the pathway from my front door, looking from side to side. But my expression was not one of a woman searching for her child. It was, without a doubt, the cool, intent expression of a hunter. The turmoil I remembered inside my mind didn't show on my face. I stepped through the gate and headed away. The film now showed an empty scene. Just dry leaves being scattered by the wind near our mailbox.

"I'm going to fast-forward it here," said Detective Yarris. "Nothing happens for the next couple of minutes. But I'll do it so that you can still see the frames and see for yourself that nothing else happened during this time."

As she'd said, the scene remained as it was during the time she fast-forwarded the footage. She glanced at her watch, seeming to be waiting for the right time to put it back into play.

And there I was again, walking back to the gate.

I had something in my hand. An envelope.

Luke's fingers pushed into the flesh on my shoulder.

I watched myself insert the envelope into the mailbox and then head back down the street again.

There was no mistake. I had done this.

I was the one who delivered the letter.

Me.

But how was that possible?

Sweat dampened my palms, making small dark patches on my white dress. What was happening? The police were supposed to tell us who'd written the letters. Instead, we'd been shown a video that made no sense. *No sense.*

Annabelle stopped the video at that point and turned to Trent. Luke's hand dropped away from me, and he studied my face in confusion.

"Now that you've seen what we've seen," Trent Gilroy told us, "I can tell you that based on this footage, we've been conducting some further enquiries."

His eyes were grave, the graph line wrinkle in his forehead forecasting that what he had was more bad news.

He eyed me directly. "Because of the nature of the letters and the reports about the man that's been loitering around, we've had to take this very seriously. We had to be absolutely sure of what's really happening. We've spoken with neighbours on your street this morning. Phoebe, we have two witness accounts that state that you were seen out on the street early on the morning you found the first letter."

Luke was on his feet before the detective finished his last word. "Don't you think we should have been informed all of this was going on?"

"We thought it best we have a more thorough understanding before calling you in," Detective Gilroy answered.

"Look, she didn't even have the letter when she left the house." Luke crossed his arms. "What the fuck is going on here?"

Trent's expression was guarded. "There's a bit more we need to tell you. Please, sit."

Luke stood there staring at him for a moment before looking defeated and slumping back into his seat. I wished he would have grabbed me and stormed out, saying that it was all nonsense, so that I could believe that this was all a mistake and that I hadn't seen myself on that video.

But that didn't happen.

I was still here, in a world more surreal than in any of my sleepwalking dreams. And I couldn't escape it by waking.

Why didn't I remember the envelope or putting it in the mailbox?

Detective Eli Haleemi took over then. "Between leaving through the front gate of the house and returning to the letterbox was a time period of just over two minutes. Long enough for Phoebe to reach her grandmother's house, get the letter, and bring it back."

"That's not enough time," Luke snapped. "My wife was sleepwalking. Nan's house is towards the harbour end of the street. It would have taken—"

"Not if she ran." Detective Yarris raised her thinly plucked eyebrows.

"She was *sleepwalking*," Luke repeated. "Not doing an Olympic sprint. And what makes you think she got the letter from her grandmother's house anyway? What if someone in the street gave it to her?"

They were talking about me in the third person. I was no longer part of this. It was all about logistics now.

Detective Haleemi took the baton again, bowing his head and crinkling his forehead as if he were thinking very hard—no, as if he were demonstrating the revolutions that should be turning in Luke's mind. "Well, I can't claim to know a lot about sleepwalking and what people are capable of in that state. But it is possible to get from your house and back in that time, if you run. And the grandmother's house just seemed the most logical place for Phoebe to have gone, seeing as that's where she ended up later. And because of one other thing. We believe that the letters were written at that house, at some point."

Ali Haleemi waited for a few seconds before continuing. "And so we went there earlier today, Detective Yarris and I, to Mrs Hoskins's house. We asked if we could take a look around, and she showed us through the house." Stopping again, his eyes rested on me. "And we discovered a typewriter in the storage area under the stairs."

I couldn't help but flinch. They'd been in my grandmother's house, going through all the things belonging to my family. I knew of the typewriter they were talking about. But I hadn't seen it for a long time. I hadn't known that Nan still had it.

"Mrs Hoskins allowed us to take the typewriter." Words continued to drip from Detective Haleemi's mouth. Nonsensical words.

Luke sucked in a shallow breath.

Haleemi straightened, as though he was about to come to his end point and needed to look official. "We had one of our experts check it out. It's the same typewriter used to write the letters."

My upper lip began quivering even before I'd fully processed what he'd said.

Luke swore under his breath, exhaling noisily. "Doesn't that mean Phoebe's *grandmother* is the one who's been writing those letters? Why the fuck would she do this to us?"

Detective Gilroy knitted his eyebrows tightly. "We don't have reason to believe that the grandmother wrote them. We only found one set of fingerprints on the third letter and envelope." His gaze lingered on me. "Phoebe, those prints were yours. Your prints shouldn't have been inside the sealed envelope at all. I think you can see where we're at."

Thoughts ground through my head, each thought turning to ashen powder before it could form anything coherent.

How? How? How? How? How? How?

How was any of this possible?

Someone needed to explain it to me. But the three detectives had grown quiet, and their attention was all focused on me, waiting for a response.

I was making movements—I wasn't sure which—shaking my head, shrinking into myself, opening my mouth to speak. Maybe all of those at once. I was too numb, too *inside my mind* to be aware of how I was presenting myself in that moment, let alone speak or defend myself against these terrible allegations.

Even Luke, who always found the right words, was silent. When I turned to him, he had his head in his hands. I didn't know how long he'd been like that. When he raised his head, his expression was different to how it had been before. "What happens now?"

Detective Gilroy's very official posture seemed to relax. "Look, all of this—these letters—have come after months of the worst kind of trauma. A week before the letters started, the six-month mark of Tommy's disappearance came. That's a terrible milestone. We understand that it must feel as though we're not doing everything we possibly can to find Tommy. We understand that. And perhaps, Phoebe felt that she would like us to do more. Our position is that this has been a cry for help, to try to make us start moving on Tommy's case again." He rubbed his temples, attempting a grim smile. "The truth is, we've never stopped moving on his case. We've thrown everything we humanly can at it. Tommy remains a top priority." Inhaling steadily, he fixed his eyes on me, softening his expression. "So, what we're going to do is to dismiss this latest wrinkle in the case. If this is a case of sleepwalking, then you're hardly to blame. We'd just like some assurance that you're going to see someone about how you've been feeling lately. Do you see anyone at the moment? A counsellor?"

"She sees Dr Leona Moran," Luke cut in. "A psychiatrist."

Detective Gilroy nodded. "Okay, good."

"I'll set up an appointment," said Luke. He then faced me with eyes that no longer knew me. "I don't understand. Did you think this would get us anywhere?"

"I didn't write those letters." There. I'd gotten the words out, pushed them out from somewhere deep in my chest.

"I watched you on the video, Feeb, putting the letter in the letterbox. Just . . . stop. Hell, imagine if we'd caught up with the guy from last night. That would have been damned difficult to explain." Luke looked away from me. I could tell he was embarrassed by what he thought I'd done.

There wasn't anything I could say to my husband right now. They had him convinced. I looked at each of the detectives in turn. "I didn't write them," I repeated.

My words sounded even hollower the second time.

No one in this room believed me.

I wanted to run home and take my pills and climb into bed and dream of Tommy. I didn't want to be here with four sets of eyes judging me, pitying me.

Detective Yarris gave me a smile that I was sure she meant to be warm, but she just wasn't capable of doing *warm*. "I used to sleepwalk when I was a kid. Ended up peeing in a cupboard one night, thinking it was the bathroom."

"Go easy on Phoebe," Trent told Luke. "She wasn't in control of this. Like I said, I'm no expert on sleepwalking, but we're guessing she just doesn't have any clear memory of writing those letters."

Luke closed his eyes briefly. "Okay. It's just . . . I came here thinking we were about to get answers, and instead I get hit with *this*." He turned to me. "Sorry I was a jerk."

I didn't answer. He still believed that I wrote the letters. Nothing had changed.

Luke looked back at the detectives. "Is everyone going to find out what really happened now? I mean, is this going to be all over the news?"

Trent Gilroy shook his head. "It won't come from us. Things have a way of getting out, but if you keep it under your hat, you'll give this the best chance of blowing over. That doesn't include Phoebe's psychiatrist, of course. She's going to need to talk this whole thing through with her. From our side of it, our official statement is going to remain that some notes were sent to your house and the café, but our new statement will be that the police don't believe they have any connection to Tommy's disappearance."

Luke exhaled quietly. I knew the most important thing to him was that no one found out about his crazy wife.

I wasn't crazy.

But people who weren't insane didn't need to tell themselves that, right?

20.   LUKE

Saturday afternoon

DRY, BROWN LEAVES DROPPED FROM AN archway of trees as I drove Phoebe to Leona Moran's clinic. The knobbed branches seemed skeletal and diseased to me.

An hour ago, there'd been some hope that a resolution to what happened to my son was in sight. That hope was dust.

I'd called Dr Moran as soon as Phoebe and I had left the police station. Dr Moran said that considering the circumstances, she'd see Phoebe straight away. Phoebe didn't want to see Dr Moran, pleading to just go home. But I wasn't going to let that happen. Someone had to look out for her, and that person obviously couldn't be herself.

Dr Moran stepped from her office to greet us as soon as we walked into the clinic. With her librarian-style smooth hair, rimless glasses and quick smile, she was a walking advertisement for her profession. She could make you shiny new and get rid of all the bad stuff cluttering your head.

I expected to wait outside, but Dr Moran surprised me by guiding me into the room along with Phoebe.

"I'd like to have a little chat with both of you." She gestured towards two comfortable-looking chairs. "Because this is happening to you both. First of all, can I get either of you a drink? A tea or coffee? Water?"

Phoebe refused the drink flatly, and I followed suit. I was thirsty for something stronger than coffee anyway.

"Okay," she started with a concerned set of wrinkles indenting the centre of her forehead. "Luke, you gave me a brief background on what's been happening over the past three days. I'd like to take it from here and see if we can't get things to a better place."

Her milky green eyes rested on Phoebe. "How are you? You've missed your last two appointments. I've been thinking about you."

"I just want to go home." Phoebe looked away from me and Dr Moran.

Anger pitted itself inside me again. She caused all this, and now she wanted to walk away from it? I didn't even know she'd been missing appointments. She'd lied to me.

"We just need to make sure you're okay," Dr Moran told her in a tone that was far gentler than I would have liked. "And you haven't been okay. I understand that both of you are hurting right now. Perhaps we can start by you telling me how you've been lately, Phoebe."

Phoebe wrapped her arms across her stomach, eyeing Dr Moran with a defensive expression. "How can I tell you when I don't understand anything right now? I need time to figure this out."

"You're feeling confused?" Dr Moran nodded.

"Confused doesn't begin to describe it. I didn't write those letters. I couldn't have. Why would. . . ." Phoebe's voice trailed away.

"Of course," said the doctor. "You're not going to untangle this straight away. Don't expect to. You've been through severe and unrelenting trauma these past few months. Have you been sleeping? How has the new sleeping medication been working for you?"

I wanted Dr Moran to drill her about the letters. Analyse why she'd done it. Instead, she was starting in a different place.

Phoebe gave a nod. "The medication's fine. I'm sleeping."

"Except for the sleepwalking episodes," I broke in.

"I had a couple of restless nights," Phoebe's voice snapped tight. "Ever since the letters started."

"That's understandable." Dr Moran paused. "The sleepwalking is definitely something new. So, these kinds of restless nights weren't happening before the letters?"

"No." Phoebe shook her head firmly.

Dr Moran looked to me for confirmation.

I didn't know why the hell we were talking as though the letters had caused Phoebe's state of mind when it was Phoebe's state of mind that had caused the letters. But I wasn't the doctor, and I decided to play along.

"As far as I know, that's right," I agreed.

The doctor chewed her lip for a second. "Okay. I knew you were having intense dreams, but this whole thing has really progressed. And not in a good way."

Phoebe lifted her head and eyed Dr Moran in an intense gaze. "I need to know something. Is it even possible for someone to write those letters while sleepwalking?"

Dr Moran seemed to think for a second, her forehead wrinkling again. "As I understand it, the letters are in rhyme, and they were written on a typewriter and delivered to your letterbox, over the course of three days. Correct?"

"The second letter was pinned to the coffee shop noticeboard," I cut in. "And the video showed that Phoebe ran to her grandmother's and back before she posted the third letter." I sounded like the prosecution in a courtroom. I stopped myself from saying any more. "I'm just trying to give you a clearer picture."

Dr Moran's frown deepened. "Well, that's a lot of complex activity. People do all kinds of things during somnambulism—sleepwalking. Just about anything you can do when you're awake, you can do sleepwalking. You can walk down the street, and you can write letters. You can even drive a car. It's not what people usually do when in that state, but it's possible. I haven't heard of carrying on an activity over several sleepwalking sessions, but I'll need to investigate that further. I'll also look into the possibility that Phoebe was in some other kind of altered state."

"What kind of altered state?" Phoebe asked, folding her arms in tightly.

"That's what we need to find out," Dr Moran told her. "Look, I'm going to book you in for a sleep study, to see what's been going on with you at night."

"What's that?" I asked.

"The patient just stays overnight in a clinic, and their sleeping phases are monitored while they sleep. And—"

"I don't want to go and stay somewhere else right now," Phoebe hurried to say.

Dr Moran gave her an understanding nod. "It won't be straight away. As you can imagine, seeing as it's an overnight stay in which you are monitored all night, the waiting lists are long. In the meantime, we might need to have a think on your sleeping medication. It might be an idea to dial back to the previous meds you were on. The new medication might be stronger than what you need."

A hint of alarm flicked through Phoebe's face, but then she swapped that for a cool expression. As if she had a mirror in front of her and could see her own face. "I'm doing well. I'm getting sleep. The old meds weren't working for me."

"We can try a different type, in that case," said Dr Moran. "I'm not happy with the way things are going with the current ones."

Phoebe plunged into silence. I could sense a cloud thickening around her.

What the hell was going on with her? She'd just been caught sending kidnapper-style letters about Tommy to our house. Anyone halfway sane would be trying to make amends, trying to fix whatever clouds of crazy were floating in her head. But not Phoebe. Instead, she was arguing with her psych over medication.

I was trying hard to play the understanding husband. Gilroy was right—the last six months had been a nightmare, and maybe I could understand that Phoebe was desperate. If she really didn't remember writing or sending the letters, she'd be in a world of confusion right now.

But I couldn't understand the way she was behaving in Dr Moran's office.

Had she written the letters intentionally and then just pretended the whole sleepwalking scenario—just in case she got found out?

She was hiding something. I was sure of it.

"I don't want to try something new," Phoebe said finally. "I'm tired of . . . change. I'm tired of everything changing and out of my control. Could I just stay on what I'm on a while longer? Just one more prescription, and we'll see how it goes?"

I stared at my wife. Her tone sounded strangely fake, but her face gave nothing away, her eyes large and slightly pleading.

Dr Moran didn't seem to catch what I did. She shot Phoebe a regretful look. "I'm sorry. I hear you—really, I do. But as your doctor, I'm afraid I can't prescribe that again for you at the moment. We need to try something else."

Phoebe gave a sigh that made no sound.

The doctor wrote out a script. "Will you be okay tonight, Phoebe? If there's a concern about you wandering around your home—or outside of it—an overnight stay in a mental health clinic might be safest for you. That might sound extreme to you right now, but what happened in the early hours of this morning was far more extreme. It's dangerous for you."

"Luke put in a new alarm," Phoebe answered. "And we have a deadlock on the front door. Everything's okay."

Phoebe sounded almost clinical.

Dr Moran eyed me quizzically.

I nodded. "Yesterday."

"That was quick. Good job." She handed the script to Phoebe, who took it reluctantly, like a child taking medicine.

Turning to me, the doctor pressed her lips together. "How are you, Luke?"

I want to strangle my wife's bony neck. That's how I am. "I'm . . . just trying to process everything. Not succeeding."

"It'll take a while. How's the real estate business?"

It was an unexpected question. But I got it. She was trying to bring things back to normal, to reorient me. Maybe she sensed my anger. Something inside me resisted. I didn't want to go back to normal. I'd been so fucking understanding with Phoebe all along. She was the one with Tommy when he vanished. It happened when *she* was supposed to be watching him, not me. But she was the one to receive the lion's share of the sympathy afterwards—from everyone. She was the mother and the one expected to suffer the most. She was the one to have ongoing visits to Dr Moran and the need for antidepressants and sleeping aids. I'd gotten past those things after the first month. Everything had been centred on Phoebe.

And now this crazy shit.

I just shook my head in response.

She hesitated for a second, her pen poised. "I'd like to make a booking to see both of you again next week. Separately this time."

Phoebe didn't answer. When I glanced at her, it seemed to me that she'd completely switched off and was no longer part of this conversation.

"We'll give you a call later and arrange something," I said.

"Please do." Dr Moran shot each of us a direct gaze.

I half-expected Phoebe to jump in and say that she didn't need to come back, but she remained silent.

"Phoebe?" questioned Dr Moran.

She smiled at the doctor. *Smiled.* "Luke will sort it out."

"I'll see you soon, then." Dr Moran nodded along with her words. I could sense her staring at us in concealed confusion as Phoebe and I left the office. At least Phoebe hadn't completely pulled the wool over her eyes. I was sure that she could see, as I could, that something was going on with my wife.

21. PHOEBE

Saturday night

LUKE DROVE STRAIGHT TO GET THE prescription filled. I wasn't trusted to do it myself. I wasn't trusted to steer myself around anymore. I was a child, and Luke, Dr Moran, and the detectives were the adults. My adult status had been stripped away.

I didn't know what was happening. At the police station and at Dr Moran's, I'd had to pack the events of today into a box and seal the lid, waiting until I was alone. Only then was I going to be able to take out the contents of the box and examine each piece in isolation.

That was what I'd always done. When I was growing up, I'd learned to pack things away. *Don't let anyone see your fear. Don't let anyone see inside.*

By the time Luke pulled up the car outside our home, his eyes had grown almost hostile. What had happened to *team Luke and Phoebe*? We'd been strong and united ever since Tommy had been taken from us. But not now. The letters had been an axe. I wanted him on my side, to tell me the police were wrong and there had to be some other explanation. But he'd already sharpened himself against me.

I headed upstairs and ran myself a bath. I wanted to soak. And wash off the terrifying scenes of the past two hours. Water surged from the tap, looking destructive. Everything seemed out to destroy me.

Mesmerised, I watched the dark water build.

Our bath was black, chosen by Luke. The entire bathroom—the whole house—was styled in masculine black and white. Luke had said this look was popular with clients when he took them to look at apartments and townhouses.

When the bath was filled, I could no longer see the bottom of it.

I needed something to help me relax. Running into the bedroom, I pulled out the shoebox in my wardrobe. I swallowed pill after pill. I didn't know how many. A dozen? I wouldn't sleepwalk after taking that many. I wouldn't be able to move from the bed.

Dropping my clothes on the floor, I stepped into the water and laid myself down.

The prospect that I really was going crazy drifted at the edges of the watery haze inside my head.

It *was* me in that footage from the police camera.

Undeniably me.

What was wrong with me? Had those terrible rhymes really come from me? Had I done those things while I was in a deep sleep?

Dr Moran had skirted around my questions. I could tell she wasn't convinced that someone could have written three rhymes and delivered them separately—to my home and to the café—all while in a deep sleep. The police didn't believe it either. I could tell.

Which only left one thing. That I'd written the letters deliberately. That I'd gone slightly nuts and concocted the whole thing (Dr Moran's euphemistic *altered state.*)

I didn't have a single memory of writing the letters. Nothing. *Where did I get the paper from? When did I drag out Nan's typewriter and start writing? How did I pin that letter to the noticeboard of the café? How did I come up with those rhymes?*

A valve slipped open in my brain, and the horror of the day flooded in fresh.

Tommy was gone, and this pain was never, never going to end. Luke and I were going to live this every day for the rest of our lives. No end. No resolution.

There was no way out.

I slipped low in the water. I'd been deceiving myself. My dreams weren't going to lead me to Tommy. I'd been trying to escape the pain by drugging myself and creating my own little make-believe world.

The one thing that had kept me going the past couple of months had just been shattered.

My head grew *heavy, heavy, heavy.*

I could *sleep.*

The water covered my face.

If I could just stay here like this for a little while . . .

Just a while . . .

22.   LUKE

Saturday night

I POURED MYSELF A BOURBON AND listened to the silence in the house.

Then pulled out my phone from my pocket and dialled my mother.

She answered with that slightly worried tone she always used when she answered the phone—to anyone, as though eternally bracing herself for bad news. "Luke?"

"Yeah, it's me." *Of course it's me. The name popping up on your phone's display right now is telling you it's me.*

"Is everything okay?" she asked.

"No, not really."

"Well, what's going on? Is it Phoebe?"

"Why do you think it's Phoebe?"

"Oh, Luke, it's always her. You're always the one picking up the pieces."

She surprised me with those words, and it took me a second to adjust. She'd never spoken of Phoebe in that negative way before.

"I've been trying to get you on the phone since this morning. So has Aunty Joan. I'm guessing you haven't heard what happened?"

"Oh my goodness, what is it? No, you know the cabin's out of range for phone calls. We're in town right now, having some dinner."

"It's all over the news, Mum. We've been getting letters. About Tommy."

"*No.* About Tommy? What kind of letters?"

"Just . . . letters. Rhymes. They make no sense."

"So you've told the police?"

"Yeah. Mum, it's *national news.*"

"Oh dear. Just who are these letters from? The kidnapper?"

"The police don't think so. Just some misguided person . . ." I wasn't going to tell my mother the whole story. Not yet anyway.

"Oh, I feel terrible. All the way down here away from everything."

"Look, I was thinking . . . Phoebe's not handling it well. Maybe I could bring her to the cabin for a bit. Give her a change of scenery."

I could almost hear Mum thinking. "I just don't know if it's the best timing."

"What's happening?"

"Your father's not well."

"Yeah? What's up with the old guy?"

"He's just going through a bit of a thing. Depression, I guess you'd call it. He really needs some quiet time so he can recharge and get back to being himself again."

"When did that start?"

"A while. What happened with little Tommy affected him deeply. I think he just can't make peace with the world at the moment."

I rubbed my forehead, not knowing if I could handle hearing about how Tommy's disappearance had affected yet someone else. Sometimes it seemed like I was the one expected to soldier on while everyone else had a licence to fall apart. "Okay, well, I'll figure out something else."

"I think that would be best."

She didn't even try to offer me any alternative. I was on my own with this. I'd been hoping my mother would welcome us with open arms and that Dad would take me fishing out on the lake. They'd had the cabin for the last sixteen years, ever since I was a teenager. Nine hours down the coast, on a lake about twenty minutes inland from the ocean. Damned freezing in winter when snow covered everything, but the best place ever in the summer. Dad had always seemed in his element there. He tolerated his trips around Europe with Mum well enough, but the cabin was his special place. He'd sit out on the porch with a grin so lazy and contented it was half sliding off his face, hands on the ballooned gut that was a sign of the good life.

Mum and I chatted briefly about nothing in particular. It was obvious she was just being polite before we ended the call.

I dropped the phone back into my pocket. It occurred to me that I didn't know when the bulk of my mother's attention had swapped from me to my father. I used to be the one that she worried and fussed about. But now it seemed that it was all about *your father*. Maybe the two of them were just getting old and afraid, and in her eyes, life had become all about keeping her husband alive for as long as possible. My dad wasn't known for his healthy eating. And he drank a lot more than was good for his liver.

Watching myself in the mirror, I set my bourbon down on the side table. I wasn't thirty yet, but already I looked older than thirty. My hairline was creeping back, and the tired look around my eyes had become a permanent fixture. For a second, I saw my dad's face merging with my own. Who was I going to be when I was in my sixties? Was I going to become a faded version of myself who sat on the porch of his cabin, drinking and staring transfixed at a lake, occasionally thinking about the toddler son he hadn't seen grow up? The son that was still missing? In all likelihood, that was my future. My parents would leave the cabin to me. What I couldn't imagine was Phoebe still by my side, fussing over me. Phoebe was never going to become like my mother or even her own mother. She was made of different stuff.

The silence of the house seemed different now. Like I was alone in it.

Leaving my drink, I headed upstairs.

The smell of vomit soured the air. The bathroom door was ajar, and I pushed it open.

Phoebe was lying fully submerged, her eyes wide open, just staring from beneath the water. A small pile of vomit sat on the tiles beside the bath, a thin trail of it leading to the toilet. A film of vomit floated in the toilet bowl. She must have flushed the rest.

It took me a moment to register what I was seeing.

In a single leap, I was across the bathroom floor. I was grabbing her, lifting her head and torso from the water. She barely registered that I was there. Just blinked at me.

"What the fuck are you doing?" I didn't recognise my voice.

"I can't . . . bear it." That was all she said.

I knelt on the floor, in the water that'd been splashed everywhere, in her vomit. "I lost Tommy too. Remember that."

"I don't understand anything. I don't understand why Tommy's gone or how the letters happened. Everything's wrong, and I can't fix it. I can't fix it. I don't want to live anymore."

As I stared at her, the urge to choke her rose from the pit of my stomach for the second time today. She'd lost Tommy, but she still had me. But I was not enough. Me—and all the things I'd given her—were not fucking enough. My hands clamped around her shoulders, thumbs on her gleaming, wet throat. A single word hissed from between my teeth. "Don't . . ."

She showed no emotion. *Nothing.*

My fingers slipped away, brushing the bath water. It had gone cool. "What were you trying to do? Drown yourself?"

"I don't know."

I brought down my fist on the side of the bath. She didn't flinch. "Tell me why. Why did you write those letters? To punish the police? Or to punish me?"

"Please . . ."

"Tell me why."

"I don't know why. I don't have any memory of it."

"How could you not remember? That makes no sense. Just admit what you did. That would be a start."

"Go to hell." It was a broken, softly spoken *go to hell*. But the look in her eyes broke me inside. A look of hate.

I was tired of saving her. When she was growing up, I'd done my best to save her from her shitty life. And I'd been saving her ever since. How long could you keep on saving a person?

But like the idiot I was, I picked her up just like I had all those times she was drunk. I wrapped her in a towel and deposited her in our bed. Her hair still smelled vaguely of vomit.

Stepping back to the bathroom, I cleaned up the mess with a bunch of toilet paper.

What was I supposed to do now? Sit downstairs and watch TV? Pretend my life was some kind of normal?

Instead, I went to lay myself down beside her. She didn't even acknowledge me. I turned to look at her, but her face was stony.

What I wanted from Phoebe was something she'd never been able to give me—a soft place to land.

Phoebe Phoebe
Not so easy
Locked up tighter
Than Ebenezer

When we were both sixteen, I used to tease her with that. Teasing her in the hope that she'd relent and fool around with me, just like Sass and Pria had already done—even Bernice. I'd felt shame years later for comparing Phoebe to Ebenezer Scrooge. But back then, when we were sixteen, I didn't think too hard about anything. I eventually wore her down. For a couple of months that same year, we used to go upstairs at number 29 and make out. Until the day that Bernice did something so damned evil at that house that none of us ever went back there.

Turning away from me, Phoebe curled herself up.

I was an intruder. In my own room. In my own bed.

Rising, I pulled on a hoodie and returned downstairs. Now I knew even less what to do with myself. So I headed out.

The front door was deadlocked, and I made sure I had both keys with me. Phoebe couldn't get out without the keys. And I'd changed the number sequence on the alarm. I didn't know if I believed in the whole sleepwalking thing, but at least my conscience was clear. She couldn't get out of the house.

Lock up your wife
She's nothing but strife

There was a rhyme I couldn't have anticipated back when I was sixteen and thinking Phoebe would be the girl I'd marry one day. Feeling like Peter the Pumpkin Eater, I jogged down to the docks.

Two homeless men passed each other's paths along the waterfront, reminding me of two ferries crossing each other on the water, carrying nothing but loneliness on board.

Before I knew what I was doing, I was on the next block, running back up the hill.

I wanted to make myself turn back. But I didn't.

Standing at Kitty's front gate, I caught my breath.

She answered the intercom, sounding sleepy.

The metal gate rolled open, and I walked up her path. Her face was all concern and comfort. "Luke! You don't look so hot. What's going on?"

"I just need some company right now. Is that okay?"

"You know it's okay."

I told myself I was going to hold back and keep the wall up—the kind of wall I kept for my business clients. But I crumbled as soon as she had a coffee in my hands and had me sitting on the sofa.

I was shaking all over, and I couldn't make myself go still.

"Oh hell, you're a mess." She touched my arm, taking the coffee from me and placing it on the low table in front of us.

My ribcage began squeezing into a series of silent sobs.

She grabbed me in a bear hug. I was grateful that she didn't speak.

"I should go home," I told her. "I've been leaning on you for months, and you don't need that."

"Nonsense. Lean on me all you need to. If you get yourself right, then you're in a better place to help Phoebe through all this."

Something inside me snapped, and I grabbed her arms "You know, that's all I ever hear. Poor Phoebe. Everyone says it. Everyone thinks it. I'm just expected to keep propping her up. No one gives a flying fuck how I'm doing."

She winced, shrinking back. "I didn't mean it that way."

"I'm just over it. Do you know what she did tonight?"

She shook her head in response, her expression tensing as if she didn't want to know the answer.

"She fucking tried to drown herself."

Her mouth dropped open. "Oh my God! What?"

"Yeah. In the bath. I dragged her out. She's sleeping now. Like a baby."

"Don't you need to call someone? She might need help. This is serious. Luke, you can't—"

"Can't what? Can't stop being her keeper? People don't drown themselves in their bathtubs, Kitty. Not if they really want to do the job. They'd cut their wrists first or take a bottle of pills, or—"

"Are you sure she didn't? The pills, I mean."

"No, she went straight into the bath. Anyway, I counted the sleeping tablets that she keeps in her drawer. I count them every few days. They were all there. She's just looking for attention."

"Look, do you want a drink?" Not waiting for a response, she went and made me a bourbon and cola and planted it in my hand.

I downed the drink. A fuzz immediately spread through me—my fourth drink in the last hour. I'd had three at home already.

"Talk to me about the notes," she said. "I can't imagine what it would be like to get those in the mail. The latest I heard on the news is that the police think they were just from a crank?"

My teeth set together. "Yeah. Just a crank. The notes are just the latest episode in my shit life."

"Sometimes, things happen that make us stop and evaluate everything in our life. Maybe you're just at a crossroads."

"I don't know where I am. I don't know what I'm supposed to be doing."

"You will. You'll find your way." She smiled tentatively. "Hey, have you had your yacht out for a spin lately?"

"Only twice in the past three months. I miss it. Dad doesn't come out on it fishing anymore. I just talked to Mum. Says he's depressed or something."

"That's no good. Hope he's doing something about it and not just trying to battle through."

"Once he's wrung the maximum amount of sympathy out of Mum, maybe."

"Depression's no joke, Luke."

"I know. But man, he's always moaning about something." I slumped back on her sofa, tilting my head back against the headrest. "Kitty, are you sure you want to go ahead with that purchase of yours?"

"Yeah, why not? I'm over investing in Sydney property."

"That's just it. It's not the wisest investment. There's much better ones out there. And it's a huge amount of money to slap down. I wouldn't touch it if I were you."

"Well, you're not me." She smiled. "I get emotionally attached to things, and that means more to me than the potential profit."

"Okay, I've said my piece. When I'm back in the office, I'll get things moving on it. I haven't been in for a couple of days."

"Of course you haven't. Don't worry about it. You've got a head full of worry right now."

"I should go." I pulled myself to my feet, feeling a bit woozy from the alcohol. "I shouldn't leave Phoebe alone too long." Hesitating, I ran my hands through my hair. "Sounds wrong, I know, but I just don't want to go back there."

In response, she rose alongside me and hugged me again.

She felt good and warm and solid. Phoebe never felt like that. Holding Phoebe always felt like trying to negotiate something that could shatter at any moment.

A thought flashed through my head, the thought of being with someone like Kitty and what that must feel like. No stepping on eggshells and no constant worry about what her mental state was like today.

Inside that thought, my mind went blank, and I kissed her on her mouth.

Immediately, she pulled back. Like I'd stung her or something. "I know you're hurting and not yourself, so I'm going to ignore that."

"Fuck, I'm sorry."

"Don't be sorry. You didn't mean it."

"That's the problem. I can't say for sure that I didn't mean it." Words were just spilling from me tonight, unchecked. What the hell was wrong with me? I wanted to blubber and be held like a little kid. I wanted to be with a woman who could give herself to me, unlike Phoebe.

She frowned, looking uncomfortable. "We'll always be close. We're friends. You're going through a ton of stuff at the moment. This is not you. You'll get past this, and we'll keep on being friends."

I swallowed hard. "Maybe I should have asked you to marry me that year we worked together at the agency. I shouldn't have let you get engaged to that jerk."

Her mouth twitched into a small smile. "You and I had a lot of fun that year. And yes, why *didn't* you steal me away and stop me from accepting his ring? What was I thinking?"

"Christ, I wanted to belt him into next week for what he did to you."

"Well, that's all in the past. I made a bad decision. But I'm happy now."

"You're happy? I don't remember what that feels like."

"You will. You'll find your way. You're a positive person." She looked certain as she nodded.

I said a quick good-bye, and she walked me to the door.

Plunging my hands into my hoodie pockets, I stepped back into the night air, feeling like a Biblical traitor. The gate closed behind me with a metallic click.

I didn't want to go back to Phoebe. But I had no choice.

A thin mist skirted the ground, slinking around the fences and yards. I jogged back to my street, the cold plunging inside my bones. It was a damned miserable winter. The most miserable one I'd ever known.

I jolted when I spotted Phoebe sitting on the low fence next to our house. She was still in the towel, her hair wet and limp over her shoulders. I sprinted the last twenty metres or so up to her.

"Feeb, what the hell?"

Her expression was calm. "Where did you go?"

"For a walk. Get inside. Haven't you brought enough attention on yourself lately?"

"Why should I stay inside, all safe and warm? Tommy isn't safe and warm."

"This ends, Phoebe. It ends now." I grasped her shoulders. "You don't have a monopoly on grieving for Tommy."

"I can smell perfume. Why do you smell of perfume, Luke?"

"You're imagining it."

"Am I? No, I really don't think I am."

"Come inside. There's no point hanging around out here."

"You've been going for runs at night a lot lately, haven't you?"

"Lots of people do."

"You're right. The people around here seem pretty nocturnal. Everyone wanders the streets at night. Bernice Wick goes out looking for her mother's cat. The homeless people walk around looking for a place to sleep. That guy that's been hanging around—who knows what he's looking for? What are *you* looking for, Luke?"

"I'm not having this conversation anymore. If I have to pick you up and throw you into the house myself, I will. How did you get out here anyway?"

"Through the powder room window. What's her name?"

"What?"

"Her name. The one you go to see, on your walks."

"Stop it, okay?"

"There's no point in us staying together anymore, is there?"

"Of course there is."

"I'll leave tomorrow."

"Come inside. You're not leaving."

"What am I? A prisoner now? You have a licence to keep me locked up? I'll go to Nan's."

Panic shot through me. Mere minutes ago, I'd been contemplating a life without her. But standing here in front of her, with her telling me she was going to leave me, I couldn't let her go. Not even to her grandmother's house. She belonged with me.

My jaw tightened. "I'm on my fucking knees, Phoebe. And you sit there, in a wet towel, like a fucking priestess, telling me you're leaving me."

For a second, she eyed me in surprise, but then her face resumed its mask. "You can't stop me." She wriggled down from the fence and walked inside.

I followed her in and upstairs. She let the towel drop like she'd shed a skin and had been reborn. Dressing in a long T-shirt, she slid into bed.

Stripping to my undershorts, I got into bed beside her. Fear whirled in my head. I didn't want her to go anywhere. I shouldn't have gone out for that walk. In the morning she'd be different. She depended on me. For everything. She couldn't just *leave*.

In the moonlight, she was insanely beautiful in a way that she wasn't in daylight. The dark light softened the angles of a face that had grown too thin. The waves that her dark hair made on the pillow were like brush strokes.

I kissed her, on the cheek and on the neck I'd come close to choking.

She didn't protest.

But she rolled over, away from me, shutting me out.

23. PHOEBE

Saturday night

I WOULDN'T SHOW HIM THE TSUNAMI inside.

I knew exactly how to contain it. I'd pack it into the box, along with everything else from today. Pack it down tight.

The bottom fell out of my world back in December. I was still falling.

If Luke hadn't pulled me from the bath, would I be dead right now? I didn't know. I'd vomited the contents of my stomach soon after getting into the bath. The residue of the pills that had been left inside me hadn't been enough to put me to sleep.

I stared at the bedroom wall, wondering how long I'd known that Luke was cheating on me. When he'd come back from some of his *runs* over these past months, he'd been distant. I'd put it down to fatigue. But his mood at those times had made me shrug and shake my head.

Until tonight.

Tonight was different. Luke had gone out and left a wife that had just attempted to kill herself. It was then that I knew. He was going to see someone to make himself feel better. Because it was always about Luke and what he wanted.

I'd been in a haze, such a long haze, since Tommy went missing. I'd told myself that everything had been perfect between Luke and me before we lost Tommy. But that wasn't true.

I recalled a time in July of last year, sitting on the sofa downstairs and drinking, long after Luke and Tommy were in bed. Out loud and drunkenly, I'd asked the gods if *my turn* with Luke was over yet. I'd had a longer turn with him than had Sass, Pria, or Kate. I'd had him for well over two years. Surely that was long enough.

But there'd been no one left to hand him over to. Sass, Kate, and Pria had all moved on with their lives. And Bernice was out of the question.

It was game over.

What went wrong with Luke and me?

Back when I lived in London, he'd appeared out of nowhere, just after Flynn had devastated me. And somehow, we'd just fallen together. It'd just happened. Things happened in a flash after that. I discovered I was pregnant. Luke announced the pregnancy to everyone, while I was still coming to terms with the fact that there was a life form growing inside of me. And then Luke got down on bended knee with a ring—just like in the movies—at a London restaurant.

It was a whirlwind romance with someone I'd known since I was eight. But while I knew the boy, I barely knew the man.

Less than three years later, it was over. As of now. The marriage gone. The baby gone. Like none of it ever happened. It had all been sucked into a vacuum and disposed of.

I'd become a sad remnant of that former life, losing my mind and writing letters about a child that (in all probability) no longer existed.

The rhymes in those letters were about me. *Of course I'd written them.* Anyone would know that, just by reading them.

No wonder Luke was cheating on me. No wonder Tommy had gone off so easily with a stranger. I couldn't be the kind of wife and mother they'd needed.

From the time Tommy vanished, I'd given a sanitised version of my life to the media. Sass had told me to. But more than that, my instincts had told me to. Show the world a different picture. Be the good woman from the commercials.

Sass and I had picked through my photos, feeding the media the pictures of Tommy and me that told the story of a happy mother and her happy child. Not just happy, but joyous. Days gilded with golden sunshine and Instagram filters. A Facebook mashup of images that showed the pearls but not the oyster shells.

That story had become mine.

Who was I, really?

I thought back to the beginning of my pregnancy with Tommy.

I'd done the usual things during pregnancy: obsessed over kick counts (the number of kicks to the guts the kid gave me every hour that told me it was still alive), raged over restaurants and stores that shunned breastfeeding mothers (I was about to join their holy ranks), cried over every sad story in the news (my body was pumped with hormones), and lived in sheer terror of this alien being that had taken over my body (and was soon to force its way out).

Luke had been too busy to tell any of this to. The baby wasn't completely real to him yet because it wasn't inside his body. To him, the baby was a shapeless mound of dough that wouldn't spring to life until it emerged, fully cooked. Luke's obsession was his business—and the house that his business might soon be able to buy for us.

The small, red, wrinkly Thomas Basko was born eight weeks early, a few weeks before Christmas. The birth itself was surprisingly silent. Neither Tommy nor I cried or screamed. Luke was the only one to shed tears.

Tommy wasn't the usual picture you saw in birth announcements. *Please join us in welcoming our alien spawn to Earth* would have been an appropriate blurb for his first photo. Tommy was in intensive care for three weeks and a humidicrib for another two weeks. He belonged to the hospital and the nurses and the routines and the beeping machinery that he was attached to. Luke and I were on the periphery of all of this.

Then, all of a sudden, he was out. He was set free of the machines, and we were going to be trusted to take him home. Slight hearing issues in his left ear. Possible ongoing respiratory problems. But in general, healthy. Still, it felt wrong to leave the job of monitoring him to a pair of fallible humans.

At home, I exhausted myself just watching him breathe. I insisted on having a breathing monitor attached to him, in case I fell asleep.

Around this time, he turned into a little snapping turtle. In the hospital, I'd had to express milk into bottles. Now, I was expected to plug him directly into the source: my boobs. My nipples cracked and bled and pained. I dreaded each breastfeed. I couldn't look at those soft-lens pastel-coloured, gloating breastfeeding photos in magazines anymore.

We engaged the services of a breastfeeding expert who *guilted* me into soldiering on for another month. When Tommy was two and a half months old, I snuck down to the grocery store and bought a can of formula. And fed it to him. I felt like a drug dealer, feeding crack to a helpless infant.

The formula healed my nipples, but it didn't help Tommy sleep any better at night—or during the day. It wasn't the golden elixir that would stop him from crying. Luke tried to help, but he'd manage to fall asleep even with a screaming baby in his arms. I didn't know how that was possible. Crying babies were as loud as 115 decibels (louder than a jackhammer).

The books about babies talked about a mystical babymoon—like a honeymoon, except with a baby and without sex. A holiday in which you and the baby shut the world out and got to know each other.

Why did I feel so ragged? Why didn't I know how to separate out Tommy's cries and know what he wanted? Where was my mother's intuition?

I was a phony. And Tommy knew it. And he cried all the harder because of it.

I had dreams. Dreams that exploded through my mind during the snatched hours of sleep in between Tommy waking and screaming. I dreamed of Tommy being in pieces all around the house. A leg here. An arm there. Like a broken doll. I'd try to collect the pieces and put him back together before Luke found out. But Luke always found out. In other dreams, I'd leave Tommy on a picnic rug in a park and I'd drive away, feeling desperate but free.

Around the four-month mark, things slowly started to get better. In some ways. In most ways, I was still lost.

Before my pregnancy with Tommy, my days had structure. I had casting calls and stage shows and parties and (languid) dinners in restaurants.

Now, after Tommy, my days were jelly. No firm ground anywhere. How had my life changed so dramatically? Luke was still doing the same things he'd been doing before Tommy. Tommy had barely altered his world.

At first, I managed my new life like an acting role. The housewife, out shopping for matching household appliances, together with her latest accessory—the baby—safely being paraded about in a sporty thousand-dollar baby pram.

I acted like the young wife loyal to her husband and his career. I acted contented to be the one with the mixed smell of baby poo and lavender soap emanating from her skin. Those other women walking their babies in prams were surely doing the same as me—pretending to be deep in mystical babymoon bliss.

I told myself that once Luke and I got Tommy past the *wake-all-night-long* stage, we could travel. Babies could travel, couldn't they? They surely weighed less than a backpack. So we could just pack our stuff and pack the baby and go.

But Luke no longer wanted to travel. Nothing interested him except the push to gain footholds into the higher end of the Sydney property market. The higher end meant more expensive real estate and bigger commissions.

By the time Tommy was five months old, we were having Saturday lunch with his parents and Sunday walks in the park and visits with Nan on weekday afternoons. We had dinners with Rob and Ellie and clients of Luke's.

That had become our life.

Visits.

Family lunches.

Client dinners.

Walks in the park.

The best times for me with Tommy were his baths. Untethered from baby clothes and wraps and accessories. Human. Soft, warm, accessible. I'd imagine escaping with him to an island in the South Pacific. Just him and me. We'd swim in the wide blue water. We'd rock to sleep in a hammock overlooking the ocean. When he was old enough, I'd feed him mashed bananas and avocadoes straight from the trees. We'd have no need of the dozens of toys and accessories that parents bought their babies.

I mentioned the jelly days and the South Pacific fantasy to my baby health clinic nurse and was promptly handed a questionnaire. The *are-you-depressed?* quiz. I scored high on the quiz, but there were no prizes. I didn't win a South Pacific holiday.

The first plan of attack by the nurse to manage my depression was a mothers' group—an organised group of mothers (and less often, fathers) who got together to share and support each other. The babies were all at a similar stage of development—four to six months old.

I started driving weekly to the group in my local area.

Swiftly, I learned there were ranks within the group.

First came the rank of wealthy mothers who swapped names of party organisers and house cleaners. They discussed the merits of private schools that their fat-faced babies would one day attend. Some had already put their little Evas and Edwards on the waiting lists for schools.

Next came the rank of achievers. Their focus was firmly on the achievements of their progeny. Baby signing, musical and mathematical ability were at the forefront of the charge. Baby milestones were old hat.

Next came the naturals—the baby-wearing attachment-parenting earth mothers who spoke a language I didn't understand. They could pronounce all the names of substances and chemicals in baby lotions and foods. They grew their own vegetables and pureed them and froze them in tiny individual glass containers (with BPA-free plastic lids). They sewed their own clever baby slings and spent a lot of time talking about the materials and designs. They were nice to a fault, but I found no connection.

I hung with the strays, the unranked, the ones who turned up with hasty hairstyles, bereft of homemade things. We'd cling together in the hall. Our prams would be turned inward in a circle, the babies propped up and facing each other—alternately glaring and giggling at each other like small maniacs.

I liked the strays. They said inappropriate things, and they overshared, and they carried mother guilt. I didn't feel conscious about my fifteen kilos of extra weight I was carrying or my stomach rolls when I was with them. They didn't care, and they weren't judging me.

Marta would tell us about her parents'-in-law shady business dealings and the nitty gritty of her prolapse surgery. She described her attempts at anal sex with her husband and the difficulties involved—she was tall and large. Her husband was much shorter than herself: *Russell has to prop himself up with pillows under his knees! It takes a bit of adjusting to get the angle right.* She and Russell were also swingers. She'd casually popped that snippet of information into the conversation like a discarded cherry seed.

"Oh goodness," Gina the ex-librarian had exclaimed. "How do you manage it? It's not for me. Mick and I invited another man into our bedroom eighteen months ago. Before I was pregnant with Cora. It was something we both wanted to do, but it turned out to be a complete disaster!"

I'd listened with the fervour of an acolyte.

A swinger at a mothers' group! And anal sex! And an extra man in the bedroom! These people were real and exposed. Nothing was hidden or shameful. None of them subscribed to any program.

They were nothing like me. I loved them all because they weren't. Through them was an escape from my *visits-and-lunches* life. They had the richness and raw honesty of the arty type of movies that won awards.

That particular conversation had brought back an image of a man I used to know. Flynn O'Callaghan. A gorgeous, eclectic Irish actor who'd broken my heart with his *open relationship* suggestion. But was I wrong and he right? Did he know something that I didn't?

Nissa, a dark-skinned lady who'd recently emigrated from India, had shaken her head at Marta and Gina. "My husband would never do any of that. But he wants to *do me* every day. I've lost all interest in sexy times since the baby. It is a desert wasteland in my privates now. His mother tells me I must give him sex or he'll leave me."

Marta had batted her chubby hand in the air. "Tell him and his mother to give you some time to get back on the horse. In the meantime, he can get himself a hobby."

Nissa had clapped a hand over her mouth and giggled like a little girl.

"I had an affair once." Those words had randomly come from the most unlikely source. The quietest one of us—Adele—a woman with a tiny waist and the most *childbearingest* hips I'd ever seen. "Your husband is nothing like mine, Nissa. He only wants sex a couple of times a month. He tells me that's normal. Maybe it is, but it's not what I want. He has an easy job—working for his father and he gets lots of time off. But he just wants to play console games or potter around when he's at home. I have to wait for him to get in the mood. If I ask for sex, he gets all defensive. I mean, men have a serious design flaw—why can't their penises just be hard all the time? Then we could have sex with them when we choose, the way they do with us. Anyway, I couldn't cope anymore. I signed up to a dating site. I didn't really mean for anything to happen. It was just meant to be a release valve. But something did happen. I met someone, and we did it."

"Just the once?" I had to know.

"No. It went on for seven months," Adele told me. "The guy kept trying to move things forward. He'd invite me out on the weekends, but I'd always make excuses. I finally admitted to him that I was married. It was awful. I felt like a bad, bad person."

Marta had dabbed at her baby daughter's dribble with a tissue. "See, that wouldn't happen in the swingers' community. Everyone knows the score. You go in with your eyes—and legs—open."

I'd thought about Luke and me then. I knew I didn't want to share him, even though the passion between us had already fizzled out like stale soda. Maybe I was territorial. I wasn't about to parcel out my land. I didn't want to bring someone else into the bedroom or join a swingers' club or have an affair. But my little sub-group within the mothers' group gave me the bravery to imagine walking away from this life if I had to. I could drop the program and get off the married-life grid.

My mother would have been horrified.

The conversation had swapped then to Marta's husband's haemorrhoids that he swore he'd developed in sympathy for his wife's pregnancy.

Mothers' group had become the unexpected bright spot in my week. For six months, it became my refuge.

But the day that Luke came home with the news that he'd just bought a house for us was the day that it all changed.

He didn't tell me where the house was—just told me that we were picking up my grandmother on the way to go and see it. I didn't suspect anything when we kept driving up Southern Sails Street after getting

Nan. I had no idea that the house was going to be on the same street, just up on the hill.

The last thing I'd wanted was to come back here to this street. But I didn't know how to begin to have that conversation with Luke. He was so proud he was beaming. The townhouse was new, it was beautiful, and it was in an incredible position. How could I say anything negative? We could barely afford it, but Luke said that if we didn't buy into the market now, we'd miss out.

My mothers' group was now on the other side of the city. I could have continued to go there. But I let it slide. It was true that Tommy's sleep times made it hard to undertake a two-hour round trip to the mothers' group. It was true that Tommy fussed on long car trips. In truth, though, I was mostly just lazy.

So, I settled into my new house with its new furniture and new appliances. Luke liked things brand new. I think one of the things that Luke especially liked about Tommy was that he was new—our own freshly created being.

When Tommy was a year old, Luke's mother began minding him often enough that I could start looking for acting roles again. And plus, we now lived on the same street, so it was convenient. Nan wasn't able to look after a baby and her house was anything but babyproof.

But the dream of gaining substantial movie roles was just about over. Due to Tommy, I couldn't turn up for casting calls on the spur of the moment anymore. I wasn't free to just walk out the door. I appeared in a couple of commercials and scored a bit part in a *made-for-TV* movie. I must have looked tired around the edges because my *sexy young girl* roles in commercials soon became *sexless-young-mother* roles.

I grew tired of the commercials and of the movie casting calls that either didn't want me or required me to be on set in another location for weeks for a small part that didn't pay well. I could no longer do that. Neither Luke nor his mother treated my acting seriously. It was a hobby, something that should never get in the way of Luke's business.

Just like mothers' group, I let my acting career slide. It seemed silly, vain even, to keep trying.

People had this notion about aspiring actors, that they were chasing a foolish dream and not a real career. It was a dream held together by stardust and face powder and boob glue.

By the time Tommy was eighteen months old, I'd walked away from acting.

I concentrated on Tommy from that point on. My world drew in tight and small. I spent Luke's money buying Tommy everything a little boy could possibly wish for. Actually, that wasn't true. Tommy wished for very little. Blocks and cardboard boxes and dirt were his favourites. And boats. He'd scream in excitement when he saw the ferries and yachts cutting across the harbour.

Being with Tommy was like being in another world. Everything slowed down to a snail's pace. A world where ladybugs and butterflies and slugs were exciting and paper boats sailed off for adventures in puddles. For a while, I was content living in Tommy's world.

But then the boredom and resentment would crawl over me like a smothering blanket. Sometimes, I hated Tommy. I wanted him to disappear.

Every day was the same thing. Every day the struggle to get him to eat healthy things instead of him screaming for ice-cream and biscuits (or cookies on the days he'd watched the Cookie Monster). Every day the endless *what's that, Mumma?* (Even though he knew perfectly well what the thing was that he was pointing to.) Every day the sticky fingers and the poo and the dressing and undressing and the miniature missing socks and the eating of dirt.

On more days than not, I found myself drinking the bottles of alcohol that Luke's clients had given him for getting a good price for their house.

No bottles of *hiphiphurray* for me. No one gave me prizes or rewards for my job, which was the job of looking after house and home and the kid. All I had were Tommy's sippy cups dribbling juice onto the carpet.

Sometimes I woke up on the sofa after I'd had a couple of drinks, not knowing where Tommy was. And I'd have to go look for him. Sometimes, he'd make a game of it and hide from me, and I'd get angry and start yelling his name.

Luke, on the other hand, went from strength to strength, winning industry awards and gaining bigger and bigger clients. The commissions got more impressive. The overseas trips got flashier—not that we ever went away for long.

Along with that, Luke started pointing out things that weren't getting done around the house. Subtly at first. Then not so subtly. He was used to seeing perfect homes that were styled for sale, and he didn't understand baskets of washing sitting on our bedroom floor or tangles of paper boats and blocks and playdough in the family room.

In Luke's view, my role was to clean the house he provided, make meals with the food that he paid for, and care for the child he'd given me (via his sperm).

I didn't remember any contract with my name on it where I'd agreed to scrub the toilet in return for a roof over my head. I didn't need Luke's roof before I had Tommy. I had my own roof, paid for with my own money. As far as I was concerned, Tommy was my day job. Luke could scrub his own damned toilet when he got home from *his* day job.

Somewhere along that road, even sex started to be on Luke's terms. He wanted it when and how he wanted it. Somehow, I'd joined the service industry. My job was servicing Luke. Servicing his house, servicing his kid, servicing his stomach, servicing his dick. Because he was paying for it all. He supplied the money, I supplied the service.

His semen became a poison thing. Poisoning my body. A potion given by an evil tyrant. Day by day making me a prisoner of the house. Because his semen had given me Tommy and made all of this happen. And he was starting to make noises about a second child. A brother or a sister for Tommy.

Resentment made of bile lined my gut. I started making excuses whenever Luke touched me: *Tommy had worn me out. It was a bad time of the month. The sciatica I'd had ever since Tommy's pregnancy was playing up.* Sometimes it was true. Mostly it wasn't.

He made comments about the wives and girlfriends of his colleagues. "Lucy Harrington really bounced back after that second baby. Rob and I couldn't believe it when we saw her in those jeans last night."

Luke flirted in front of me. Even with Sass. I didn't blame Sass. Flirting was like breathing to her. It was Luke I blamed.

I was still flabby a whole year after having Tommy. Luke never mentioned it outright. It would have been better if he had. Each subtle dig dug me deeper into the hole.

It was only after Tommy went missing that I dropped the baby weight—within weeks.

Silently, I made plans for tomorrow.

24. PHOEBE

Sunday morning

NAN STIRRED HER TEA AROUND AND around, clinking the spoon against the inside of the cup until my bones felt raw and exposed.

Clink, clink of the spoon on my spine.

Clink, clink on my shoulder bones.

Clink, clink on my skull.

I didn't know anyone who stirred their tea as vigorously as Nan did. The tiny square of Nan's kitchen seemed to close in around me, the century-old cupboards giving off a faint mouldy musk.

"Women stayed and fought for their man in my day," she informed me, the hollow of her cheeks severe in the dim light.

"There's nothing to fight for, Nan. He's seeing someone else."

She didn't blink or miss a beat. "Then give him a reason to stay married to you."

"The reason we had for staying together was Tommy . . ." My voice fell away like crumbling earth. I hadn't admitted that to myself until now.

For a moment, there was something bright and soft in her eyes. But it didn't stay. I knew it was for Tommy. She loved him in her own way. I wondered if she ever wished she'd been nicer to him on the day he vanished. Probably not. If Tommy wandered back in through the door right now, within five minutes she'd be scolding him for touching the ornaments.

Luke had threatened me with all kinds of things earlier this morning. Saying he'd call Dr Moran and have me committed to a mental health facility. Freeze our bank accounts. He'd even threatened to call a reporter and tell them it was me who sent the letters. Then he'd broken down and said he didn't mean any of it. Finally, he'd agreed to me having a short break, and he'd insisted on driving me up the street to Nan's house.

"How long do you intend staying here for?" Nan sipped her tea noisily, her gaze skewering me.

We'd reached the business end of things now.

"Not long," I told her. "I just need to get myself together. Then I'll organise somewhere else to go. I need a bit of time. I've had . . . issues with my medication, as you know. But all I need is just some rest."

Her mouth pursed in the way it always did when someone was doing something she didn't approve of. "Just remember that you made your bed with your husband and you can't just flit away." Then she did her signature huffy sigh. "Look, you're likely to be feeling a bit upside-down at the moment, due to those silly letters. Stay here for a few days if you need to, but then you've got to go back to him."

I took the cup of tea that Nan offered me—she never had coffee here. "What if he doesn't want me back?"

"That boy was always obsessed with you, Phoebe. It was obvious."

"Well, not anymore."

Another sigh. Extra huff. "Well, I've said my piece. What about this sleepwalking trouble of yours? How are we going to manage that? I need to know that the whole incident with the toolshed isn't going to happen again."

"It won't. I promise. My psychiatrist changed my medication."

"That's a relief to hear. I wouldn't know what to do with you. You were quite frightening."

"I was? I'm sorry."

Her sparse eyebrows pulled together. "The police took some odd things from the house yesterday. Some notepads. My old typewriter and ink. I didn't know what they were after. Thought it had something to do with that strange fellow that's been hanging about."

"Yes, the police are . . . being very thorough." I winced, wondering if she'd end up figuring out that I'd written the letters.

"They asked me not to mention it to anyone. All very odd."

"Yeah. Odd. Nan, who's the *strange fellow* that you said has been hanging about?"

"A couple of the neighbours said there's a man who walks up and down the streets quite a lot at night. Could be homeless, though they usually don't come all the way up here."

"Okay. Think I'll head upstairs for a nap." Taking my cup of tea with me, I stepped out to the hallway and made my way up the narrow stairs to my old bedroom. It'd been my room from the time I was born right up until my first year of university. My childhood books still occupied their spot on a shelf: *Charlotte's Web, Anne of Green Gables, Lemony Snicket,* and a host of other dog-eared volumes. A poster of an anonymous ballerina still hung on the wall—the same ballerina silhouette you saw on the internet, turning around and around and you couldn't tell if she was turning left or right. The room carried the dust of many times the number of decades I'd lived in it, the dust lying thick in the cracks in the floorboards. This had been my mother's room when she was a baby. Her childhood doll sat on my shelf alongside the books, dull eyes staring out from a brittle plastic face.

My phone buzzed in my pocket, and I slipped it out. It was Sass. I knew exactly what her reaction was going to be to the news that I'd separated from Luke: tightly controlled excitement. She hadn't been as impressed with *married-Phoebe* as much as she had been with *fancy-free-Phoebe.*

"Hey, babe," came Saskia's voice brightly through the phone, "how are you doing today?"

"I left Luke this morning." Might as well get it out of the way.

"You *what?*"

"He's been seeing some other woman."

There was silence on the other end of the phone. Before she exploded. "What! *No.* How could he? God, Phoebe, I'm sorry." She paused, and I could almost hear the thoughts running wild through her head. "Where are you? Look, if you want to bunk in with me—"

"I'm at Nan's."

"You'll die there. Get your stuff together. You're coming to my place."

"I appreciate it. You know I do. But I'm fine."

"Sorry, babe, but I'm not leaving you alone to deal with this. You didn't deserve this on top of everything else. It's fucking cruel of him."

"I know. But to be honest, I don't even know if I care. I mean, I thought we were still a couple and everything—up until I knew about the other woman that is—but we weren't. We were Tommy's parents and that's all." I didn't need to say the rest. Without Tommy, we were nothing. If Tommy hadn't vanished and if life had gone on as normal, would either of us have guessed that our marriage wasn't real?

"I'm coming down to see you after work. You'll be there at Nan's?" All my friends called my grandmother Nan.

I hesitated. I wasn't ready to see anyone. I didn't deserve anyone's sympathy. The video of me placing the envelope in the mailbox kept looping in my head.

"I'm sorry, Sass. I'm just really, really tired."

"You poor thing. You looked so tired yesterday. We put a blanket on you and tiptoed out."

"I'm sorry for falling asleep on all of you."

"Don't be sorry. Don't you dare. I have to go away for work tonight, but I'm coming to see you the minute I'm back. Get some good rest, okay? I'll call you later."

The line went dead. Sass was always the one to end the conversation and hang up. It was like an unspoken rule between us.

The phone rang again almost as soon as I'd dropped the phone back in my pocket.

I expected Sass again. She often forgot to tell me something and she'd call back five times in a row to rush out a couple of sentences and then hang up again just as quickly.

But it was Detective Gilroy.

"Phoebe, Luke told me you'd left to go stay at your grandmother's."

"That's right. I have. Hey, it's Sunday. Don't you ever have a day off?"

"I am off work today. But I'm a little worried about you, so I thought I'd call. Is her house secure?"

"Yes. She's had deadlocks for years. And she's home during the day. Unlike Luke."

He seemed to hesitate. "Luke said you two had a series of arguments last night?"

"Yes, we did. I just found out Luke's been seeing someone else."

"Seriously?" I heard exasperation in his voice. "That makes things difficult. Well, I'm very sorry to hear it. I think I need to call Luke back and have a chat."

"Don't you believe me?"

"Of course. It's just that this throws in an unexpected twist. As I said, I'm worried. I'd like to think that you're going to be somewhere where someone can look out for you. You'll be putting yourself in danger if you head outside sleepwalking again."

"Obviously, the person to look out for me can't be Luke. He's got other priorities."

"Do you have some other family that you could stay with? Somewhere away from here might be good. A change of scene."

"A few aunties and uncles and cousins, but I don't want to go and stay with any of them. I want to stay on my street."

"Okay, it's your decision. Luke told me you saw Dr Moran yesterday. That's good."

"She put me on new medication. I'm feeling better."

"Well, keep getting better. I'll stay in contact. We'll get back to concentrating on Tommy's case. You need to focus on yourself."

"I will."

The call ended.

I heard heavy scraping sounds coming from outside in the courtyard, setting my teeth on edge. I didn't have a view of the backyard from here. My bedroom window looked out onto the street.

Gulping down the tea, I headed back downstairs. Nan wasn't in her armchair as usual.

I stepped out through the back door. My tiny grandmother was struggling to shift a large pot of ivy against the shed. I'd tidied and swept up all the broken pots and dirt earlier this morning.

"It won't get any sun there, Nan," I pointed out.

"It's ivy. It'll do just fine." She turned to me, a smear of dirt embedded in her lined cheek.

"You should wait and ask me for help if you want to move things that heavy."

"I'm perfectly capable. I've been living here alone a long time." Her voice held a note of sad astonishment, as though she herself couldn't believe how long she'd lasted by herself in this house.

I frowned, noticing that she'd roughly hammered a large piece of wire mesh onto the shed door. Stooping, she began winding the ivy tendrils from the pot into the mesh.

Fine threads of panic pulled tight in my veins. It had just been a dream that Tommy had wanted desperately to get inside the shed, but the dream had stayed with me. "Nan, you won't be able to access the shed ever again once that takes hold."

"I've told you there's nothing in there that's of any use. I might as well use the shed to grow my vines on, the ugly old eyesore that it is." She continued to insert the ivy into the mesh.

I wanted to stop her. But I had no reason to. It was probably just an old memory of Tommy playing in Nan's yard that had surfaced in my sleepwalking dream. I couldn't insist that she stop what she was doing. It was her shed and her ivy.

High above the yard, the morning sun made the top-storey windows of Mrs Wick's townhouse opaque. But not so opaque that I didn't catch the blurred sight of Bernie Wick's large frame as she stared down at us from her bedroom window, her mother's cat in her arms. She moved away as soon as she saw me looking at her.

25. LUKE

Monday morning

TYING THE TOWEL AROUND MY MIDSECTION, I dripped water to the bedroom. It felt wrong, standing in this room without Phoebe. Like there was only half of me here. There was no Phoebe asleep in the bed like every other morning. The house was empty—just a house made of brick and wood.

I was just going through the motions as I dressed and stepped in front of the full-length mirror. I straightened my tie and stared at the face that stared back at me, my skin reddened in patches by the hot shower.

Who the hell was I? I'd lost my son and now my wife.

I needed to talk sense into Phoebe. She'd stayed overnight at Nan's— that was enough time to get her head a bit straight. Just days ago, I thought we were starting to get our lives sorted again. She'd come out to a work dinner with me, and she'd handled it well. And she'd been taking care of the wall garden. Little steps, but positive ones.

But all along, this thing with the notes had been happening, and I'd had no clue. Until it all exploded.

I almost wished the police had charged her and put her into my custody. House arrest, or something like that. But I guessed they couldn't do that. Hell, I remembered reading about a guy who faked his own death and he didn't get charged. They'd called it pseudocide. Did they have a fancy name for what my wife had just done? Probably not. Probably no one in the history of kids being abducted had ever done what she had.

I tried to ignore the voice hammering at the back of my brain, telling me things were never going to be okay with Phoebe again, let alone Phoebe and me.

Picking up my briefcase, I headed out of the house. My first stop was the local hardware store to pick up some pots and plants and potting mix. Then I drove to Phoebe's grandmother's.

Bernice Wick stared at me curiously from the front step of her house as I parked my car outside Phoebe's nan's. Bernice seemed to spend a crazy amount of time out there, just watching people go past. She revolted me. People who threw their lives away were bloody wastes of space.

I lugged the stuff from the hardware store up Nan's path, taking me three trips. I rapped on the door.

Phoebe answered it.

I wanted to see relief on her face. Or regret. Something. But her eyes showed nothing at all.

"I got some pots and things to replace the broken ones," I started. "And I'll fix up the yard."

"I already did that yesterday. You can leave the new stuff here on the porch, and I'll take it inside."

"I'll help you."

"No, it's okay."

"Phoebe, please, don't be like that. I'm your husband. I just want things to get back to normal."

She pulled her mouth in tight in a way that reminded me of her grandmother. "You mean with you and me and *her*? That kind of normal?"

"There is no *her*. Look . . . it was wrong of me to say I didn't drop in on someone that night. But she's just a client. We talked business. It helped get my mind off things." It was a carefully rehearsed speech that I'd made up while I was at home. I tried to make it sound ad lib.

"And you got close enough to rub bodies and smell of her perfume?"

"What? No. We shook hands."

"And somehow the perfume jumped onto your neck."

"I—"

"Don't bother." She crinkled her eyebrows together. "You know what, I just realised that I know that perfume. *I remember it*. She's someone I know, isn't she?"

"Stop making something out of this that it isn't. Yes, you've probably met her. You've met a lot of my clients."

"If she's just a client, then why are you so secretive about her name?"

"Because I'm not dragging her into this, that's why."

"You think I'm going to go and do something nuts if I find out who she is, is that it? Start sending her letters or something?"

"No, I don't think you'd do that."

"Why not? I just wrote those letters about Tommy, right?" Her shoulders slumped then, and she looked defeated. Was that her admission that she'd written them? It was probably the best I was going to get from her.

"Phoebe, I'll forget those letters if you will. We don't have to talk about them ever again. And I know you don't believe me, but I haven't been seeing another woman—not in any romantic way. Trust me, I wasn't."

"Even if that's true, and I don't know if it is, you've been seeing a woman you haven't told me about. Lots of times. The same woman."

Those wide eyes of hers—so like Tommy's—were drilling into me. "Okay, yes." *Why did I just admit that?*

"And talking about me—all your problems with me."

"It wasn't like that." *It was exactly like that.*

"Just go, Luke."

I inhaled the cold winter air, knowing I needed to change tactics. "You can't stay here. You know you'll start going around the bend spending all that time with Nan by yourself. No offence to Nan. Speaking of which, how is she going to cope if you have another sleepwalk episode?"

"I was fine last night. I've got the new meds now." She crossed her arms.

"You've got another appointment with Dr Moran this afternoon. I'll take you."

"No, I'll get there myself."

"Why are you being so difficult? I'm just trying to help."

"I'm not being difficult. I just don't need your help."

I wasn't getting anywhere with her. The more I was trying, the more she was digging her heels in. Maybe it was better to leave her be for a couple of days and then she'd be ready to come back home.

26.   PHOEBE

Monday afternoon

DR. MORAN'S OFFICE SMELLED OF LAVENDER. The walls were deeply lilac. The framed paintings were that type they call naïve art, with the perspective all wrong, giving it a childlike look. I was never sure if Dr Moran thought the paintings would help people get in touch with their inner child or if she'd bought them because she genuinely liked them.

In this office, I always had the feeling I was in a dollhouse and that her patients were the dolls she played with.

How are you today, Mrs PoppyFlower? You look sad. Never mind, here's your medicine . . .

Dr Moran was dressed in a crisp white shirt and perfectly pressed pants. Even the smile on her face was perfectly pressed. "It's good to see you today. How are you? How have you been sleeping at night?"

"Much better." I wriggled back in the chair and placed my feet on the footrest. Dr Moran was a big believer in footrests. She had one herself.

Dr Moran had called me earlier to make sure I was coming today. It felt like I was being managed between her, Luke, and Trent Gilroy.

"The new medication's been okay?" she asked.

"Yes. I slept straight through. No waking, no sleepwalking."

"That's very good to hear. So, what's been happening?"

"I . . . I've been . . . existing."

"Getting by?"

"Yes."

"Are you ready to chat about the letters?"

"I am."

"Good. What do you remember?"

"I still don't remember anything. Maybe I made myself forget?"

"That's possible. How about we talk about how you've been feeling the past month or so."

"Okay. But there's not much to tell. I've just been . . . numb."

"Anything else?"

"And angry. It's been a whole six months without Tommy. With no resolution."

"Can you tell me what kinds of things you thought about when you were feeling angry?"

"I just felt like the police weren't doing enough."

"They weren't coming up with any answers?"

"Yes, that. It was their job to find him, and they hadn't done that."

"You were angry at them?"

"Not exactly. Just . . . I just felt rage. In general."

"Phoebe, were you keeping a journal or diary or anything this year?"

"No."

"Poetry? Ever write that?"

"I'm not a poet."

"I was trying to help jog your memory of the letters. You must have had the paper and envelopes somewhere. A sleepwalker has to start somewhere. In your waking hours before all this happened, you would have known where to find those things."

"I don't remember ever seeing them before."

She sucked in her lips, moistening them. "I'll let you know that Detective Gilroy invited me to view the film of you putting the envelope in your mailbox. It was helpful for me to see what you were like that night."

"What did you think?" I said, hiding the fact that a tiny part of me hoped that she'd have noticed something different to everyone else.

"Well, you were certainly in some other kind of state. It seems to me that you need yet more time before any memories return to you. If we can figure out how you came to write the letters, it might help us to discuss your feelings at the time. It can be difficult to heal things sometimes if we can't see them clearly. Also, you seem to want to remember."

"I do." I eyed the clean, white ceiling. "Do you have any idea why I would choose to use Nan's old typewriter to write the letters on, when I've never used it before? I mean, I didn't even know she still had the thing. I haven't seen it since I was a kid. I'm not even sure I'd know how to use it."

"Well, I can't claim to have used one either. But they don't look very technical." She gave a half grin. "It is an interesting point, though. There must have been something in your subconscious that drew you to it." Dropping the grin, her eyes grew quizzical.

"You ended up in your grandmother's yard that night, right? Trying to get inside her toolshed? What was that all about?"

"I honestly don't know. I dreamed that Tommy was there and he wanted to get into the shed. So I was trying to help him."

"Looks like the sleepwalking is connected with old memories."

"That's what I thought. But none of it really makes sense."

"Well, people do a lot of things when sleepwalking that don't make a lot of sense. They drive cars and crash them. They write nonsensical stories. They can even get violent."

"I did something worse. I wrote notes that made me believe that we were close to finding Tommy's abductor."

"Maybe that's the real reason you wrote them," she said gently. "Perhaps you wanted so badly to get answers that you invented this person."

"Maybe. It terrifies me to think I've done something like this and I can't recall it. I could do something else and not remember it. Something worse."

"Well, we're going to work on making sure that doesn't happen. Like I said, it seems you need a little more time. We'll return to this at the next appointment. Let's just concentrate on you for the rest of this session. How are things between you and Luke? Things were quite . . . tense when you two came in."

Thinking of Luke made me suck in a breath of resentment. "Things got even tenser. I found out that Luke's been fucking some other woman."

I didn't know for certain that he'd been fucking her, but he'd smelled of her perfume. That, and the cringing look on his face, was enough to tell me that something had happened between him and her.

She gasped, her fingers touching her lips. "Oh no. . . ." She straightened herself then, nodding in a more business-like way. "You've had an extremely rough couple of days."

"You could say that."

"Do you want to tell me what happened?"

"When Luke and I got home from our visit with you, we had an argument. Luke went out for a walk and came back an hour later smelling of perfume. He admitted he's been going to see someone. I moved out, and I'm at my grandmother's now."

It hurt retelling those scenes. It seemed like someone else's life.

I could tell that she was searching for something to say that was free of bias. She was recalibrating her vision of Luke in her head, trying to match what I'd previously told her of him with this new, tarnished vision. Since I'd started seeing her, soon after Tommy's disappearance, I'd told her the same *perfect couple* story that I'd told the police.

"Oh . . . Phoebe . . ." She breathed in and out heavily. "I'm sorry."

"I'm sorry too."

"Tell me, how has all this been affecting you? What are you feeling?"

"Empty."

"So, you're living with your grandmother now?" She furrowed her brow. "I remember that you haven't had the smoothest relationship with your grandmother in the past."

"She can be a hard person to be around. But she's been okay." *No, she hasn't been okay. She's been her usual critical self.*

"You're planning on staying with her? No plans to head anywhere else?"

"No plans yet."

"Of course. I'm sure you're still feeling numb and bruised. So, all of this with Luke came as a complete shock?"

I chewed my top lip. "I knew something was happening before the night I found out. But I didn't admit it to myself. I didn't want to see it."

"What didn't you want to see, Phoebe?"

I tried to hold back. I didn't want to talk about this. I wanted her to make me remember writing those rhymes, but we'd gotten nowhere with that.

"I didn't want to see that I'm a disappointment to him," I found myself saying in answer to her. I folded my arms, trying to barricade myself.

"Why did you think you disappointed Luke?"

My eyes closed, betraying the barrier I'd tried to put up. "Because I'm not all he thought I was."

"Luke had a different picture of you?"

"Yes."

"Why do you think he had a different picture?"

I hesitated, the truth of Luke and me welling inside my chest.

I wanted to talk.

"Because he never knew me," I said, the words flattening as I spoke them.

"He didn't know you?"

"No. Luke had always pursued me, I mean, from the time we were teenagers. But I didn't give in. And I think, because of that, he built me up in his mind to be something more than what I was. Every year that he didn't have me, the more special I became—in his eyes."

"In other words, he put you on a pedestal?"

"Exactly. And in a way, that was his biggest criticism of me. I wasn't good enough as I was. He just saw some ideal of me."

She sat back, eyeing me thoughtfully. "What things about you do you think Luke doesn't know?"

"He doesn't know what drives me."

"What drives you, Phoebe?"

"It's hard to explain. It's that feeling of having a warm body. Of feeling totally alive and awake."

"Can you tell me the last times you felt that way?"

"When I lived in London I felt like that. As a theatrical actor. It didn't pay much, but I felt alive in those days. There was an energy. I travelled a lot. Travel is easy from London. Things were constantly moving."

"When do you think things stopped moving?"

"I guess, when I became pregnant with Tommy. Luke and I married, and we moved back to where we started. Everything became centred on Luke, and he expected that I'd be happy with that. He was working around the clock to be able to afford the house we have now. There was no time or room for anything else."

"And then when Tommy was born?"

I stared out the window, at the arch of bare-branched trees that lined the avenue. Dark, brittle sunlight had turned the scene sepia. "When Tommy was born, he was like this little squashy alien being who I knew nothing about, and who knew nothing about himself. He was sick for the first few weeks. It was hard for me to accept that he was even mine."

"Am I right in saying you felt a bit of distance from your baby?"

"Yes. I wasn't an instant mother. At least, I didn't feel like one."

"And in the months after the birth? How were things then?"

"I guess . . . I always felt like a bit of an imposter being a mother. It wasn't something I was qualified for."

A smile stretched the edges of her pink-lipstick mouth. "It's a job none of us feel qualified for."

"I just wasn't the mother I should have been."

"You didn't feel adequate?"

"No."

She hesitated, tapping her pen lightly on her notebook. "It's a common experience for mothers to feel inadequate."

I stared at her. "I wasn't just *inadequate*. I didn't protect him from someone stealing him away." Something inside me broke. "I can't stand it. The weight of it. I can't do this anymore. After the first weeks, people started saying that time would find me in a better place. I'm not in a better place."

"Can you tell me the place you're in?"

"It's so deep. There's no light. I feel . . . *hate*. Hate for everyone this hasn't happened to. Because they get to live in a different world to me. Hate for myself for not protecting Tommy."

I cried, listening to myself speak words that I didn't know I'd been holding inside. *I hated people for not being me?*

Dr Moran fetched me tissues, saying soothing things I could barely hear.

A lull fell in the room. I'd given away too much of myself. I could see that her eyes had changed.

"Phoebe, I'm going to ask this directly. Have you had thoughts of harming yourself lately?"

"No," I lied. I wasn't ready to tell about what I'd done. If I did, she might want to put me in a facility somewhere. And I didn't want that. I needed my own space. A cocoon.

She didn't look convinced. "I always wondered in our earlier sessions if you were holding things back. I want you to get the most out of these sessions, and you won't if you hold back. I've sensed anger from you, but you haven't brought those feelings to the surface. Except for little bits and pieces."

"I'm trying to put it behind me, I guess."

"It's hard to put things behind us when they're following us everywhere. Sometimes we need to stop and turn around and face those things."

"I don't want to talk about this stuff anymore."

"Okay, but we'll return to it at your next session. I think we'll make another appointment in three days. Right now, we'll concentrate on small steps to get you back on that road of having a warm body again. Tell me, how often do you do things you enjoy doing? And how often do you see your friends?"

"I can't say I really have hobbies anymore. I don't see my friends very much. I don't have much in common with them anymore. They have *lives*, and I don't. They're all doing things and going places, and I'm not. It makes me feel worse, so I avoid seeing them."

"You have a life. It's what you do every day that makes up your life. If you stay home every day and stare at the four walls, well, then that becomes your life. Sometimes, when you've reached rock bottom, it takes going step by step to get yourself out of there. But you *can* do it. We're going to make a plan for you. Just small steps."

Handing me a piece of paper, she asked me to write down things I could do over the next week that were different to what I usually did. *Small steps.*

I wrote:

Go swimming.
Have my hair cut.
Have dinner with friends.
Go to Bingo with Nan.
Go see a movie.

I planned on doing none of those things.

When I glanced up from the page, Dr Moran was eyeing me fixedly. "Phoebe, I'm going to be in close contact. I'm going to want to know that you are doing these things, okay? I'll be calling you each day to see how you're going. You're going to need to have your phone switched on. I'll be calling at four in the afternoon every day. Just to see how you're going with your small steps." She smiled warmly, taking my sheet of paper and quickly reading it.

"I'd like that," I said, lying to her for the second time.

She copied down what I'd written and then returned the page to me. "See this as a contract. I will tell you that I'm concerned about you. In my experience, you're at a tipping point. If something else happens, you might well need to have a stay at a place where you can rest—and be monitored. Yes, I'm that worried. I need to know that you're going to take these steps to reconnect with yourself."

Straightening my jacket distractedly, I nodded. I had to be more careful at future sessions. I'd revealed too much, and now I'd won myself daily phone calls from my psych.

27.   PHOEBE

Tuesday afternoon

NAN SAT IN HER ARMCHAIR, MAKING a scratching sound with her pencil as she did the puzzles from a women's magazine. She wore a green cardigan that had been pulled out of shape around the collar, from all the years she'd scrunched up the cardigan around her neck to keep out the cold. I knew that the cardigan would smell musty — everything in this house did. Even Nan. She had no care for new things. Behind her, on the wall, a sixty-year-old clock ticked loudly, winding its way around to two in the afternoon. I hated the ticking. But Nan didn't seem to even notice the sound.

The whole day had passed slowly. I sat reading a book, wishing I'd put *reading* on Dr Moran's *small steps* list yesterday. She probably wouldn't have been happy with it, though. She wanted me to see people, get out of the house. Anyway, I'd read the same paragraph six times over. I couldn't get into it, and this was only the second page. The book was one of my mother's old historical romance novels. I used to like them when I was a teenager. Now, it seemed that romantic love was a lie.

"It's soup for dinner," Nan announced out of the blue.

"Okay."

"It'll be pumpkin."

"Pumpkin's good."

"Sass called around while you were out at the doctor's."

"Okay. I told her I'd be at Dr Moran's. Must have forgotten."

Nan peered over the top of her reading glasses at me. "She's still flitting about unattached, I see. Should be married off by now, that girl."

"The man she was engaged to years ago is in prison, Nan. I think she dodged a bullet."

"Well, she'd better find someone else, quick smart, before she turns thirty. She didn't look crash-hot when she stopped in here last week, and I told her so. Too much makeup. She's lost that glow of youth, she has."

I stifled a sigh. "There's no race to get married by thirty anymore. Why did Sass come by last week?"

Her expression softened a touch. "Drops in all the time. I guess I'm like family to her. She was forever in this house as a child, cheeky little so-and-so she was."

Nan didn't add that kids only used to come here when my father wasn't around. It was an unspoken understanding. She hadn't thought much of Morris—my father—but she'd forced herself to tolerate him because he was her daughter's husband.

I used to spend a lot of time at Saskia's house. Her parents and grandparents were relaxed and happy people. The house wasn't there anymore. It had been pulled down years ago, to make way for the apartment blocks that were coming. Saskia's parents and grandparents had moved way up north to Queensland.

All the old houses would be gone soon. Including Nan's.

Nan switched on the TV. She flicked from channel to channel, complaining about the quality of the TV shows these days. She settled upon an old sitcom.

The canned laughter of the show ate its way under my skin. The whole thing was a manufactured experience, the audience instructed when something was funny and what to feel. *Laugh. Stop. Be sad (cue slow music when the character says something poignant) Stop being sad. Laugh.*

Nan scowled when the show finished and a home renovation program began. I knew exactly what she was thinking, because she often said the same thing when those shows were on: *People want change for the sake of change. Why fix something that isn't falling down?*

Nan put another sitcom on. More canned laughter. I thought of heading upstairs just to lie on the bed and get away from the noise.

My phone buzzed in my pocket.

It was Pria—all sympathy and comfort. Saskia had told her about what happened with Luke. Typical Sass. She couldn't keep anything to herself for more than a day. Pria begged me to come up to her house so she could hug me in person. She couldn't come to me because she was waiting on Jessie to get home from school. Kate was on her way there, too. Sass couldn't make it, Pria said.

I was about to make an excuse when I remembered Dr Moran's *small steps* again. It would be something to tell her when she called later. Plus, I enjoyed hanging out with the girls when I made the effort. I told Pria I'd come up there for a few minutes.

"Be back in time for dinner!" Nan called as I left the house. I suppressed a smile. It was like I was ten again.

I ran my hands through my hair as I walked down Nan's garden path and out onto the street.

Deliberately, I looked away from the Wick house and number 29 when I walked past. If Bernice was peeking through her window, I didn't want to see her. And if a curtain shifted at number 29, I didn't want to know. And I didn't look at Luke's parents' house or my own house either. If Luke wasn't going to be in my future, then I had to start separating myself emotionally.

I couldn't stay here in this street for very long—too many reminders of the past. But I'd need a job if I were to move somewhere else. I couldn't imagine what my resume would say. *Out-of-work actor. No experience in any field other than acting. Needs to answer to her psychiatrist on a daily basis. Not good with children.*

Yes, that should get me a decent job.

A chill breeze blew around my ears. I continued on up the hill.

Before I could think of leaving Nan's, I had to concentrate on getting better. I'd try Dr Moran's small steps and see where it took me.

It took less than ten minutes to reach Pria's house, but it wasn't a walk for the faint-hearted. The hill rose sharply, and the vigorous roots of Moreton Bay figs lifted up the pathway everywhere. The house lots became larger and more impressive the farther up the hill you went, the homes high and imposing and kept behind ivy-covered walls. The gardens looked healthier and more abundant, as though the very air up here nourished them.

I didn't know many of the people on the highest part of the hill, apart from Pria and Kate. The people mostly kept to themselves. I knew everyone at the lower end.

After Tommy had gone missing, it hadn't been any different. The people from the high end would gently grasp my arm and hand me platitudes in lowered tones. *Oh, it's shocking. I don't know how you're managing.* The people on the lower end would march right up to me and they'd say, *If I get my hands on the animal who took Tommy, I won't think twice before ripping his guts out and stuffing them down his throat until he chokes.* Intellectual-me wanted no such thing. Gouging out someone's entrails wouldn't do a single thing to change the terrible thing they'd done. But the dark-night-of-the-soul-me fed hungrily on the *entrails* rants. The rants were raw and on the same level as my rage. The people at the high end brought me food on pretty plates and left like angels in the night. I didn't want their food. I had no appetite. I wanted rage. I needed rage. Because the rage would sustain me.

But in truth, the *force-feed him his own guts* people didn't share my pain. They wanted retribution for the sake of it. I didn't want retribution as much as I wanted Tommy. A memory flashed through my mind of his soft little cheek against mine and the sound of him whispering in his croaky toddler voice, *Mama. Sssh, Mama shweep now . . .*

I reached Pria's house and climbed the time-worn stairs that had been cut into the boulders. I smiled at the alcove in the rockery where Pria kept a collection of naughty gnomes that mooned the unwary.

I heard Kate's kids charging about the moment Pria opened the door, their voices ear splitting as they squealed.

Pria and Kate pulled me inside—Pria still in her work gear and Kate in her usual gym clothing.

"Oh, honey." Pria hugged me.

Kate threw her arms around me next. "I can't believe it. Seriously. It's just—" She shook her head.

"It's been going on for a while," I admitted. "I just ignored it, I think."

"You're the best thing that happened to Luke," Kate told me, her eyes wet. "Really. What was he thinking?"

"He'll make the right decision, in the end." Pria pulled her hair loose of its tight bun. "That's one thing about him that's always stood."

It was almost strange hearing Kate and Pria talk about Luke in such knowing terms. But of course, they'd both known him as long as I had. They'd each even been his girlfriend.

"Any more news about the letters?" Kate asked me.

"Not a thing. My psych advised me to try to stop thinking about them. Leave it to the police." I knew that talking about letting the police do their job and following my psych's advice would appeal to Kate and Pria.

"Good idea. They'll get it sorted," Kate said, as I expected she would.

"Your psych sounds wise." Pria indicated towards the other end of the house. "C'mon, I think we all need a nice glass of chilled wine." She took us through to the kitchen and poured three glasses of white wine.

The house had barely changed since I was a kid. Mahogany wood surfaces gleamed everywhere. Enormous paintings of the harbour claimed the walls, and the same ornate furniture stood in the rooms. A steady hum of air flowed from the air conditioning vents. The clocks were new—they ticked in every room. Pria had told me she held her psychotherapy sessions in different downstairs rooms, wherever a client felt most comfortable—and she liked the clocks so that she could keep an inconspicuous eye on the time, rather than checking her watch. Some clients preferred to stretch out on the sofa. Others liked to sit and drink coffee at the kitchen bench. Still others liked the plant-filled atmosphere of the sunroom.

Instinctively, Pria led Kate and me along the long, dark hallway to the sunroom. We curled up our legs on the round wicker chairs, letting the afternoon sun spill on our faces from the skylight.

Kate's twin girl and boy—Orianthe and Otto—giggled as they played hide-and-seek around the large potted ferns. They were three. Not that much older than Tommy would be now. Orianthe had her father's blond hair and determined eyes. Otto had his mother's softer, dark-haired looks. Orianthe was the definite boss of the game, staunchly refusing to be the one to seek. She insisted on being the one to hide.

"Kids, go play outside," called Kate. She shot me a look that I was sure was meant to look exasperated, but instead it looked apologetic. I'd only seen the twins three times since Tommy went missing, and each time, Kate had looked apologetic. As though she needed to be sorry that she had kids that hadn't been abducted, like my child had.

"They're having fun," I protested. But the kids had already run from the room. In truth, I was glad. I *did* find it hard just looking at them, feeling the absence of Tommy crush me even more.

I glanced around the sunroom. This room was my favourite. The wood-panelled walls, wicker chairs, hat stand, and ferns had always reminded me of a detective noir movie. It occurred to me that Detective Trent Gilroy would look at home here, dressed in a double-breasted suit, the statistical-blip crease in his forehead deeply furrowed as he puzzled over a case.

My fantasy detective noir Trent would figure out a vital clue about Tommy's disappearance, and he'd leave in a hurry, hot on the trail. And he'd find the kidnapper. Because in a movie, the detective always found the kidnapper.

A sharp half sigh caught in my chest.

Pria tilted her head, a sad, warm expression entering her eyes. "How are you? We didn't get that much of a chance to talk to you on Saturday. Too much to catch up on with all of us together. Plus, you fell asleep on us!"

I smiled. "Getting by."

"I've missed you."

"Missed you too. I've just been so. . ."

"I get it. People distance themselves sometimes. It's a kind of protective shield."

"Yes, it's been like that. How about you? What's been happening? Didn't you say you met someone new?"

An uncertain but happy smile dimpled her cheeks. "Yep. It's mostly a long-distance thing, so we're both trying to figure out how this is going to work."

"Is there a possibility he might leave the navy?"

She looked hopeful for a moment then shrugged a shoulder almost defensively. "Well, who knows? That would be fantastic, but it's his career. I'd like to think that we can meet somewhere in the middle and make some kind of new beginning, whatever that means."

I gave Pria a crossed-fingers gesture then turned to Kate. "How about you, Kate? What's happening?"

"I'm just flat out with the twins, I guess," she told me. "I did some work for a Kmart clothing catalogue last week. I get two or three jobs a fortnight, usually. Elliot doesn't like me to do too many jobs. He fractured his foot a few days ago, running after some little ratbag fourteen-year-old who was spraying graffiti on a wall. So, he's been at home for a while, doing a Netflix marathon."

"Does Elliot know you graffitied a wall once?" Pria teased.

Kate sipped her wine. "Someone should have arrested me."

Kate was so different to how she used to be. I wasn't sure, but it seemed to me that she changed after that day at house number 29, thirteen years ago. Maybe she felt bad that we never told the police what really happened. Now, anyone breaking the law was a criminal in her eyes. No shades of grey. And it wasn't just that. Kate used to be bold and independent, but now Elliot's decisions ruled her. She had an almost child/parent relationship with her husband. She actually called him her captain and herself his co-captain.

Footsteps echoed from the floorboards in the hall.

Jessie—pigtailed hair tucked under a straw hat and school bag on her shoulder—poked her head around the sunroom door. Her face lit up when she saw Kate and me.

"Phoebe!" She circled around the ferns to hug her mother and then Kate and me.

I squeezed her small body. "How was school?"

"It was okay," she answered.

Pria checked her watch. "You're six minutes late."

She turned to her mother. "I stopped to play with Mrs Wick's cat. And then Bernice started talking to me."

A frown crossed Pria's forehead. "Don't do that again. And don't talk to Bernice either. She isn't a very nice person."

Pria, Kate, and I exchanged glances. We—along with Sass and Luke—knew things about Bernice Wick that no one else did. A faint queasiness rose in my stomach.

"She's nice to *me*." Jessie looked from her mother to me. "She told me she makes model ships with matchsticks and I could come in and see them, if I was allowed to."

"You're not allowed," Pria said quickly.

Jessie nodded, though her eyes were dubious. I knew she wanted backup from Kate and me, but we had none to offer.

"Sweetie," I said. "I just don't think she's someone you should be talking to. I'd listen to your mum."

Kate screwed up her forehead. "She's just *strange*."

I snatched Jessie's hat playfully from her head. "Anyway, tell me what you did at school today."

Jessie let her bag slide from her shoulder. The thought niggled at me that she didn't quite believe either of us about Bernice, but it was hard to tell with Jess. She often seemed secretive.

Dropping her bag next to one of the wicker chairs, Jessie wriggled back on the chair's cushion and sat cross-legged. "We practised for our school play."

"A play?" I raised my eyebrows. "Cool. I used to love those when I was at school. What's this one about?"

"It's from the book, *Little Women*."

"And what are you doing in the play?" I asked.

She cast a sideways glance at her mother before looking back at me. "I'm Beth."

"Beth?" Pria shook her head, setting her glass of wine down on the table. "You were supposed to be playing *Josephine*."

"I know. But Bree wanted to play Josephine really, really bad. And the drama teacher agreed that she'd be better as her. So we swapped."

"She knows just how to get around you, that Bree." Pria was still shaking her head. "She's a piece of work. She and her mother. All sweetness to your face and lemons behind your back. Well, you can march down there tomorrow and tell Bree you changed your mind."

"I can't change my mind. We already told Mrs Simmons." Jessie drew her knees up to her chest, half-hiding her face.

"Mrs Simmons gave you the role of Josephine for a reason," Pria snapped. "You're perfect for the part. Are you now supposed to play a bit part just because Bree wants the spotlight?"

I watched the exchange between mother and daughter, surprised at Pria's strident tone.

"I don't want to talk about the play anymore." Jessie's voice grew small and tight. She left her chair, heading out of the room. "Going to get something to eat."

Pria sighed loudly, throwing up her hands. "I don't know what to do with her. She's done two years of drama, and she's excellent. She finally gets a role where she can show what she can do, and she lets Miss Bossy Boots Bree walk all over her."

"Maybe you can talk to her teacher." I tried to understand Pria's tone with Jessie. The scene had been uncomfortable to watch.

A deeper part of me wondered how much further I could have gone if my mother had been like Pria. The kids who acted in movies had parents who were behind them every step of the way, if not pushing, at least encouraging them forward. I'd had none of that. My mother had been fearful of the world. In her eyes, the day wasn't something to seize, it was something to survive.

"You betcha. I can't believe Mrs Simmons just let this happen." Pria squeezed her eyes closed then, giving a short laugh. "Okay, I'm not going to let this get to me. Jessie's on her own journey. Sooner or later, she's going to have to figure out that if you want something, you have to go for it. If you keep giving things away, you'll end up with nothing but regret."

Kate shrugged at me. "Well, I know one thing about my twins. They're not going to be models. I already tried them out for catalogue work. Within the first ten minutes, Orianthe informed me that she doesn't like to do boring things and that modelling's boring. And she's not going to let her brother do boring things either."

I laughed.

The cries of the twins pealed down the hallway as they bounded inside and called Jessie's name. They must have discovered she was home.

"Hey, where's the pup?" I asked Pria. "Can I see him? Jessie said he's growing big."

Immediately, Pria rolled her eyes and made a low disparaging sound. "I sent Buster out with the dog walker as soon as I knew Kate was coming over with the kids. He'd knock them flying. Wish I'd never bought him, to tell you the truth. After the break-in, I wanted a watchdog, but I should have paid more attention to the breed. He's damned strong—even though he's only nine months old. And he snaps. To tell you the truth, I'm a bit scared of the mutt. I'm having a dog trainer try to rein him in, but if that doesn't work, he's gone."

"What a shame," I said. "Jess told me she'd like to walk the dog sometimes, but that's not sounding good."

"Nope. The only thing I got right about him is his name. Because Buster has busted everything from doors to shoes." She shook her head, a sorry smile on her face.

The sound of the three children playing became too much. Tommy had once run through this house, too.

I stayed for a while longer then made an excuse to leave.

28. PHOEBE

Tuesday night

STORM CLOUDS PUSHED INTO THE SKY, making the day darken a good hour before the incoming night. The heavy atmosphere pressed down on me. I opened the window of my bedroom upstairs at Nan's house, letting the chill air stream in.

I could only just catch a glimpse of the water from here. An enormous cruise liner dominated the harbour, staining the water red and blue with its lights.

Maybe my small step in seeing Pria and Kate earlier had helped my frame of mind, but I didn't feel it yet. I was back at square one. I began pacing the room, feeling unhinged. Things were all so *in between*.

Dr Moran hadn't succeeded in jogging my memory about the letters. She'd said she didn't think it was possible to do all that I'd done in sleepwalking sessions and so the memory should still be in my mind somewhere. True sleepwalkers rarely remembered their dreams.

Not remembering any of it was the most disturbing thing of all.

It wasn't the first time I'd forgotten things. With the binge drinking and the trauma of losing Tommy, there were gaps in my memory. But not a *fucking chasm*. And forgetting the writing of three notes and delivering them was a fucking chasm.

Nan called me for dinner, and we ate the pumpkin soup together. I'd tried watching one of her sitcoms with her after that, but I gave up halfway through. I headed back upstairs. Surprisingly, I was tired enough to sleep. I crawled into bed and let myself drift off.

I woke just before four thirty in the morning. The temperature had plummeted—I guessed it was below ten degrees.

I'd been dreaming. The dream had been of the last day that Sass, Luke, Pria, Kate, and I had ever been to house number 29. I used to have nightmares about it all the time. But not since I was a teenager.

I'd spent my life blocking out that memory.

The only adults who knew about the terrible thing that Bernice did that day were Luke and Bernice's mothers. They'd told us it was best for everyone to just let it go. And so we'd let it go.

But you couldn't really fully ever let go of something that had hold of you.

There were two things that Bernice did—when she was fourteen and when she was nineteen. The first thing was not so bad. But the second was something only God could forgive.

I could almost smell the dust and slight odour of mould and the old musky aftershave in the bedrooms of that house.

That was our place back then. No one ever came there but us.

We started coming to number 29 when Kate, Pria, Luke, and I were ten and Sass was eleven and Bernice was thirteen. We made the abandoned house our own. Each of us either brought something there or changed things in order to put our individual stamp on the house.

Sass decorated it with signs that she'd pilfered. She was hugely into signage.

Pria drew rude things on the prints hanging on the walls.

Kate rescued some sad-looking pot plants from the courtyard and nursed them back to life then arranged them in the living room—to clean the foul air, she'd said. She glued together a large, broken dollhouse she'd found in an upstairs room, and then she posed rat skeletons on the furniture. Kate used to be weird like that.

Luke painted the living room walls red with the same paint he'd once stolen from his parents' garage (to paint our billycarts, back when we were eight).

My contribution was to set up the living room like a murder scene on a film set. I dragged in a mannequin that a fashion store had thrown out in a Dumpster, and I dressed it in a vintage suit from an upstairs closet. I positioned the dummy on a chair like he were dead, a whiskey bottle taped to his hand and a cigar hanging from his mouth—and a knife in his back.

I videoed vignettes of us every time we were there at number 29. Like a recorded history of who we were. Sometimes, I made everyone act in skits, and I videotaped those too.

Bernice did pretty much nothing but just hang around on the fringes, sometimes helping with exploits to get signs or things for the house. She was a thin, gangly girl then, on the cusp of becoming a teenager.

A year after we started coming to number 29, we discovered that the knives were missing from the kitchen. There had been six pearl-handled knives sitting in a knife block on the narrow, dirty bench top. We used them sometimes to scratch messages into the wall. Someone else had been in the house, and they'd taken our knives.

We were rattled about the knives for a week or two, until we forgot all about them.

Then came the day we found out that Bernice had chosen to do something in secret to make the house her own, something we didn't find until the day Sass decided we should all play dress ups with the old clothing in an upstairs bedroom. When we pulled the clothing out, we found that the back of the wardrobe had been hacked away with a saw, exposing the wall. On the wall, all our names were written in capital letters. All six. Embedded in each of our names was a pearl-handled knife. Except for Bernice's name. That solved the mystery of what had happened to the kitchen knives.

Bernice put on the waterworks after the discovery and said that she hadn't meant anything bad. She told us she'd been feeling left out of the group.

Kate and Pria were the first to forgive her. Sass and Luke and I were not so merciful. We held a meeting and decided that Bernice was out.

Three against two. Luke declared that the knives should stay in place as a reminder of what he called Bernice's *traitorous treachery*.

Bernice started hanging around the local boys after that.

When Bernice turned eighteen, she suddenly became useful to us again—she was old enough to buy the alcohol that we couldn't. She got invited back to number 29.

A few months later, after she'd turned nineteen, she did the thing that made all of us stop going there.

It was late afternoon, almost sunset. Number 29 was dim as always, thin slashes of light spearing through broken blinds, the smell of cigarettes and pot and bourbon dominating the mustiness of the old timber and furniture. Sass had sourced the pot. Bernice had bought the cigarettes and booze. The house stunk of cat piss too—Pria often brought her rescue cats there. Sometimes, we dressed the (indignant) cats up in doll's clothing and laughed at them like drunken idiots (which we often were).

We were lounging on the broken, propped-up furniture, already drunk and stoned. I stumbled out to the kitchen to pour myself another shot of bourbon.

Luke came up behind me and kissed my ear then turned me around to kiss me fully. He'd asked me to be his girlfriend the month before—I hadn't been sure if I wanted that. But it was the year of experimentation, and I told him we'd try it out and see what happens. And so he and I had been going upstairs to make out over the past weeks. Even Kate and I had decided to kiss one drunken night three months back—we'd both decided that we liked it but didn't want it to go further. Kids' stuff, I guess.

Luke took my hand and led me upstairs. I didn't know why it was always like that, why I never took his hand and led him upstairs. Maybe, with him taking the lead, I never had to take responsibility. This thing between us, whatever it was, could remain Luke's idea and I didn't have to think about it or consider whether it was a good thing or not.

We went to the largest bedroom, because it was the only room with a bed. And we kissed more and rolled around on the bed together and made the old springs protest and squeak.

A sharp noise rang out from the bedroom at the end of the hall. An alarm clock. Luke and I ran together down the hall to check it out.

Luke pushed the bedroom door open.

Immediately, a coppery stench hit me in the face. I recoiled, gagging.

A single clock sat on the middle of the bedroom floor.

Around the clock, five large rats—black and grey—were sprawled on the floor around the clock, eviscerated. A kitchen knife was stuck in the belly of each of them.

The broken wardrobe was open, and we could see the names that Bernice had drawn on the wall there years ago. But the knives were missing. The knives were now in the bodies of the rats. Pearl-handled knives.

Luke yanked out one of the knives, his face darkening as he roared with anger. He ran from the room.

With vomit swilling from my stomach, I stumbled backwards, needing to get back downstairs and away from that sight and smell. Luke followed, the knife in his fist.

I knocked hard into someone behind me. I spun around to see a woman of about sixty. A bag lady. Dressed in dirty, worn clothing. The door of the middle bedroom was now open, and I could see a large handbag and an empty bottle of alcohol and gear on the floor. The homeless woman must have been drunk and sleeping it off in there. I guessed the alarm clock had woken her.

Her hooded eyes filled with raw fear as she glanced from me to Luke, her eyes fixing on the bloodied knife.

She rushed ahead of us to the stairs.

A loud cracking sound rang out. She shrieked as the stairs gave way.

The middle of the staircase just disappeared, crashing downward. The woman's arms flew into the air as she fell into the dark space that had opened up, dust and dirt spraying as the stairs landed on the floor below.

Luke flung the knife down. He and I raced along the bottom edge of the staircase railing. Moths flew up from the huge gap in the destroyed stairs, fluttering manically all around us, their wings torn ragged by the falling wood.

Sass, Kate and Pria were already flinging open the door that led to the area underneath the stairs. Kate shone a light from her phone in the interior of the dusky space. Bernice moved up behind them, peering over their shoulders. She turned and ran from the house, slamming the door behind her.

Luke and I stopped midway on the stairs, shocked rigid at what we could see of the woman.

She was lying on her back, splayed over the broken stairs. Her head had hit something hard on the way down and had bent sideways at a macabre angle. The worst thing was her eyes. Her pale-blue eyes were open and staring up at us, as wild as the fluttering of the moths' wings. But then her eyes glazed and dulled. Slowly, slowly, specks of dirt that were swirling in the air settled on her eyes and face.

We'd witnessed the last seconds of the woman's life.

We didn't know who she was or why she'd been there in the house, but she was dead.

We should have called the police straight away, but we didn't.

The only person who could have done this was Bernice. But we were all here, too. And we were underage and drinking and smoking pot. Not to mention defacing a house that wasn't ours.

Instead, we told Mrs Wick what her daughter had done. And Luke told his own mother. I didn't dare tell my parents.

Luke's mother commenced a clean-up operation, rushing to number 29 with gloves and a bucket. She was scarily efficient. Our alcohol, cigarettes, and pot were disposed of, except for a small amount of it that she placed beside the bag lady's gear in the second bedroom. Our names were scrubbed off the wall behind the wardrobe. Even the rats were taken away and the blood cleaned. Only then did she call the police herself and tell them she'd heard a disturbance next door in the house that was supposed to be empty.

The police found that the stairs appeared to have been cut with an electric saw rather than just rotting away. The cuts were fresh underneath the old carpet runner. The stairs had been held up underneath by two A-frame ladders. The ladders had somehow collapsed right at the time the woman was running down the stairs. We guessed that Bernice had pushed them over right at the time that the lady was coming down the stairs. The police said they believed a broom had been used to tip the ladders over.

The police carried out a door knock on our street as part of their investigation. None of us told them anything about that day. Mrs Basko—Luke's mother—didn't let anything slip either.

We saw the bag lady in the newspaper a few days after her death. She was Grace Louelle Clark, aged forty-four. Not anywhere near sixty, as we'd thought. Plagued by an untreated mental illness, she'd been homeless for eleven years. She was known to the police for multiple counts of petty theft. The only photographs of her from the past fifteen years were mug shots, and the mug shots were what the newspapers printed.

The police, unable to discover what had happened in house number 29, eventually let the case drop. No friends or relatives of the woman came forward to demand that the police keep investigating.

Even Kate and Pria had no forgiveness for Bernice this time. Bernice swore she had nothing to do with the rats or the stairs. But it didn't shock us that she didn't admit to it. Who would admit to killing someone? She was over the age of eighteen and no longer a minor. She would have been tried as an adult in court.

We were sure she'd wanted to get us back for throwing her out of our group when she was fourteen. Maybe she didn't think someone was going to die. Maybe she just wanted to scare us.

We'd never know for sure.

I sat up in bed, scenes of that incident from thirteen years ago still flashing through my mind.

A sudden cold sweat pricked my skin.

The moths with the damaged wings.

The woman's wild, fearful eyes.

The pearl-handled knife.

The three things I'd been handed in my dreams—I'd seen them all that day in number 29.

And I'd been dreaming of them over the past few days. I'd dreamed them so intensely. So vividly.

I'd ended up convincing myself that the dreams were random. Meaningless.

I was wrong.

Those images were all connected to number 29.

But why had I dreamed of things connected to number 29 and Tommy in the same dreams?

The answer flashed into my mind.

Whatever had happened to Tommy was linked with that house.

Was it Bernice who took Tommy? Was *she* the abductor?

Panic tightened my chest. Even all these years later, she might still be holding onto her hatred.

At dawn, I had to do the thing I said I'd never do again.

Go back to number 29.

I had to.

I waited out the next hour between four thirty and five thirty.

Then it was time to go. Dressing in dark colours, I pulled a hood over my head.

If Nan heard me leaving, I'd say I was going for a walk. The sun would be rising soon.

Misting rain coated my skin as soon as I left the house. The sky was moonless, dead dark. The street quiet. I stepped quickly down Nan's path, hoping no one who knew me was about at this early hour. I closed the gate.

I jumped as a figure seemed to appear from nowhere, walking towards me. We both stopped short, each of us startled by each other. A man, hooded like me, stood in the street a short distance away.

I ran a checklist through my head. Was this the man I'd seen that night near my mailbox? He wasn't wearing the same cap or a jacket—he was wearing a dark, hooded raincoat. From here, I couldn't tell if he had a beard.

He began walking again. I tried to see him as he passed, but it was between streetlights and he kept his head down. All I saw was that he had facial hair. More than a goatee. A full beard. If he was the same man Kate had seen, his beard might have grown. In one hand, he held a briefcase. In the other, an umbrella. I stared after him. The umbrella had the carved head of a duck on the wooden handle.

Bernice had the same type of umbrella. The *exact* same umbrella.

The night swallowed him, and I couldn't see him any longer.

I made my way past Mrs Wick's house to number 29.

The gate was unlatched, swinging on its hinges. I glanced back down the street. The man had come out of number 29. I was sure of it. The street had been empty, and then he'd just materialised in this spot. There was no other house he could have sprung from.

A rash of nerves crawled over my skin as I continued down the path. The front door was locked. It'd always been locked. The key—if it was still in the same place as it used to be—was under the welcome mat. Luke had once painted *un* in front of the word *welcome* on the rubber mat, but it had washed away, probably a long time ago.

Crouching, I lifted a corner of the mat. An object glinted dully. The key was there. When I picked it up, the metal didn't seem as cold as it should. Did the man just have the key in his hand?

I unlocked the door and pushed it open. The thought of closing it behind me made a shiver pass down my back, but I had no choice. I didn't want anyone to pass by and notice the door open.

Slipping my mobile phone from my pocket, I switched its light on and shone it around the room.

The walls were still red, just as Luke had painted them. The store dummy still sat on an armchair, the sole occupant of the house. (At least, I hoped he was the sole occupant of the house right now.) Saskia's stolen signs were still in place.

I sucked in a cold, musty breath of air as I trained the light on the staircase. The missing section of stairs was back in place. Maybe the police had put it back when they were investigating the case of the dead woman all those years ago. Or maybe someone else had put it back. The section would have to have been repaired—because it had broken apart when it'd smashed to the ground.

I stepped closer. Were the stairs sturdy enough to walk on? I couldn't trust that they were.

My heart squeezed as I went to open the door that led to the small storage area underneath the stairs. I was sixteen again, seeing the face of the dead woman, watching dirt particles settle onto the whites of her eyes.

I shone my phone light inside the space.

The two ladders were in place again.

Surely it would be impossible for one person to have replaced the section of stairs by themselves? If Bernice had done this, had she had help? But who would help her?

I checked the kitchen and the laundry next—all the nooks and cupboards. The laundry was external to the house. There used to be an outside toilet room too, but it had fallen down long ago, when I was still a kid. There was nothing else downstairs.

Biting down so hard on my bottom lip that it hurt, I headed back to the stairs.

I collected myself. I was here in this house looking for my own child. But it wasn't a game of hide-and-seek. If I did find Tommy's remains here, would I be wishing like hell it hadn't been me who found him?

I'd lost all credibility with the police. I wouldn't be able to convince them to come and search. I had no evidence whatsoever—just my dreams and an old memory.

I had to force myself to climb the stairs.

Clutching the railing, I made my way up slowly. I couldn't stop myself from turning back every few steps, terrified that the stairs would collapse. Terrified that the man might appear behind me. Why had he even come in here? Was he looking for something? Or was he trying to hide something?

The room Luke and I used to make out in when we were sixteen looked exactly the same as it had before. I moved quickly, looking under the bed and in the wardrobe and drawers.

The second bedroom seemed to be the victim of a roof leak. An overpowering smell of mould made me gasp. The dead woman's belongings were still lying on the floor, covered in black mildew. If any friends or family who'd known the lady had heard about her death, none of them had cared enough to come and collect her things. Holding my breath tight and wishing I'd brought gloves, I checked the room.

The only room left was the third bedroom. It stood at the far end of the hall, its door closed. I could still remember the fetid stench of the mutilated rats and their stiff, open mouths.

The old boards of the hallway were rickety beneath my feet as I made my way along them. I kept picturing the boards giving way and me falling to the bottom floor, like the bag lady had done. Two days ago, I'd wanted to die. But I didn't want to die here in this house. And there was a chance that I had something to hang onto again now: my dreams hadn't been random.

I turned the handle of the third bedroom. An almost sweet, pungent odour met me. Marijuana.

There were objects all over the floor. Not dead rats. Just . . . things.

Bric-a-brac mostly. *Books. Framed photographs. A funeral wreath. A vase of dead flowers. A government demolition sign. A kewpie doll. A garden gnome. Men's jackets and hats. A frilly corset. Umbrellas hanging on hooks on the walls. Golf clubs and tennis racquets. Used shoes — all types and sizes.*

Why would anyone want to go to the trouble of bringing all of this up here? The room didn't give the appearance that a squatter was living here. It didn't look like anyone was actually living here at all. The things were old but clean and neatly ordered. Like a collection.

I walked among the items, poking through them with one of four walking sticks that I'd found against a wall.

The photographs ranged from old black-and-white pictures to modern, all seemingly random. None of them seemed to be of the same family. I recognised a few people who used to live on the street.

A book sat on the dresser, its cover reflected in the mirror. I recognised the image on the cover. A moose. It was a children's book, simply called The Moose. When Sass and I and the others first came to this house as ten-year-olds, we'd found this book. It was about an ancient American Indian myth, in which the east wind brought mists and a change in weather. Saskia invented the game, and she made us take it seriously. If there was a change in the weather, one of us could *invoke The Moose.* We had to then write down our names and throw them into a hat. Whoever's name you pulled out, you had to become that person all day. Luke had struggled with the game the most, having no choice but to act *like a princess* (his words) for a day. There were no other boys in our little group.

It seemed odd that the book was on its own and not piled up with the other books.

I kept looking around the room.

A couple of pot-smoking devices occupied a corner, in the only clear space.

The man must be coming in here to smoke his pot and look at his collection of junk. But why?

I thought of Bernice then. She wore mismatched clothing — clothing that looked like it came from a thrift shop. And she often wore different hats and had different umbrellas on her arm, including the duck-head umbrella.

Did she and the man come up here and smoke pot together? Was he her boyfriend? Maybe I'd been wrong to think she wasn't seeing anyone. If the two of them *were* a couple, why was Bernice hiding it? Unless it was just a friends-with-benefits arrangement and she was trying to hide the fact from her mother.

A muffled noise made me whip around. The man might become violent if he caught me looking at his strange treasures.

No, it was just the creak and sway of the house. Still, I shouldn't stay here long. He was bound to return, sooner or later. I hadn't seen any evidence that he was sleeping here, but he obviously came here often.

A tiny wooden boat half lying beneath the kewpie doll caught my eye. Tommy had loved boats. I picked it up from the floor.

My breath stilled. I'd seen this boat before. It was exactly the same as the boats from a nightlight belonging to Tommy. The nightlight was large and round, with wooden waves the whole way around, and with red-and-yellow striped boats riding the waves. The waves and the boats would bob up and down as the nightlight slowly turned, making a pattern of waves and boats on the walls, together with dreamy, tinkling music.

Tommy had spotted the nightlight in a city toy store window when he was around eighteen months old. He'd been desperate for it, and I'd bought it for him, ignoring for once the enormous price tag. *Over eight hundred dollars!* The nightlight had been a limited, hand-carved edition.

I stared down at the boat in my palm. I could see where it had broken off from its stem on the nightlight.

My heart pulsed against my ribs.

I needed to call Trent Gilroy.

As I was about to bring up his number on my phone, I stopped myself. It was too early. He wouldn't be in his office yet. And would he think this was just another desperate ploy from me? All I would have to do was to break off a piece of the nightlight and plant it in this house and then claim I'd found it here.

First, I had to find out if the nightlight was still in Tommy's bedroom, or whether it'd been stolen.

29. PHOEBE

Wednesday morning

LEAVES THAT HAD BEEN DAMPENED BY the light rain whirled in a plodding dance around my ankles. A wind had crept up while I'd been searching number 29. The dim light of dawn exposed a darkly bruised sky.

Pulling my jacket tightly around my chest, I walked up the street to my house.

Luke would have left for work by now. I was sure that he worked longer hours than any other real estate wheeler and dealer in the city.

When I stepped inside the front door, I realised I'd forgotten all about the alarm. But no high-pitched sound pealed in my ears. Luke must have either turned it off before he left, or he hadn't been bothering with it at all since I'd left him.

Like an intruder, I stole upstairs. Into my own son's bedroom.

Tommy's room was so *lifeless* it made me skip a breath. Coming back here after having been away for a while brought the sadness of his unused room back threefold.

I eyed the room. It was perfectly tidy, with barely any toy or item on display. Luke's mother had put all of Tommy's things away, throwing away most of the soft toys. She'd told me once they were just dust mite carriers.

I didn't know exactly where the nightlight was. I'd barely been able to look at Tommy's things since he'd been gone—except for the night I'd dragged out his train set in a sleepwalking haze.

I opened his walk-in wardrobe. Tommy used to hide in here and shout *shuprisesh* when I stepped into the room. He'd often substituted a *sh* for a *s* when speaking. In the mornings, sometimes he'd climb up onto my bed, try to pry open my eyes, and whisper *shhh, mummy'sh ashweep*. All while doing his best to wake me.

The nightlight wasn't on any of the shelves in the walk-in wardrobe. And it was far too big to be in any of his drawers.

It wasn't there.

Surely Luke's mother wouldn't have thrown out the nightlight. It was special, and she knew that.

Someone must have stolen it from the room.

My fingers froze on the shelf as I heard the click of the front door downstairs and then heard the sound of keys being tossed into the ceramic dish on the hall table.

What was Luke doing home again?

He was coming upstairs now. He walked into our bedroom, and it sounded like he'd laid himself down on the bed and kicked off his shoes.

Then I heard his voice.

Hey, Kitty.

He was on the phone. Who was Kitty?

Is it too early?

You sure?

Sorry, I just wanted to talk.

I appreciate it. I offload too much on you.

A knot twisted in my chest. He had to be talking to the other woman. Kitty. I instantly hated the name. He sounded so close to her.

I got into work and I just can't concentrate. I sent myself home.

Yeah.

I don't know. I just can't get my head straight. I'm a wreck.

Come over now? But what about your—?

Are you sure about that?

Okay.

Okay, see you soon.

Kitty was obviously a woman who was there for him at any time of night or day. Mopping up his problems and anxieties in her no doubt warm bosom.

Who or what had he been referring to when he'd said *but what about your*? She must have interrupted him, because he hadn't finished that sentence. Did she have a husband at home and Luke had been worried he'd be there? And had she reassured him that her husband wasn't there?

A sense of ridiculousness swept through me. I was in my own home, hiding in my own son's room, trying to decipher my own husband's phone conversation. How did everything change so fast?

There was a short interval before he bounded back down the stairs. The front door slammed shut.

It was time for me to leave. I waited five minutes first in case he came back for something—Luke was often forgetting something.

I casually strolled from the house and down the street again. No one was going to find it strange that I'd been in my own home at the same time as Luke, even if they did know I'd left Luke. They would just assume we'd been talking. I was quite sure that the street gossip machine was already in action.

I felt for the wooden boat in my jacket pocket. It was real. I hadn't conjured it up in a dream like I'd conjured up the injured moth. But I needed something more before I went to Trent. Some solid evidence. After the debacle with the letters, I had to make sure not to mess this up.

I spotted Bernice walking up ahead of me, heading towards the docks.

She was connected to this somehow. She and the stranger.

I made the decision to follow her.

Bernice headed to the end of the street and then turned right. Into the Southern Sails Café. I was disappointed she wasn't headed somewhere else.

Committed now to tracking her, I made my way to the same point, stepping into the café through a different entrance. But I doubted I'd find out anything in here. Maybe she'd go somewhere else afterwards. But Bernice barely left our neighbourhood. If she bothered to go to another place, it would have to be important to her.

I had to try to ensure she didn't see me. I kept my hood down low over my forehead. I didn't want anyone else to recognise me either. My face had been all over the news lately. Plus, I wasn't supposed to even be here. Detective Gilroy had warned me not to come back here.

I caught a brief glimpse of Bernice at the café counter. Quickly, I turned my face and stepped away behind the three-quarter wall that divided part of the café. I could hide here for a while. Moving up to the noticeboard, my gaze swept over it.

There were no more letters about Tommy.

I needed to walk to the other end of the wall so that I had a better view of everything that was happening in the café. I didn't want Bernice to leave without me knowing, and I couldn't very well just stand there and watch her directly. I also wanted to know if the man I'd seen earlier was in here somewhere and if Bernice was meeting up with him.

I browsed the paintings on the divider wall as I moved along. The Southern Sails Café allowed local artists to hang their work on the wall in return for a possible commission. Some of the work was good. Some of it was not. Some were just not my taste at all. The painting in front of my nose was an ugly hack'n'slash of dark lines: *Here's my anger and frustration at the world on canvas. For the small price of $345, you can take it home, hang it on your wall, and enjoy.*

If I were to paint my inner self on a canvas, I doubted I'd be able to confine it. Sometimes I wanted to coat the whole world in ugly colours.

I'd earned the right to glance about the café now. I'd shown an appropriate amount of interest in the paintings. I hadn't just marched over and started eye-stalking people.

There were mostly businesspeople dotting the café. In suits and winter dresses and muted colours.

Bernice was sitting on her own, with her back to me. She had a different umbrella with her today—a gaudily patterned one with a white plastic handle. The man wasn't with her. If he was here, I couldn't spot him.

People were starting to glance my way. I couldn't just stand here peering around the café any longer without drawing attention. I decided to go and grab a coffee. Bernice wouldn't be able to see me from where she was now.

Digging in my hands into my jeans pockets, I found a five-dollar bill and three dollars in coins. It was enough.

I ordered a mochaccino and then went to sit in a position where I could see both exits from the café, next to a tall pot plant that helped conceal me.

I'd barely taken a sip when two people walked towards each of the exits at the same time. Bernice and a man in a grey business suit. I stood, waiting for the businessman to pass by me so that I could leave and follow Bernice. I sipped my coffee again, trying not to look like I was watching anyone.

The man's eyes seemed strangely distracted. His face was slightly hidden by his facial hair—something in between a three-day-growth and a light beard.

A thought flashed in my mind. Was it him? The man I'd seen earlier out in the street? He was the right height and had the right amount of facial hair. He could have stashed the raincoat in his briefcase. Maybe even the umbrella, if it folded up small—or he could have thrown it away. Was the briefcase the same as the type the other man had been carrying? I couldn't remember. My attention had been on his face and the umbrella.

Then another thought: Were he and Bernice leaving at the same time, to meet up at a different location? Was there some kind of weird thing going on between them where they didn't want to be seen together?

When I turned to watch Bernice, she'd already left.

I swung back around.

The man lifted his satchel briefcase over a chair that was jutting out in his path. Something small and furry hung from the satchel. The arm of a blue teddy bear.

A prickle imbedded itself in the back of my neck.

He had a toddler's toy with him.

My cup of coffee slipped through my fingers, clattering to the floor.

Fragments of white ceramic swam in a pond of dark liquid.

The man glanced back over his shoulder, staring at me for a moment and then continuing on his way.

A café staff member rushed from behind the counter with a small bucket and a fistful of paper towels.

An elderly man half-rose from his chair, touching my arm. "Do you need some help?"

"I—no. I'm okay," I spluttered.

"You might get a nasty burn out of that. You only just bought it." He indicated towards my leg, sounding like a grandfather admonishing a grandchild.

Looking down, I saw the large, wet stain of coffee on my thigh, soaking through my jeans. Immediately, I felt the sting.

"I'm fine," I told him. "But thank you."

Café patrons gawked, waiting and watching to see what the crazy lady would do next. *Dropped boiling coffee on herself and barely noticed! What type of crazy is she?*

"I'm really sorry," I told the woman who'd come to clean up the mess. "I must be butterfingers today."

Her mouth stretched thinly, almost to the point of grimacing. "Don't worry about it." Her expression changed as she eyed me closely. "Excuse me, but aren't you—?"

"I have to go." Rudely, I backed away and left the shop. The woman had recognised me, and I didn't want to have to tell her that yes, I was Tommy's mother and yes, I'd been receiving strange letters, and yes, one of those letters had been right here at the café.

I couldn't see the man.

Breaking into a run, I crossed the street to the docks. Grey ghost boats sailed out on the harbour. The salty air that blew into my face still carried a light rain. A smattering of people walked up ahead towards the business district, holding umbrellas over their heads and obscuring my view.

I ran.

Rain pattered down harder now. I reached the cover of the office buildings and their awnings before my clothing became drenched.

I almost walked straight past the man from the café. He'd stopped at a combined tobacconist/magazine stand to buy a packet of cigarettes.

I stopped too, pretending to browse the newspapers. On page one of a newspaper, there was a small headline that said: *Can you crack the code of the Tommy Basko letters? Page Five.*

I jerked my gaze away, to the cookery magazines.

The notes about Tommy had become a type of entertainment. Just like the crosswords Nan liked to solve. Amateur armchair detectives, treating Tommy's case like an episode of *Miss Marple* or *CSI*.

But none of them knew yet that I'd written them. If people knew, it would destroy their amateur detective fun.

The man walked a short distance away, stopped again, and lit up a cigarette.

He turned in my direction. I busied myself, peering into the nearest shop window. The man continued on, disappearing around a corner. I was going to lose sight of him. I hurried to the corner and headed into the much busier, wider street ahead.

I twisted my head to search both sides of the streets.

"Looking for me?" A deep voice to the left of me.

Just a couple of feet away, the man with the suitcase was leaning against a wall. Still smoking his cigarette.

I turned to face him directly. "What? No, I'm not—"

"You were following me. All the way from the coffee shop. Straight after you did *that* to yourself." He pointed at my coffee-soaked leg.

"I was heading off to buy some new jeans." That sounded weak.

"Well, I'd say you passed a few clothing stores already."

It was obvious that I'd been doing exactly as he'd said I had—following him. There was no point in pretending.

"Is there something you want from me?" he added before I could reply.

My shoulders slackened as I lost the conviction I'd had in the café. He didn't look like an abductor up close. But then, what did a child abductor look like?

"I don't know," I told him. "Do you know Bernice?"

"Who?"

"Never mind. I'm just . . . looking for someone."

"And you think that person is me?"

"Do you have my son?" I blurted out. *God, what was wrong with me?*

He'd been going to take another puff on his cigarette but his arm froze midair at my question. "What?"

Words stumbled from my mouth. "My son is two. He's been missing for six months."

"Well, I had you pegged wrong. I thought you must be someone my ex-wife sent to spy on me. I'm sorry about your kid, but why on earth do you think I've got him?"

I decided I might as well go for broke. "I have reason to believe that someone local took my son. And you—"

"*Tommy Basko.* You're Tommy Basko's mother."

"Yes."

"Thought I'd seen your face before, but you looked . . . ah—"

"A bit more groomed than today?"

"Yeah."

"Well, this is me. I'm sorry, but there's a man I was looking for."

I sounded crazy. Or desperate. *Both.*

He stubbed out his cigarette, then picked up the stub and flicked it into a nearby bin. "I don't have your son. In all honesty, I don't know how much longer I'm going to have my own. My little boy's in the Children's hospital. I was off to see him right now. Then I noticed someone following me." He shot me a pointed look.

He had an ill son in the hospital? My gaze was drawn to the teddy bear arm that was still sticking out of the man's briefcase.

"How old is he?" My voice fell away to a half whisper.

"Just a baby. Fourteen months. Heart problems."

"That's awful. I'm sorry."

"Yeah."

"I'd better let you get on your way. I shouldn't have—"

"Look, if my kid was missing, I'd probably be doing the same as you. I'm just glad it wasn't my ex who sent you. We split up about ten months ago. It's her that wants a divorce, but she's acting completely nuts. One minute she wants me back, and the next I'm the worst person in the world. I think the pressure of Jake being so sick is getting to her. He's been sick since he was born." His voice had changed. He sounded broken.

In that instant, I understood. He hadn't spoken about his problems with his wife with anyone. So he was telling a stranger on the street. In a morbid connection, we were both losing our sons. Three days ago, I would have said it wasn't possible for Luke and me to fall apart like this man and his wife. We'd been solid, a united force. Not anymore.

He checked his watch. "I have to go. Good luck." He stopped after a few steps and turned back to me. "Your stalking skills need a lot of work, by the way." He shot me a smile that was friendlier than I deserved.

I watched him thread his way into the city crowds.

He wasn't Tommy's abductor.

I started walking in the opposite direction. I didn't know where Bernice had gone. She might have headed back home for all I knew.

Rain slashed through the city now, washing along the street and making everyone move faster.

30.   PHOEBE

Wednesday morning

IT WAS ONLY WHEN I WAS trudging back to Nan's house in the rain that I saw the link between the little boat in my pocket and the third letter.

I was watching the torrents of rainwater rush along the gutter of my street. Bits of torn, saturated newspaper and a food wrapper were caught in the flow.

In the past, I'd let Tommy sail a boat along that gutter in the rain. Never his favourite yacht—just paper boats that wouldn't make him bawl if I failed to run and save them from the drain in time.

Back when Luke had asked Trent Gilroy if the third rhyme could mean that Tommy was at the bottom of the harbour or that his body was being concealed on a boat, the thought had made me want to drink a bottle of Luke's bourbon and curl up on my bed and force my mind to shut down. I hadn't thought enough about what else the rhyme could mean.

But now I knew exactly what the rhyme of the third letter meant.

I was sure of it.

Little Boy Blue
Why'd she let you go?
On red ships and yellow boats
'Round and 'round you row

The rhyme was talking about Tommy's nightlight.

The boats on the nightlight went around and around, with little wooden children rowing them. And the ships and boats were red and yellow.

I stopped dead still.

If I'd written that rhyme, I would have seen that connection straight away.

I didn't write that rhyme.

I didn't write any of them.

I had no memory of writing the letters because I didn't write them.

But how did my fingerprints come to be on the paper inside the third letter?

My breaths quickened. Whoever the person was, maybe they'd given me the paper to hold when I was sleepwalking. Yes, that could well be what happened. I had long periods of time that I couldn't account for.

The police video didn't show where I'd gotten the letter from. Someone might have given it to me. Someone who was out of the frame of the camera. I'd thought I'd been given a knife that night, and I thought I'd returned to my house to put it away for safekeeping. But what if I'd put the knife in the letterbox, thinking that the letterbox was something else—just a safe place?

The rain drenched me while thoughts raced through my head.

The same person who wrote the letters had stolen the nightlight. And they knew that I would understand the rhyme. I was the one who had bought the nightlight. I was the one to switch it on for Tommy each night.

Why was this person signalling me with the nightlight clue?

I thought back to the first letter. The letter-writer had deliberately impregnated it with a coffee aroma. The person knew that I knew the café well. And they must have known that I'd always been able to pinpoint even a vague scent. And they knew that the words about

Tommy not remembering his mother would cut me especially deep. I'd always thought I wasn't good enough as a mother.

This person had to know me very, very well. All of this was meant for me. The rhymes were meant for me and me alone.

This person was trying to crush me.

They'd sent me the letters, and they'd framed me.

Why were they doing this?

Was Tommy really dead and this person was trying to torture me, making me believe I could find him?

Would Bernice know about the nightlight? She'd never been in my house.

I had no evidence to tie Bernice to the letters. The only evidence that I could possibly take to the police was if I found the paper that the letters were written on. The police hadn't found the paper or envelopes at Nan's house. They had to be *somewhere.*

If the stationery was at number 29, I hadn't seen it. Maybe it was—it was too hard to search every single hiding place. And I hadn't been looking for stationery then.

And if Bernice had the stationery, she'd hardly be keeping it at number 29. She'd be secretly storing it away in her own house. But I couldn't search Bernice's house. *Could I?*

Even if I could summon up the daring to actually do it, Bernice and her mother hardly ever left the house. They only went out twice a week. Once for groceries and once for the bingo and trivia night down at the local club. Occasionally, they made trips to the doctor's surgery.

Nan had a key to the Wick house—she'd had that long before I was even born. And Mrs Wick had a key to Nan's house. The idea being that if either of them went into hospital, then the other could fetch some clothing and toiletries and take them into the hospital.

God, if Mrs Wick had access to Nan's house, then Bernice also had access to Nan's house. She'd had access to the typewriter and the ink.

I had to take a look inside their house. I wouldn't be breaking in, *exactly.* Not if I went in there with a key.

The trivia comp at the club was on tomorrow night. Mrs Wick and Bernice would be gone for three or so hours. Bernice was good at trivia, and she'd stay until the end, trying to grab the prizes.

Nan wouldn't be at home either. She almost always went with Mrs Wick and Bernice, unless her arthritis was acting up.

There was no going back now. I was going to see this through to the end.

I hurried up to Nan's house and ran inside and upstairs to the shower, ignoring the look of dismay that Nan shot me. I'd clean my wet footprints from the stairs later.

Standing in the shower, I let the warm water sink into my bones while I planned what I would do the following night. It felt almost good to have a plan, after so much uncertainty.

I deposited the tiny nightlight boat into a trinket box on top of my dresser and then spent the rest of the day cleaning Nan's house. When Nan cleaned the house herself, she missed all the corners and dark, dim spots. I made sure I missed none of them.

Nan stepped up behind me when I was on my hands and knees scrubbing the grime from the cupboard underneath the kitchen sink.

"Don't become your mother," she said.

Her words sent hackles between my shoulder blades. I turned. "Just because I'm cleaning?"

"Cleaning every speck won't make any difference. If it's clean enough, it's clean."

I was about to answer when a sharp series of knocks carried through the hallway.

Nan stood back and let me go to the door.

Sass rushed in, red knotted scarf and red lipstick and clatter. She squealed a hello. "Ohhh, Phoebe. You poor thing!" Grabbing me, she hugged me tightly. "He never deserved you. He just never did." Stepping back, she brushed hair back from my face. "How are you? Don't even answer that. You're not okay. I can see that."

I managed a smile. "Sass, I'm doing okay. I think."

"I'll be the judge of that." She eyed the plastic kitchen gloves in my hand. "Doing some cleaning?"

"Yeah. Anything to keep my mind off things."

"I know what you need. The girls and I have arranged a special dinner for Friday night. It's a Christmas in July thing."

I grinned, wondering which one of them had come up with that idea. "Sounds festive. But I'm not feeling very . . . festive."

She put on a fake shocked face. "You can't say no to celebrating Christmas with your oldest friend!"

"I just don't know if I can face . . . *people*."

"Hey, don't worry. There won't be anyone you know there. It'll be the perfect Christmas, without any drunk, over-friendly uncles or family arguments. It's a touristy thing. People from around the world. It'll be fun."

We headed upstairs to my room then, on some kind of unspoken signal, just like we used to do when we were teenagers. We talked on for an hour.

Sass, with her red high heels kicked off, padded over to the window. "I miss waving at you from my window."

Sass's house used to be directly across from mine, and her bedroom window faced mine. We'd wave to each other each night before going to bed. There was just flattened rubble on that side of the street now.

She peered down onto the footpath. "Ugh. There's Bernice. She wears the weirdest gear."

I crossed the floorboards and looked down over Sass's shoulder. Bernice was walking in through her gate—her head and her shoulders tilted forward like she were burrowing an invisible tunnel. She wore a fuzzy blue jacket with a long, shapeless dress and boots.

Sass pulled a face at Bernice's retreating figure.

"Hey," I said. "Have you seen Bernice about lately, with a man?"

Sass paused as she tucked her scarf into her vest, her eyes widening. "Bernice has a *man*? Lord above. Poor guy. Someone needs to warn him."

"No, I haven't actually seen her with anyone."

Sass frowned at me, giving a slight confused shake of her head.

I hesitated. Sass already hated Bernice, and if I were to tell her about the duck-head umbrella and what I'd found at number 29, she might well turn into a bull in a china shop. But I decided to take the risk. My past and Saskia's were bound up with Bernice and that house. She'd understand more than anyone what Bernice was capable of.

Sass's confused look had already turned to worry by the time I took a breath and began telling her everything, taking the boat out of my trinket box to show her.

"I'm coming with you," she told me as I finished my last sentence. "I'm not letting you go in there alone." Taking the boat from me, she studied it. "I remember the nightlight. This is definitely a piece of it."

"You can't come with me. I'm not involving you in this."

She eyed me steadily. "I've been involved ever since Bernice stuck those knives in each of our names. I grew up on this street. Trust me, I'm involved."

Tilting her chin, her gaze travelled out to the grey sky beyond the skyscrapers in the distance.

31. PHOEBE

Thursday night

I MADE NAN EGGS AND TOAST for dinner and then headed into the living room to wait. The day had been long, with nothing to fill it.

Dr Moran had rung at 4:00 p.m., to check on my *small steps*. I lied and said that I'd been out to see a movie. She might have been more impressed if I'd told her *I searched an abandoned house yesterday morning, stalked a man, and was about to search my neighbour's house.*

Finally, it was almost eight o'clock. Time for the Wicks and Nan to head down to the club.

Nan dressed herself in her usual thick tartan jacket and *smart trousers* for her trip out.

"Will you be all right here on your own?" she said, her eyes crinkling. "You really should come along with us. I think you'd enjoy yourself."

"Trivia's not my thing, Nan. I have the memory of a gnat. I wouldn't be able to answer a single question."

"Well, you could just enjoy the socialising. I'm sure Bernice would like your company, rather than just hanging with us oldies."

You mean, Bernice would like a chance to gloat on my suffering, firsthand? I didn't know for sure if Bernice had done anything wrong. But whether she had or she hadn't, she'd still gloat on my suffering.

"I'd rather just stay here." I smiled to soften my words.

She sighed. Triple the huff volume. "All right, then."

I watched as she headed out the door. As soon as she closed the door, I peeked through the living room blinds. I needed to make sure that both Bernice and her mother were going tonight. They were both standing at Nan's mailbox.

I ran upstairs to change into dark leggings and a black jacket. As long as I was going to break into someone's house, it felt right to be dressed like I imagined a thief would. Returning downstairs, I took out the key to the Wick house from Nan's collection of keys in the top drawer of her dining buffet and started to prepare the things I'd need.

A rap at the door made me jump.

For a moment, it seemed that the police were here, knowing ahead of time that I was about to commit a crime.

But it was Sass at the door, dressed in black. She looked more like a movie villain than a house thief—with a tight leather jacket and shiny skin-tight pants and boots. She'd tucked her thick red-blond hair under a ski cap.

"Do you have gloves?" she asked.

I nodded. "Yes."

"Zip lock bags?"

"Yeah." I gave a half smile. We sounded like criminals already.

Outside, the night was still and clear. We pushed the gate open and stepped along the path to the Wick house.

Sass clung unhelpfully to my arm as I inserted the key and unlocked the front door.

Sass walked in first. She gasped—*loudly.*

Closing the door, I turned to see what she had.

Boxes. *Boxes and boxes and boxes.* All sizes. Piled high. And *things.* Vases, ornaments, and trinkets—even paintings that I recognised from the café.

"Wow," Sass remarked, finally remembering to lower her voice. "Someone's a hoarder."

"How are we even going to search this?" I eyed Sass in frustration.

"I don't know. I'm not even sure how we're going to hack a path through it."

A narrow pathway through the boxes led to a small space where a two-seater sofa and the TV stood. This tiny space had to be where Mrs Wick and Bernice watched TV.

Boxes and containers were stacked up in the kitchen and on the stairs.

Sass blinked at me. "So, which one of them do you think is the packrat?"

I ran my bottom lip through my teeth, trying not to accidentally elbow any of the boxes and tip them over. "Has to be Bernice."

"Why her?"

"You'll understand when you see the room at number 29. This is like that, multiplied."

I couldn't imagine Mrs Wick being the hoarder. Sass and I had been in this house when we were kids. It'd been neat and clutter free.

"It's bizarre," said Sass. "Like a TV show where people come in and clean up the hoarder's house. It's that bad. Did you have any idea?"

I shook my head. "I've seen boxes being delivered here lots. But I didn't expect *this*."

Either Mrs Wick was holding back on telling Nan about the hoarding, or Nan was keeping her secret well.

Deciding to look in Bernice's room only, we picked our way up the stairs. Every room was filled with boxes, except for Mrs Wick's bedroom. The third bedroom was packed to the ceiling.

I edged inside Bernice's room.

A dark shape jumped at me from behind a column of boxes. A scream caught in my throat.

A furry grey creature stood on the floor with an arched back, hissing. Mrs Wick's cat.

Stepping over to the window, I looked through it and down onto Nan's yard. Bernice had a clear view.

Sass squeezed in behind me. "Let's get started."

But her voice had an air of defeat. Our mission was impossible. We couldn't search every box in this house for a set of stationery. The only thing we could have a try of looking for was the nightlight. At least it was large.

We poked around for a while but found nothing.

Sass groaned as she lifted a large box back into place. "Maybe she destroyed it."

I sat on Bernice's bed. "I don't know. It looks to me like she just doesn't throw anything away. And all this stuff, it's just so organised." I exhaled. "There's no toys here in the house. No kids' stuff. I know it sounds crazy, but Tommy's nightlight doesn't belong here."

To my surprise, she nodded. "It's not here. So where is she keeping it?"

I rubbed my eyes with the palms of my hands. "I feel like just waiting here and asking her."

Sass's eyes opened large in alarm. "Don't do that. Bernice will deny it, just like she denied what she did to that bag lady. You know she will. All that will happen is that she'll know what you know. We have to be smarter."

I felt my anxiety ease a little. Sass was here to organise me. Like she used to when we were kids. Like she had when I first lost Tommy. It had been Sass who had masterminded quite a few of our childhood exploits.

"What we need to do," said Sass, "is to set up cameras in number 29. Motion-detect cameras. I'll talk to the guys who film our home renovation shows and see what we need to do."

"Cameras—Damn, I should have thought of that."

Cameras didn't tell the whole truth, though. They hadn't told the truth about me and the letters.

"Just be sure not to tell Kate what we're doing," Sass said. "I trust her but not the guy she married. If he finds out what we're doing, he'll try to stop us. He's the police. And once they get involved, it's all over. I'm not sure about telling Pria, either. She starts crying if we even mention number 29. It's just you and me, okay?"

"Okay." I drew in a breath that reached all the way to the pit of my stomach.

"I'll get the cameras organised. On Saturday, after we go to the Christmas in July thing."

"I seriously have to go to that?"

"You seriously do. Your doc was right about one thing. You've been by yourself too much. Luke's chosen to go his own way. And now you need to go yours." Sitting beside me, she slung an arm around my shoulder and squeezed it. "And along the way, we'll find out just what Bernice Wick is up to."

32. LUKE

Thursday night

MY FINGERS TANGLED IN KITTY'S HAIR. She made me feel real. Substantial. Like everything about me wasn't about to dissolve.

With Phoebe, I was salt, watching the sky for storm clouds.

We were lying in Kitty's bed, a jumble of sheets and pillows all around.

Jazz music piped from vents. She was a music lover. She'd played violin in the nude earlier, sitting in the corner armchair of the bedroom, and it was the sexiest thing I'd ever seen. She wasn't as pretty as Phoebe, but she had an earthiness that was raw and sexual.

If I had made a life with her all those years ago, I could have had a real life. Not a broken life. I wouldn't be here comparing her to a woman who never gave me what I needed.

I didn't even know how we'd ended up like this tonight. It had just happened. Organically. I'd tried calling Phoebe earlier tonight, but her mobile phone wasn't answering, and neither was the home phone. I'd remembered then that it was trivia night at the club—Nan would be out. Maybe Phoebe had gone with her.

Bored and lonely, I'd come around to Kitty's for some company. We'd started drinking, and then somehow, we'd moved closer and closer to each other. I'd kissed her again, and this time, she didn't resist. I guessed that now that my wife had left me, Kitty didn't feel like she was pushing into the middle of a marriage.

But I still sensed a reluctance in Kitty. Maybe it was me. Luke Basko—the guy who had no trouble picking up women but just didn't have what it took to keep them.

I shifted my body close to hers. "This is crazy, but I want this all the time."

"Luke . . ." She gazed up at me with her large eyes. "It just doesn't seem right. Not yet anyway."

"I know what you're saying. I've thought the same thing. You and me, it wouldn't be easy. But tonight, I don't know. I'm different. I want to be different. I don't want the same life."

"I know you probably don't want to hear this, but I feel for Phoebe. She's been through hell. I don't want to cause her pain."

"Me either. I still . . . love my wife. She's the mother of Tommy."

"I know you do. It was just supposed to be a separation between you and her, right? Not a divorce."

"Yeah. But you should see the way she looks at me. She's never coming back."

"People change their minds."

"Maybe," I said. "But what's in it for me? Fuck, I fought her so hard when she left. But now, I don't know. I've had time to think. I'm tired of the crazy."

"I'd go 'round the twist if I'd lost my kid like she did."

"She was like that before. I've never said this to anyone . . . but the day we lost Tommy, she was already going off her head. My mother was staying with us because Phoebe wasn't capable of watching Tommy. I haven't even fucking told the police that. I asked my mother to keep it to herself, too. I shouldn't have left Phoebe alone with Tommy that morning in the playground. She was too scattered."

She laid herself on top of me, holding me tightly. "Oh hell, Luke. I didn't know."

"Nobody knows. Except my mother. But she doesn't know it all."

"Look, I'm here for you. I'll be your rock, whatever you need. When things feel right, maybe we can start planning something."

I lifted my head. "Seriously?"

"Yes. Maybe a complete change. Go somewhere where there are no reminders of your old life. I just want you to be happy."

"Where? Let's talk about it. I need something good to look forward to."

She ran her fingers through my hair. "I don't know where. It's just a thought. How about we just go one step at a time? We've got this for now. You and me. Maybe we shouldn't push it any further just yet."

I let my eyes close, feeling the warmth and weight of her body on mine. She was right. I was shooting off my mouth. I had to enjoy the moment. I'd never really learned how to do that.

33. PHOEBE

Friday night

I FELT LIKE TIPTOEING IN WHEN Sass opened the door to her apartment. I hadn't seen it since she'd renovated. It was all white. Dazzling white. Sterile, with splashes of bright colour, like a modern art museum. Everything new and flashy.

Beauty. Calm. Everything in its place.

So Saskia.

She'd insisted I come over to her place to get ready for the Christmas in July dinner party.

I put my bag of clothing down (I'd hastily thrown in some stuff). The old duffel bag squatted in a guilty clump on the tiled floor.

Sass seated herself on her red Arne Jacobsen egg chair, holding court, her yoga-pants legs tucked under her.

"Sit," she instructed me. "We're going to meditate for the first five minutes. Everything's going to be different from now on."

"Sass, I don't know if I can get into that head space right now."

She grinned, winding her hair into a knot. "Yes, you can. You're not going to think about your life right now. Leave that to sessions with your psych. We're going to just bliss out. And then we're going out on the town. Woo hoo! This town won't know what hit it. Phoebe Vance on the loose again!"

"Oh god, I really—"

"Trust."

I breathed out slowly.

"Take a seat," she insisted.

I perched on the edge of an art deco chair, feeling like I was interfering with an art exhibit.

"Get comfy." Reaching back, she picked up a remote control from a small table and pressed a button. Ethereal music began to pipe through hidden speakers—soft at first and then growing in intensity.

I wriggled back in the chair.

"Close your eyes," she instructed. "Let your mind free itself. Thoughts will wander in. Let them. Imagine a broom, sweeping them out again."

Pinning my eyelids down, I wondered why Dr Moran didn't go in for this sort of thing. It would be less work for her. I imagined a broom, sweeping out Dr Moran and her small steps. Luke's face intruded, his critical face with his beautiful eyes—Luke didn't realise how handsome he was (his criticism extended to himself). And the old lady and her birthday-money envelope. I watched the envelope tearing in half, fluttering over the water.

"You're not at rest," said Sass. "I can see your eyes moving. Use your broom. You're in a temple. Thoughts can only enter through the door straight before you. Where you can easily whisk them out at will."

I concentrated on the broom.

The broom split into many. Like the broom had in *The Sorcerer's Apprentice*.

Sweeping. Sweeping. Frantically sweeping.

"Phoebe." Sass's voice was gentler this time. "Forget the broom. Concentrate on your breathing. Think of nothing else. Slow breaths. In. Out. Repeat. You might feel bored, but that's normal. That's your mind resisting."

I shifted my mind to my breathing.

Sass was right that I might feel bored. Because I was bored.

The sound of the clock ticking away on the wall irritated me.

It was only later, when I was putting my things away in the spare bedroom that I noticed my heart rate had slowed. I'd been aware of my heartbeat on and off all day.

Saskia stood in the doorway, arms folded. "Did you bring any sex-ay dresses? Something you can rock with a jacket and boots?"

I shook my head. "My old stuff doesn't fit, and I'm going to be more comfortable in jeans anyway."

"No way. You're dressing up tonight, girl!"

"I just want to wear something that lets me fade into the background, y'know?"

"Seriously? Because I can loan you clothes."

We both knew that Sass was a lot taller than me. I was safe from having her dress me up tonight.

I shook my head, not giving her anything else to argue with.

She sighed loudly. "Well, we'll head down there in another couple of hours. The girls are meeting us at seven."

I showered and changed into the jeans and a black zippered jacket. Sass tried to persuade me to *do something* with my hair, but these days my hair had become just a nuisance that needed tying back. I couldn't cope with the thought of anything else.

We walked through the crisp dark air to the boardwalk at Darling Harbour.

The boardwalk was a sweep of hundreds of trendy cafes and restaurants. Part undercover and part open to the salt and sea spray, ghostly boats swaying along the dark pier. One end held an aquarium, a zoo, and a wax museum. At the opposite end, an IMAX theatre and a shopping centre filled with yet more eateries and stores.

And a playground. *The playground from which Tommy had vanished.*

I knew that Sass wouldn't have thought of that when she asked me to come to the dinner tonight. Darling Harbour was just close and convenient. We could walk, therefore drink. And it was filled with tourists who didn't know me.

Sass headed towards a restaurant named Billy Coachman. Like the other restaurants, it was undercover but open to the water, with most of its tables outside. The tables were already full.

The restaurant was totally themed like an English Christmas. In Australia, we had so many images of white Christmases pushed at us that I was sure we all had fake childhood memories of actually having had them. Even now, it didn't seem like Christmas unless I saw snow (even if that snow was that spray-on stuff on windows).

Christmas snow globes as tall as me whirled fake snow around tiny villages. Outdoor heaters, shaped like vintage street lamps, stood between the busy, full tables and potted pine trees that were decorated with baubles. A Christmas tune pumped from a live band inside. Alcohol-soaked voices of different nationalities competed for air space as they banged out the lyrics to the music.

Two women rose from a table and waved wildly, their cheeks bright from the nearby heaters. Kate and Pria.

Sass and I threaded our way through the tables.

"I think this calls for a round of champagne—to celebrate us!" Kate pinched her pretty face into a smile. Kate often gave the impression of squeezing a smile out, as if the smile came from somewhere deep. She seemed to coast through life in her own private happy place—a place from which smiles could be extracted at will. Tonight, she was wearing a pale-blue dress and headband, giving her a dark-haired *Alice in Wonderland* look.

"Correct. That's exactly what we need." Pria buried her nose in the wine list. "My shout for the first round. And God, I need it. My last client today told me his life story. And worst thing? I don't think it would be possible for anyone to have done less with their life but take so long to tell the story of it." She tucked her pale hair behind both ears as she shook her head in frustration. "I don't mean to be mean, but sometimes . . . you wish you could pop on headphones and play some music."

Saskia laughed out loud. "You couldn't pay me enough."

Pria ordered a bottle of Krug Vintage from the drinks waiter.

I bit my lip, grinning. "Remember when we used to get bottles of that el cheapo berry-flavoured champagne?"

Pria wrinkled her nose in amusement. "I got drunk more times than I can remember on that stuff."

"I miss those days." Kate toyed with her Christmas-tree-shaped napkin.

"Do you remember that we used to run everywhere?" mused Saskia. "We didn't have to. But we just ran. Like, somehow we knew those days were precious and we didn't have time to waste."

"So true," said Pria. "These days, we know how fast the time goes, but we never run. We walk, like life is forever. If we run, we're not actually going anywhere. Just going for a run to keep our thighs from jiggling."

A waiter presented the bottle of Krug to Pria and then poured each of us a glass. Another waiter brought us a plate of tiny squares of Christmas fruitcake, with white almond icing and glacé cherries.

At the table next to us, a bunch of rowdy American guys held their drinks out in victorious poses, inviting us to clink glasses with them.

The tallest of them, with a mop of blond hair, half-stood and leaned across to clink glasses with Saskia. "To new friends this Christmas. May the year ahead be bright and merry. Or at least for the next six months until we have Christmas again." He winked.

"To new friends!" Saskia clinked his glass.

The six guys then all leaned over for a round of glass clinking.

A guy with intense dark eyes and a slow grin leaned across and touched my shoulder. "I've seen you before, somewhere."

I went rigid. I was used to people recognising me, but I hadn't expected it tonight. "Wherever you think you've seen me, you haven't." I forced a snarky smile.

"I'll remember, sooner or later. I'm Dashiell."

I shook the hand that he offered. "I'm . . . happy to meet you."

"Oh, great pickup line." Pria smirked at the man. "Leave her alone. She just got here."

The man's eyebrows hooked into a wry frown—a very attractive expression, probably well practised—as he noted four sets of female eyes suddenly on him. Shaking his head and grinning, he revolved around to his friends.

I relaxed. *A pickup line.* Nothing more. He hadn't seen my picture anywhere.

"To us." Pria raised her glass.

Sass, Kate, and I lifted our glasses.

A fog rolled in fast over the harbour, hanging back only when it reached the water's edge. All the people at the tables around us stared at the sudden mist, watching it rise and gather.

A mischievous glint entered Saskia's eyes. She pushed her hair back over both shoulders like it was some kind of ceremonial cape. "Girls, can you feel it? I think The Moose is back."

Setting her drink down, Pria held up both hands in a stop gesture. "The Moose isn't back."

"Yes, I'm pretty sure he is." Sass raised her eyebrows high.

"You invoked The Moose? I don't believe it." Kate's rosebud lips formed a small circle. "The Moose hasn't been back since we were, what, sixteen?"

"We can't," I protested. "Sass, c'mon, we don't do The Moose anymore." I hadn't told her I'd found the old moose storybook in number 29. I'd forgotten about it as soon as I'd found the nightlight boat. The book had brought up instant memories of all of us as children, invoking the moose and then pretending to be each other for the day.

Sass gave a playful shrug. "Once he's invoked, we can't un-invoke him. Sorry."

"Wait, what about Luke?" I said. "We can't play this game without including him. So, the game is off."

"The rules were we could invoke the moose in someone's absence. The absent person doesn't get to play." Grabbing our drink coasters, Sass flipped them and scrawled our names on each of them. She shuffled them then, like a pack of square, awkward cards and handed them out to each of us.

The name on my coaster, in tall letters, said *SASS*. With a love heart.

Fuck the moose, I thought.

But no one was listening to my thoughts.

Sass dragged me off to the women's bathroom to start the process of becoming *her.*

I stood in front of the small square bathroom mirror, under dim lighting. The bathroom walls were wallpapered, the toilet cubicles having black curtains instead of doors. The cubicles reminded me of Catholic confessional boxes.

"I can't do this," I said as she laid out her arsenal of lipstick, eye shadow, and fake eyelashes on top of her handbag.

"You've got to make a change, and it starts tonight."

"You haven't told me which one of us you are. Because if you're me, then you wouldn't be doing this. I would definitely say no to this."

"Lucky I'm not you, then. I'm Kate. And Kate approves."

She was right that Kate would approve of a makeover. Kate kept her hair and makeup perfect for a living. Even when her twins were babies.

My fingers fumbled as I applied the red lipstick. I'd barely worn any makeup since I'd been pregnant with Tommy. Taking over, Sass lined my eyes and then stuck on false eyelashes. She brushed colour onto my cheeks. Then she tugged the elastic from my hair and brushed my hair out. My hair fell around my face, a deep brown beside my pale-brown eyes.

Sass reached around me from behind and yanked my top down, exposing the cups of my bra. Sass was very hands-on. I pulled it back up again. She tugged at it again. We compromised on halfway. She then undid my shirt and tied it into a knot underneath my boobs.

Kate and Pria stepped inside the bathroom, stopping and blinking at me like I was one of the *afters* on a makeover show. Sass had her hand on my shoulder like the show's proud presenter.

"You look like . . . *you* again," Kate told me. She didn't add, *before you had a baby and got fat, and then got too skinny and stopped wearing makeup.*

Kate had given birth to twins without looking any different afterwards. I almost felt like I had to excuse all the weight I'd gained and lost. It was a weird thing, weight-guilt. You felt you had to go around apologising for every extra kilo you were carrying or for every loss of a kilo that made people think you were one step closer to becoming anorexic. Your body belonged to other people.

"Yep, she looks like the old Phoebe Vance. Thanks to me." Grinning widely, Sass snatched Kate's headband and fixed it onto her own head.

"Hey," said Kate. "I would have asked first. Maybe I should analyse why you're so grabby."

Kate was either Luke or Pria. Pria analysed people for a job. Luke analysed them for a hobby. Then I remembered that Luke wasn't in this.

"You're Pria," I told Kate. Then I turned around to Pria. "That means you're me."

Pria took my hands in hers, her warm eyes suddenly serious. "I know you, Phoebe. You'd take someone else's burden if you could. So, for a night, offload everything. Hand it over to me."

"Wish I could," I told her.

"Pretend that you just did." She gave my fingers a gentle squeeze. "Just . . . don't go too crazy being our resident wild child, Sass. Use your new powers wisely." She shot Sass a pointed sideways glance.

"Hey!" Saskia pretended to look offended.

We used to carry out a clothing swap then at this point. When The Moose was invoked, clothing always used to be swapped. Luke had been the only one who was exempt from the swap. But we'd all been around the same height and weight then. Now, Sass had grown tall, and I'd grown thin, and Kate had model-slim hips, and Pria had boobs that made the rest of us jealous. The clothing swap wasn't going to happen, and as we looked at each other, I knew each of us could tell we had the same thought.

"Woo!" cried Saskia. "Let's go get our party started!"

Sass grabbed my reluctant hand, and we headed back to our table.

The guy with the intense eyes looked up as we headed in his direction, and he did something close to a vaudevillian double take.

"Remember," Saskia said close to my ear, "you're me. Just think, what would Sass do?"

"That's the problem," I told her quietly. "I know exactly what Sass would do."

A thought half-formed in my mind. *The guy didn't look at me like that before Sass slapped the contents of her makeup kit on me.* But that was only partly true. He'd still spoken to me. I couldn't even wallow in a pond of murky, indignant water.

"If you were me, you'd be telling me to stay right away from him right now," I said under my breath.

"Once again, just lucky I'm not you," Sass said flippantly.

"Did you hear his lame pickup line earlier?"

"So what? He's hot, and he probably knows how to make a girl laugh."

And that was when I knew that Sass had engineered the call of the Moose. *Of course she had. To help me step out of my skin for a while. The fog had just made it easy for her.*

We hadn't yet seated ourselves when a guy wearing what I could only describe as a hipster Santa suit stepped out from the restaurant and boomed a hello to everyone. "Hear ye. Hear ye. Christmas dinner is served. And afterwards, we dance! And merry-make! And celebrate! Rumour has it that there might be mistletoe."

Everyone surged inside. People tended to behave like they were in some Dickenson novel when food was announced.

The tables and chairs had all been cleared away inside the covered section of the restaurant, leaving open spaces of shiny wooden flooring. A buffet of Christmas foods ran the lengths of long rectangular tables that were dressed with white cloth and silver-sprayed flowers.

People loaded their plates, ate fast, and mingled. The air grew increasingly warm, and coats were shed.

Dessert consisted of sweet creations from the chef that were mostly admired and not eaten, because everyone was stuffed full of rich food and alcohol already.

The band switched back and forth from piano and drums to violins to the accordion, playing festive songs from around the world. Right now they were playing some kind of German folk music.

People were instantly drawn to the dance floor.

"He's looking over at you—the guy," Sass narrated to me. "Wait, now he's walking this way."

"I don't—" I started.

"Life will happen with or without you . . ." Sass stepped lightly away. That was such a Kate thing to say. Sass had chosen her words well. Kate was full of pithy, Zen-like sayings. All delivered with a *freshly-squeezed-orange-juice* smile.

The man stopped in front of me, forcing me to look at him.

Fashionable stubble. Carefully tousled hair. A mouth just on the edge of flickering into a grin.

"You didn't have to go to so much trouble for me," he said, gesturing towards my hair and clothing. "I was already sold."

Flirting. Right. Yes. I can do this. Sass-style.

"I can go to a lot more trouble than this," I told him, raising my eyebrows

His face showed momentary surprise, but he recovered quickly. "Bet you can." He shot me an amused frown. "I want to ask you to dance, but I don't know if I can drop my standards for a girl who doesn't iron her clothing."

He tugged at my shirt. I glanced down. I hadn't ironed it, but it was made of a material that didn't look bad unironed. At least, that's what I'd told myself.

Touching me lightly under the chin, he tilted my chin up. "But hey, I'll forgive it."

His hand closed around mine, and I let him lead me onto the dance floor. Straight away, he was holding me, dancing close. A warm charge sped through my chest and up to my neck.

"Relax," he whispered close to my ear. "I've got you."

If I were eighteen, I'd be falling for his routine—hook, line, and sinker. If I were really Sass, I'd let myself fall for it. Saskia was all about experiences and losing herself in the moment.

I'd never lost myself. Not in any good way. Not voluntarily. Except when I was acting in a role.

A new song started, but the guy—*what was his name?*—didn't let go.

Dashiell. I remembered now. His name was Dashiell.

I caught sight of Pria. She was dancing with a tall, bearded, arty-looking man. That kind of guy used to be my type.

Panic began to make the food in my stomach feel like poison. I couldn't hand the job of being *me* over to Pria, not even for a night. The cloak of worry and anguish was mine. I needed to plan what I was going to do tomorrow night. Pria didn't know about the duck-head umbrella or the nightlight boat or the scent of caramel mochaccino. She didn't know how to be me. She couldn't.

I turned my head, looking out past the people to the dark mist over the water.

I desperately, desperately didn't want to be me. I didn't want to count down the days and hours since my son went missing. I didn't want to feel the terror of not knowing. Where he was and what had happened to him. I didn't want to feel the hollowness of my husband's deceit. I wanted to disappear from all of that. Let the war go on without me. Maybe, in the deepest part of me, I was worried that if I was someone else for too long, I'd want to run away and never be Phoebe Basko again.

I was startled out of my thoughts as bunches of silver leaves on silver strings were let down from the ceiling. Like oxygen masks suddenly appearing from above on a plane, fifty or so bunches of leaves now dangled above everyone's heads.

"Ladies and gentlemen, we have mistletoe," announced the hipster Santa.

When I glanced back at my dance partner, a wide grin had spread across his face. He moved in to kiss me. A long and lingering kiss that took my breath.

Tiny flakes of white tinsel floated down from above.

"You feel tense." He ran his hands up and down my arms. "I think I need to kiss you again."

"I'm a bit woozy. Too much wine, I think."

"Oh yeah? Come outside—we'll get you some air. Getting a bit hot in here."

Phoebe would refuse his offer.

But Sass would just go. No hesitation.

I walked with him through the restaurant and across the boardwalk to the water. The cold, damp air cooled my skin instantly.

"What's your name?" he asked.

"Fee . . . Saskia."

"Say what?"

"Saskia."

"Nice. You know my name already."

"Dashiell."

"You remembered. Dash for short."

"Cute."

"It's a curse. I know I sound like something out of a Christmas musical." He opened his arms wide and sang in a deep, almost operatic voice: *Dashing through the snow, in a one-horse open sleigh. . .*

I laughed. "I wasn't thinking that."

"What were you thinking? That you'd like to take a man named Dash home? Imagine the bragging rights."

"Damn, you're smooth. *Not.*"

"Just being me."

"Must take a lot of practice to be you."

He gave a wry laugh, stepping in front of me. "Do you like the end result?"

"Do you ever give the pickup lines a rest?"

Stop, Phoebe. This isn't Sass. Sass isn't this cynical. She's open. Open and free.

He snorted, staring up at the inky sky for a moment. "Okay. But would you do something for me?"

I shrugged, smiling. "Maybe?"

"Can we finish our dance out here?" Shooting me a dejected look, he took a pretend-timid step towards me. He put his arms around me again the same as he'd done inside the restaurant and started a kind of waltz.

His hands slipped into the back pockets of my jeans. He pulled something from my pocket.

I gasped at the sight of my notebook in his hand.

Hell, I'd forgotten I left it in this pair of jeans.

Spinning around, he opened the notebook. Ignoring my attempts to get the book back, he read, "*Midforties man, in a suit that's seen better days. Probably working in low-level management.*" Dash flipped through a few more pages. "*Something, something about a woman in a red coat.*"

He turned back around to me, his eyes different. Snapping the book shut, he handed it back to me. "Okay, I get it now."

Hurriedly, I shoved the notebook back into my pocket, my heart bumping against my ribs. "What are you talking about?"

"You're a journalist."

"What?"

"You can drop the act. You're a player, just like me."

"They're just notes about imaginary people. For a book."

"Complete with times and dates? Not buying it."

I gave myself time to breathe and put a smile back on my face. "What would it matter if I was a journalist anyway? Have you got something against them?"

"No. But you played me well."

"That's kind of nuts. I'm just out with friends."

"Yeah? So, here we have a woman who goes out at night in a button-up shirt and jeans, without a scrap of makeup on her pretty face.

Suddenly, she does a one-eighty and she looks like a bombshell. Seems to me that she sniffed an opportunity for a story and went for it."

Bombshell? "Why would anyone want to do a story on you? Who are you, anyway?"

"You can cut the act."

"I would if I knew what the act was. Are you that notorious that journalists would bother chasing you down?"

"Maybe. Evolutionary psychology is always good for inspiring a bit of outrage."

"Evolutionary psychology? You mean like the study of human nature?"

"Exactly."

"That's what you do?"

"Yup. We're out here in Australia to run a series of seminars."

"All of you? The guys you're with?"

"Yes."

"And why would you think me changing my look would get me a story with you?"

"I specialise in relationships between men and women. The science of attraction. So, you thought you'd turn it around on me and get one of those sneaky undercover stories. Wouldn't be the first time a female journalist has done it to one of us."

"So," I said, "what ideas do you believe in that get people so worked up?"

"I see straight through people. No one likes that. Everyone likes to think they're so deep and mysterious. And you, lady, are either a journalist or a whacko who takes notes on strangers. Which is it?"

"How about we just forget this? Let's head back inside."

"You're giving up that easily? What are you, new to the job? A rookie?"

I decided it didn't matter if he thought I was a writer, but it *did* matter if he thought I was taking notes on people. No one was supposed to know that.

"I just write for a website," I told him. "Nothing special."

"Okay, well, I'll do you a deal. You can tag along with me to the seminars and get your story. But it's got to be fair. Deal?"

"Seminars aren't really my thing. Hey, I'm going to go back—"

"Sure?"

"Yes. Sure."

We walked together towards the Billy Coachman restaurant.

Sass, Kate, and Pria were gathered together out the front. Sass seemed to be crying. Excusing myself, I rushed up to them.

Sass turned to me with reddened eyes. "I have to go, Feeb."

"What happened?"

"Nanna Rosie died."

I gasped, hugging Sass tightly. We'd all called Sass's grandmother Nanna Rosie. She was the warmest person I could name.

"I'm coming back home with you." I brushed her hair back from her face.

She shook her head. "I'm catching a cab straight for the airport. Mum sounded a mess over the phone. I have to get up there."

"But you don't have a bag packed, or—" I started.

Sass wiped her tear-stained face and managed a sad smile. "Gives me an excuse to go shopping for new things when I get there."

"I'll wait with you at the airport," I insisted. "I don't want you to go alone."

"No, sweetie, there's a flight coming soon. I've already rung and checked. I'll be gone soon after I get there. Stay here. Be me and have fun for me for the rest of the night, okay? Please?"

We stepped arm in arm to the taxi stand and waved Sass good-bye. Sass blew each of us a kiss from the taxi as it drove away.

Pria glanced across at Kate and me. "I think this calls for a toast to Nanna Rosie."

"Correct." Kate bunched her arms in close to her chest, shivering. "Let's head back."

Fog wisped around us as we made our way to the restaurant again. The band belted out an old Irish song. The music seemed appropriate. Nanna Rosie had come to Australia from Ireland as a young woman.

At a table inside, I ordered a bottle of wine. Red. Strong.

Kate raised her glass. "To Nanna Rosie. She made the best banana cake and told the best stories, especially the racy ones."

Pria and I raised our glasses.

I was wobbly on my feet when I headed off to the bathroom. I needed a moment by myself, to still the waves of raw panic coursing through me. Saskia wasn't going to be around for a few days. The cameras for number 29 weren't going to happen.

In the bathroom, I held my face low to the sink, vomiting a small amount of watery liquid.

Too much time was racing past.

If the cameras weren't going to be keeping watch, then I had to somehow arrange it myself. Only, I didn't know the first thing about stop-motion cameras or how to conceal them.

Every night, I had to be out there, looking for the stranger man, watching Bernice, watching number 29.

I cleaned my face with paper towels and drank enough water to get rid of the sour taste in my mouth.

On the way back to the table, someone tugged my shirtsleeve. I spun around to Dash's amused eyes.

"You're not walking straight," he said. "Hey, was your friend okay?"

"Her grandmother just died."

"That's rough."

"Yeah, it is."

"I was thinking. We both gotta eat, right? How about just dinner? Tomorrow night? My shout. You can ask me anything you want. All I ask is that you don't twist my quotes."

This guy didn't give up easily.

"Thanks for the offer, but no."

"You are damned hard to work out, Saskia."

"I thought you said people were easy to see through."

"True. But I need a bit of time to warm up."

A thought pushed into my head. If I went out to dinner with him, it would give me a cover for tomorrow night. I could go to dinner and then head off to watch number 29. It would give me time to figure something else out—something that wouldn't make Nan or Dr Moran or Trent Gilroy suspicious that I was doing something I shouldn't be.

"Okay. Dinner." I held my breath. It wasn't a *date*. But it was still dinner out with a man who wasn't my husband. *A husband who was busily dating another woman.*

"Eight good with you?"

"Eight's perfect."

"Somewhere at Darling Harbour?"

"Yeah. How about we meet outside here, at the spot we were at earlier?"

"Too easy."

"Great."

As I walked away, he caught hold of my sleeve again. "Wait, what's your last name?"

The question caught me with my guard down. "I prefer not to reveal that."

"I prefer that you tell me."

"Nope."

"Just like that? *Nope?*"

I nodded.

Letting go of me, he held his chin between his thumb and fingers, studying me with his dark gaze. "Isn't it fair to let me know who you are so I can look you up? Else I might think you're trying to hide something. Maybe you're the kind of writer who's trying to make a name for herself by writing scathing exposés."

"Maybe you'd better give me enough material so that I can." I flashed him a smile.

There was a delay before he threw his head back and roared with laughter. "Okay, do your worst. The more moral outrage spread around about me, the better for my career. Gets my name known."

"I'll do my best." I stretched out my hand to shake his.

He reciprocated. But instead of letting go after a polite second, he hung on and squeezed my fingers lightly. "Make sure you wear something other than a wrinkly denim shirt."

34. PHOEBE

Saturday afternoon

IN THE CORNER OF NAN'S SHOWER, I sank to the floor, my knees drawn up tight to my chest.

The anxiety inside me was a cresting wave that refused to break on the shore.

What am I doing?

I can't go to dinner with that man. I can't do it.

Last night I'd been emboldened by a few drinks of champagne and wine and eggnog, and by being Sass.

I let the water run over me until Nan banged on the bathroom and demanded that I stop wasting all the hot water. Too late. The water was already starting to run cold.

I had to call Dash and tell him I couldn't make it.

No, I couldn't. I didn't know his number. Or his last name (even though he thought I knew him).

After I'd dressed and come downstairs, I found Nan outside working on getting her precious ivy to grow over the toolshed, twisting it through the wire mesh that she'd put up before.

"You slept past lunch," she told me over her shoulder. "There's a chicken curry in the fridge."

"Thanks, Nan."

"You must have had an awful lot to drink, to sleep this late."

"We had a few toasts to Nanna Rosie. Nan, she died last night."

She winced. "Oh no. Not Rosie."

I knew that Nan hearing of deaths of the older group of people she'd known hit her particularly hard. Each death was like a nail in her own coffin. Nan hadn't even been good friends with Rosie. Rosie had been a firm believer in happiness, not in duty and stoicism, like Nan.

"Sad news, but Sass told me she enjoyed her life 'til the end," I said, trying to soften the blow. "Saskia flew up to Queensland already."

"I'll send a card." She resumed threading the ivy.

"Nan," I said hesitantly. "I'm going out tonight. Just to dinner."

She stopped, her shoulder bones drawing in together. "Who with?"

"A man that I met."

She started shaking her head even before she turned around. "That's not the right thing to do."

"Why isn't it?"

"You have a husband."

"A husband who's dating another woman."

"You're not going to fix this by going after other men."

"I didn't go after him. He asked me. And anyway, Luke already broke our marriage."

"A good woman knows to be patient and show her best side. Her husband will see sense, sooner or later."

I frowned at her with sudden realisation. "Granddad cheated on you, didn't he?"

Her face crumpled. "Why would you say such a terrible thing?"

"He did, didn't he? And you just waited it out, right?"

"I don't want to talk about this, Phoebe. It's none of your business. In any case, sometimes men stray. If a woman wants to keep the marriage solid, she'll pull out all stops to get him back."

"That's the same kind of advice you used to give Mum. Stay with your husband, no matter how abusive he is. She was your own daughter, Nan. How could you do that?"

She pulled her lips in, dusting her hands of dirt. "I was raised to be strong. Not like you young women of today."

"You and I have a different idea of what it is to be strong."

"I was twenty-six, and I already had the two boys," Nan said with a tremble in her voice. "Your grandfather started chasing a seamstress around. She worked in the textiles factory. What was I going to do? There wasn't any help back then. I stuck it out. And we ended up having a good life, your grandfather and I."

I bit my lip. Hard. "Were you happy?"

"Happiness is a fleeting thing. No one has hold of it for long. But a marriage keeps a family together and provides stability. That's worth a lot. And your grandfather and I were very fond of each other."

I was about to point out that Mum was never fond of my dad, but in truth, I didn't know that for certain. Mum was always so guarded about her real feelings.

Leaving Nan to her ivy, I headed into the kitchen to heat up the curry. I took it up to my bedroom.

Down on the street, Bernice was walking home. She was sporting a large, floppy purple handbag. I recognised it from the stash of second-hand wares at number 29.

Damn. If I'd been out of bed earlier, I could have followed her to see where she was going.

I needed to try to find the stranger tonight.

Closing my eyes, I told myself I needed to get through the dinner with Dash. So that I could head out and search without Nan getting suspicious.

Three hours later, I began getting everything ready. I'd wear tight black pants, a nice red top, boots, and a black jacket tonight. In my bag, I packed a knit cap, warm gloves, and my notebook. I spent ten minutes researching evolutionary psychology on the internet. If I was going to pretend to interview a scientist, I needed to know a bit about my subject.

Dr Moran called me on the phone just as I was packing two of Nan's sharpest kitchen knives into my bag. She was surprised when I told her about my *big step* of going out on a date night. I could tell by her voice that she didn't know whether to cheer or be alarmed. If she could see me right now, she'd definitely swing to the alarmed side.

Another three hours after that, I was ready to leave. It would take me the better part of half an hour to walk to Darling Harbour.

Nan seemed to control her glaring expression somewhat as I headed for the front door.

"I'll be back before midnight," I told her.

"Where is he? Isn't he picking you up?"

"I'm meeting him just down the road."

"You stay safe and make him bring you home," she told me.

I nodded, not wanting to verbalise yet another lie.

The night sky was clearer than the sky during the day had been. Thank God, the ever-present rain and fog were holding off tonight.

I walked to the pier and waited. I wanted to be the first one there. I needed to be the one to set the tone for the date. If I could control everything with Dash tonight, I could get through it. *Maybe.*

Seagulls burst from the dark sky as I stood by the pylon. Like harbingers of doom from an apocalypse movie.

Minutes ticked. He was late.

I waited longer. Until he was so late that I was starting to feel a bit like an idiot. People in the outdoor cafes and bars were watching me. They all had a good view. I shouldn't have made this the meeting place. Last night, in the deep of the fog, it hadn't seemed quite so public.

So, he'd ditched me for a better option.

I'd have to fill in some time before I headed back to my street.

I walked the loser's walk of shame towards the nearest bar and ordered a drink. I seated myself on a bar stool. Within the space of five minutes, I was hit upon by two men.

Look, here she is. The poor loser girl who got stood up. She's an easy target now that she's got the stink of rejection on her.

Yet another man made his move. He parked himself on the stool next to mine, doing a quick, nervous lick of his bottom lip. He was bulky underneath his too-tight shirt. It was obvious he worked out. A lot. Too much. Sleeping with him must be like sleeping next to a bundle of boulders.

I forced myself to grin and make light conversation. I tried to channel Sass. Sass flirted with everyone. Even women. Even with my nan.

"Are you meeting with friends?" the bulky man asked me.

"A guy. But it looks like he found something better to do."

The man stared at me with interest. "So, are you coming home with me instead?"

I straightened, confused. "How did the conversation get *there*?"

"Just want to know where I stand. We could be wasting your time and mine if this isn't headed anywhere."

I felt so, so far out of the singles scene. It all felt as impersonal as a transaction. Only no money was being exchanged. Just time. And cheap conversation. And most of all, bodies.

"Okay, I'll give you an answer," I told him. "In respect of your time, the answer's no."

He barely missed a beat. "Your answer doesn't have to be no. Let's break this down. What are your reasons for saying no to me?"

"A second ago, you were worried about wasting your time. Well, you're not going to get productive here. You might as well go try your luck with someone else."

"You'd be surprised how many women respond to being asked straight out if they want to sleep with me. It gives them a direction. But maybe you're not like that and I took this too fast. Let's dial it back a bit. What do you do for work?"

I leaned towards him slightly and spoke slowly and concisely. "I don't want to talk to you anymore."

"That's a bitchy thing to say." But he remained sitting there, sipping his drink, as though he believed that getting past my defences was just a matter of persistence. "You don't even know me, but you're just dismissing me."

"I'm not dismissing you. Just your offer."

I was completely out of my depth. Sass would have handled it like an expert. I wasn't Sass.

I needed to get out of here. It was too crowded. Airless. The body heat of the packed crowed was mixing with perfume and sweat and sour alcohol. The music was hammering my ears. Sass had no problem entering bars alone. I didn't know how she did it. I didn't know *why* she did it.

The bulky man was obviously still not satisfied. He didn't leave. "You damned women get it too easy. You just get to sit there like a princess and wait for men to come to you."

I eyed him directly. "What if I just wanted a drink or two to drown my sorrows before I head home? What makes you think I'm some kind of man-processing factory?"

He chewed his lip, not answering. His eyes were round and strangely childlike in that meaty, square-jawed face. I realised he was probably only twenty-two. I felt a weird twinge of pity for him.

"Hey bud, she's with me," came a voice from the other side of me. An American voice.

I turned, and it was Dash.

Dash, in a midnight-blue shirt and his hair smoother than it had been last night, was even better looking than I'd remembered. He had a kind of young Keanu Reeves look to his features.

The bulky guy pulled himself up from the stool, but then stopped, peering at Dash. "Hey, I went to a seminar today. Aren't you Dash Cit—?"

"Whatever," Dash cut in. "Get lost and stop bugging people."

Shaking his head, Mr Bulky began making his way back to wherever he came from. I stared after him. Mr Bulky hadn't left when I'd asked him to. He'd only left when another male had basically claimed me. I resisted an urge to follow and kick him in the shin.

Dash slid onto the stool that Mr Bulky had deserted "I caught the last couple of things that jerk said."

"I think he's just a bit of a stupid kid, trying out pickup lines."

"Sorry I'm late. Got caught up and couldn't get away."

"Don't sweat it. After all, I had a bar buddy to keep me company." I made a wry face.

A grin caught at the edges of his mouth. "Hungry?"

"Yeah." I was never hungry.

I walked with him to a restaurant that I'd chosen. I'd been to it years ago with Sass, Pria, and Kate. I remembered the food had been good.

I'd booked a table outside. Being outside made me feel less anxious. Like if I needed to get up and run, I could.

The night remained clear, lights from the boats reflecting on the water. A large two-level boat filled with diners in formal dress sat at the edge of the boardwalk. A wedding maybe.

Dash ordered a bottle of wine before we'd even seated ourselves.

"So, should we get started on the interview?" I asked.

"I worked a three-hour seminar today. We'll eat first. Talk shop later."

"I'm cool with that."

"Why don't you tell me about you? You know stuff about me. I know zero about you."

"That wasn't the point of coming here tonight."

"Yeah, but even I get bored talking about myself."

"Maybe you should work on your notoriety, so you don't run out of material."

He laughed at my joke. He laughed so easily. So naturally. Luke wasn't like that. Luke had a pre-approved list of comedians and comic actors that he found funny, and all other attempts at humour were met with stone-cold silence. Including mine. Especially mine. He never found me funny.

A waiter came with the wine then, rescuing me from talking about myself for the moment.

Straight after we ordered, my phone buzzed. It was Luke. The message said *Urgent*.

"Would you excuse me?" I asked Dash.

"Go right ahead."

Stepping away out of Dash's earshot, I called Luke.

When Luke answered, he sounded a little lazy, as though he was lying around somewhere.

Probably her bed.

He was somewhere next to a clock. I could hear the *tick tick tick*. We had no analog clocks at our house.

"Did Gilroy get in contact with you yesterday afternoon?" he asked.

"No. I was probably at Sass's. What was it about?"

"Don't know. He didn't tell me."

"If it was about Tommy, he would have told you. Why'd you text me to say this was urgent?"

He paused and then sighed. "I just wanted to hear your voice. And know that you're okay."

I exhaled in annoyance. "I'm okay."

"Where are you tonight? I called you at your nan's, but she said you were out again. She told me what happened with Nanna Rosie. So, I know you're not with Sass."

"I'm just out with a friend."

"What? *A guy?*"

"What does it matter?"

"Who is he?"

"You don't have the right to ask me that."

He sighed in a low, drawn-out voice. "I don't want you to start seeing other men. If you care about our marriage at all, you won't do this."

"But you—"

"Phoebe . . . I'm so fucking confused right now. I feel like if we don't get together and talk this out now, then things are going to go so far that we can't fix it. We need to talk. Please?"

"I'm sorry you're confused about which woman you want," I said dryly.

"That's not what I meant."

"That's exactly what you meant."

"Phoebe . . ."

"I don't even care. And I don't want to talk to you."

I ended the call.

Luke's idea of relationships was as strange as Nan's. He obviously didn't think that him seeing another woman had irreparably damaged our marriage. But he thought that me seeing another man would.

I felt *burned* after the conversation. I didn't know him anymore.

I'd call Gilroy in the morning to see what he wanted to talk to me about. He was probably just keeping an eye on me. To check that I wasn't up to more crazy stuff.

Like what I was planning to do later.

I returned to the table.

"Anything wrong? You look like you just swallowed a lemon," Dash remarked.

"Everything's all right." I waved a hand in front of my face. "Okay, I just reset my expression. No more sour lemon."

He shot me an amused glance. "Maybe a bit less sour."

"What's that supposed to mean?"

"Well, you do kind of have that *resting bitch face* thing going on."

"Seriously?"

"Yeah."

"Fine. You'll just have to put up with it."

"I ordered for you while you were on the phone."

"What did you order for me?"

"Something nice."

"Guess I'll find out." I relaxed, smiling. Ruining my resting bitch face. "So, what do you think of Sydney so far?"

"I've been here before."

"Oh yeah?"

"Yup. Last December."

"You were?"

"Sure was. Setting things up for the seminars that are happening now. Choosing the venues and all of that. I left a New York winter to head straight into blistering heat. This time, I left the sunshine to head into your doom-and-gloom winter."

"It's been a nasty one."

"Hey, I think that's when I saw you before. In December. Can't remember where, though."

Okay, so he really did see me before? Maybe it hadn't been a pickup line. My face had been all over the news back then. I swallowed. "I live in Sydney. Maybe we walked past each other?"

"Or maybe I saw you in a newspaper."

"What?" My voice went weak.

"Maybe your photo was with one of your articles or something. Either a newspaper or online. But your hair was different."

I relaxed again. He still didn't remember me as being the mother of an abducted boy. My hair had been cut in a shoulder-length layered style then. And I was carrying a lot more weight—I was one of those people whose faces looked very different when they gained or lost weight. I needed to change the subject. "Maybe. Hey, I didn't get an answer to my question earlier. About Sydney?"

"Okay, yeah. I haven't had a lot of time to look around, either time I've been here. But I like what I've seen. You guys are spoiled. It's a sexy-looking city. And the wait staff are nice even though you don't tip them. But the bad thing is that everything starts shutting down just as I'm ready to head out. The place is like a teenager on curfew."

"Good analogy, I guess. Sydney *is* a bit like a teenager. Subject to curfews, a bit awkward, a bit self-conscious about its pimples." I shrugged. "But a lot of fun to be around."

"Maybe you could show me some of the fun places I haven't seen."

"Don't you have a tight schedule?" I tried to keep a hopeful note out of my voice. I wanted him to be too busy.

"I still gotta eat and have some downtime."

"And spend some time working on being notorious." I laughed.

He laughed with me, but then his eyes grew serious. "Well, don't go believing all that you've heard about me."

He had no idea that I didn't know who he was. Without knowing his last name, I wasn't able to look him up earlier. I lifted my chin, studying his face. "I don't take anything at face value. There's always more to a story than you know."

"I'm warming to you." He kept his gaze on me. "I bet you're someone who does interesting things in their spare time."

My one and only hobby is the relentless search for a little boy. "I do amateur theatre. I guess that's my big love."

"I like that."

"What about you?"

He grinned. "Cause mayhem. Gotta keep the notoriety going somehow."

I grinned back. "I like that."

The scent of steaming-hot food reached me before the waiter placed the plates on our table. I already knew what we were having before I laid eyes on it. Dash had chosen pumpkin ravioli for the two of us.

"Did I choose good, Phoebe?" Dash asked.

I jerked my head up, stunned. "My name's Saskia."

He shook his head, rubbing his temple. "Dammit, sorry. *Saskia.* I must have heard someone calling out that other name last night. Somehow, the two names got mixed in my brain."

He glanced away, somehow not looking convincingly apologetic. Or was I imagining that?

"No problem," I told him.

He dug into his dinner. I followed suit. I needed this dinner over and done with.

Pouring us both another glass of wine, he frowned suddenly. "Forgot to tell you. You got pipped at the post. A female journo called me this morning. I agreed to a Skype interview. So, you're not going to get the first interview with me."

"How did it go?"

"She went for the jugular."

"What did she say?"

"I'm not giving you ammunition, girl. You should have done your own research."

"Maybe my article can be an examination of her interview. Complete with quotes from you."

"Direct quotes, no twisting of words?"

"Direct quotes. No twisting."

"My *spidey senses* tell me not to believe you."

"My *resting bitch face* stares down your *spidey senses* and annihilates them."

"Ha! Okay. Whatever. I'll believe you when I see what you write in black and white. And if you want to know what Ms Palmer wrote about me, it's in black and white already." He thumbed through screens on his phone and then handed it to me. "Here, read this bit."

I read through the paragraph. The paragraph described him as having shifty eyes and possible cheekbone implants in his *too-pretty-for-a-man* face. And his *spray tan* had apparently come from a bottle on the shelves of Evo Pysch headquarters.

The journalist had certainly been brutal in her summary of Dash.

My eyes flicked upwards, and I looked closely at Dash's features. His eyes were deep and penetrating, but they had a directness that I would never call *shifty*. If he had cheek implants, they were perfect; he didn't have implants. His tan was even and natural. Not something from a bottle.

Sucking his lips in, he smiled knowingly. "Do you agree with her appraisal of me?"

Heat rose behind my neck and ears. He might just be the most attractive man I'd ever spoken to. He was the kind of guy that the more you looked at him, the more you noticed how attractive he was. Luke's looks were more angelic and innocent (even if he wasn't those things at all).

"You'd pass muster in a herd," I muttered. "That's something my grandmother says."

To cover up my embarrassment, I decided to begin the interview. I whipped out the notebook and pen.

"What would you most want people to know about your field of work?" I began. "About evolutionary psychology."

He brushed his chin over the back of his fingers. "Hmmm. That we're animals, I guess. Our behaviours and culture can all be traced back to things we needed to survive in prehistory."

I scribbled down a note. "So, you consider that we're creatures of our past?"

"Yes. Certainly."

"What kind of behaviours?"

"All. Including love. Sex. Relationships."

"So, what is it about how we love that can be traced to our past?"

Sipping his wine, he nodded thoughtfully. "Would it surprise you that I believe that women can't love men?"

I tilted my head, giving him a bemused grin. "They can't?"

"No. They think they do, but they can never love a man the way in which a man loves a woman. His love is simple and complete. He loves her softness, her weaknesses, her beauty. But she can only love him up to a point, depending on what he provides for her. When he stops providing what she needs, she's gone."

"Okay. And what are the historical reasons she wants those things from a man?"

His mouth flicked upward. "Think about women being carted off into harems or sent into arranged marriages. She had to adapt—and quickly. Her whole tribe might have got slaughtered when she got taken away. She had to be able to leave the past behind quickly and move on. She couldn't remain loyal to the life she had before."

"But women today have their own resources and money."

He hooked an eyebrow. "How many college-educated women in good jobs do you know who are marrying men in casual, dead-end jobs?"

"I know women in high-paying jobs whose husbands are at home with the kids. You know, house husbands."

"Is that the usual?"

"Nope."

"I rest my case."

"Okay, Dash, you said men love women for their softness and beauty. How can you call it actual *love*, if it's just her visual appeal that makes him love her?"

"That's just the initial point of attraction. But it's not just the physical—her personality should be gentle, too. After marriage, she just needs to be *nice*. And his love for her will be unconditional."

Shaking my head lightly, I wrote his words down. "And what is it that women need from men?"

"What they've always needed. Stability, strength, protection, resources, good looks . . . *excitement*."

He knew exactly how to say the word, excitement. With a low murmur that almost made me shiver. "That's what a woman wants?"

"That's exactly what a woman wants."

"And after marriage, does he just have to be nice and everything will just hum along like a Disney movie?"

"Not a chance. He's going to have to prove his worth every day of his life."

"Every day?"

"Every day."

"How?"

"Men have to constantly prove that they're men. Be strong, don't cry, improve, build assets, gain respect, raise yourself up in the male pecking order . . . and that starts from boyhood."

"Sounds kind of sad."

He shrugged, the expression in his eyes slightly distant. "I was a geeky teenager with a bad haircut once. Girls didn't like me then." Pulling himself out of his reverie, he said, "It's the way it is. It's our human evolution."

"Okay"—I made a show of scribbling things down—"but what about the industrial and pre-industrial era? People were too busy for any of that. If my history knowledge serves me right, men and women worked alongside each other on farms. Her softness and weakness weren't assets. And her beauty was soon gone. Damn hard work hoeing fields and milking cows. And he didn't have to prove to the cows each day how much of a man he was—and his wife was too worn out to care."

He took three sips of his wine before answering. "I'll concede that point."

"Just like that? You concede my point? No argument?"

"Sometimes, you're better off not entering an argument."

"I want an argument." I surprised myself. I never had conversations like this with Luke. Luke had little interest in talk that didn't involve money and real estate. With Flynn, I used to stay up debating him until three in the morning, drunk on cocktails and concepts. I missed that like crazy.

"You. I like you." Dash winked, drumming on the table with the fingers of one hand. "Okay, I'd argue that what attracted the farmer to his farm girl wife in the first place was her softness and beauty."

"But concepts of beauty change, and they're different from culture to culture. A Rubenesque woman used to be thought of as sublime. Or a tribal woman with six rings around her neck."

"But it's all still thought of as feminine."

"What is *feminine* and what is *beauty*, if it can change so much?"

"You're destroying my argument, girl."

"Then my mission is complete."

He smiled, gulping the rest of his wine. "I'll give you something for free. I've been thinking of giving up the seminar circuit."

"Oh, yeah?"

"Yeah."

"You do this a lot? The seminars?"

"It's practically all I do. I think I've got burnout. And maybe I don't believe everything my colleagues do. Maybe I'm just waiting for something to send me in a different direction." He paused. "Or someone."

I exhaled, downing the rest of my glass of wine, too. Trying to avoid his sudden intense stare.

"So, are you," he said, "looking for a change?"

"My life is very . . . complicated."

"Ah, the *complicated* word. Sounds legit."

"I'm not just saying that."

I heard him sigh under his breath. Eyeing me directly, he shot me a dry grin. "Let me guess the trajectory of your life."

"Uh, okay."

"You're about thirty—"

"Close." *Not yet. God, but close. Too close. Next year. I used to look young for my age. What happened?*

"You did an arts degree in college, and you took a year or two off after that to travel. The usual tourist haunts, but places that are far enough off the beaten track to claim you went the road less travelled and have the photos look sufficiently quirky on Instagram. Then you pottered around the hipster crowd for years—acting in amateur theatre and maybe some slam poetry. You dated the men who excited you. Invariably, they disappointed you. Then you blundered into writing. But you'll probably get bored with that sooner or later. You'll decide at age thirty-two that what you need is to marry and pump out a couple of kids. You'll take a year or two to find a man with assets and resources and pin him down. When the brats are old enough, you'll enter the corporate world, and in your downtime, post sage and lyrical memes on Facebook." A broad but cynical smile spread across his face. "How am I doing?"

I tried to conquer the tight feeling in my jaw and throat. I had to sit here pretending to have never had a child. His analysis was missing the sudden and unexpected injection of Luke when I was twenty-six. "Sounds like a feminist wet dream. Sign me up."

He laughed.

We talked on for another half hour. I took more notes—enough to look convincing.

Moments of awkwardness followed the end of the interview. We'd had dinner, and I'd asked my questions. It was time to leave.

Dash had his eyes on me. "So, what happens now? You choose."

"Uh, isn't this where we shake hands and go our separate ways, each of us richer for the experience?"

"Hmmm. What if—*just say*—this was a date? Then what would happen?"

I thought for a moment. "I guess we'd have some after-dinner drinks in a quiet bar and have a bit of aimless chat. And then you'd ask me back to your hotel room, and I'd politely turn you down, and then after a weird silence we'd both regret the whole night, and I'd go home, and you to your hotel, and we'd each watch some unsatisfying movie and fall asleep before it ended . . ."

He lifted an eyebrow. "Interesting prediction. And hey, you've got tickets on yourself, imagining that I'd ask you back to my room."

"So, you wouldn't?" Despite everything, I was enjoying bantering with Dash. It reminded me of the person I was years ago.

"I don't know. Let's try it. We'll see what happens." He half-winked.

"Unfortunately, I have to go. I enjoyed tonight."

"Maybe we can try this again? As a date."

"Sorry, I can't."

His eyes became completely serious for perhaps the first time tonight. "Can I ask why? Do you have a husband? A kid?"

I was about to lie and answer *no* when I realised that *no* might be the truth. I didn't know for certain whether I had a husband or a child. I existed in a kind of limbo.

"I just . . . want to keep this professional," I finally answered.

When he nodded, I could see that his earlier cheer was gone.

35.   PHOEBE

Saturday night

ZIPPING MY JACKET UP TO MY neck, I paid the cab and jumped out in a quiet street near the Southern Sails Café.

The salty punch of the harbour swept past my face in a dark breeze. I ran into a quiet alley, pulling the cap over my head and tucking my hair in. Next, I wrapped a woollen scarf around my neck and up to my mouth then put on my thin hooded raincoat. It would be difficult for anyone to recognise me now.

I slipped the sheathed knife into the pocket of my jacket.

Now I was ready.

Had Dash gone straight back to his hotel room, or had he gone to a bar by himself? I guessed he hadn't gone back to his room—he had too much wiry energy. I hadn't expected to enjoy myself at dinner with him, but I had. More than I wanted to admit. It wasn't right to enjoy myself while Tommy was still missing. I had to focus.

I began walking up a block that ran parallel to my own block. Kate, and a few of the neighbours, had said they usually saw the man between nine and midnight. If I didn't spot him, I'd have to steal inside number 29. And wait.

That house had featured in my nightmares for years. And now the nightmares were back.

A rush of fear pricked the back of my legs.

I made my way around four blocks in my neighbourhood. I'd seen joggers and lone men and families bustling from their cars into their houses—trying to avoid the cold—but I hadn't seen the man. I knew his body shape and his walk. I knew the intense feeling I'd had last time I'd seen him.

I could hide myself in a neighbour's yard and wait and see if I could spot him. But if anyone saw me, they'd call the police. I could hide in Luke's parents' yard, if not for the fact that it was so damned neat, with its low, two-foot-high hedges and rows of flowers. No trees or overgrown shrubs to conceal myself behind.

There was nothing else to do but to steal inside number 29.

I rounded the corner and stepped past the houses where Kate and Pria lived. Then on past my own house and Luke's parents' house.

Bringing my arms in close to my chest, I hurried in through the gate and along the path of number 29.

I unlocked the door and replaced the key exactly in the same place under the mat. Once inside, I locked the door behind me.

The house was dead dark. I could see nothing.

Immediately, I wanted to run out again. Flee.

Any sane person would.

The room felt so cold. Colder than the street.

I had to force myself to stay here. In the darkness, with the odours of age and mildew and death in the air. Maybe I imagined I could smell death, but it was as much a part of this house as the wood and the walls and the vintage furniture.

I found my way to the sofa, almost jumping out of my skin at the feel of a cold arm. I sucked in a quick breath. The arm belonged to the store dummy. Of course it did. I'd put the dummy here, so long ago.

Don't be scared of this house, Phoebe. You and Sass, Kate, Pria, and Luke made it what it is. Bernice too. Whatever it is, you all created it.

Positioning myself behind the sofa, I knelt where I could see over the dummy's arm.

Minutes passed, measured in breaths and heartbeats.

Then came the sound of a key at the front door.

I held my breath.

A figure entered, but I could barely see their outline.

A dim light flashed on. Some kind of LED lamp that gave off a white glow.

I could see him. The man.

He carried a garbage bag in his hand—filled with bulky things.

The floorboards creaked underfoot as he crossed to the stairs. He glanced back over his broad shoulder towards the living room. And stopped.

I edged back.

What was he looking at?

From the corner of my eye I looked down at the floor. My body was casting a faint shadow. And I made that shadow move when I'd pulled myself back.

My fingers felt weak as they found their way into my pocket and unsheathed the knife.

What was he doing now?

Slowly stealing over towards me?

Waiting for me to show myself?

Did he have a knife, too?

I suppressed a scream as I heard his footsteps rushing my way.

He stopped suddenly and then walked in the opposite direction.

The door slammed.

He'd gone?

Or had he just pretended to leave, to make me come running out?

With panting breaths, I crawled to the window and peered out.

The man was walking away. Fast.

I had to follow him—the man who had just terrified me.

Shoving the knife back into my pocket, I ran out after him.

The street was already empty. I craned my head, scanning the street both ways.

Not knowing which way he'd gone, I decided to head down the hill. Breaking into a run, I reached the docks within a couple of minutes.

A shuffle of footsteps made a muted scraping sound behind me.

I looked back over my shoulder, expecting to see one of the homeless men.

There was no one.

I kept walking, sensing that someone was following me, but each time I turned, I couldn't see anything.

Crouching to the ground, I pretended to adjust my boot. With my head angled down, I raised my eyes and peered along the docks.

A stone dropped in my stomach as a tall shadow slipped behind a Moreton Bay fig tree.

The man I'd been trying to follow was following *me*.

I sprinted to the tree.

"Who are you? *Who are you?*" I demanded, my hand in my pocket, clutching the knife handle. *I have a knife, and I AM afraid to use it.*

I circled the tree.

There was no man.

Not even a shadow.

36.   PHOEBE

Sunday midday

THE MORNING SUN COMING THROUGH MY bedroom window was warm, as though the coming spring had found a pocket to spill into.

In contrast, Nan's house felt too dark and enclosed.

Looking for clothes to put on, I picked out tights, a short dress, and a thigh-length jacket. Usually, I just pulled on one of two pairs of jeans. I didn't know why I'd chosen something different today. This was the kind of gear I used to wear when I lived in London. I hadn't worn the dress since those days. Maybe the dinner with Dash had woken a dormant part of me and reminded me of my former life.

I headed downstairs. Nan sat watching a morning variety show. Two presenters were discussing funeral plans. Morning television was filled with advertisements for funeral plans and life insurance. The advertisements must seem like a constant reminder for someone nearing eighty, like Nan.

"There's porridge in the pot," she told me.

"Thanks. I'm not hungry."

She shot me a brittle look. "Are you going out again?"

"Yeah, I thought I'd—"

"With the new man?"

"No, Nan. I won't be seeing him again."

"Oh? It didn't go well last night?"

What if I needed to make the excuse of having dinner with him on another night that I wanted to watch number 29?

"It was fun," I answered. "I just meant we're not dating. It was just dinner."

"So, just what sort of thing is it?"

"It's not a thing." I exhaled, shoving my hands in my pockets. "I'm going out for a walk. Do you need anything?"

"Bring back some bread. Light rye. None of that stuff with seeds in it."

"Okay. I'll grab some."

Stepping outside, I began walking.

I found myself down at The Domain. I walked through the wide pathways of the park. Bright displays of flowers punctuated the expanses of grass.

Parents tugged small children along, the children clutching balloon animals. There must be some kind of event happening.

Jazz music saturated the air. I remembered then seeing a poster for a coming jazz festival.

I used to take Tommy to the outdoor festivals in the city. Didn't matter what it was. Tommy just enjoyed the music and people and energy. He used to be one of those children nursing a balloon animal.

Tommy's tiny bare feet had once walked here. He might have walked in the exact spot where I walked now, on his dimply toddler legs. His eyes used to open in round wonder at the sound of the St. Mary's church bells pealing. He'd danced on the pavers to the tunes of the street buskers in his uncoordinated way—he couldn't decide whether to clap or to bob up and down or to wiggle his bottom like Beyoncé. So he'd do all three at once.

A couple strolled towards me with an exuberant little boy running alongside them.

Involuntarily, I held my breath.

Tommy's size.

Hair like Tommy.

Not Tommy.

I averted my eyes like a priest stepping through a bikini parade.

I didn't want to see any more happy parents and their happy toddlers.

Threading my way through the crowds, I found an out-of-the-way spot on the grass. I sat myself down.

Once I felt strong enough, I'd walk home again. It was stupid coming here, where there were so many people.

I remembered then Luke telling me that Detective Gilroy had been trying to contact me. I took out my phone. There were four missed messages from Trent.

I returned the call.

"Hi, Phoebe," came Trent's voice over the phone.

He sounded normal. I was right—there was nothing out of the ordinary that he had to tell me.

"How are you," he asked, and he sounded like he cared.

"I'm doing well. It's Sunday again. We seem to be making a habit of these Sunday catch ups."

"I don't mind. I'll be off at a family barbeque later, but I'm just chilling now. So, still no more sleepwalking?"

"No. No sleepwalking."

"Good to hear."

He seemed to be lingering on the phone. It began to make me uneasy. If enquiring after my health was all he'd called me for, he should be winding things up now.

"Phoebe, you know that we have a team continuously working on Tommy's case, right? That process hasn't stopped since December."

"Yes?"

"Well, the team has brought something to my attention. A phone call."

"A phone call?"

"A call that you received. According to our data, it was right at the time Tommy went missing."

I froze in the silence that followed.

"Phoebe?"

"I don't know about any call."

"It's right there on the printout in my office. I can show it to you on Monday. In the exact space of minutes in which Tommy disappeared, you answered a call. I don't have any record of a call in your statement to us, but small things are easily overlooked when you're dealing with traumatic events. There was a woman at the scene who told a reporter that she witnessed you on the phone. We dismissed it back then. Reporters sometimes throw things in that aren't exactly true, just trying to find a different angle for their story. But, in the end, it checks out."

"But, didn't you talk to that woman yourself and she denied it? I don't remember her name."

"Elizabeth Farrell. She was the first person to call the police and report that Tommy was missing."

"The red-haired woman with the baby."

"Yes, that was her. When we interviewed her back then, she said you and Tommy had been in her view just before she saw you running around looking for him. She didn't mention that you'd taken a phone call. But after our team checked your phone records, just yesterday, they found the call. I paid a visit to Elizabeth personally, yesterday afternoon. She had a slightly different story."

"She did?"

"Yes. She told me that the reporter was correct. You had been on the phone. She was distressed, saying that she'd held back telling us that before because she felt sorry for you. She didn't want you to look like a . . . bad mother. She said the call was super short. That your son shouldn't have had time to wander off during such a short call."

"Who was the call from?"

"Well, we were hoping you could tell us that. We've been unable to track the call. You only spoke to this person for around a minute."

"I don't remember this at all. I didn't even have my phone—"

"As far as I understand, you lost your phone sometime that day? You told me that's why you weren't the one to call us first—because you'd lost your phone?"

"That's right."

"Well, you must have lost it sometime after that call. I'd like you to have a think on who it was. It's probably not important, but we'd like to know."

"Okay, I'll try."

"Thank you. I'd appreciate it."

When I finished the phone call to Trent, my mind was churning.

I had been on the phone when Tommy disappeared?

God. I'd let myself become distracted by a call?

Who was it?

No one had come forward to say they'd been talking to me that day on the phone. It couldn't have been Sass or Kate or Pria. Trent said the call was just a minute long. Had it just been a spam call? Some salesperson selling timeshare apartments or life insurance? Even the big banks spammed you. One of those calls could account for the short duration of the conversation and why I'd forgotten it.

Trent said it was probably not important, but why would he call specifically to ask me about it?

Prickles ran along my arms. Could the person on the phone have been the kidnapper?

Were they on the phone to me when they took Tommy, deliberately distracting me?

I gazed up at the canopy of trees.

Think.

I pictured the phone I'd had back then. It had a deep-green, diamond-patterned protective case. And a ring tone that was from David Bowie's "Rebel Rebel."

And then there it was.

A memory.

A memory of me taking my phone out at the park that day. Of me answering a call.

My lungs squeezed down, clogged with dust from the past.

Whose voice was it on the other end of the phone?

Think.

It wouldn't come to me.

I needed to go back to the beginning of that day.

The sanitised version of the day Tommy vanished began to disintegrate. The picture that I'd painted for the police and the media wasn't real. Yet, I'd ended up believing it myself.

I remembered the morning, before we left for Nan's house. I'd drunk two furtive mixer cans of bourbon from a stash I kept in the kitchen cupboard. Luke's mother had rearranged the cupboards the day before, and it had taken me ten minutes to find the cans. She'd praised me for the way I'd dressed Tommy. Her constant praise was irritating, and I was glad to be going to Nan's, even though taking a toddler to Nan's was always a trial.

I remembered walking to Nan's with Luke and sitting in her living room, watching Tommy trying to conceal the fact that he desperately wanted to touch Nan's ornaments. And Nan getting cross with him. No, not with him. With *us*. In her eyes, Luke and I were lazy parents.

In my mind, I could see Tommy's large brown eyes and his tufty blond hair that was so like Luke's, all his dimply toddler beauty.

A dull ache had started in my head that wasn't a headache. More like the boom of a drum. A slow, monotonous beat.

We left Nan's house to take Tommy to the playground.

Luke had lifted Tommy onto his shoulders. "Well, we've got the grandma thing out of the way for this week," he'd said.

"Don't even," I snapped at Luke, but in a lowered tone that diminished any power in my voice. I didn't want Tommy to tune into the change of conversation.

Luke cringed. Actually physically cringed. He knew exactly what I was referring to. His mother—Tommy's grandmother—had been staying with us for three weeks now.

"My mother won't be at our house forever," he told me. "Just until things are a bit better."

"You mean, until I'm not crazy anymore?" I said under my breath.

"You're not crazy." Luke didn't bother to quieten his voice. There was nothing in his tone that made me believe he really meant it. He sounded more like a parent trying to placate a child.

In Luke's opinion, I was on the train to crazy-town. Especially after *the incident* three weeks ago, when he came home to find me locked away in our bedroom with a bottle of scotch that one of his clients had given him. I'd been crying into my pillow, while Tommy was running loose in the house. The house was upside down, even more than usual.

Enter Luke's mother. He installed her in the spare bedroom and set her function dial to cooking, cleaning, and childcare mode.

I was the one who didn't cook. Or clean. Or look after the kid. Worse, I'd proven myself unable to cope with motherhood. The defective woman.

Luke's mother—June—was bright and cheery, with her yellow-framed glasses and cruise ship clothing (floral shirts and white capri pants).

I was never at fault in her eyes. That sounded better than it actually was.

She'd gush that I was doing a *super job* if I had a shower. She'd stand behind me and whisper that I had *mother's intuition* when I knew that Tommy was ready for sleep (the times that he started spinning in circles). She'd even tell me I was *a wonderful mother* if Tommy just survived the day.

All I could think was, no wonder Luke's father drank. Living with her would be like living with Pollyanna on steroids.

"Look." Luke gave a heavy, exaggerated, beleaguered-husband sigh. "We'll set a time-frame. How about another week? My mother stays just one more week."

I knew what would happen if I disagreed. He and his mother would gang up against me. His mother would never say anything nasty, but she'd beat me down with her cheery platitudes until I begged for mercy. Neither of them trusted me alone with my own son. Luke's parents had come back three weeks early from an overseas trip just so that June could move in with us for a while and care for Tommy (and supervise me).

From atop Luke's shoulders, Tommy yelled with excitement when he first spotted the playground.

Luke set him on the ground and let him run ahead.

A suffocating bitterness tightened around me. "Instead of her staying on, how about you change your work schedule so you can actually be at home with Tommy sometimes? So that I can go and do things? So that, oh, I don't know, so that Tommy can get to know you and we can be an actual family?"

"You know we have to make sacrifices."

I didn't know when individual Luke and individual me had become *we*.

Luke had begun speaking for both of us sometime after Tommy was born. When Luke spoke of things that he was doing, he used the *we* pronoun. Luke couldn't change his plans because *we* needed him to do exactly what he was doing.

Taking his eyes off Tommy for a moment, Luke glanced at me. "We've still got a long road ahead of us to get where we want to be."

There it was again. *We.*

"Other couples manage," I said. "You don't have to work twelve hours a day."

Tommy ran a short way then turned to check that his parents were still close behind him.

"To hell with just managing." Luke's voice rose in order to make his point. "We'll be in a very good position a few years from now if we hang tight."

"Even if it's killing me?" My words fell like a rock, dragging space and time into a vacuum. I hadn't spoken those words before. I hadn't told him how I really felt.

He stopped still. I could sense the rising irritation in his raised shoulders, in the stubborn set to his jaw. "It's fucking killing you to live in a great house in a great suburb and have your days free to do whatever you fucking want?"

"I never asked for a great house in a great suburb. And I am not *free.*"

Tommy was too far ahead now. We both jogged along the path to catch up to him.

Luke and I clamped down on our angry words as soon as we reached the playground. That's what we did. Put on the *nice* show in public. Rip strips off each other at home after Tommy was asleep for the night.

When we reached the playground, Tommy made a beeline for the water-play canals.

Squatting, Tommy zoomed his plastic yacht backwards and forwards in a canal like it was a car.

Luke's phone rang. I could tell by the almost supplicating, reassuring tone he'd swapped to that it was his mother.

Anger flashed through me. "Tell her to be gone by the time we get back."

He held his hand over the phone. "Phoebe, we'll talk about this later." He sounded so *nice*, so fucking endearing. He always pretended to be something he wasn't in front of her.

And now, if I started yelling here in front of all these people, I'd be the raving lunatic. Look at what her poor husband and child have to put up with. I had to conceal, conceal, conceal. An actor, pretending everything was wonderful.

"Tommy, do you want an ice-cream?" Luke said as he put his phone away.

Tommy thought for a second, his fist tightening on the boat, then shook his head.

"Okay, well I'm going to get one." Luke fished his sunglasses out from a pocket and put them on.

I shielded my eyes from the sun. "Just get one scoop in Tommy's."

"He just said he didn't want one."

"He thinks he'll have to leave the water to get ice-cream. Of course he wants one."

"Then he should learn to say what he wants, not make other people guess."

"He wants a fucking ice-cream, Luke."

People gawked. My voice had inexplicably carried. How my voice had amplified like that in the middle of all this noise, I didn't know. Maybe all my rage had condensed into that one sentence.

"Not in front of all the kids," he mumbled.

Of course. He was on show now. People were looking and watching. *Who was at fault here? Which one of them started it? Who should we direct our disgust at?*

Shaking his head, Luke moved off. And with that, he sealed it. I was the one to blame. Everyone here knew the story: *He was the hapless husband who was used to defusing his wife's irrational outbursts. He was the one who never struck back. His wife might even be violent. Did the kid have any bruises on him?*

When no further entertainment was forthcoming, the people turned back to their own kids. A couple of the mothers gave their children grabby hugs and kisses on foreheads. Just to demonstrate they were nothing like me. They loved their kids. Even their husbands. Hot meals on the table every night and sex on Sundays. They wore long cargo shorts and long pastel T-shirts and pastel hats. Which proved their devotion. No cleavages or cut-off shorts. Their husbands wore the same outfits their tiny sons did. Everyone looked so *good* and pure and shapeless. You could bottle them and sell them on a supermarket shelf like jars of applesauce. How would any of them know if their kid or husband was replaced with another? They wouldn't.

Tommy splashed in the canal, oblivious to my loud, angry words. He was used to them. Used to Luke and I screaming at each other. We weren't always careful. Things slipped through.

I wanted to give Tommy a different mother. It was a gift—giving your child a good mother. But you couldn't give what you didn't have.

It was okay for Luke. He got the guy card. As long as he paid the mortgage, he was good. In the eyes of the pastel T-shirt brigade, there wasn't one thing more he needed to do to be husband-and-father material. But the wife and mother, she needed to turn herself inside out, empty herself completely. Everything in life she'd been trained to do so far was useless. Her career, her personal time, her motivation to succeed—she had to let all that go.

Something was stirring in my head. The heat of the day and the pastel clothing and the slow sound of a drum.

The phone buzzed in my pocket, and I slid it out to answer it.

A voice asked me, *"Are you going to go ahead with it?"*

*

I was ripped back to present time.

Sitting in the park, staring at a phone in my hand that existed only in my memory.

A fuse blew in my head, and my brain turned to static.

Cold, dead static.

There *had* been a phone call that day.

Who was it?

I couldn't recall the sound of the voice. Just what they'd said.

What had I been *going to go ahead with*?

What had I done?

37. PHOEBE

Sunday midday

I STOOD, TERRIFIED OF THE MEMORY.

Terrified of myself.

I began walking, blundering. I had nowhere to go to be alone. If I went back to Nan's like this, she'd be examining me with her uncannily sharp senses, putting me like an ant under her magnifying glass.

Rain misted in the air, making people fan out and look for shelter.

"Whoa!" A hand reached out from the crowd and took possession of my arm.

Dash materialised in front of me. "Finished writing up lies about me yet?"

I stared at him uncomprehendingly for a moment, until my mind adjusted.

The dinner last night.

The interview.

The story.

"Dash. Hi. I haven't written it yet."

"No?"

I made an attempt to sound light-hearted. "Not quite. It's Sunday. I can't be nasty on a Sunday. Better leave it to Monday."

"Hey, are you okay? You look kind of—"

"I've got a lot on my mind."

"Need a friendly ear?"

"Thanks. But I just want to . . . walk. If you don't mind, I'll just keep going." I moved off.

He stepped beside me. "Walking's good. I can walk with you."

"Don't you have seminars to run?"

"I'm not speaking at one until nine tonight. Baxter and Eddie are doing the talks this morning. And the rest of the troops abandoned me. So, I decided to come down here and soak in a bit of the blues."

"You like this stuff?"

"You don't?"

"It's not my favourite."

"Maybe you just haven't heard the best of it."

"Maybe."

"I've been down here for a couple of hours, all alone. I was going a bit stir-crazy."

I glanced his way. "I thought stir-crazy was when you were forced into a tight situation with people you didn't want to be with."

"Yeah. I get stir-crazy in my own company. It's a curse." He glanced at me. "I'm guessing you're not like that."

"No, I'm pretty comfortable being alone."

"Is that a hint?"

Sighing softly, I stopped.

Behind us, between the exposed roots of a tree, an elderly homeless man slept. The branches of the tree above him were spread out wide. He'd be protected from the coming rain. Still, it seemed a miserable place to sleep. Briefly, I wondered if he'd ever stepped through this park when he was young, holding the hand of a woman.

"I'm just not feeling good," I told Dash.

"Why don't you come back to my hotel with me? You can relax, and we can watch a movie together. And if it's boring, we can fall asleep before it ends . . ."

I gave him a small smile. "I can't. Bye, Dash."

Walking away quickly, I headed towards the cathedral. The spired sandstone building stood across the road from the park. Maybe I could just sit in there on a pew for a while. You were allowed to be upset in a church. I watched a series of cars pull up and park beside the kerb. People in suits and evening wear bustled from the cars. There must be a wedding on. There were always weddings at the church. The church let you in sometimes when it was a funeral. But not a wedding. You were on your own in terms of sanctuary when someone was getting hitched.

I spun around.

Dash was still standing there, watching me.

His expression swapped to surprise as I walked back along the path towards him.

I didn't understand myself right now.

Didn't know myself. I didn't know what I'd done in the past, but it must have been wrong. So very wrong. I wanted something—anything—to numb the terror inside my chest. The crash of the drum—the noise and reverberation through my head.

Waking straight up to him, I took his hand. *"Let's go."*

He didn't ask questions. Wordlessly, we stepped through the streets. The city seemed restless to me. Darkening, and gathering a storm.

Our hair and clothing were damp by the time we reached Dash's hotel.

We took the elevator up to the fourteenth floor. Dash took my hand this time, leading me to his room.

His room was small, with a wide balcony that overlooked Darling Harbour.

He switched on the TV. "Any preference in movies? Comedy? Sci-fi?"

In response, I walked over and kissed him.

His hands closed around my upper arms. Pulling back slightly, he drew his eyebrows in tight as if he were figuring out a maths equation. "You said you weren't feeling well?"

I kissed him again. Deeply this time. I didn't know what I wanted or why I was even here. I just desperately needed to lose myself for a while. I didn't want to speak.

He eyed me intently, as though waiting for affirmation. When it didn't come, his eyes changed. He unbuttoned his shirt just enough to pull it over his head. His chest was as smooth and tanned as his face. He peeled off his shoes and socks and went to stretch out on the bed.

Propping himself on one elbow, he watched me, keeping his expression neutral. But his chest rose and fell at an increasing rate.

I pulled off my jacket and top and crawled onto the bed beside him.

Cradling my face, he kissed my forehead. It felt almost religious. Like he were sanctifying me. My cheeks were wet before I understood that I was crying.

He drew back, alarmed.

I shook my head faintly. "Ignore it."

He shut his eyes, exhaling. "Would I sound like the worst person ever if I said I'll ignore it if you want me to? But I can't say I've ever slept with a sad woman before. Their sadness usually comes afterward."

"I'm not sad."

"You're *something*."

I half-smiled. "I don't want to talk."

*

I woke with his arms firmly around me.

We'd had lunch together, slept together again, watched a movie, and fallen asleep again. I hadn't slept so deeply in a long time. I'd lost countless hours of sleep over the past few months, and I'd never seemed to catch it up.

He was so close I could see the tiny furrows and lines on his forehead and under his eyes and the curves of his mouth. A man who would never disappoint me (because I'd never see him again).

I didn't feel better. Anxiety still raced through my veins, burning me. I hated myself and everything about me.

I glanced at my watch. Dr Moran would be contacting me soon. I needed to get out of here within the hour. I imagined taking her call here, with Dash listening in, and the conversation I'd have with him afterwards.

Why, yes, my psych does call me every day to check on me. Doesn't everyone's?

Gently, I wriggled from his grasp. If I could leave without waking him, that would be best. No small talk or awkwardness.

My clothes were hanging over a chair on the balcony. They'd been damp with rain, and the room didn't have a clothes dryer.

He roused, and I stilled myself. With a short, deep breath, he woke fully.

Brushing back a lock of hair from my forehead, a small smile indented his cheek. "Happier?"

"Yes, happier," I lied.

He rested his head on the crook of his elbow. "*Stay.*"

"I can't."

"Why not? It's Sunday."

"Didn't you have a show to do later?"

"Yeah. I'll smuggle you in. It'd give you more to write about. You'd see me in action."

"And have to hang out with nerdy scientist geeks? No, thanks."

A vague look of confusion entered his eyes. "You think we're running seminars for *scientists*?"

"Aren't you?"

He coughed. "I . . . There's a lot of science involved."

"Well, yeah. You talk about the study of human relationships, right?" I hesitated. "Please don't talk about me."

"Can I think about you?"

I grinned, in spite of myself. "No. Wipe me from your memory banks. I was never here. You never met me."

"Okay, I'll lock you away in my heart, then."

"How sweet. But hearts can be replaced by mechanical devices, you know. They're not that special."

"Okay, you got me. You're dead to me."

I kissed him on the forehead—"Good"—and padded across to the balcony door in my underwear.

I whirled around at a sudden noise behind me.

People burst into the room. Half a dozen. Men and a giggling woman in a shiny red nightclub dress, her makeup half-on. I recognised the men from Dash's group at the Christmas in July event.

Dash jumped up from the bed. Grabbing a cushion, he held it in front of his groin. "Saskia, quick, save yourself," he said playfully. "It's too late for me. They've seen my naked body, and they won't be able to control themselves."

I hurried out to the balcony.

But the small crowd followed, cheering me.

I now had the choice of squeezing through a wall of men in my underwear or putting my dress on here. I decided to pull the dress on.

Dash, now in underwear, pushed through the middle of them. "Give her some breathing space."

"Isn't that the reporter chick from the other night?" A tall, Black American man squinted at me, like I was a strange species of animal he'd never seen before.

"Yeah, Baxter," Dash told him. "Now if you could all give us five minutes, I'd like to say good-bye to her properly—"

"No, babe." The woman pulled me by the hand. "Don't go. Stay and party. I'm outnumbered by the boys." She had a pretty (if smudged by makeup) face and was somewhere in her late thirties, her breath smelling of vodka and lemon.

"Better get out and pull some more women before the seminar tonight." A rotund man (that I remembered was named Eddie) slapped Dash on the back. "That's what we're here for."

Dash shot me an uncomfortable look. He gestured to me to leave, and I tried, but the woman was hanging onto me for grim death.

A tall man with a hawkish nose above small blue eyes and a buzz cut nodded. His name had been—what?—Billy. "Get some tail, Dash, or you're going to have nuthin' to talk about. Can't convince the people if you're all talk, no walk."

"You didn't get any last night yourself." Eddie leaned back against the balcony railing. "The tail turned tail."

A round of laughs followed.

Billy shrugged. "My game was tight. I don't know what happened with that blond bitch at the second bar. She was flirting back. I was heading toward sealing the deal. Then she went cold on me."

"Awww," squealed the woman. "Must've been worried her boyfriend was going to turn up any second."

"I snatch 'em away from underneath their boyfriend's noses," Billy told her.

"My man, you do not," scoffed Baxter.

"Dash could." The woman eyed Dash openly, flirtatiously. "He's cute. Super cute. Not really fair for the rest of you to wheel him out as an example of a guy who can pull chicks just by using a few pickup tricks."

I stared at Dash. "That's what you guys are? *Pickup artists?*"

"Please," said Eddie, pulling a fake affronted face. "*Professional* pickup artists."

"No." Dash swallowed tightly, his voice flattened. "We're not *that*. We don't use cheap tricks. We don't cheat. We call ourselves relationship experts. We give advice, and we take it seriously. And yeah, we use evolutionary psychology."

They weren't scientists.

I thought back. He'd never claimed that they were.

"Were you lying to the poor girl, Dash?" The woman used a tone that was more teasing than scolding.

"I didn't lie to her." Taking firm hold of my hand, Dash pulled me away from the group and led me inside.

I grabbed my shoes from the floor.

"I don't get it," he told me quietly, his eyes hurt. "You researched me. Dash Citrone, right? You knew what I do for a living."

"Can we just go back ten minutes? We were about to forget each other. Please."

"If that's what you want. And I'll go back to being confused as hell by you."

"Thank you."

"Are you still doing the article?"

His face fell as I shook my head. He swung the door open for me as I left.

"Shame you're not doing the write-up," he called down the corridor. "I would have liked to know what you thought of me."

I looked back over my shoulder. "Good things. *Mostly.*"

38. LUKE

Sunday afternoon

ROB KEPT HIS EYES GLUED TO a short-legged woman with petite boobs and big hips as she walked from the bar, four glasses of wine carefully balanced between her fingers. "Nice."

"Bit stumpy for my taste, mate." I shrugged.

"I like 'em like that."

The bartender handed two beers to us. We remained sitting on the stools. We'd met with a new client ten minutes ago. He'd wanted to meet at the bar of the hotel he was staying at, but he hadn't actually wanted to drink. Rob and I were left high and dry and thirsty.

I sipped my beer. "Then explain Ellie." Everything about Ellie was slim and lanky—even her hair. She was slightly taller than Rob, and when she wore high shoes, the height difference was noticeable.

"Ellie just happened. I was with a little, short girl before her. Charlotte. Something about the way she made me feel in bed was hot, like I was this big rampaging bear or something. It really turned me on."

"So, what do you feel like with Ellie? The smallest of the three bears?" I turned back to the bar, chuckling to myself.

"Real funny, Basko." Rob loosened his collar, tugging at his tie. He hated what he called his monkey suit.

"You don't appreciate Ellie enough."

"Yeah, I do. I can look at other girls, but she's the best. Anyway, she'd cut me off at the knees if I ever cheated on her."

I smiled. "She's certainly the best when it comes to sales at the agency. Ever gonna let her run the auctions?"

He shrugged to hide his sudden and obvious discomfort. "She's not ready for that."

"We'll lose her."

"She won't go to another agency."

"Won't she?"

He didn't look so sure.

Immediately, I thought about Phoebe and what I'd done with Kitty. I was going to lose Phoebe. No, I'd already lost her. I'd slept with another woman and Phoebe had been on a date with another man. Did what I'd done even count as cheating if the marriage was over? I didn't want it to be over. Maybe Kitty was what I needed for a while to get my head straight. Any man trying to deal with Phoebe would be sent around the twist. It'd cut me in two when Phoebe had asked if I was trying to decide which woman I wanted. She'd been right—I was. If Phoebe wanted me, then it was her I wanted, always. But if she didn't want me as fully as I wanted her, then I had to look elsewhere.

Three guys about our age walked past and seated themselves on the stools on the right side of me. Two of them were talking in loud, American voices about the girl they'd nailed the night before—both in the same bed, apparently. I couldn't help a mental picture from jumping into my head. One of the two was short and chubby. The other a tall, slim Black American.

The third, sitting on the stool next to me, was concentrating on his phone. I caught the message he was texting. *Change of heart. Need to see you again. Tomorrow? Please?*

I wanted to tell him to run. Don't get caught up with a woman. Be like his buddies. He was a good-looking guy. Yet he was the one running after a girl.

He glanced up and grinned, putting his mobile away. "Apologies for my friends. They shoot their mouths off everywhere they go."

I nodded, returning the smile. "Sounds like an interesting night."

"They're just making the most of it. We're only here for nine days, then to Brisbane, then home."

"What part of the US are you from?"

"Maine originally. In Seattle now."

"Loved Seattle. Haven't seen Maine. Except maybe in a mental picture when reading Stephen King novels."

He laughed. "Yep, they seem to be set in Maine. You've travelled America?"

"Not for a holiday. Just for business. We've bought up quite a few US properties, and we're sitting on them. I own a real estate business."

"Yeah? We're a lot cheaper over there than you guys. But I wouldn't mind investing here if prices are going up fast. What's a one-bedroom apartment go for near the harbour?"

"Sydney real estate's a mecca for overseas investors. But like you said, it's hell expensive. You're not going to see as much of a rise from a one-bedroom apartment as you would for a two-bedder. People want that extra bedroom and more space in general, and they're prepared to pay for it." Leaning across, I shook his hand. "I'm Luke. If you have any questions at any time, just give me a call." I pulled out a business card from my wallet.

"Thanks." He took the card. "I'm Dash. Dash Citrone."

"Yo! Dash!" One of the guys that Dash had come in with hollered at him, even though he was only a couple of feet away. "You famous, man. You're on TV!"

I glanced up at the TV. The guy sitting beside me was indeed up there on the screen. On a hotel balcony no less, pulling up his trousers. A group of five men stood there with Dash, clapping and cheering. The other two that were at the bar were there on the balcony, too. There were two women, one of them facing away from the camera, shimmying into a tight dress. Some wild party that must have been.

Six men. Two girls.

"Oh, man, no . . ." Dash groaned. He jumped from the stool, watching the screen in shock. "How the hell did anyone get footage of *that*?"

"They must've been filming from the balcony straight across from ours." The tall dark guy beamed.

The girl in the tight dress turned.

She had Phoebe's face.

But she couldn't be Phoebe.

"There's that chick you porked," the fat guy snorted. "She got out of there fast after we showed up."

My brain refused to catch up with what was happening on the screen. My thoughts stuck in wet cement.

A voiceover began on the TV while the scenes repeated in a loop.

In the latest of a series of bizarre incidents, Phoebe Basko—the mother of missing Sydney toddler Tommy Basko—was seen cavorting half-naked with a group of notorious American pickup artists. The men are here to run seminars that instruct men on how to pick up women for sex.

Just days ago, Phoebe Basko was taken away by police from a Cremorne-bound ferry for accosting an elderly woman. Mrs Basko reportedly believed that the woman was sending her kidnapper-style letters about her missing son. This belief was found by police to be baseless.

Last week, Mrs Basko and her husband, Luke, received three letters in rhyme about their son, Tommy, and the day he disappeared from a Sydney playground. Police investigations have so far been unable to uncover the identity of the writer of these letters.

Pictures of Phoebe flashed on the screen. Pictures of Tommy.

Citrone threw up his hands as he turned back to his friends. "Her name's *Phoebe*? And she's married? *And* she's got a missing son? Fuck, I had no idea. Explains why she was so secretive."

Dots connected in my head, each point firing and exploding.

The man standing beside me had sex with my wife. And who knows how many of the others she'd slept with? But I had one name for certain. Dash Citrone. It was Phoebe he'd been texting.

By the time I pulled myself to my feet, I could no longer think or breathe. Swinging my clenched fist, I punched Citrone in the jaw. He crashed backward over the stool.

Arms grabbed me from behind. "Luke! Leave it alone!" Rob wrestled me away.

I should have been grateful that Rob was pulling me towards the exit. Because I wanted to smash Citrone into the ground until there was nothing left of him.

Rob insisted on driving me home, telling me he'd go back to the bar and smooth things over and make sure that Citrone didn't lay charges.

Finally, I agreed. Rob was right. Something like this could blow up bigger than Ben Hur. Especially if the media got hold of it. Our company could be affected.

What the hell was Phoebe doing in a hotel room with American pickup artists? Was it an attempt to get back at me?

Rob dropped me outside my house.

I should have headed straight inside. But the rage I felt inside kept me there on the street. As Rob pulled away, I took out my phone, my mind raging, calling Phoebe every name under the sun as I tried repeatedly to get her on the phone. As I expected, she didn't answer. If she wasn't with Citrone anymore, where was she? Out partying with other men?

My chest sank as I turned and walked to my gate.

Something was in the mailbox. I realised I hadn't checked the mail since last Thursday. I pushed the mailbox key in and retrieved three letters. Two bills and one plain envelope.

One plain blue envelope.

Phoebe wouldn't, would she? She wouldn't send yet another letter?

The answer came to me.

Yes, she would.

My wife was batshit crazy.

I tore the envelope open. And unfolded the thick blue paper inside.

My knees buckled when I saw what was on the page. I fell to my hands and knees, vomiting into the garden.

39.   PHOEBE

Sunday afternoon

I WALKED THE BUSY CITY STREET, barely feeling the cold air on my bare legs. I wasn't wearing the tights that I'd been wearing when I left Nan's house this morning. I'd dressed in a flash when Dash's crowd had turned up.

God, they were *pickup artists*. Why hadn't I guessed? Or at least found out Dash's full name and looked him up. I'd been too focused on my own things.

Switching on my phone, I smiled at a text from Dash: *Change of heart. Need to see you again. Tomorrow? Please?*

He'd sent the message half an hour ago. I'd been making my way through the city since I left his hotel, and I was about to enter the playground. Normally, I avoided this area—the anxiety attacks that it triggered made me visibly tremble.

But I needed to remember more about the phone calls.

After grabbing a coffee and croissant from a café, I continued on to the water play canals. The area was largely empty, the rain having driven most families away. And night was drawing in fast. In July, night fell by five. Only a scattering of children and their parents wandered through the playground.

Sitting at the edge of one of the canals, in the exact place where I'd last seen Tommy, I set my coffee and paper bag down beside me. I slipped off my shoes and let my toes slide down into the frigid water. Tommy had played with his yacht here.

People stared at the strange woman sticking her feet in the water on a winter's day, but I didn't care.

I watched the tiny, trickling stream. Desperately trying to remember the voice on the phone that day six months ago. I ate a portion of the croissant and tossed the uneaten part to the pigeons.

I became aware of people on the edges of the playground that didn't seem like parents or tourists. They were looking for someone.

One of them looked my way and froze.

Suddenly, I knew who they were looking for.

They jogged straight towards me, as though I was about to flee instead of sitting here quietly with my shoes off. Something about them told me they were police. Plainclothes police.

Something was wrong. Something new and terrifying.

The shorter of the two reached me first. "Mrs Basko? Phoebe Basko?"

"Yes?"

"I'm Detective Gillian Farley. And this is Detective Kelsey Donahue." She gestured towards the second woman who'd arrived. "We'd like you to come down to the station with us. There's an urgent matter."

"About Tommy?"

Detective Farley eyed the other detective before looking back at me. "I'm afraid we don't have any information about this. Detective Gilroy needs to see you. That's all we know."

This wasn't about Tommy directly. It was about me. Was it the phone call from six months ago? Had they worked out who was at the other end of the call?

Holding my breath, I gave a sharp nod. I walked with them to their car—unmarked, of course. It was obvious to me that they knew exactly why I was being brought in. It was obvious in every attempt they made to talk about the weather and the jazz festival as Detective Farley drove the busy city roads.

I refused to talk.

I'd had enough of games.

There was an eeriness about the police station when I walked inside with the detectives. Everything seemed to be swept up, everything concentrated on one point. And that one point centred on me. The faces of the police throughout the station turned to me as I was escorted by the two detectives into the interview room.

Elliot—Kate's husband—was one of the constables behind the counter today. I avoided his face.

Three detectives with deadpan expressions waited inside the interview room. Trent Gilroy, Annabelle Yarris and Ali Haleemi.

I knew all their names, like characters in a TV series.

Luke was there, too. Just like another character. He eyed me with the same deadly serious expression as the detectives. Nothing like a husband would look at a wife. No sense of familiarity there.

What was happening? Why wouldn't anyone tell me? What was it that had dragged Trent Gilroy into the station on a Sunday?

Trent asked me to take a seat. "Phoebe, I'm going to ask you a question, and then I'm going to ask you to look at something."

I seated myself without answering.

"Firstly, the question," he said. "Did you send another letter?"

Was he testing me in some way? Or was there really, actually, another letter? I shook my head.

"Are you certain?"

"Why are you asking me?"

"Because of this." He turned his laptop computer around so that I could see the screen.

I cried out loud.

An image of a piece of blue paper with fold marks.

A rhyme, like the others.

But more than that.

A large splash of dried blood—droplets of it sprayed across the printed words.

My stomach gripped itself as I turned my head, bile shooting into the back of my throat.

"Forensics has already made a number of findings about the blood," Trent continued in a matter-of-fact tone. "Is there anything you want to tell us about the blood on this letter?"

"God, please don't let it be Tommy's."

"We've run tests," Trent said. "I have to tell you that it *is* Tommy's blood."

I covered my mouth with both hands, scarcely able to breathe.

Tommy's blood.

I stared across at Luke. He stared back, his eyes grown fierce.

Trent watched the exchange between Luke and me and then spoke again. "The next thing I have to tell you is that the blood is not fresh. It's old. The lab says it could be as many as six months old."

Six months.

My eyes tracked back to the computer screen as I realised I hadn't yet read the rhyme:

Little Boy Blue
Lie down to sleep
Unwanted baby
Rest in peace

A raw, physical pain tore through my body.

Rest in peace.

Tommy wasn't supposed to be resting in peace. He was a little boy.

In desperation, I looked to Luke again.

There was no comfort in Luke.

No warm place in this room.

"Phoebe," came Trent's voice. "Your doctor is on her way here. I need to tell you that the case with these letters has now taken a very different turn."

"Wait," I cried, "you have a camera. You can see who put the letter there. You can see for yourself."

By the look on Detective Haleemi's face, I could tell there was a problem. "We took the camera away yesterday," he told me. "We didn't believe that it was needed anymore."

Trent walked across to stand in front of me. "Forget the camera, Phoebe. We've already been through all that. We'd like to ask you some questions. I'll inform you of your rights first. You have the right to remain silent and engage a lawyer before you communicate with us again."

40. PHOEBE

Sunday night

I WAS INSTRUCTED NOT TO LEAVE my neighbourhood. The police were in the process of gathering evidence. I wasn't under arrest, but in all possibility, it was a matter of time before I was.

The process of searching the two houses I'd lived at had begun. I was to stay in the house while they were searching, next to Detective Annabelle Yarris, who'd been assigned to watch me.

Annabelle turned on the TV, either bored or to give me something to take my mind off the search. I discovered that the whole world knew about Dash and me and the hotel room. She switched the channel, but not before I'd seen exactly what the world had seen.

I had no secrets left. No privacy.

I wasn't a person with rights anymore.

No quiet space in which to mourn Tommy.

No time to grapple with the contents of the fourth letter.

The police took three hours to search my marital home. Luke doled out tea and coffee to everyone from the kitchen, avoiding me completely.

The police made a mess of Tommy's room. All of his things, everywhere. Things his little hands had touched tossed carelessly to the floor. They took away with them a book that had been passed down to me by my mother—a book of old rhymes: *Peter, Peter Pumpkin Eater, Georgie Porgie, Little Miss Muffet, Little Boy Blue* . . .

Outside, a machine drilled down in Luke's perfect lawn and took soil samples.

Having found nothing, they turned their attention to Nan's house.

Nan's face was chalky as I was brought inside. She'd already had a visit from the detectives—telling her what had happened and what was about to happen to her house.

She grabbed my hand, squeezing my fingers together. "I don't understand this, Phoebe. Any of it." It was a phrase she was to repeat over and over as the day wore on.

Annabelle steered Nan and I into the living room before the police flooded in.

I sat next to Nan on the sofa, too numb to speak.

Annabelle stayed with us, seeming oblivious to the state Nan and I were in. I guessed it was normal for her, seeing people like this, people in the worst situations of their lives.

With a rigid expression, Nan handed me a letter. An official government letter. It had been hand-delivered today. She had three months in which to find another place to live. The date for the demolition of her house was set. I reached for her hand, but I couldn't give her any real comfort. All I had done was to add to her trauma.

The media appeared out of nowhere outside, like leeches in damp weather. Nan looked as though she wanted to go out and shoo them all away. The media had already had their juicy piece of scandal today. But now they were getting bonus gifts. Tommy Basko's mother had not only *cavorted* with men in a hotel room, but she was the one who'd penned the kidnapper letters, *and* she was on the brink of being charged with her own son's murder.

Bang. Clatter. Bang.

Doors and drawers being opened and closed. Nan trembled with every sound the police made through the house.

I noticed the chipped edges on the walls where the wallpaper met and the frayed edges of the carpet—things I was normally immune to.

The house hadn't seen anything new since my mother was alive. I knew that these were the things that the police were seeing. When you walked through a house for the first time, you zeroed in on all its spots and scars and wrinkles. Just like when you met a new person for the first time. But once you'd lived in a house for a while, or once you'd known a person for a while, you stopped seeing the faults. Luke always said that it was impossible for homeowners to see their own homes with fresh eyes—when they went to sell their house, they always overvalued it because all they saw were the memories.

Bang. Clatter. Bang.

I couldn't bear the noises anymore.

With my arms over my ears and head, I tried to close it all out. I was an animal whose burrow was being torn apart by rampaging ferrets on the trail of a rabbit.

They'd forced their way in, and no one could get them out.

The sounds, the sounds the sounds. The hammering, the hollow echoes of walls, the protests of hundred-year-old floorboards as they were wrenched from their moorings. The ferrets were moving between the walls, beneath the floorboards, scurrying across the roof, digging in the yard.

Clatter. Clatter. Smash. There went another of Nan's pot plants. They weren't careful, the ferrets. They didn't need to be. The ferrets had a licence to destroy your home.

But they'd never find Tommy.

Because they didn't know where to look.

The ferrets didn't know where to find the rabbit.

Nan clutched the arms of her chair as the sharp sound of metal on metal rang from outside. She rose to her feet. Annabelle tried to stop her.

"This is my property," Nan reminded her curtly, her voice ragged.

Annabelle hesitated then stepped aside.

I stepped along the hallway after Nan.

In the courtyard, two police were on bended knee, breaking the lock of the toolshed. The ivy had already been ripped from the exterior of the shed.

Dread and blood rushed into my head until all I could hear was a drum thrashing. That drumbeat. I'd heard it at the back of my mind for so long. So long.

"Surely this is unnecessary? It's just an old shed," Nan said bitterly, to no one in particular. She stepped in front of Trent.

Detective Yarris tried to lead Nan away. "Mrs Hoskins, if you'll just step over here for a moment. This won't take long."

"Take your hand off me," Nan told her.

Annabelle surveyed Nan coolly. "If I do that, will you stand here quietly?"

Nan reluctantly moved a few inches, not completely giving way.

A final hammering at the lock made it fall away.

Detective Gilroy strode forward.

The old shed seemed startled as Trent pushed its doors open and the glare of police spotlights streamed inside. All of its spades and rusted tins of paint and crates of tools exposed.

Everything grew quiet.

Dead quiet.

There was something in the shed that I couldn't see.

Trent turned back to glance at me questioningly.

The dozen or so police in the tiny yard moved aside as I stepped to the shed.

I now had a view of two large plastic bags that I'd never seen in there before. The bags weren't old. They hadn't gathered the signs of age that the other things in the shed had.

There were mangled shapes inside the bags. Twisted things.

Pulling plastic gloves on, Trent edged his way in around the crates. Carefully, he untied each bag.

A police photographer stepped inside, snapping pictures.

Trent dragged out a large teddy bear—Tommy's bear—half-destroyed, its stuffing spilling out. Trent pulled more things from the bags. All toys. The missing stuffed toys and trucks that had belonged to Tommy. Either smashed or cut open.

There was something large in the second bag. Detective Gilroy spread the plastic back.

Tommy's nightlight.

Mangled.

My mind in chaos, I twisted around to Nan. "Who did this to Tommy's things?"

She folded her arms in against her chest. "You did."

I shook my head. She hadn't understood my question.

"It was you, Phoebe," she repeated.

"Why are you lying?" I didn't understand why my own grandmother would say such a thing.

Lifting her glasses, she rubbed away the wet that had gathered under her eyes. "It was in November of last year. You weren't well. Not well at all. You tore up the cushions in the house and smashed the vases and plates. And yes, you did this to Tommy's toys."

"I didn't . . ."

"I know you don't remember. You'd been drinking heavily. The drinking made you forget things all the time back then. On this day, you called me on the phone and begged me to make you stop. I rushed straight up there with Bernice and her mother. We cleaned everything up. But you wouldn't let us throw anything away. You said you wanted to fix it all and make it right again, when you were better. So I had to keep them. But there was no possible way of fixing those things."

It couldn't be true. It couldn't be. My voice weakened. "Where was Tommy when this was happening?"

She moistened her lips. "He was there. He was very frightened. Bernice took him with her back to her house while Mrs Wick and I did the clean-up. We had it all sorted before Luke came home from work."

Hot tears burned the edges of my eyes. The memory was vague. But I remembered snatches of it now. I'd been drinking since that morning, rage slowly building inside me. The sound of the drum relentless in my head.

Stepping to Nan, I took her arm. "But why would you keep it so secret? The toys in the shed?"

Nan took in a shuddering breath. "That day, after you calmed down and realised what you'd done, you went hysterical. You threatened to kill yourself. Said you were no good as a mother. I was afraid for you. The next day, when you didn't seem to recall what you'd done or what had happened to the toys, I thought it was all best forgotten."

"I'm sorry, Nan," I whispered to her.

Her fingers shook as she unfolded her arms and twisted her fingers together. "I never understood what the trouble was with you, but I did try to help you. Maybe I just didn't do enough."

I saw fear bright in her eyes. Did she believe that I'd killed Tommy? She knew about the fourth letter and the rhyme and the blood—everybody did.

No, I had no memory of hurting Tommy. No memory . . .

But was my memory enough?

I hadn't remembered what was in the tool shed. No wonder I'd dreamed of Tommy trying to get in there. He'd wanted his toys.

"I thought Luke's mother threw Tommy's things away," I said, my voice falling away.

"I know. In the weeks after that day, you had another episode," Nan told me. "Luke came home to find you'd been drinking and not watching Tommy. I tried to get him to have you sent somewhere to get better. But instead, he got his mother to come stay with you. You blamed her for taking away Tommy's toys. But they were already gone."

"But I did get better," I said. "I know I got better." But was that only because I'd had Luke's mother to feel resentful of, rather than my own life?

"Yes, you did get better," she agreed, but she didn't sound entirely convinced.

The detectives were all observing me closely as the conversation between Nan and me ended.

"Phoebe," Trent Gilroy said, "I have to inform you that you have become the primary person of interest in this case. Do you know what that means?"

I swallowed, feeling dry and burned inside. "It means you think I'm the one who hurt Tommy."

He hesitated, the blip line in his forehead deepening. "I'd suggest you get yourself a good lawyer, Phoebe. We're going to need to have you in for questioning. Within the week."

Trent Gilroy's face was very different to the way I'd always seen it before. This was a grim, masked face that was closed to me.

I gave a dazed nod.

Police were carrying the destroyed toys out of the shed. I watched them carry the nightlight past me.

Sleep, Tommy. Sleep.

I no longer needed to find out where the nightlight had gone.

And I didn't even want to remember who I'd been on the phone with the day Tommy went missing anymore.

But it was too late.

I remembered.

41. LUKE

Sunday night

IT SEEMED LIKE A GIANT STICK had pried the whole neighbourhood out of their burrows. There was nothing like red and blue police lights to tear people away from their TV sets.

I sat on the low brick wall outside Nan's house, not caring who saw me or who filmed me. I couldn't stand another minute of being inside Nan's house or yard. The sight of Tommy's destroyed playthings had sickened me.

I wanted to go to Kitty's. But as much as I didn't care who was watching me, I couldn't bring her into it. And a camera crew might decide to follow me.

My wife was a monster. Nan had done way too much covering up for her.

I'd married a woman who'd murdered our son.

What had she done to Tommy? Who had helped her? Someone else had to have been there that day at the playground to abduct Tommy. Phoebe had planned this.

Maybe soon, when I found out what happened to him, I could finally grieve. I'd kept it all locked up tight for so long. There'd been no closure. No funeral.

A car pulled up across the road, behind the police cars. A middle-aged woman rushed out. My mother. My father followed, a lot slower in gait.

Mum crushed me to her in a bear hug. "My God, Luke. We were on our way home when we heard the news. We'd planned to stay overnight at your Aunty Felicity's on the way, but when we heard the news, we just kept driving."

"Mum . . . it was her. All along."

"I didn't want to tell you this before, but I always suspected her. But let's not talk about that here. Too many people about. Let's get you back to our house and leave them all to it. We'll take Phoebe's grandmother with us too. She's probably half having a heart attack by this, poor old lady."

"We'll be looking after her," came a sharp voice from next door.

It was Mrs Wick. Bernice and her mother were on their front lawn in their dressing gowns.

Mrs Wick stepped from her lawn across to Nan's. "Bernie and I'll be right there with Coral, helping get her place back in order. Coral and I have always lived in our own homes. We don't just up and leave when there's trouble. Now get away with you."

"Tommy was our grandchild," Mum said coldly. "We have a right to be here."

"Not on Coral's property, you don't," Mrs Wick informed her.

"Fuck off." I took a step towards Mrs Wick.

My mother took hold of my arm. "It's not the time or the place, Luke. People are watching."

Bernice moved from the shadows of her house into the light. She shot my parents a look of what I could only describe as barely concealed hatred. She'd been a weird girl, and she'd become an even weirder woman. I could guess that Bernice hated me and my family because we were not fucked up in the head, like she was.

My mother led me away, past the Wick house and past number 29 to their house. Dad trailed behind.

"Bernice is unusual. I'll say that for her," my mother said quietly, even though she no longer needed to be quiet. Bernice was way out of earshot. "She should have got herself away from here and started her life a long time ago."

"Yes, that would have been for the best. Poor Bernice," my father said in a defeated voice.

I wanted to punch him in his soft gut. I hated the way he spoke through a sigh. He hadn't stood up for my mother against Mrs Wick. He was always so damned placid.

And why the hell were either of them wasting energy talking about Bernice? They'd often said the same things about her over the years. What kind of catastrophe would have to happen before their normal lines of conversation swapped to the present moment instead of the past? An earthquake? *Jesus.*

Mum unlocked the door and herded us inside. The house smelled a little musty, but it looked the same as always. Everything in place.

While Dad settled into his armchair, Mum buzzed about, getting tea and coffee.

It was only after Dad had dozed off to sleep and Mum had mentioned Tommy's name to me that I cried like a baby in her arms.

42. PHOEBE

Monday morning

I SLEPT FITFULLY, MY MIND ROARING with nightmares and then snapping awake. My dreams rushed and jumped from scene to scene.

My mother, sitting on her bed, counting her collection of buttons. Calmly, she looks up at me and asks, "What did you do to Tommy?"

I can't answer. My mouth is too dry, and my head hurts, and I can't remember. Bending her head over her tin of buttons, she returns to counting. I run from the room, catching my reflection in the hall mirror.

I'm gawky and reedy in my school uniform, and I'm no older than twelve or thirteen. Stomping back to her bedroom, I want to scream at her to stop counting the damned buttons, but she's gone. The tin of buttons remains on the bed, half uncounted.

JUMP.

A nightclub. Frenetic, pulsing electronic music. Saskia and Pria's hair flying as they dance, red and yellow lights strobing across their faces. Sass is in her element.

It's December last year. I've been leaving Tommy with Luke on Friday nights and heading out with Saskia. Pria doesn't come along often.

Sass thinks I should leave Luke. Says he's no good for me. Sass and I get drunk and wild on our nights out, just like in the old days.

I'm wearing a new dress and feeling good. I've lost a lot of the pregnancy weight, though I've still got a long way to go. My hair's been newly shaped and layered to just above my shoulders, and it swings when I move. I love, love, love the feeling of my hair swinging as I dance. I'm also very drunk. And Sass gave me a party pill earlier. The lights of the dance floor pop before my eyes, and I'm sure the music is plugged into every nerve in my body.

Sass is sick suddenly and needs to go home—the pill had a bad effect on her. I stay at the nightclub with Pria, having too much fun to go home.

Someone taps my shoulder. I whirl around to a handsome face. We dance. He moves closer. Asks my name. Wants to know if he can have my number. I shake my head, but I'm laughing. Happy.

We kiss. He grins at me. Stays with me all night at the club. Says he wants to take me home with him. To the USA. His face . . . is Dash's face.

Dash is visiting Sydney, but I don't hear the reason why over the pumping music.

JUMP.

Tommy splashes near my feet. We're in the playground. Luke's gone to get ice-creams. My phone rings. Rebel rebel, goes the ring tone. I'd forgotten I was supposed to be taking a phone call right now. I'd planned it the day before. The cans of bourbon had made me forget. Squeezing my eyes shut, I pull out my phone and answer.

The man who speaks is Flynn O'Callaghan. Calling me from London. His voice floods inside me, into every part of me. I can picture him as he speaks. He's glorious, with his Irish accent and his crooked way of lifting his eyebrow at me.

He called me up out of the blue six weeks ago. Just friends, just catching up. At first. But it soon became clear to both of us that the spark between us had never extinguished. The following weeks, things became hot, heavy, and delirious over the phone.

Until the day he asked me if I'd leave Luke and go live with him in London.

Now, at the playground, I'm listening to the drumming inside my mind and chest as I hold the phone to my ear.

"Are you going to go ahead with it?" he asks.

"I want to," I tell him, my voice uncertain.

"Then please, Phoebe. You know what you need to do."

I'm nodding even before I answer.

JUMP.

I'm plunging scissors into the giant bear, tearing into it, letting its stuffing spill free. Then, Tommy's face is there, his wide eyes staring up at me, and I've still got the scissors . . .

With a gasping scream, I woke. Not a terrified scream but an enraged yell.

God, what had I done?

I ran to the shower and wrenched the tap around with both hands. I stood under the too-hot water in my sleep shirt, wanting to burn myself. Shaking, I slid to the floor of the shower and let my tears flow with the scalding water.

It had been Flynn on the phone that day. Flynn urging me to jump on a plane and meet him in London. I'd blanked that out. Yes, I'd sneaked a few drinks that morning before Luke and I left home (to help me deal with Luke's mother now being my live-in guardian) but I wasn't drunk. It must have been the intense shock of losing Tommy (and then Saskia urging me to look like the perfect wife and mother) that had caused the blank. Whenever I'd thought back to that day over the past few months, my mind had switched off during the point Flynn had called me. Like a TV set momentarily losing reception.

Nan tapped on the door. "Phoebe! Are you all right?"

"Yes," I rasped.

I wound the water off again. Wrapping a towel around myself, I headed back for my room and balled myself up on the bed. When the heat left my body, I began shivering in the chilled early-morning air.

I remained like that, in my wet clothing, until I heard angry voices outside.

Crossing the floor, I glanced down from my window into the street. The reporters were still there from yesterday, but they'd been joined now by a crowd of at least thirty people. They were yelling things I couldn't quite hear, except for one word. One clear word. *Murderer.*

I shrunk back when two of them spotted me at the window.

Taking the damp towel from the bed, I hung it over a chair and then dressed myself. I couldn't go out. I was a prisoner. Not that I had anywhere to go.

My phone buzzed, and I switched it on. There was a message from Kate. But I couldn't bear to talk to anyone right now. I was about to switch the phone off again when an alert jumped up on my news app. An alert about Phoebe Basko. I tapped on it.

My heart sank through my chest as I read the short article:

The blood-soaked "kidnapper" letter is the fourth letter to be sent to Luke and Phoebe Basko. Police forensics have confirmed that the blood on the letter belongs to Tommy Basko. The blood is estimated to be six months old, possibly from around the time that Tommy was first reported missing.

Police allege that the letters were written by Phoebe Basko herself, the mother of Tommy. Her fingerprints were found inside all four envelopes, the last two of which were sealed at the time that either the police or Mr Basko gained access to them. A hidden police camera recorded Mrs Basko placing the third letter in her own mailbox.

In another twist to this explosive case, it's been confirmed that Mrs Basko received a phone call from a mysterious person in the minutes before Tommy vanished from the inner city playground.

Police investigations are expected to concentrate on finding the identity of the person on the other end of this phone call. It is assumed that this person is connected with Tommy's disappearance, possibly having abducted Tommy under Mrs Basko's direction.

Police are confident they're closing in on a resolution to the case and finding out what happened to Tommy.

It is expected that Mrs Basko will be under arrest by this afternoon.

I was going to be under arrest today . . .

Of course, what else did I expect? Murderers got arrested. Even if I arranged for someone else to do it, I was still a murderer.

But how could they be talking about Tommy and me? It was surely a news story about another mother and child, one of those stories that you read in the news that was so terrible you couldn't believe it had really happened.

I scrolled down the page to a battery of reader comments under the story.

Slaughter the murdering slut the way she slaughtered her kid!

Drop her in prison, from a great height. Then let the prisoners rip into what's left of her!

I never trusted that po-faced bitch!

The comments got worse. People hoping I'd get raped and disembowelled. Hundreds more comments followed. I threw the phone onto my bed like it had seared my hand.

I heard someone talking to Nan, downstairs. *Mrs Wick.* I guessed she'd come over to help Nan tidy the house.

I needed to go and help Nan, too. If I was going to be leaving this house today, I had to do this one last thing. To help clean up the mess caused by me.

Mrs Wick met me with a lingering gaze as I descended the stairs. She never held back on staring at people with her tiny, caustic eyes.

"I feel awful for your nan," she informed me.

"I'm sorry for her, too." I kept walking, out to the kitchen.

"She shouldn't have to deal with something like this at this stage of her life. She'll go down, you know. And once old people go down, they often don't get up again. Like Gladys at number 26. I knew that once they put her in a wheelchair, she was gone." She paused, only to end with, "Dead within weeks."

Her voice followed me along the hallway. She'd put it as though I were a disease that would end up killing Nan. I'd sensed fear in Mrs Wick's tone. Fear that yet another old person that she knew was going to die.

Nan came in from the yard. She'd been pegging out clothes on the line. It was Nan's washing day, and she was obviously determined to stick with her routine. She nodded an acknowledgement at me as she passed into the living room. Her eyes were red, and I guessed she'd been crying while hanging out the clothes. I wanted to hug her, but Mrs Wick's words rung in my head. I was a disease. There was no comfort in me. Only hurt and pain.

I started on the kitchen first. All of the cupboards had been emptied by the police.

The process of putting all Nan's things away felt oddly like trying to put the meat back onto bones. It couldn't be done. The memories of the house had been stripped away. New memories replaced the old. Scenes of police tramping through the hallways and rooms, touching everything and disturbing the time-worn order.

Nan and I didn't speak much. And we stayed away from the windows. The media were ready to feed on the rotting meat.

When there was nothing left to put away, I headed upstairs. Mrs Wick eyed me with a hostile gaze, a possessive hand on Nan's shoulder.

Kate called again, and this time I answered. She gave me the name and number of a lawyer that she and Elliot knew. The conversation was short and awkward, Kate steering clear of all topics except the lawyer's reputation and to ask how I was.

Pria called shortly afterwards, and although she wasn't awkward, it was far from a normal conversation. She simply said that I was in her thoughts. It didn't take rocket science for me to guess that she and Kate were together, either at her house or Kate's, talking about me and then making the calls.

Sass hadn't called. But suddenly, I wanted to hear her voice. She'd always billed herself as my oldest friend. And it was true that she was. We'd first met each other as newborn babies. We were like family. And I had no siblings, no parents. Today was maybe the last time I'd ever speak to her, and I wanted to say good-bye.

I dialled her number, but her phone kept ringing. I was about to hang up when she answered.

"Hi . . . Phoebe." Her voice was stiff. Was I imagining that? No, I wasn't imagining it.

"How did the funeral go?"

"You know us. We made a bit of a celebration of it. Like Nanna Rosie would have wanted."

"How's your mum doing?"

"She's coping with it a lot better now."

"That's good."

A pause followed before she spoke again. "I have to go, Phoebe. Family stuff."

She wasn't convincing. I didn't blame her. And I didn't even know what I had hoped for in calling her. It wasn't like Sass not to want to take control of the conversation and run on about everything that happened. Nothing, not even a funeral, dampened what everyone unkindly called her motor mouth. Sass dealt with everything by talking—whether she was happy or sad.

"You've heard the news here?" I ventured, my voice as thin as burned paper.

Another pause. "I didn't want to say this to you, but you brought it up. Yes, I heard the whole thing. About the letters. And the toys. I—" She stopped and started again. "*Why?*"

I felt like I'd been punched in the throat. "Sass, I don't remember . . . anything."

"He was beautiful." Her voice caught.

"I know."

"I can't . . . talk to you right now. I'm sorry. Bye, Phoebe."

The phone went dead.

I collapsed into my chair.

The trembling started up again fresh.

Dr Moran called at two in the afternoon. I had the stupid thought that it was too early for her to call for the *small steps* program. She told me that she'd spoken with Detective Gilroy and delayed my arrest, organising instead for me to go to a mental health facility. Luke had just been to see her. He'd barged into her clinic demanding to know if I'd admitted murdering Tommy to her. He'd told her I was nuts. That I'd tried drowning myself in the bath. Worried that I was at risk of suicide, she'd responded by ordering him out and arranging for me to go somewhere where I could be watched. Which had enraged Luke more, accusing her of trying to have me declared insane, to make it easier for a lawyer to get me off a charge of murder.

I sat in my room, waiting.

There was no more *looking for Tommy*. By anyone. The focus was all on me, waiting for me to get a bit less crazy and tell everyone where he was.

When the staff from the Greensthorne facility came to get me, I took my packed bag downstairs and kissed Nan good-bye. She clung to my arm for a moment then turned her face away from me.

Tall buildings blurred past me as I was driven to the facility at North Sydney. My room was small and painted blue, with a painting of a rainforest on the wall. No glass covering the painting of course and nowhere high within the room to hang anything from—nothing for a resident to use to kill themselves.

A broad-faced man with a tiny, pursed mouth showed me around Greensthorne. It looked like a small country hospital, except for the view of the city from the upstairs floors. Long halls smelling faintly of antiseptic. Lots of paintings of sultry rainforests and tropical birds. Outside, high black metal fences surrounded the entire property, the bushy bamboo failing to hide the spikes on top of the fences.

The residents gazed at me with either probing or open stares. I'd been instructed to wear sunglasses and a large hat or hooded top—even inside the facility. If people recognised me, they might try to hurt me. No one took a good view of child killers.

I stayed in my room after the tour.

Visiting hours were until half past eight at night. Luke tried to come and see me at seven, but I refused his visit. I knew what he wanted from me. To tell him where his son was.

At ten o'clock, I peered around the corner of my doorframe to ensure no one was coming and then knelt down next to my suitcase. In a locked, zippered pocket, I'd hidden my sleeping pills. I knew they wouldn't like for me to bring my own pills. They'd be deciding what medication I had and when. They'd already looked through my bag— *just standard procedure, they'd said*—but they hadn't found the hidden compartment. Luke used to joke that this was my drug-runner suitcase.

I'd take the last of the pills every night until there were none left. Just so that I could see Tommy. It would be the last time I'd ever see his face so vividly.

I locked the compartment securely and swallowed the pills with a drink of water from the plastic jug beside the bed.

It didn't matter if I sleepwalked here. I couldn't get out, and they were used to people acting strange here. I had nothing to hide, anymore.

All I wanted now was to sleep and dream.

I spent Tuesday and Wednesday in a haze, hidden behind my hat and sunglasses.

When the nights came, I returned to my stash of sleeping pills, to begin the dreams again and find my way back to Tommy.

This was all I had now. This was all I wanted.

43. PHOEBE

Wednesday night

SOMEONE WAS TOUCHING MY HAIR.

Inhaling a sharp breath, I rolled over.

Tommy stood next to the bed, stroking my hair. *"Shweep, mumma, shweep."*

"Tommy," I whispered. "Where have you been? I've missed you."

"I been gone."

"I know. You've been gone too long. Too long . . ." I wriggled to a sitting position, rubbing my heavy forehead in a small circle.

I didn't have time to think about Tommy's long absence because he'd already slipped out of the room. I caught sight of his shadow out in the hall, just before it vanished from view.

Jumping from bed, I ran after him.

In the narrow corridor, Tommy pushed through a door, leaving it swinging behind him.

God, where was I? I didn't recognise this place.

Sprinting, I pushed through the same door that Tommy had. Another corridor lay ahead. Rooms led off the corridor—two with their lights on. I turned and looked the other way. The corridor extended even longer in this direction. Tommy was there, running—towards a tall woman.

Saskia.

In a long, dark jacket, scarf, and jeans.

Tommy ran and encircled her legs.

Why was she here in this strange place?

"Tommy! Tommy!" I called. "Come back to me."

Saskia's eyes became strange. "Phoebe, Tommy isn't here."

Tommy squished his shoulders and nudged his head around to look back at me. I froze. His features were gone. No mouth. No church-pew eyes.

He was wearing the exact same clothing he had been when he first went missing. He always wore those clothes. Why didn't I notice that before?

He wasn't real. I'd been chasing a ghost.

As I raised my eyes to Sass, Tommy faded from view.

I'd lost him again. This time, he wasn't coming back.

Putting a finger to her mouth to tell me to be quiet, Sass waved me forward.

"They weren't going to let me in," she said quietly. "Visiting hours are closed. But I told a small lie and said I had to fly out of the country tomorrow."

"Do you know this place?" I gripped her forearms.

She stared at me, her expression growing sad. "Oh, Phoebe, they've pumped you full of drugs, haven't they?"

"Where are we?" I asked her.

"You're in a special place where you can rest," she told me. "But you can't rest yet. I have to take you somewhere."

"I want to leave here."

"Good. But you have to trust me. The people here don't want you to leave. We have to be careful."

I turned my head back in the direction of my room. "I have a bag—"

"It's best we don't go back for it. They were about to change over shifts when I came in, and they'll probably do a room check."

Shrugging off the calf-length jacket that she wore, she handed it to me. "Put this on."

I obeyed and buttoned it up.

She brushed my hair and knotted her scarf around my neck.

Taking my hand, she led me along the corridor, peeking briefly into each room that had an open door. In one room, an elderly woman was sitting in an armchair with her legs tucked up to her chest, fast asleep, a plastic princess crown lopsided on her head. Sass grabbed her shoes. "These might fit."

We stepped into an empty room, and I squeezed my feet into the lace-up orthopaedics. They *hurt*.

"Phoebe, you're not walking straight. I need you to act normal, or you won't get out of here."

I wanted to get out. I didn't like this place. I nodded at her.

We took the stairs to the bottom floor. Sass didn't want to take the elevator. She hung back in the dim corridor as we neared what looked like a reception desk.

"It's a new person at the desk," she told me quietly. "Hopefully they don't know that only one person came in. I need you to walk straight and tall beside me. You get one shot at this, okay?"

"Okay." I could *pretend* this, like an acting role. Pretend that my mind wasn't fog and my heart hadn't been torn away by Tommy's deception—leading me to believe that he was here when he wasn't.

She eyed me fixedly. "Here we go."

I copied her, walking in step.

"Thanks!" Sass called to the woman at the front desk.

The woman nodded at her. "Use the card you were given when you came in. And keep it, for further visits."

Sass shot her a broad smile and then continued on to the glass door. A tiny light flashed above a round lime-green button. Sass pressed it. We went through to yet another glass door. A light flashed above a green button here, too. Again, Sass pressed it.

We were out.

I inhaled the cold night air.

"C'mon." I followed Sass to the first fence. Beyond that lay a parking lot.

Sass inserted her visitor's card into the slot. The gate buzzed and clicked open. We threaded our way through the parked cars to the last gate. Again, Sass inserted her card.

I recognised her car parked on the street, even though it was half enveloped by mist.

As we drove away, I remembered something. "You hate me," I told her. But I didn't remember why she hated me.

"I was wrong," she said.

"Why—?"

"Phoebe, let's not talk about it now. You're not yourself. Whatever they gave you, it's made you pretty damned dopey."

I decided to let it go. "Are you taking me back to Luke?"

"Is that where you want to go?"

"No." Why didn't I want to go back to Luke?

"That's good, because we can't go there."

"Then where are we going?"

She pressed her lips in, lights of an oncoming car washing over her face. "Number 29."

"*No.* I don't want to go there."

"Just trust me."

That house was the last place I wanted to go. But my mind was sludge and ash. And my head too heavy to argue.

I fell back into sleep.

*

I woke alone.

I knew exactly where I was even before I opened my eyes. Those overpowering scents of age, mildew, second-hand clothing, and the new scent of pot. I was upstairs at number 29, in the third bedroom.

A soft light shone from a corner, but most of the room was a palette of deep shadows.

My voice sounded hollow as I called for Sass.

No answer came.

My heart thudded in the silence.

Of course she wasn't here.

I'd been dreaming.

I was meant to be at Greensthorne. And Sass was a thousand miles away, with her family.

How did I get here from Greensthorne? How did I get out? I remembered taking the pills and getting into bed. I remembered Sass . . . and Tommy.

I glanced down at my clothing. I was wearing a long jacket and the old lady's shoes. I'd stolen all of that. Wincing, I pulled my feet free of the restricting shoes.

Someone was coming.

I heard the *creak, creak, creak* on the stairs.

Crawling around a rack of framed paintings, I bent my head low. The rack was just high enough to hide me. I had to be still. There were spaces through which I could be seen.

The floorboards groaned along the hall.

A man walked into the room, a large canvas satchel over his shoulder. The same man as before. He dumped out the contents of the bag on the floor and then set about arranging the items. He hummed as he added to his collection—his voice odd.

He stopped and frowned as he lifted two black shoes from the floor.

I sucked in a rapid breath. I'd left the old lady's shoes out there.

He turned his head, looking around. I watched his shoulders shrug then as he gave the shoes a place.

Seeming satisfied that everything was in order, he hung his hat on a free-standing coat rack, then his jacket.

He peeled a wig from his head. *A wig?*

Shoulder-length hair dropped. I knew who he was even before he removed the goatee and moustache.

Bernice.

I edged back a fraction as she stepped across the small room to put the wig on a shelf. As I moved, the floorboards made a tiny shifting sound under my feet.

I had no time to react before she marched to the painting rack and peered around it. Her eyes were intense as she grabbed hold of my arm and yanked me from my hiding place.

"Phoebe Basko. What are you doing here?"

"Let go of me."

"Tell me why you're here, and maybe I will."

Words blurred in my head. "I don't know why I'm here."

She made a derisive sound under her breath. "I'm supposed to believe that?"

I sensed a shadow behind us. I twisted around at the waist.

Sass emerged from the darkness of the hallway into the doorframe. Sass, shoeless and with a pearl-handled knife in her hand.

I stared at her like she were a hallucination.

"Leave her alone." Sass's voice was calm, icy. *"You freak.* I should have guessed that the strange man around the neighbourhood was *you."*

"Get out of my house," Bernice roared. "You don't belong here. Either of you. Not anymore."

"This place was always ours." Sass took a bold step forward.

"You left it, and you didn't come back." Bernice shifted her gaze to me. "And Phoebe's going to be going away for a long time. She can't hide here."

"She didn't come here to hide." Sass took another step.

"Sass, be careful!" I cried, trying to wrench my arm from Bernice. Sass had a knife, but Bernice was larger and stronger than either of us.

"Don't worry about me," Sass said. "I can deal with Bernice."

"I thought I dreamed you," I breathed at her.

"You were certainly in a drug haze." Sass nodded at me. "I had to help you inside and up the stairs, then I went to move my car. I didn't want anyone to know I was here." She paused for a moment, biting her lip anxiously. "I'm sorry about how I was when you called me on the phone. I was just so angry with you. More than angry. I've always seen you as a sister. Which made Tommy my family. When I saw all the evidence against you, I can't even explain how I felt—"

Bernice tightened her grip on my arm. "If Phoebe didn't come here to hide, then why is she here? And why the hell are you here?"

Saskia's expression hardened. With her eyes on Bernice, she pushed her hand into the front pocket of her jeans and pulled out a small object.

The boat from Tommy's nightlight.

"This is why," Sass said.

I felt Bernice's shoulder shrug beside me. "What's that got to do with me?"

"Phoebe found this here. In this room. With your things," said Sass.

I shook my head slightly. "It doesn't matter anymore, Sass. They found the nightlight in Nan's toolshed. It was me who—"

"No, it does matter." Saskia held up the boat between the thumb and forefinger of her free hand. "If there's one thing I'm good at, it's colour and patterns. It's what I do for a job. And this boat has red stripes in straight lines. But Tommy's didn't. The stripes on Tommy's boats had a curve that followed the curve of the boats. Those kinds of small details are important when you're a designer. Most people don't notice. But *we* do."

"You're both insane," said Bernice. "Phoebe's about to be charged with *murder*. While you're trying to make up some ballyhoo about stripes on a kid's toy. Not to mention, you've got a knife pointed at me. I'm pretty sure that's a crime in itself."

Sass slipped the boat back into her pocket, holding the knife out straight. "Are you going to call the police on us? I don't think so. Not after you hear what I have to say. On my flight home, the on-board TV on the plane was showing the news. I saw a close up of the nightlight. And I thought back, to the day that I played on the floor with Tommy and that nightlight. The boats had all been uniform. You know, curved stripes. Not like the boat Phoebe found here at number 29."

I eyed the metamorphosed Bernice from my side vision. The scoffing look hadn't left her face. My mind was still processing seeing her change from a man to a woman. Sluggishly, I tried to concentrate on what Sass was saying.

"But, I needed to know for sure," Sass continued. "When I got home, I went straight to see Phoebe's nan. I told her I'd left a scarf behind in Phoebe's room. And I went up there and grabbed the boat. It was just like I thought. Straight lines. Which means this boat came from another nightlight. I already knew from Phoebe that the nightlights were limited edition and how much they cost. You're just not going to find broken bits of them everywhere. So, I raced home and looked up the toy shop where Phoebe bought it. And I called them. I pretended to be the police needing urgent information about the sales of the nightlight. It wasn't difficult for me to do. I mean, the nightlight had already been splashed on the news everywhere. The store owner looked up the sales records for me. He had a record of one being sold in December last year. To someone on this street. He even remembered the woman who bought it. She was blonde, Bernice. Like you."

I gasped, my mind racing, unable to put any pieces together. Had Bernice bought one of the nightlights? Why did Sass find it so important that someone on this street had bought one of them?

"What are you trying to say?" Bernice's voice was cold but also oddly curious.

Sass locked eyes with Bernice. "You bought the exact same nightlight that Tommy had, and you brought it here. To this abandoned house. Pretty strange, wouldn't you say? What did you do with Tommy? That's what I'm trying to say."

Bernice made a low sound under her breath. "You found a piece of a nightlight here, and suddenly I'm the one who took Tommy?"

"Did you?" Sass raised her eyebrows, waiting.

"I wouldn't hurt Tommy," Bernice said.

"How do we know that?" Sass demanded, taking a bold step into the room.

"I loved Tommy, too," Bernice said quietly. "When Phoebe's nan would mind Tommy—all those times that Phoebe was too strung out to take care of him—I used to take him for walks and play with him."

"I didn't know that." I hated the thought of Bernice anywhere near Tommy.

"Your grandmother didn't tell you," said Bernice, "because she knew you wouldn't want Tommy with me."

"My grandmother was right," I told her.

God, was it possible that it wasn't me who hurt Tommy? Back at Greensthorne, I'd been prepared to accept that it was me. But standing here in this house again brought back my dreams of it. The sense that the terrible day at number 29 was somehow connected to Tommy solidified again in my mind. The injured moth and the woman's terrified eyes and the pearl-handled knives. Whoever had carried out those things was responsible for whatever had happened to Tommy. I was sure of it. They'd tried to hurt me when I was sixteen, and now they'd hurt me again, in the worst way possible.

"You can't fool us. We knew you," said Saskia. "*We knew you.* You like cutting things. You stabbed knives in our names. You cut up the rats. And you cut up the stairs and murdered that woman. But she wasn't supposed to be here in the house that day—*was she*? So, was it Luke or Phoebe you wanted to kill that day?"

My heart jumped as Sass walked forward. "I think it was Phoebe you wanted dead. You wanted Luke, and he didn't want you. So, you tried to hurt his girlfriend. It didn't work. But you kept the hate inside you. You took her son, Bernice. Didn't you?"

I held a breath so long my lungs began hurting. I shot Bernice a hard stare.

She shook her head in response, the muscles in her face drawing tight.

Releasing her grip on me, she rushed at Sass, shoving her hard against the wall. "Leave me alone. Both of you." The knife clattered along the floor.

She ran out.

Sass grabbed the knife and charged out after her.

"No, Sass! Let her go!" I followed, but my movements were syrupy, as they always were after I'd taken the sleeping pills.

"Sass!" I called.

Bernice bounded down the stairs, Sass on her heels. Sass wouldn't listen to me, wouldn't stop.

I screamed at the groaning sound of the stairs shifting. Beneath Sass, the stairs tipped.

Sass fell, crying out sharply as she rolled over and over down the stairs to the floor.

Not thinking clearly, I rushed after her, the stairs swaying precariously.

The stairs held.

Sass hugged her leg. "*Hell.* I think I broke it."

Bernice, with her hand on the front-door handle, stood in the darkness, staring at Saskia's crumpled figure. I expected her to keep running, slamming the door behind her. But she didn't.

She took swift but uncertain steps back to the bottom of the stairs. "Let me see."

"Get away from me." Sass's face creased in pain.

I rushed to Sass. "God, are you okay?" I swivelled my head back to Bernice. "Don't touch her."

But Bernice silently knelt and felt Sass's leg with both hands. "It's not broken. I'd make a guess it's badly sprained. Maybe a hairline fracture or two."

"Take your hands off me," Sass ordered her.

Bernice did as she was asked. "You'd be crazy to try to walk on it. You should stay put and call an ambulance. I know I was only a yachties' safety officer for a short while, but I did learn a few things. There were quite a few broken bones in the races, even a snapped neck once."

"I'll manage," said Sass icily. She squeezed her eyes shut, alternately panting and gasping.

"All right then, I'll leave you to it." Bernice raised her face to me. "I didn't hurt your son, Phoebe."

"Was it you who bought the nightlight?" I tried to keep my words even, but I failed, my voice dissolving into a coarse whisper.

"No," she answered.

"Then why did you have a piece of it?"

"I found it. Just like all of the stuff that I have here. I collect the things that people throw away."

"Then where did you find it?"

"In the trash. At Kitty's house on this street."

I flinched at the name. Luke had a *Kitty*. "Kitty? There's no Kitty on this street. You're lying."

Sass grasped my arm. "God. That was the name the toy store guy gave me. No last name. Just that. Kitty. I just assumed it was Bernice, giving herself a fake name. She likes cats." She levelled her gaze at Bernice. "Are you Kitty?"

"No, I'm not Kitty," she answered.

"Which house does Kitty live in?" I asked Bernice in a rigid voice.

"Oh, you know the house," she told me. "Luke goes there often. I see him go in there when I'm walking the streets at night, looking for things. I'll give you a hint. Kitty used to be a collector, like I am now. Except she didn't collect things. She collected strays. The lost and lonely cats and kittens. She'd take them home with her."

I swallowed, exchanging glances with Sass.

Sass's eyes widened. "*Pria*. But her name isn't—"

Bernice nodded, sucking her mouth in. "Yes, her other name is Kitty. Do you remember when she was briefly Luke's girlfriend, back when she was sixteen? Luke had a pet name for her. *Kitty.* Because of the cats. No one knew that. But I overheard him calling her that a few times."

I sat back, the air pinched from my lungs.

Bernice watched our reactions for a moment, and then she continued. "Another thing that people don't know is that each cat seemed to disappoint Pria. I'd see her taking them in her school bag and dumping them back on the docks. She tell the cats that they didn't love her enough and that she didn't want them anymore. And sometimes, if they really disappointed her, she'd dump them straight in the water. I rescued some of the poor things myself."

"Oh hell, *that's* what she was doing with the poor cats?" Sass gaped at Bernice. "She used to tell us she'd found homes for them."

"Yep," Bernice said.

I couldn't breathe. "Is *she* the woman Luke's been seeing? *Pria?*"

"Of course it's Pria," Bernice told me. "He's been going there for months. Even last year. I thought it was strange, even though they were friends. It looks like Luke's been keeping big secrets."

"How could he? And Pria . . ."

"*Bitch,*" Sass mouthed silently.

My mind couldn't fit the two of them together. Luke and Pria. Luke and *Kitty.* It didn't make sense.

But then I remembered the scent of the perfume on Luke's neck.

It was Pria's perfume.

It had been Pria Luke had been to see that night.

How did Luke manage to persuade his way into her bed? And how could she keep pretending to be my friend while all the while she was—

No, don't let yourself think about what they did together. It doesn't matter.

He could have her. She could have him.

Closing my eyes for a moment, I breathed deeply. "Bernice, are you certain that you found the boat at Pria's house?"

"In her garbage bin," she answered. "Alongside a bunch of flowers that Luke gave her."

I recalled the dead flowers upstairs. "How do I know I can believe you?"

"Why would I lie? The nightlight meant nothing to me. I didn't even know about it. You never asked me into your house."

"But why did you keep a broken piece of a toy?" I pressed. "Why do you collect all this . . . useless stuff?" I gazed up the tilted stairs at the upper storey.

"It's not useless to me." She crossed her arms defensively. "Things have stories attached to them. They've got memories. I don't have much of a life, myself. So I collect pieces of other people's."

If she was lying, she was doing a good job of it.

Saskia stared at her openly. "I'm not buying it. Maybe Luke and Pria have been total dirtbags. But you didn't find the boat at her house. I've got you figured out. Everything points to you."

"You can think what you like," Bernice said, her words slow and wound tight on each other.

"I don't have to just think it," said Sass. "You admitted to writing our names on the wall and then skewering the names with the knives. Why did you hate us so much?" The whites of Sass's eyes shone in the dark light.

Bernice's chest visibly sank, her bottom lip trembling. "You really want to know? I didn't hate any of you. I just hated the pain I was carrying. I think I just wanted to offload some of it. Something happened to me, that year. When I was thirteen."

"Are you going to tell us more lies?" Saskia said.

"It's not a lie," Bernice told her. "But I wish it was."

Sass eyed her dubiously, trying to stretch out her leg and then redoubling, wincing.

"It was here that it happened," Bernice said. "In this house. I came here looking for you guys. None of you ever told me where you were hanging out. I was just lucky if I chanced across some of you and you let me tag along. So, I just waited in the house, having a cigarette. Mr Basko came by, looking for Luke. He told me he'd tell my mother he'd seen me smoking. I begged him not to. He said I'd have to show him I could be a good girl. And then he—" She stopped abruptly, taking a slow, shuddering breath. "And then he pushed himself on top of me. On the lounge. I pleaded with him to get off me, and he just kept saying I had to be quiet. I have to be quiet. Be a good girl. I went numb. He raped me. At the time, I didn't even understand what was happening."

I gasped out loud, my memories of Bernice from that year disconnecting from the version she was telling me now.

"Luke's dad did *that* to you?" Sass held a hand over her mouth. "Oh God. I caught him staring at me sometimes, or at Phoebe or Kate, but I never thought—" She shook her head. "Why didn't you go to the police?"

Bernice raised her shoulders in a silent sigh. "It's hard to explain. I didn't tell anyone at first. I felt so numb that I just wanted to disappear. Days went by in a blur. And it got harder and harder to say anything. But one day Mum demanded to know what was wrong with me, and I told her. She marched me up to the Basko house. She told the Baskos what I told her. Mr Basko acted as though I was a silly girl making things up. Luke's mother said that I was making it up to cover up the fact that I'd been caught smoking. *But she knew.* I could tell that she knew. My mother asked me if I wanted to go to the police. Right in front of the man who raped me. I was too scared to speak. My mother just didn't stop to think. She should have taken me straight down to the police station. But she didn't."

"All these years." I shook my head, studying her face intently. "Why didn't you tell us? If not the police, why not us?"

"I thought you'd all hate me or you wouldn't believe me. It was Luke's *father*, not some random stranger. I wanted to fit in. So I kept it to myself." She stared hard down at the cracked floorboards.

An uncomfortable quiet followed. What she'd just said might've been true. We might have shunned her if she'd told us. Luke had been one of us, and she'd been on the outside of our group.

It was Sass who spoke first. "Is that why you did what you did to the stairs? Because of the pain inside?"

Moving around us, Bernice sat heavily on the edge of the staircase, her face shuttered in darkness. "For the last time. No. I didn't cut up the stairs. I didn't stab the rats. I did fix the stairs and put them back into place though, a few months ago. It wasn't easy, but I managed. I just wanted somewhere to come and smoke some pot and be alone. I can't do that anywhere else. And . . . I've run out of room to put things in my mother's house."

Bernice looked fragile as she leaned forward, brushing her hair back with both hands and licking her lips uneasily.

Sass and I exchanged guilty glances. We'd seen the cramped conditions at the Wick house for ourselves.

"Don't blame me for things I didn't do," said Bernice. "I've been through enough."

Saskia shivered. "Maybe it was the old man who used to live here, the man who owns the house. Maybe he was a weirdo who cut the stairs as a warning to intruders. Maybe the stairs just chose to fall at that moment."

"Both ladders at once?" Bernice shook her head. "How could the safety lock on both ladders collapse at once? I put the ladders back up. They're not faulty." She exhaled, staring at us fixedly. "It had to have been one of you."

Sass shook her head, shrinking back from Bernice's stare. "Don't look at me like that. All I remember is being in the living room drinking when the stairs fell. I was pretty smashed."

"Hang on." Bernice glanced at the store mannequin that was sitting in the armchair. "Phoebe, weren't you videotaping at the time? I remember you sticking your camera on the lap of that dummy."

I tried to think back. Was Bernice trying to pull a trick on us? Was she trying to make us think she hadn't done it because she was prepared to have video evidence of the day shown?

"Like Sass, I was smashed," I told her. "I think that's partly why we all made such a bad decision that day, in not going to the police. We were young, drunk, and not thinking clearly. But I know I couldn't have been videotaping at the time it happened though. I was upstairs, with Luke."

Bernice sighed. "Yeah, true. But maybe there's something on the tape from that day that gives some sort of clue. I tried to talk to you about that, in the days after it happened. But you refused to listen to me."

"The tape's long gone," I said. "Luke's mother did the big clean-up in here. I asked her about the camera afterwards. She said she destroyed the tape that was inside it, just in case. And then she stored the camera away in a cupboard. The police were all over this house in the days after that lady died. I couldn't come back for the camera. And I didn't want to. This house just makes me feel sick every time I look at it."

She knew the tape got destroyed, I thought darkly. A memory pushed in. I *was* filming that day. I'd been (drunkenly) pressing everyone to tell me where they thought they were going to be by the time they were twenty. *Twenty* had seemed so far away. It'd only been a year away for Bernice, but over three years for the rest of us. The tape had run out. I remembered giving the camera to the dummy for safekeeping before I'd gone out to the kitchen for yet another drink. But I didn't remember turning the camera off. A chill ran along my back. Whenever a tape would get full, then the on-board flash memory of the camera would take over. The camera probably didn't have anything telling on it, but it might have *something*.

Sass was staring at me with a wary expression. "Phoebe?"

I turned to Bernice. "Have you seen the camera here?"

Bernice shrugged. "Yeah. I found it in the linen cupboard. I took it upstairs with the rest of my stuff. There's no tape in it. I was hoping maybe you came back and took it."

"Is the camera okay?" I asked her, my eyes locked on hers.

She gave a confused nod. "As good as a thirteen-year-old camera could be, I guess."

"Have you used it?" I tried not to let hope rise in my chest.

Bernice looked at me oddly, glancing at Sass for answers but being met with a shake of Sass's head. "Nope. What have I got to take video of? Why?"

I blew out a tense stream of air. "I can't recharge the camera anyway. I threw the charger away."

"You want batteries?" asked Bernice. "There's sure to be batteries in some of the things upstairs. Maybe some with some charge left. What type of battery?"

"I never used batteries for it. I don't even know what type it took."

Bernice heaved herself to her feet. "Want to go check?"

"Don't leave me here alone," said Sass quickly. Her eyes shifted to me. "And don't go up there with Bernice."

"Yeah, fine. Keep hating me," Bernice told her. "Who knows, maybe your hate is the glue keeping me together. Because fuck knows what else is keeping me going."

With a shake of her head, she headed back up the stairs.

Sass and I met each other's stare, neither of us volunteering our thoughts.

A series of knocks and dull bumps echoed down the stairs. Bernice returned with the camera, her eyes quietly triumphant.

I held my hand out for it.

"Fuck you," Bernice muttered, fiddling with the buttons and refusing to give it to me. A light sprang on at the top of the camera. And then the viewing screen.

Bernice sat on the bottom stair, watching it herself, forcing Sass and I to move around to either side of her, Sass crawling sideways on the floor.

I felt my stomach lurch at the scene it showed. This house. On the day Grace Clark died. The position of the camera was fixed, people moving around in front of it.

God, there was Luke, taking me by the hand up the stairs. I watched myself looking back over my shoulder, half-dazed, continuing on to the top of the stairs with Luke. Bernice, Kate, Sass, and Pria were sprawled on the lounges. But it wasn't a clear view. Just their legs. All wearing dark-coloured jeans. Someone got up. A person in black jeans and a hooded jacket. That person walked along the hall and disappeared into the dark space next to the stairs.

I could feel every beat of my heart as the person opened the door that led to the storage underneath the stairs.

The metallic sound of an alarm clock pealed out in the film.

Shuffling and shouts from upstairs.

Grace appearing on the stairs. Terrified and white-faced as she ran to the middle of the staircase.

And the stairs collapsing inwards, dust and splinters exploding in the air.

The door to the stairs had already been closed, the person running from the direction of the outside courtyard at the time that the others were running from the living room to the stairs. No one was looking up the hallway. All focus on the destroyed staircase.

Then I saw the face that emerged from the dark hallway.

Pria.

Unmistakably Pria.

Bernice set the camera down on the stair, her face chalky in the dark light.

In the long silence that followed, Sass and I looked to each other first, Sass's expression a mirror of the shock and guilt flooding through me.

"Bernice . . ." Sass began.

"Don't," Bernice snapped.

Tears brightened Sass's eyes. "It wasn't you. I'm so sorry."

My gaze fell to the rush of bodies on the camera viewfinder. All of us running in different directions not knowing what to do. All this time, it had been Pria that caused all that. My lips quivered. "There's nothing I can say to make this better. We were so damned . . . *wrong*."

"You can start by shutting the hell up," said Bernice. "Do you think I want the soppy apologies of you two now? You can both go to hell. But I care about Tommy. So stop blubbering and start figuring things out."

My mind began spinning away. If Pria had been the one to set the trap on the stairs, what else was she capable of? *What else?*

Sass's head dropped low, her blonde hair touching the floor. "Phoebe, some stuff about Pria is making terrible sense now. The night we went out to the Christmas dinner, it was my idea, but it was Pria who decided where we should go. She told me she'd read that a guy you'd met and liked at a club last year was going to be there. I thought it would be a bit of fun for you. I didn't know who it was. I'm guessing now it was one of those men you were filmed with at the hotel. That Dash guy. Before . . . before we went out, she said we should call up The Moose. She said she'd be you for a night, to try to take some of the pressure off you. And that you should be me for the night. She's a psychologist, Phoebe. I thought, of anyone, she'd know the best thing to do."

I closed my eyes, knowing with all certainty who'd called the media when I was with Dash. I could see all of us, when we were kids, playing *Moose* at number 29. Pretending to be each other. It was a dangerous game to play with Pria, only none of us knew.

"And something else," said Sass, raising her eyes to me. "When I was at Pria's once, about five months back, Jessie told me that Pria was keeping their dog upstairs in the playroom, and that she'd never seen it. I thought that was strange. But Pria told Jessie to go and do her homework, and then Pria was kind of dismissive about the dog thing. As if Jessie was making it up."

"Phoebe," came Bernice's cautious voice, "I swear to you that where I told you I found that nightlight piece is the truth. You can choose to do what you damned well please with that piece of information. But I think you need to find out a bit more about your good friend *Kitty*."

44.   LUKE

TWO NIGHTS AGO
Monday night

KITTY SLID A LAZY LEG OVER my stomach and drew close against me in her bed. "Hate seeing you so stressed."

Staring up at the intricate vintage rose on her ceiling, I stroked her bare waist and thigh. Outside the high window, fog pressed in.

She ran a finger along my temple, tucking a lock of hair behind my ear. "Maybe you were right before. About getting away. Why don't we? Just sail away."

I glanced at her in surprise. She was too close for me to see her face clearly. "Really?"

"Yes."

I sighed, drumming on her hip with my fingertips now. "Wish I could."

"Sometimes, the best choice is to run away. You've been fighting to stay afloat for too long."

"Until the police have got her under arrest and this is all over, I can't leave. They should have arrested her as soon as they got their hands on the last note. Not stuck her in a clinic."

"I guess they have their procedures to follow. They need to be sure."

"What fucking else do they need? That's Tommy's blood on that letter. My son's—" Pain welled inside me, making my chest hurt.

"Luke . . ." She hugged me in silence for a moment.

"I need to know what happened to Tommy," I told her in a hoarse voice that didn't sound like my own. "What she did and who helped her. When they bring her in for questioning and rip the truth out of her, at least I'll know. And I can finally start to grieve."

"I know. Of course you want that."

Leaning over, I went to pick up my mobile phone from the bedside table, but it wasn't there. "Have you seen my phone? I need to check if there's any updates. On the news or from Gilroy."

She put her hand over mine. "I haven't seen it. But you know that he'll call you if anything comes up. I'm worried about you. You're showing all the classic signs of someone who's about to go under. Seriously, I didn't want to say this, but I'm worried about your state of mind."

I moved away from her a fraction, scanning her face. "I'm keeping it together."

"No, you're not. And you mutter in your sleep all night long. About . . . well, about murdering your wife. You're actually scaring me." She untangled herself from me.

I grasped her arm. "I know I talk in my sleep, but—"

A vague look of fear visited her eyes. "Last night, you were tossing to and fro, so restless. I caught pieces of what you said. You wanted to cut her into tiny pieces like what she'd done to Tommy's toys. The next thing I knew . . . you were on top of me, your hands around my neck . . ."

"I did *that*?"

"Yes."

"Fuck."

"I told you I wasn't Phoebe and managed to roll you off me. You didn't do it again, but you kept making angry noises under your breath. I admit, I was a bit scared."

I sat up, drawing in a deep breath. "That can't happen again. I won't come here for a while. Until I'm past this."

She shook her head. "I'm worried that would make you worse right now. You'd be taking yourself away from the one person you turn to for support. At the worst point in your life. You've told me that your parents aren't capable of giving you the shoulder you need. Look, I know what I'm talking about with this."

I'd already come to the point of putting my hands on Phoebe's throat and wanting the release of strangling her. Last night, I could have killed the woman beside me in the bed. Kitty was right that I needed her—more right than she knew. I could admit to myself that I'd always needed a cheer squad behind me. The cheer squad used to be my mother. In my teen years, it was the Southern Sails Street gang—it felt like I had a team of beautiful girls under my wings (even when they rejected me). And then it was Phoebe, even though she never quite knew how to wave the pom-poms.

I turned to Kitty. "So, what the hell do I do?"

"Trust your instincts. You wanted to get away, and I think you should listen to yourself. You're a smart man, Luke. Look at the business you built up from nothing. You know what you need to do."

"I just . . . can't go right now."

"Why not now? Everyone would understand. Your wife has been accused of murdering your own son. You need some time to get your head around that. Phoebe's psychiatrist will probably be able to buy her quite a bit of time before the police bring her in. In the meantime, you're here waiting and suffering. I tell you what. Why don't we go away just until she gets arrested?"

"I'm not prepared to put you in harm's way to help myself."

"You need a change of environment, and you'll be fine. That's all. This street has too many reminders."

I stared at her, thinking.

"I'll get packed. You've got lots of your clothes here. Enough to take away. You don't need to do a thing." Her smile was warm as she left the bed and stood naked in the soft glow of her bedside lamp.

"Where would we go?"

"Why not the property I just bought?"

"Seriously?"

Kitty had bought a damned island, a tiny piece of Australia far off the windswept coast of Victoria. I'd negotiated the deal, but I'd tried hard to talk her out of it. She'd paid way more than I thought she could sell it for in the future. But she'd seemed set on it.

"Yes, seriously. What could be better?"

"That's a long sailing trip."

"It's not that long. What, two or three days?"

"About that."

"Just long enough to get your head in a different place. You love sailing. And I do, too."

This was moving too fast.

"What about Jessie? And school?"

"She can have a week off. She'll be so excited."

"Kitty, Jessie doesn't even know about us. This might not be the best way of telling her."

"She has to find out some time or other. It's been damned hard keeping you a secret."

"It's going to come as a shock to her."

"Yes, but I know her. She'll adapt. And she gets a trip away in your yacht. It'll be an adventure for her."

I laid myself back on the bed. "I think I'd better start calling you *Pria*. Might be an extra point of confusion for Jessie if I call you *Kitty* in front of her."

"I like *Kitty*. You gave me that name. It's special to me."

"Suits you." I smiled up at her. "But it's going to sound weird to Jess. Trust me." I was going to have to make myself think of Pria only as *Pria* from now on.

"I trust you. You're the one steering this ship." Grabbing some clothes, she headed into the ensuite bathroom to get dressed.

Maybe she was right about what she'd said earlier about my wife. Phoebe wasn't in jail—yet—but she was locked away. There was nothing for me to do until she was arrested or until she admitted everything under police questioning—whichever came first.

Pushing into my chaotic thoughts about Phoebe were thoughts about the preparation of the yacht for the trip ahead.

45.   JESSIE

TWO NIGHTS AGO
Monday night

I HEARD THE JANGLE OF KEYS in the lock of my bedroom door.

Mum always kept it locked at night—ever since we had thieves in the house in January. She didn't want anything bad to happen to me.

Light spilled in as she cracked the door open. I sat up in my bed. "Mum?"

"Jess, I have the best news. We're going on a little trip."

"Where to?"

"Somewhere you've never been before. You'll love it. We need to get you packed up and ready to go."

"We're going now?"

"Yes, right now. Jump up and help me pack your suitcase."

"What about school tomorrow?"

She dragged the suitcase out of my wardrobe and lumped it on my bed. "You get a few days off school. Lucky, huh?"

"But . . . the play?"

"Oh, don't worry about that. You don't care about it, do you? You ended up with a rotten part anyway."

"But they're expecting me to be Beth. I've learned all the lines."

"Don't worry, sweetie. Just imagine the look on Bossy Boots Bree when she finds out you won't be there. She won't get to act like she owns the whole play, right in front of your face."

"She's not like that," I mumbled. Mum didn't hear me, and it was better that she didn't. She really dug her heels in over some things.

The floorboards were cold under my feet as I went to my tallboy to start collecting clothes. "How long are we going for? I don't know how much stuff to get out."

"I'm not sure. I mean, who knows?" Her voice rose, thin and kind of nervously happy. "Just bring enough for a couple of weeks. And bring lots of warm clothing."

"A couple of weeks? Wow."

Her eyes danced as she folded my raincoat into the suitcase. "Yes, *wow*. I knew you'd be excited. This is going to be incredible. For all of us."

My arms, full with a pile of jeans and T-shirts, hung in the air. "All of us? Who's all of us?"

She drew in a long breath that I could hear. "You know that I've been seeing someone."

"Yes?"

"We're going away with him."

"The man from the navy?"

She took the pile of clothing from me and pressed it into the bag. "Well, that was a little fib. This is kind of difficult. And you're going to find it hard to understand."

"What am I going to find hard to understand?"

"Maybe it's best you see for yourself. He's here right now."

"He's *here*?"

As far as I knew, he'd barely been to our house. He was away all the time at sea. No, that was wrong. Mum just said that was a lie. Why did she lie to me about him?

She packed my underwear and socks and zipped up the bag.

"Bring books," she said.

"And my iPad?"

"No, honey. There's no internet where we're going. Okay, let's go."

"I need to get dressed."

"No, stay in your pyjamas. You'll be going back to bed anyway. Just put shoes and your winter dressing gown on."

Her sleeve slipped up as she bent to pick up a pair of my shoes. She had a bandage wrapped around her wrist.

"What happened?" I touched her arm.

"Oh, I just bumped it. Racing around like crazy trying to get this trip sorted."

She didn't insist on me making my bed as we left my room, like she normally would. I rolled my suitcase behind me, following Mum down the hallway.

Standing in our living room was a man, his back to us as he looked at our photos on the mantelpiece.

"Jessie," Mum said in a careful tone. "I know you know Luke."

As he turned, I was confused. This was Tommy's father, not *Mum's boyfriend*. But there was no other man in the room.

"Hi, Jessie." He gave me half a smile and half a shrug.

"Hi, Mr Basko." I sounded weird, like I was greeting a stranger.

Mum nodded at me. "I know this is going to take a little while to get used to. You know that Luke and Phoebe are no longer together. Well, now Luke and I are together."

"Like boyfriend and girlfriend?" I managed to squeak.

"I guess so." Tommy's dad shoved his hands in his pockets and switched to looking at Mum. "We like each other a lot. I've been feeling very, very sad for a long time. Your mum has helped me feel a lot better. She's been a good friend, and I really needed a good friend. I hope you and I can be friends, too."

My mouth felt too dry and my head still fuzzy. I'd been asleep just a few minutes ago. "Will Phoebe be going to jail?" I hadn't meant to say that. It just *slipped*.

"I'm not sure," said Mr Basko. "But when people do something wrong, then yes, they go to prison."

Mum shot Mr Basko an anxious look. "We'd better get moving, before it gets any later."

I noticed then that there were three suitcases and two boxes of food next to the sofa. They were already ready to go. All this had been happening while I was sleeping.

"I don't like the look of the fog out there." Mr Basko seemed worried.

"Once we get through it, we'll be fine." Stepping over to the suitcases, Mum grabbed two of the handles. "I used to go out sailing all the time with my parents."

"Wait," I said. "What about the puppy?"

Even though we'd had it so long it wasn't really still a puppy, that's what I called it. I still hadn't even seen it, so my mind couldn't make the leap to picturing a fully-grown dog.

"You have a dog?" Tommy's dad frowned at Mum.

She sighed. "We don't now." She tilted her head at me, like she was trying to get a different view. "Oh honey, I didn't want to tell you, but I had to give the dog away. A couple of days ago."

I bit into my bottom lip. "It's gone?"

"I'm so sorry. But we couldn't keep it any longer. I promise we'll get another one soon. A nice puppy this time."

"Must have been a well-behaved mutt," said Mr Basko. "I never heard it."

"It wasn't well-behaved at all." Mum sounded exasperated. "It'd run itself ragged during the day until it dropped. Then it slept so heavy you couldn't wake it. A terrible guard dog. I got it as a rescue from the pound."

Mr Basko grinned then. "It's just like you to be rescuing animals."

"Okay, we'd better move it." Mum pulled out her phone and called a taxi.

The cab came quickly. A large-size transit cab that would fit all our stuff. From the conversation Mum had with the driver, it sounded like she'd paid him a lot extra to get here so fast. He stopped at Mr Basko's house first, and Mr Basko ran in to collect some stuff. His boat licence and keys for the yacht. Next we headed down to the docks. I didn't believe we were really going until the cab drove away, disappearing into the mist.

We walked down towards Mr Basko's yacht with the suitcases. The water made a lapping sound against the jetty, the air putting a briny taste in my mouth and making me feel sick. Mr Basko went back for the boxes while Mum and I boarded the yacht. She got me to help her take the suitcases down the stairs into the cabin. There were two rooms and a bathroom and a small dining area, everything bolted to the floor. Humming, Mum made the beds. She told me to go back up on deck and wait for Mr Basko to see if he needed help.

An old man moved out of the foggy air on the dock, scaring me. He was one of the homeless people, with his long tangled beard and staring eyes. I wondered if he was looking for a yacht to sleep on for the night.

He pointed towards the yacht's cabin. "She's one of the bad 'uns."

"Excuse me?" I didn't want to be here, alone on the deck.

He kept pointing as my mother moved out of the cabin. "I been 'round and 'round this city longer than anyone. I seen 'er since she was your age. She's a bad 'un."

"Move along and stop talking to my daughter," Mum called to him sharply. I wasn't sure if she'd heard what he'd said.

The old man shuffled away, past Mr Basko, who'd returned with more of our things.

Mr Basko seemed a lot less awkward once he was on his yacht. Like he had a job to do and he had to concentrate. He jumped here and ran there, loosening and tying ropes and moving things about.

Mum helped him until the sails were up and the yacht began to tug away from the docks.

The fog crowded everything else out. Like we were about to head off into a world where there was only mist and nothing else. A world of dark, dark nothing.

Mr Basko sounded the boat's horn every couple of minutes. Stepping up behind me, Mum enveloped me in a bear hug, telling me that he only needed to do that until we were through the fog and in the clear. Excitement seemed to run through her arms and fingers, and she could barely stay still or stop herself from squeezing me too hard.

I wanted to feel the same excitement as she did as I watched solid ground slip away. But instead I was anxious as the fog claimed the space between the land and the yacht. I lost sight of everything except for the upper-storey lights of the high-rises. There was no one in the high-rises at this time of night.

The yacht speared out into the ocean. The air grew colder and colder, whipping around my face as the yacht picked up speed. Mum told me I needed to get used to the sway and pitch of the yacht before we could go into the cabin below, else I'd get seasick. She left me to go and stand with Mr Basko at the wheel. She hugged him just like she hugged me. I think she had too much excitement inside her and she had to let some of it out.

I didn't understand the rush to get away on this trip or why Mum was with Tommy's dad or how she could give the pup away without even telling me.

I didn't want to look at this fog anymore.

Mum's attention was all on Tommy's dad right now. Deciding to head into the cabin myself, I made my way around to the cabin's entrance.

I didn't know which bedroom was for Mum and me and which bedroom was for Mr Basko, but my bags were in the smaller room, and so I headed for that one. If I went back to bed, maybe I could sleep all the way through this foggy night and wake up to a clear sky.

A tiny thrill sped through me: no school tomorrow. Or the day after that. Or all week. I wished I could have told the kids at school that I was going away on a yacht tonight. But I felt heavy inside when I thought about the play again. Mrs Simmons and kids were going to be disappointed with me, and I hated disappointing people.

Despite the lack of breezy air, it was cold in the cabin. Leaving my dressing gown on, I climbed into bed. Even with the blankets pulled over me, I was shivering.

46.   PHOEBE

PRESENT TIME
Wednesday night

THE LIGHTS WERE ALL OFF AT Pria's house.

A sickening feeling ran along my arms and into the centre of my back. We were too late.

They'd gone.

Bernice had driven Sass in her car to the home of an old boyfriend of Sass's earlier. She'd remained friends with him since they'd broken up years ago. Her leg was too bad to come with us, and she needed to be at a place where the police couldn't contact her. If they didn't know by now that I'd escaped from Greensthorne, they soon would. Bernice and I had caught a taxi to the top of our street, near Pria's house, our identities concealed with Bernice's disguises.

I took Bernice around to the side door that led into the sunroom. I knew how to disable the alarm going in this way. I'd seen Pria do it many times. Breaking the lock with a hammer, we entered the house.

We peeled away the wigs, hats and beards, leaving them on the chairs in the sunroom.

"Let's go," said Bernice quietly, whistling in awe under her breath at the interior of the house.

We crept through the corridor and past the living room.

The door to Jessie's room was open. Jessie wasn't in it. Next we made our way to the upper floor. Pria's bedroom was empty also, a strange odour that I couldn't place wafting from it. The third, fourth, and fifth bedrooms looked as they always had—full of Pria's parents' old furniture.

All that was left was the rumpus room. We stole along the worn carpet of the hallway. The door clicked open when Bernice turned the handle, into the large, empty space. It smelled of strong cleaning fluid.

What was I meant to do now? Go chasing after Pria? I didn't have any clue where she'd gone. I had no proof she'd had anything to do with Tommy's disappearance. Just a broken piece of a nightlight.

Bernice had her flashlight's beam trained on a small section of wall, at about my head height, and she was staring intently at it.

"What is it?" I asked her.

"I'm not totally sure"—she flicked the beam up and down—"but I think I see a handprint."

Running over, I squinted at the wooden surface. The spot was small, and it looked greasy. Bernice stepped up next to me, raising the light to get another angle. "See that?" She spread her fingers out and put her hand sideways, almost touching it to the wall. "It's like my hand, only much, much smaller."

"You're right. It's a handprint. Must be an old one of Jessie's." I stood back, thinking. "No, it can't be an old print. Pria didn't have this thick panelling on the walls last time I was up here. And that was maybe in November last year. Pria and I were playing hide-and-seek with Jessie and Tommy, and they ran up here."

A chill ran underneath my thick layers of winter clothing. An image flashed through my mind of a small child struggling to get away from an adult, and desperately spreading their hand out on the wall as they were being carried into the room.

Could that child have been Tommy? Could he have been struggling to get away from Pria all those months ago, and she'd forgotten he'd touched the wall up here? The walls seemed to have been so carefully cleaned everywhere else, right down to the ground level.

It was still no proof. The print was smudged.

"Let's try downstairs." Bernice took another peering look at the print before heading out of the room.

On the bottom floor again, we entered Pria's office.

Folders and papers were stacked high on the two desks. A desktop computer and a laptop sat together on one desk.

Bernice switched them both on. She looked back over her shoulder at me when the password screens booted up. "Know how to get past these screens?"

I shook my head. "No idea."

We tried typing in a few different passwords—*pria, jessie, kitty, luke, tommy*—but none of them worked.

"Going to look outside," Bernice told me.

I continued looking through the office, but I didn't know what I was looking for.

On Pria's main desk, I peered at a large A3 work jotter and diary— one of those pads with dates on each page and tear-off pages that companies gave out as promotions. This one was from a society of psychologists. I flipped through the pages. The top few had appointments, doodles, and messages from Jessie's school that Pria had written down. The page after that had nothing but a pencil drawing—of an island. It seemed that Pria had spent a lot of time sitting here and drawing this. It wasn't that the picture was detailed, but every line appeared to have been retraced several times over. As though the image was important to Pria.

Underneath the picture, she'd written:

sanctuary

eden

refuge

ab ovo

It looked as though the island represented some kind of freedom to her.

Bernice walked in and looked over my shoulder, making me jump. "Isn't that what we all want?"

Smiling grimly at her, I tore the page out, folded it, and slipped it into my pocket.

"Find anything?" I asked her.

"These," she said, producing two mobile phones from her pocket. "Found them in the garage."

I took the phones. "Those belong to Pria and Luke. Why did they leave them behind?" Seeing the phones together made it real that Pria and Luke were together—a couple.

"It's a puzzle," she agreed. "Pria's car was there, too. Didn't find anything in the second garage. Just a whole lotta furniture. Looks like someone liked making bush furniture from logs. Pria?"

"Her dad. It was his hobby."

She shrugged, walking away again, knocking a book down from the pile at the edge of the desk.

I remembered Tommy knocking a pile of Pria's books and stationery down from there before, the day Pria and I had played hide-and-seek with the kids. And I remembered the stationery now. Sheets and envelopes of coloured paper. Pink, yellow . . . *and blue.*

"You look like you've seen a ghost," Bernice commented, picking up the book and flipping it back onto the stack.

"The blue stationery," I said. "I've seen it here."

"What stationery?"

"The paper that the kidnapper letters were written on."

"Hell. Here in the office?"

"Yes. Near the end of last year. Tommy knocked some stuff over. Pria picked up the books. I picked up the paper and envelopes."

"Putting your fingerprints all over it." Bernice didn't waste any time before she was moving about the office again, searching. "Let's find it."

I stared uselessly for a moment, my fingers touching. It had been an easily forgotten thing. Pria had meant it to be. Sometimes in the days or weeks after Tommy and I had left her house, she'd taken that stationery to my grandmother's house and typed up those letters. She must have asked Nan about the typewriter, and Nan would have mentioned to her where it was. I could even imagine what Nan would have said: *Useless old piece of garbage. But it belonged to my husband, and he used it to write all his scathing letters to the newspaper editors, so it's got sentimental value.* But it was so many months ago that Nan wouldn't have connected it, probably didn't even remember. And Pria had planned it that way. *What had Nan been doing while Pria was busily typing away?* Probably sleeping. Everyone knew that Nan napped during the day. Nan would have been none the wiser.

After ten minutes of trying to find the stationery, we hadn't found anything blue.

"Maybe she's keeping it upstairs in her room," Bernice suggested.

I nodded. We hadn't checked drawers or wardrobes.

We headed back upstairs. This time, I flicked on the bedroom light. It was too difficult to search for something small using just the light from my phone and Bernice's small torch. The room smelled wrong. I'd thought so before, but we'd been moving quickly through the house.

The light illuminated a spray of dark fluid on the cream-coloured wall, spreading onto the half-open door of the ensuite bathroom.

Rushing across the plush carpet, I turned the bathroom light on.

Blood.

In the bathtub.

Bright. Watery. Dried at the extreme edges where it had splashed up the sides of the tub.

I gripped the doorframe.

Bernice looked in and drew straight back. "Jesus."

"*Why?* Why is there . . . *blood?*"

"Don't think the worst."

Specks of blood dotted the white tiles and mirror and basin. There was no conceivable reason for all that blood to be everywhere. *None.* Unless something awful happened here.

A sharp knocking sounded downstairs. At the front door.

I gasped. "Oh God. I think we've been seen."

"By who?"

"I don't know. But if someone was walking up the path a minute ago, they would have seen us in Pria's bedroom."

"Let's go find out," said Bernice grimly.

We sprinted downstairs and to the front door. Whoever it was didn't have a key. Could it be Luke?

Bernice pressed her eye to the door's peephole then looked back. "It's your friend, Kate."

"No," I rasped. "She'll call the police for sure."

I pulled the door open. "Kate!"

Kate was heading away down the stone steps when she stopped and turned, fear edging into her eyes. "What are you two doing here?"

I breathed out. "There's a lot to explain."

"Where's Pria?" she asked nervously.

"I don't know. Listen—"

"They're looking for you, Phoebe." She stepped back, barely looking around to see where she was going on the steep stairs.

"Be careful!" I called. Desperation rose inside me. "Kate, do you know where Pria went? Did she tell you?"

The wariness didn't leave Kate's pale eyes or voice. Not a single one of her kind phrases or *orange juice* smiles for me now. "She called me earlier. Saying she was a bit scared. She heard noises outside. Elliot and I were out at a kids' party, but I said I'd check in on her when I got home. She's not answering her phone, and now I find that she's not even here."

Kate drew her teeth through her bottom lip, plunging her hands into her jacket pockets. "I've already called the police, Phoebe. I'm sorry." Spinning around, she began walking, breaking into a run.

*

I sat in the same police room where they'd shown me the image of the fourth letter. The same room where I'd watched the video of me at my letterbox. Detectives Trent Gilroy and Annabelle Yarris sat at the table opposite me. Bernice had already been taken for questioning in a different room.

Bernice and I hadn't run when we heard the police sirens. I couldn't guess at Bernice's reasons, but I had nowhere to run. I didn't know where Pria had gone or how to find her.

Trent studied my face with his intense eyes, as if he could bypass the questions and read my mind. "I'm going to ask you again, Phoebe, and I need you to give me a straight answer this time. Whose blood is it in the tub?"

In my mind's eye, I could still see the blood, red against the white bathtub. "You tell *me*. You're the police."

"But we want *you* to tell us," said Detective Yarris.

"I don't know. I already told you. I saw it when I went upstairs with Bernice." I tried and failed to conquer the quivering of my arms as I folded them against my chest. My voice closed to a whisper. "Don't you understand? You're torturing me. I need to know if it belongs to Tommy. Just tell me. Please . . ."

"Did you have one of your episodes where you do things and then don't remember?" Annabelle Yarris lifted her eyebrows, her tone so cut and dried it was mocking.

"No. And I had someone with me. Bernice. She can tell you exactly what happened."

Detective Gilroy gave a slight shrug, his mouth in a firm line. "What if she's giving us a different version than you?"

"You're just saying that." But I didn't sound entirely certain. I couldn't be entirely certain of anything or anyone.

"How long has your husband been seeing Pria?" Annabelle leaned her back into her chair.

"I'm not sure. He's been going out for walks at night since late last year."

"And you think he was seeing Pria?"

"Yes. Certainly he has been in recent months."

Her eyes needled me inquisitively. "How does that make you feel?"

"Shocked. But I have bigger things on my mind. I—"

"I'd be shocked too if I found out my husband and good friend were having an affair. I can imagine you going to Pria's house in a rage, and—"

I stopped her. "No. That's not why I went there."

"Look, it's understandable you were angry," she continued, as though I hadn't spoken. "And then when you confronted her about sleeping with Luke, things got heavy fast, didn't they?"

"You think I hurt Pria?" I breathed. "You think *I'm* the reason there's blood everywhere in the bathroom upstairs?"

"So it *is* Pria's blood?" she said.

"I don't know. *I don't know.* Why do you keep asking me? She wasn't there when I went to the house. And neither were Jessie or Luke." I squeezed my eyes shut. "God, please don't let it be Jessie."

"We were able to gain access to Jessie's health records online," said Trent. "It's not Jessie's."

"Thank you," I mouthed at him

The questions paused for a moment while I closed my eyes, grateful to know the blood didn't belong to her. Tommy's blood had already been spilled months ago—it couldn't be his.

"Are you and Bernice lovers?" Annabelle fired at me then.

"What?" My eyes shot open.

"Our team found sex play gear and marijuana at the house you and Bernice have been frequenting," she told me.

"What you found is Bernice's *disguises*. Apparently, she dresses as a man so she can walk the streets at night in relative safety. And so that people don't know it's her going through their trash. I knew nothing about all that until tonight. And I haven't been frequenting number 29."

Annabelle and Trent exchanged looks.

"Then why did you and Saskia choose to go there after you left Greensthorne?" asked Trent.

"Because I found something belonging to Tommy there—days ago. A piece of his nightlight. Except, it didn't end up being from his nightlight. It belongs to another version of it. Slightly different." Taking the boat from my pocket, I placed it on the table.

Annabelle creased her face in a cynical expression, not even bothering to look at the boat. "Sorry, but I'm not following. What does it matter? You found a piece of a kids' toy that was similar to your kid's toy?"

"Yes. But the nightlight was expensive. And limited, numbered edition. There isn't going to be bits of them everywhere. They're not McDonald's toys."

"Let's move on from the nightlight." Trent seemed impatient while trying hard to appear to be the opposite. If it was true that police worked in good cop/bad cop pairs, then he was making an attempt at being the good one.

"No," I said unwilling to let it go. "You can go to the toy store and find out who bought the last one they had, six months ago. This person lives on our street, but I don't know their name. But you can find that out. You're the police"

"How do you know all that?" Annabelle frowned at me.

I couldn't tell them Sass had been impersonating a police officer. "It's not important."

"Leave it for us to decide what's important," Annabelle told me.

"Okay, then we'll make a deal," I said boldly. "You listen to what I have to say, and I'll answer your questions." I needed them to know what I knew. Urgently. So far, they hadn't given me a chance to explain myself.

Detective Gilroy nodded. "All right, Phoebe, what do you want to tell us?"

"I have reason to believe that the abductor of my son is Pria Seville."

"You told us that when we first brought you in," he said. "But we have no reason to believe that she is."

"Because you're not listening to me." I clasped and unclasped my hands, not knowing where to put them, a desire to *run* increasing inside me. "There's a toy room upstairs in her house. It's been locked all year. She told Jessie that she'd bought a puppy to help guard the house, but that the puppy was too aggressive and needed to be taught how to behave before Jessie could meet it. But Jessie never got to meet it. And when Bernice and I went up there, there's no sign of a dog ever having been there. In fact, there's nothing in there at all. But Bernice found a toddler-sized handprint high up on the wall."

The cynical look hadn't shifted from Detective Yarris's face. "You and Pria were friends. Even if it was Tommy's print, he could have been in that room before."

"The room's been totally renovated since he's been in there. And besides, it smells of cleaning liquid, like it's all been thoroughly cleaned recently."

"Understandable if she had a dog in there," said Annabelle.

"Who would keep a dog locked in a room for six months?" I shot back.

"We don't know if this is even true." Annabelle tapped her pen on the table, obviously not liking the direction the conversation had taken. "Is the handprint clear?"

"It's smudged," I said.

She sighed, sounding annoyed. "So, we can't use it. Is this all you wanted to tell us?"

"No, there's more. I remembered something. Late last year, I was visiting Pria with Tommy. We were playing hide-and-seek. All of us— Jessie too. A pile of books and stationery crashed to the floor in Pria's office. I assumed Tommy did it, even though it would have been hard for him to reach that high. I didn't think about it at the time. Anyway, I helped her pick it all up. There were some loose sheets of paper and envelopes. They were blue. I touched them when I put them back on the desk."

I noted a vague interest in Trent's eyes. "You're saying this stationery was the same as that used in the kidnapper letters?"

"Yes. I'm certain."

Detective Yarris shook her head, a slight alarm in her eyes at the turn the conversation had taken. "Why wouldn't you have told us that before?"

"It was one of those tiny things," I said, "that you forget almost as soon as they happen. And it was a long time ago. November last year. I didn't connect it until I was back in her office again."

"Did you find that stationery tonight? In Pria's office?" asked Trent.

"No. Maybe she threw it away."

"That gives us nothing to go on." Annabelle rubbed her forehead. "Okay, well, if that's all you have to tell us, then—"

"There's something else." A secret that I could no longer keep. That I should never have kept.

"Go ahead," said Trent.

"This was years ago," I started.

"Then how is it relevant?" Annabelle raised her eyebrows, glancing at Trent with a weary expression. She wanted him to tell me my time was up. No more of me having free time to speak.

"It could be," I told her quickly. "I know how Grace Clark died."

My words got their attention, but neither of them seemed to recognise the name. No one remembered the poor woman. Not even the police.

"She died in number 29," I said. "About thirteen years ago. Fell through the stairs onto the floor below. A homeless lady."

"I wasn't working here then," said Annabelle. "Hell, I wasn't even a police officer, actually."

"I was here," said Trent, looking deeply engaged in thought. "The stairs had been purposely cut."

"Yes, they were. And me, Pria, Luke, Saskia, Kate, and Bernice were all there."

"You what? You were there in the house when Grace died?" Detective Gilroy's eyes widened, and he waited for me to continue.

"Yes, we were. We'd been drinking. The usual teenage stuff. Luke and I went upstairs to hook up. We heard an alarm clock go off in one of the other rooms. We went to check, and what we found"—I sucked in a breath, remembering the terrible smell yet again—"was a circle of dead rats on the floor, surrounding the clock. Each one with a knife in its belly."

Neither Annabelle nor Trent was interrupting me with questions now.

"Luke was angry. He grabbed a knife from one of the rats and charged out into the hall. Unfortunately, the lady—Grace—came running out of the middle bedroom then. We didn't even know she was there. The alarm clock must have woken her. She saw Luke with the knife, and she ran away from us. Onto the stairs. That's when they collapsed."

Trent scratched his temple—a distracted, thinking gesture. "What happened to the rats?"

"Luke's mother came and cleaned it all up."

He blew out a long breath. "She was the one who reported hearing something next door at number 29. Bloody hell. All of you kept this a secret all this time."

"Yes," I said, watching both their faces.

"So, how does Pria come into this?" Annabelle's tone had changed, but I couldn't guess what she was thinking.

"Someone had to be underneath the stairs, waiting to collapse the ladders that held up the stairs. We were sure it was Bernice at the time. But we were too scared to tell the police anything. But tonight, we watched an old video. The camera had been running at the time. The video shows it was Pria who was the one who went into the space under the stairs, the second before the stairs collapsed."

"Why didn't you watch the video before?" Annabelle's eyes sharpened.

"It was a shocking thing, what happened to the woman. Things happened so fast after she died that all of us forgot the camera. Luke's mother put it away when she came in and cleaned up. She destroyed the tape that was in the camera, but the camera films on its on-board memory when the tape is full or when there's no tape. The video was still there."

Trent and Annabelle exchanged glances again.

He turned his face to me. "Where's the camera now?"

"It's still upstairs, in a room at number 29."

"Why would Pria cut the stairs, though?" he asked. "And how? It's a pretty impressive feat—cutting the stairs and concealing the cuts, and at the same time making sure the stairs were stable enough to walk on."

"I'm not sure. Pria's father made furniture from tree logs. A hobby. She used to help him. I don't know why she cut up the stairs, though. I always assumed that Bernice did it because she liked Luke or something and wanted to hurt me."

"Damn," said Trent. "Was that the reason you thought Bernice had a grudge against you? You know back when I asked you who could be writing the letters? You named Bernice, but wouldn't tell me why."

"Yes, that's why. But we found out tonight that it wasn't her."

Detective Yarris studied my face. "Do you have anything else? Anything else you remembered?"

Trent seemed surprised at her question.

When Annabelle noticed his confusion, she took a quick breath in and out. "I'm feeling like we've been looking at the tip of an iceberg in this case all along," she told him. "I'm happy to go and bring in the camera—if it really exists. And run a check on the nightlight tomorrow."

He still seemed hesitant when he nodded. I wondered if because he'd been on my side all along, when all evidence had ended up pointing to me as Tommy's killer, he'd grown especially hard against me.

"Thank you," I breathed. "There's probably lots more I could tell you, but my head isn't working properly. Because of the sleeping pills I took. For what it's worth, I found this in Pria's office, but it's just a drawing." Pulling out the folded pencil sketch of the mountain, I pushed it across to them.

Frowning, Annabelle unfolded the large piece of paper.

Trent bent his head over it. "Yeah, that's not telling us any—"

"Wait." Annabelle traced a finger over the words, *sanctuary*, *eden*, and *refuge*. "Those mean something if you're into sailing yachts down to

Victoria. Those are all stops along the way. Sanctuary Point. Eden. And Refuge Cove. People stop at those because they're beautiful. And safe. *Ab ovo* I don't know about. I'm not saying that's what these are, but . . ."

I gaped at her. "I know where Eden is. Not far from where Luke's parents have a holiday house. But I've never sailed that far with Luke. I get seasick. But he's been with his father a few times."

"My husband's parents are yachties," she said. "I made the trip once with them down to Victoria. Never again. I'd rather drive it."

Trent pulled out his phone and tapped on the screen. "Hmmm, *Ab ovo* . . . doesn't look like it's a place anywhere in Australia. Lemme look up the dictionary meaning. Okay, it's *something, something* about Helen of Troy and an egg. Apparently it means new beginnings." He raised his eyes to Annabelle. "So, where are the other two places?"

"From Sydney, Sanctuary Point is the first, Eden the second," Annabelle told him. "The third one on that list is Refuge Cove. But it's way past Eden. It's on the southernmost tip of Victoria."

"Hell of a long way down," agreed Trent. "If that's your last port of call, where would you be headed?"

"The Bass Strait," said Annabelle simply, staring down at the picture. "That's if you were headed out to sea. Next port of call, Tasmania." Her forehead pulled into a frown. "Unless you're stopping at one of the islands along the way. There's quite a few. There's about three hundred kilometres between the mainland and Tasmania."

God, where were they and where were they headed? Beyond Tasmania, there was only Antarctica. Tasmania was a relatively small island compared to the open vastness of Australia, but there were still too many places they could hide.

Detective Gilroy's expression was troubled as he eyed me. "Does Pria own a yacht?"

"Not as far as I know. She sold her parents' yacht a long time ago. But Luke does. He keeps it moored at the docks."

"I don't know what's going on here, but I tell you what. We're going to follow up on what you've told us tonight. First thing, we'll find out if Luke's yacht is still moored."

47.   JESSIE

TWO NIGHTS AGO
Monday night

ROUSING, I THOUGHT I HEARD A horn. A ship's horn.

I sat up in bed. Where was I?

It took me a few moments to remember. I wasn't at home anymore. I'd left that far behind.

I'd woken too soon. Through the porthole, I could see that it was still dark. I watched the porthole lights of a large ship pass us by.

I stretched and slid from the bed. Mum was lying asleep on the bed in the other room—Mr Basko's room. Maybe she didn't want to wake me by coming in here. Would Mr Basko get angry with her for being in his room—like Mum did when I was where I wasn't supposed to be?

I decided to go back to sleep. I didn't want to go up on deck alone and talk to Mr Basko. I'd never been shy of him before, but I was now.

When I woke again, we were docked. I thought we'd arrived at our mysterious destination, but Mum told me it was just a stop off. Somewhere called Sanctuary Point.

My stomach was woozy as I left the yacht. The sunrise lit the water pink and yellow. The first day of my holiday. We were already a long way from home, Mr Basko told me.

We had breakfast at a small café—sausages and eggs. But I couldn't eat much.

Mum and Mr Basko carried boxes of food and drinks onto the yacht and filled the fridge. I took a walk along the beach, scuffing the sand with my toe.

"Help me put the things away, Jess," Mum called from the cabin.

Regretfully, I left the sand and returned to the yacht. Mum's cheeks were bright from the cold, but she was smiling. I couldn't remember ever seeing her this happy. Working beside her, I put the frozen food away in the freezer and the milk and cheese in the fridge. She told me there was no point putting anything else away as we'd be taking it all off the yacht again.

I felt the buzz of excitement return. Where were we going? Mum was still keeping it a big surprise.

"Just put the cereal in a cupboard, honey, so it doesn't knock around," she told me.

The box wasn't heavy, but it was big, filled with ten or so different types of cereal. I tried to open a rounded plastic door in a recess under the cabin stairs. It reminded me of a hobbit door. I noticed then that the turnstile wheel had a padlock.

"What are you doing?" Her voice turned sharp.

"Just trying to find somewhere to shove this box."

"Well, aren't you lazy? You could have just taken the boxes of cereal out of the big box and put them in a kitchen cupboard."

"But you said you didn't want stuff unpacked."

"Well, use your brains. Anything loose has to be taken out of the boxes."

"I didn't know."

"Okay, well, just don't touch that door. Luke might get cranky. It's a place to keep important things secure. So that if you dock the boat and leave it, no one can steal your money and things." She switched back to her happy face. "Why don't you go back up on deck? I'll finish up here."

I didn't need to be told twice. Mum could go on and on sometimes if I got things wrong. I walked out to the bow of the boat.

Mr Basko grinned at me from the steering wheel. "How's your stomach? Handling it better?"

"Not too bad I guess."

"Good." He took in a deep breath as he eyed the ocean. "We'll make a sailor of you yet."

"Mum told me that you were a sailor. She was fibbing."

One side of his face creased into a wink. "I'm kind of a sailor. I just don't get paid for it. So, do you like it out here? Or would you rather be sitting at a school desk doing fractions?"

"I'm terrible at fractions."

"Maybe I can teach you."

His eyes looked sad then, and I wondered if he was thinking of Tommy. Maybe he was thinking it should be Tommy on this boat instead of me, and he should be teaching Tommy how to do things.

"Mr Basko, how long until we get there?"

"I'm hoping to get there in a few hours. There's some bad weather coming." A quick smile spread across his face. "But nothing we can't handle. We're sailors, right? And hey, call me Luke."

"Okay." But I didn't know if I could get used to calling him that. Phoebe was Phoebe, but Luke had always been Mr Basko or Tommy's dad. I didn't know him like I knew Phoebe.

White clouds spun across the sky overhead. There was just ocean all around now. No land at all. It was beautiful and scary at the same time. I hoped Mr Basko knew where he was going. How did anyone find their way out in the middle of all this water?

*

My sea sickness went away sometime on Wednesday. Which was just as well, Mum said, as she brought out a chocolate cake to celebrate our first trip together.

We'd made another stop on land, this time overnight, at a spot called Eden. Mr Basko and Mum slept in the same bed that night, the door closed.

I wanted to stay in Eden, the coastline looked so beautiful. But Mr Basko was steering the yacht back out to the endless ocean.

We played monopoly out on the deck in the afternoon. Mum won. She almost always won games when we played at home. Mr Basko tried to help me work out what to sell and buy, but my mother stopped him, telling him the best way for me to learn was on my own.

When the game was done and Mr Basko started steering the yacht again, Mum started cuddling him, telling him he was a different man than the one that'd left Sydney. She kissed him a few times on the cheek, the kisses getting longer each time.

"Going to go read my book," I mumbled.

I was surprised she heard me. "Stay on the deck. You'll start getting seasick again if you go in the cabin. Okay?"

"Yeah, okay."

Taking my book, I wandered down to the other end of the yacht. I didn't want to watch her kissing Tommy's father. *Phoebe's husband.* Maybe it was okay because Phoebe was going to jail and she couldn't be Mr Basko's wife anymore, but it was all so mixed up.

I hated to think of Phoebe going to jail. She'd been a friend to me.

I picked a sunny spot on the deck and sat cross-legged.

Mum glanced down to check on me a few times, but then she stretched out on a deck chair, content to watch Mr Basko and the ocean.

I'd only had three chapters left to read of *The Girl Who Circumnavigated Fairyland in a Ship of Her Own Making,* and I finished the chapters quickly. Proud that I was up to the second book in the series already, I thought of going to tell Mum. But she seemed to have dozed off in her deck chair.

I hummed the tune from a song I liked as I headed down into the cabin.

A knocking sound made me pause mid-stair.

Tap tap tap tap

It was dull. But I heard it.

Did a bird get in and was trapped in a cupboard? Continuing down, I checked the cupboards and rooms. There was nothing at all here.

Looking through my box of books, I picked out the book I was reading next. Tracing a finger over the shiny new cover, I returned to the stairs.

Tap tap

The noise was coming from under the stairs.

From inside the cupboard with the hobbit door.

A thought flashed in my head. What if Mum was only pretending that she'd given the dog away and she'd actually brought it with us? Or maybe she'd already bought the new puppy that she promised me?

Something was making that sound.

I remembered Mum bringing home a few rescue dogs and cats before from the pound. But they'd always ended up running away or something. I'd been small then.

The lock had the key still in it. I could open the door and take a quick peek. But if it was a pup, I'd be ruining her surprise.

Tap tap tap tap tap

If it was a pup, maybe it was stuck. And I'd almost convinced myself it was a pup. If I went and told Mum about the tapping, she'd only be annoyed. I wasn't supposed to go below deck at all.

I was going to peek.

Tiptoeing around and under the stairs, I ducked my head until there was enough space above me to stand almost straight. The key in the padlock was tiny. I had to be careful that it didn't fall out and get lost. Because then the padlock could never be opened again. And Mum would know I'd tampered with it.

Gently, I rotated the key and removed the heavy padlock. Now, there was a wheel thing to spin around. It made a squeaking sound as I wrenched it.

My heart started to jump as I cracked the door open.

The cupboard was large, going deeper and higher than I expected. A soft-glowing light hung on the wall. There was nothing in there.

Wait. There was a yoga mat on the floor. A thick blanket hid whatever was sleeping under it.

It moved.

Its foot was under the blanket, kicking a metal tin that was as big as a barrel.

Tap tap tap

I drew closer.

I could see soft fur—very light in colour.

A golden retriever? A Maltese?

I knew all the dog breeds. I'd wanted a puppy forever.

The head was large and round. Too big for the small size of the dog. What kind of dog had—?

My feet glued to the floor.

It wasn't a dog.

It was a boy. A little boy.

Here.

I didn't even think about getting in trouble anymore as I knelt down beside him. He was asleep. Kicking the tin in his sleep. Sweat beaded on his forehead.

He was too hot. I tugged the blanket back. There were straps—wide straps around his arms and legs.

My throat hurt as I swallowed.

I felt the same way I did at Mia's sleepover party, when her teenage sister put on a horror movie to scare us. We thought it was a joke at first, until we were too scared to speak or move.

This was all kinds of wrong.

And then I knew one of the things that were wrong.

I knew who he was.

He was a little bigger and different than last time I saw him.

He was Tommy Basko.

I couldn't catch my breath as I backed away, the little boy's name roaring inside my head. Hot tears sprung into my eyes and ran down my cheeks.

Why was he here?

I hated closing the door on him, but I didn't know what else to do.

As I fumbled with the padlock, I heard someone on the stairs.

Mum rushed down the stairs, gasping angrily.

Her hands were around my shoulders and throat before I could even turn around. She shook me. Hard. Her fingers pressing in deeper.

"*Luke!*" I cried out. But my voice was muffled, spluttering.

She released me, roughly turning me to face her.

I coughed and breathed in sharply, holding my throat, protecting it from her.

Her upper lip trembled, her eyes switching from angry to alarmed and fearful. "Oh, Jessie, what did you make me do that for? It's not me to do that. You know that. I didn't expect you to disobey me. You caught me off guard."

"You hurt me," I accused.

She crushed me to her, stroking the back of my head. "Parents get pushed too far sometimes. I'm sorry. *I'm sorry.* Okay?"

Her hold felt suffocating. I wriggled out of her arms.

"Jessie, are you upset by what you saw in there? We need to talk about this."

I breathed in a tiny measure of courage, pointing at the hobbit door. "That's Tommy Basko in there."

"Yes, it is." Tears wet her eyes as she nodded.

"Why? Why is he here?"

"Because he's ours, that's why."

"He's *not* ours. He's Phoebe's."

"No, you don't understand. Phoebe's not well. She did bad things to Tommy. She wasn't a good mother. So we had to rescue him."

"The police think she killed Tommy. That's why she's going to jail. But she didn't."

"If he was there with her for much longer, she would have. You saw the news and all the cut-up teddy bears? That would have been Tommy. Someone had to keep him safe."

I panted, leaning against the door. The cut-up toys had terrified me. A Phoebe that I didn't know had ruined those toys. There'd been groups of strangers on our street for days, yelling out horrible things about Phoebe. I'd heard them when I was walking home from school. Everyone thought bad things about Phoebe.

I swallowed, tasting my own tears. "Tommy was the puppy upstairs, wasn't he? We never had a dog."

"It killed me not being able to tell you the truth. Yes, Tommy's been part of our family all along. It's been rough on me just looking after him."

"What about Mr Basko? Does he know Tommy's here?"

"Of course. But he was worried about how you'd react. He wanted it kept secret until we get where we're going. You mustn't say a word to him."

She spun the wheel around and then replaced the padlock. Dropping the key in her pocket, she guided me away. "Go and dry your face. And remember, not a word to Luke."

"Wait, we can't leave Tommy in there. There's not enough air."

"The room has lots of air. He's just one little boy. Boats are not safe for little ones to be running around on. He's a lot safer where he is."

"His dad thinks it's okay?"

"It was his idea. Now go get yourself tidied up. We're almost there. Not long now."

48. LUKE

YESTERDAY
Wednesday afternoon

MY FIRST CLEAR VIEW OF *AB OVO* terrified me.

What the hell was I thinking? It was remote, wild, *empty*. Jagged, rocky hills rose beyond a white beach peppered with sticks and orange-hued rocks. Wind had blasted the trees bare along the shoreline, thrusting their branches up and backwards like women's skirts.

I'd brought a woman and her child here, and now I was responsible for them.

Pria said she'd organised someone to bring supplies each week from the mainland. But what if something happened and they didn't? We had no phones with us, no point of contact, except for the yacht. We'd somehow lost both our mobile phones in the rush to get ready, but I doubted they'd work here on the island anyway. I'd been carried along in Pria's bubble on the way here. But that bubble had burst on those forbidding hills ahead.

Ab ovo didn't strike me as a place abounding in nature's milk and honey. I went through a mental checklist of the fishing gear my father and I had on board. If things went badly wrong, at least we'd have fish. We had cooking facilities on the boat, lots of fire starters, and rope.

I calmed myself. I had backup. For the past few years, I'd operated to a plan. I needed that. The schedule. The planning. It was the way my father had done it. And he'd done all right for himself. Mum had always seemed happy and secure. I'd wanted that for Phoebe and Tommy. And now I had to provide it for Pria and Jessie.

Relaxing, I allowed myself to take in the beauty of the place. It was a wild, remote postcard view of a kind that few people would see in their lifetimes.

I sighted a spot to anchor the yacht and steered towards it.

Stepping up behind me, Pria put her arms around my waist, her face against my back. Jessie stood at the bow, her face more apprehensive than excited when she looked back at us.

"Land ho!" I called to Jessie, trying to cheer her.

Finally, she grinned, wind blowing her hair to and fro around her small face. I had to become like a father to this girl, but I didn't know how. She reminded me of Phoebe at the same age. That wasn't good. I much preferred she'd be like Pria and my mother. Open, with their emotions all on show. I could deal with displays of emotion. It was when those emotions were locked away I was at a loss.

Pria helped me anchor the yacht and get the blow-up boat ready to motor across to the island.

A family of brownish rabbits watched us take the first step on the shore.

Jessie ran to them straight away. I was relieved to see her do something childlike, instead of acting so adult as she did. The rabbits scattered among the orange-lichen-covered rocks.

Mentally, I added the rabbits to my list of food sources if everything went haywire.

Pria's eyes were more alive than I'd ever seen them. She was extremely pretty with the sun on her pale hair. I grabbed her for a quick kiss while Jessie wasn't looking. "Hey . . . we're here."

"Isn't it incredible? Our own island."

I stole another kiss. "Let's go find the cabin."

It wasn't hard to find. Sharp steps led up from the beach to the house, half concealed behind trees. It would be murder taking all our stuff up those stairs. There was another way up, on the slope of a ridge.

The three of us dragged our bags up a grassy slope and along a barely visible track. The house, made of wood and stone, was larger than it'd looked from the photographs, with a clear view of the ocean. I could guess why the previous owners of the island hadn't built at the highest point, even though it would have given them a 360-degree ocean view—the winds would probably have blasted them from all sides.

Inside, everything seemed clean and sturdy. It just needed a good airing. There were three bedrooms—one of those a loft, which Jessie immediately claimed. The furniture was comfortable, if old and dusty.

I whistled at the sight of the fireplace. Made of stone, it was a thing of beauty, soaring up to the high ceiling. "Gotta get a fire started."

"Better check it for animals first." Pria smiled. 'Don't want to scorch some possum's butt."

"I'll head back to the yacht for the fire starters and matches. I'll grab whatever else too."

"No, I'll go," Pria told me. "You and Jess can get it stocked with wood."

"Sure?"

"Yes, sure. I can see you're excited to look around." Tilting her head back, she looked up at the loft, where Jessie was investigating her new bedroom. "Jess, I want you to help Luke. And remember what we talked about, okay?"

Jessie glanced at me with tense eyes before nodding at her mother. I wondered if Jessie had been disobedient on the yacht or if she'd told her mother she didn't like me. Either way, there was going to be a settling-in period. I wasn't going to just fit in with Pria and Jessie overnight.

After Pria left the cabin, Jessie didn't look at me much. I guessed the issue was that she was uncomfortable with me. I made a few attempts at conversation while we went out to collect firewood, but she kept giving me short answers and then busying herself, her back turned to me. I decided to give her some space.

Pria returned with a backpack and a large suitcase on wheels, which she took directly into the spare bedroom. She handed me the fire starters. "I brought across some boxes of food, too. They're back on shore."

"I'll go grab them." Glad to be relieved of the edgy atmosphere between Jessie and me, I quickly lit the fire and then left the cabin, jogging back down to the beach. I took three trips to lug the boxes up the hill.

Flames roared in the fireplace. A low, steady hum came from the generator—Pria had got it cranked up for the fridge and lights. She poured us both a glass of red wine. "To us and *Ab ovo*."

"Cheers." I grinned, clinking my glass against hers. "Where's Jess?"

"She's gone out to poke around."

"On her own?"

Pria smiled widely. "There's nothing that can hurt her here. It's a sanctuary." With a hand on my shoulder, she kissed me deeply and then tugged me into the bedroom. She had fresh sheets on the bed already.

We made love, breathing in the heady, enticing scent of wood smoke. I could make an easy guess that most of Pria's barely controlled enthusiasm and energy during sex came from the excitement of her first day here at the island.

Afterwards, I stepped out onto the verandah, stretching. I imagined long days of sitting out here just taking in the view, like my dad on the porch at his cabin. I could hear Pria humming inside, putting things away in the kitchen cupboards.

I spotted Jessie down near the rocks, tossing a ball around. I'd have to put up a basketball hoop for her. It was lucky she was such a bookworm. I could see a young kid getting bored here after a few days.

Jessie rolled the ball along the sand, the ball disappearing behind a rock. She seemed to be gesturing to the ball, willing it to come back to her. She was either playing make-believe games, or there was a rabbit or something she thought she could train. Good luck with that one.

The ball rolled back. I straightened, mystified.

There must be another kid on the island. Pria was wrong that no one was living here—unless there were day trippers. But why would day trippers come here? There wasn't anything special to see here.

Thoughts of drug smugglers flashed through my mind.

Get away from civilisation for a minute, and all crazy thoughts come flooding in.

Jessie rolled the ball a bit short.

The other kid came running out. A very young child.

A felt a twinge of disappointment for Jessie. The kid was maybe not even three years old. Rugged up in a knit hat and thick jacket.

The kid's parents must be close by. Surely no one would let a kid this age wander an island on its own?

Shoving my hands in my pockets, I wandered down for the meet and greet of the family. If they did live here, I wanted to know who they were. I was starting to feel a bit territorial already. This was *my* island. Even if by association.

Jessie turned to me as I stepped onto the sand, her expression guarded, almost . . . *scared.*

I'd understood before when she was uncomfortable around me. But what was it that I'd done or said that had made her scared of me?

The child seemed scared of me, too, ducking behind the rock and peeking out.

There was no one up the broad stretch of beach in either direction. Okay, maybe they did just let their kids wander here. Who knows, maybe there's a family on the other side of the island, raising up their brood like wild things, pushing them from the nest as soon as they could walk. After you'd had four or five kids, maybe you stopped helicoptering them.

For Jess's sake, at least, I hoped there was a brood.

Jessie rolled the ball to him again.

Forgetting his shyness, he ran and tried to kick it, missing and then trying again.

Something about the way he moved reminded me of Tommy. But he was more confident than Tommy—better control of his body. Similar face, too, only his hair was much blonder, almost white.

He got it wrong when his kick connected with the ball, sending it in my direction instead of Jessie's. He ran my way and then stopped dead still, staring with wide eyes.

I couldn't look away. *His eyes.* Eyes just like Tommy's. Just like Phoebe's.

He pointed at me, the way Tommy used to point at everything.

"Daddy," he said.

His word tore at me. I shook my head. "No, I'm not—"

The wind collected his hair and blew it back from his face.

I saw him properly.

I saw Tommy.

His full, rounded cheeks, stung pink by the cold. His large, expressive eyes and dark eyelashes. His tiny, naturally pouting mouth.

Sinking to my knees, I knelt heavily on the sand. I didn't know anything right now except that this boy was my son.

He stepped towards me, an uncertain look on his face now. Raising his small chin, he looked beyond me.

I turned. Pria had stepped from the cottage.

Tommy bolted straight for her.

Pria scooped him up, hugging him.

I loped across the sand, my mind caught in a storm.

A nervous smile appeared on her face. "Luke, I can finally tell you!" Her smile faltered at the edges.

Words refused to come. I held out my arms, demanding Tommy. She delivered him to me, and I held him up, staring into his face—the face I hadn't seen for so long.

Becoming shy, he dropped his forehead down to mine. I cradled his small body, and he nestled in tight against my shoulder, coyly tapping my neck with his finger.

"How? How is it that he's here?" Inside, my mind was roaring, but my voice pushed out low and broken.

"We brought him to the island, Luke."

"We what?"

"He was on the yacht. He slept the whole way. There's a lot I need to tell you. Let's go for a walk." She glanced towards Jessie's still figure on the beach. "Jessie will be fine."

"No. Pria, you need to tell me now. Because I have all kinds of things running through my head. And none of them are good."

Tears made her eyes wet and shining. "I don't even know how to tell you. But you have to know. I found Tommy, just a day ago."

"What? You *found* him? Where? *Where?*"

"Please, walk with me, and I'll tell you everything."

I could scarcely breathe, as if my lungs had grown rigid.

We walked along the top of the hill, higher and higher. Until Jessie was a tiny figure on the beach, sitting and watching the ocean.

Tommy burrowed into me, clinging. He fell asleep the way he always used to do, in an instant. I had the irrational urge to shake him, force him to wake and open his eyes and assure me that he was alive.

Pria stopped and turned her tearstained face to me. "This is what I know. I've been noticing Phoebe coming in and out of a certain house on our street for a few weeks now. Sometimes with a strange man. Sometimes on her own. At first, I just thought she was having an affair. But then, after the fourth letter, I was terrified, knowing what she'd done. I decided to look for myself. Luke, you know the house. Number 29."

"*That's* where you found Tommy?"

"Yes. He was there. She had him locked in one of the rooms. There were toys. And some food and water. But . . ." Her voice caught in her throat. "It was cold, and he wasn't wearing much. Just a little summer top and a nappy. He was dirty, and the room itself just stank of mildew."

"*Fuck*. She was keeping him there? Like that?"

"I'm afraid so."

"Why didn't you call the—?"

"I did. I mean, that was my intention. I took Tommy from that horrible room, and I went downstairs. I was about to call the police when Phoebe burst into the house."

Pria gently brushed a lock of Tommy's hair from his cheek. "Luke, she was frightening. She demanded I give Tommy back to her. When I refused, she grabbed a knife from inside her jacket and waved it at me. I lied and told her that I'd already called the police. She backed off then, telling me that the police would end up giving Tommy to her, because she was the mother and she'd been suffering a mental illness. And you know, she's right. They would. They have little choice. They'd keep her away from him for a while, and she'd go into a facility while she recovers. But eventually, she'd get him back."

I kissed Tommy's forehead. His skin warm under my lips. My thoughts dark. "No judge in the land would give Tommy back to her after what she did."

"But she didn't murder Tommy. She didn't kidnap him either. You can't kidnap a child you have custody of. There are a few things she could be charged and jailed for—including serious neglect of Tommy and concocting the whole kidnapping drama. But there's a strong possibility she could get off those charges. I've witnessed the court proceedings for quite a few cases of child neglect. If the mother has a mental illness, they can't hold it against her. You and I know that it wasn't just an episode of mental illness though. It's Phoebe. Something about her is very wrong. She never wanted Tommy, but she couldn't give him up either."

"No, she never wanted him," I repeated. There hadn't been anyone in the past that I could tell that to. Her unhappiness at being a mother had been my burden to bear alone. It was a relief to finally say it. In the last months of the year before, she'd started heading out with damned Saskia, nightclubbing and who knew what else? I was the sucker at home with Tommy while she was leading the single life again.

Pria was sobbing now. "That's right." She wiped her face with her hands. "I hope you can find a way to understand. As a mother, I couldn't allow it. I couldn't let her have him back. *Ever*. I told her I was taking Tommy to the police, and I left. I put him in my car, and I drove away. In desperation, I came up with the plan to head to the island. Where Tommy would be safe. I knew you'd go straight to the police. I just wanted to give you time to think. So that you didn't make a decision you'd regret later."

I stared down at Tommy, still expecting him to be a mirage and vanish from my arms. "How could a little boy live in that house and no one knew? How could no one hear him?"

"He was drugged when I found him."

"*Drugged?*"

"I'm sorry. Yes, he was lethargic and floppy. But I don't know if she kept him there the whole time. I think she had help. I mean, someone must have been helping her, right? That phone call when Tommy disappeared? Someone had to take him from the playground. She must have paid someone well."

"*Hell.* I'll kill her with my bare hands when I see her again. Her and whoever else was involved in this. Fuck, why didn't I know? Her sleepwalking thing—that was probably just a cover for her going out at night to look in on Tommy. What was she hoping to achieve with this? *Attention?*"

"I think so. She wanted to rid herself of the responsibility of caring for Tommy, and she wanted the spotlight back for herself. So she came up with a plan in which Tommy would be snatched. She would receive enormous public attention and sympathy, and she could use her acting skills to play the part. Months later, when the attention began dying off, she started sending herself the letters. More attention on Phoebe."

"Well, she got what she damned wanted."

Every muscle in my body started shaking, and I couldn't gain control of it.

Gently, Pria took Tommy from me. "It's a reaction to the news. When people get news that overwhelms them, this can happen. You need time. Just sit, Luke. I'll sit with you. It's okay. Tommy's here. He's not going anywhere now. He's safe with us."

Not taking my eyes from Tommy for a moment, I did as she said. She was the one who'd brought my son back to me. I sat on the stringy, rough grass. "How did you even manage to smuggle Tommy here without me knowing?"

"He was among my bundles of things. And he slept in the cabin with Jessie. Anyway, he's here now. You've got him back."

"I appreciate what you've done. We'll stay overnight. But we've got to head back tomorrow. You know that we can't do this."

She looked alarmed, but then she wriggled down beside me, taking care not to wake Tommy. "We already have done this. Sometimes you have to do desperate things to keep your children safe. I know all of this is going to take a long while to sink in. You're in shock right now. For the past six months, everything has been about the police finding Tommy. Well, Tommy has been found. The police can't help you now. The only thing that would happen if the police get involved is Tommy getting back in Phoebe's hands."

"Pria, you're getting yourself in up to your neck doing this. Tommy's not your kid."

"How could I not? I love you, Luke. And I love Tommy. I want what's best for you both."

She hadn't said *I love you* before. If she'd said it an hour ago, it would have surprised me. Now, I was just numb.

Down on the beach, Jessie pulled herself to her feet and turned and watched us for a moment. Then she headed towards the house.

49. PHOEBE

AN OFFICER ESCORTED ME FROM THE cell back into the interview room. It had been a long, drawn-out night, sleeping on a hard bed. And an even longer day. It was now midday. The wheels were turning too slowly. Far, far too slowly.

"It's called Whale Rest." Detective Yarris slapped a photocopied map onto the table.

"What is?" I glanced from her to Trent Gilroy, confused.

"Phoebe," said Trent, "did you know Pria bought an island?"

"I—No. A whole island?"

"Yes," he said. "Within the last couple of weeks, in the name of her deceased father's company. It's located in the Bass Strait. She might have renamed it. Which might be where the name *Ab ovo* comes in."

"Oh God." I waited for him to say more.

"We checked Luke's yacht at the mooring. It's gone. We spoke to Luke's father to ensure that he hadn't taken it out. He told us that he wasn't aware that his son was going out on a sailing trip."

"Can you find out where he went?" I asked.

"We're on it right now," Trent told me. "We have a team making calls and trying to track the yacht. We've also been making other enquiries. We've found out that Pria contracted a building company to soundproof the walls and floor of the upstairs playroom in November of last year." He took a breath. "We spoke with your friend Saskia a bit earlier. She contacted us when she heard you'd been brought in. She corroborated everything you and Bernice said, including what Pria's daughter told her about the dog."

"And I went to your toy shop," Annabelle said, taking over. "Yes, there was a sale in January under the name of Kitty. It was bought with cash. No paper trail. But, when I showed him photographs of six different women, including Pria, he picked Pria out straight away. And we have the camera. It showed exactly what you said it did."

"And one more thing," said Detective Gilroy. "Forensics went over Pria's house and the playroom with a fine-tooth comb. The handprint was too smeared, but they did find a hair. And it appears to belong to Tommy."

I nodded, swallowing. I'd given them a lock of his baby hair when he'd first gone missing. "What's next?"

"I promise you this," he said. "We're moving on this as fast as we can. We don't have all the pieces, but we're not waiting for them before we act. As I said, we're making enquiries to see if we can locate Luke's yacht. We're also trying to find out if either Luke or Pria is on board and if Jessie's with them. We're getting two helicopters readied. If we get an affirmative, we'll be on our way."

I lowered my eyes. They weren't looking for Tommy. The chase was all about finding out what happened to Tommy. The *after*.

As if they knew what I was thinking, a lull came over the room. No one spoke.

It also wasn't lost on me that he'd said *either Luke or Pria*. The police still didn't know whose blood had been spilled in that bathtub.

It was moments later that a call came through on Detective Gilroy's phone. The yacht had been sighted at Refuge Cove. Early yesterday morning. A young couple and a girl of about ten on board.

"Hang on," said Annabelle. "So, all three of them? Alive and well?"

"Yep." Trent gave half a shake of his head, exhaling a stream of air. "This gets stranger."

They rose from the table together.

"Phoebe," Trent said, softening his tone. "We apologise for doubting you in the beginning. And for—Well, there's going to be a lot of conversations between us to come. But right now, we need to leave. Are you ready?"

"Yes, ready. Can I ask two things?"

"Name them," he said.

"Could you call Nan? Tell her I'm okay."

He nodded. "Sure thing."

"And the second thing is, I want Bernice to come with me."

"Bernice?" He looked puzzled.

"She didn't have to do what she did for me tonight. She had every reason not to. But she did. And if I find out the worst, I want someone there who actually loved Tommy. Nan can't make the trip. Sass can't either. And Kate—well—she abandoned me. Please."

He held me in his gaze for a moment then nodded at Annabelle. "The chopper can take five passengers. Three police. Phoebe and Bernice. We've got backup from Victorian police. We're good."

It took another hour from that point until we were seated in the helicopter, listening to the general emergency procedures.

Bernice's face somehow retained that look of disbelief from when the police had first taken me to her cell to ask if she'd come. As if the surprise had imprinted on her so deeply that it had worn through all her layers.

Like a scene from some TV police drama, the helicopter swept past the patchwork of towns and fields below. While I'd been in Greensthorne, Luke and Pria had been travelling all this way.

After three hours, the ride in the helicopter became increasingly bumpy.

The pilot twisted around to face Detective Gilroy. "Weather's turned foul. Going to have to land."

Trent leaned forward. "Now?"

"Yeah," the pilot confirmed. "Sorry, mate. We can take it to Refuge Cove. I'm not heading out to sea." He radioed a message while the helicopter continued to bump and drop.

Below, the land spread out wild and green, with open-space camping areas. We landed high above the bay, next to an old sandstone lighthouse. A sign said Wilson's Promontory.

Bernice stood blinking in the bright sunlight, peering down at the curved bay. A large police boat cut a white line through the water.

50. LUKE

PRESENT TIME
Thursday

PRIA STIRRED SOUP ON THE COOKTOP while Jessie and I bathed Tommy in a small tub in front of the fire. I'd found the tub outside this morning, and I'd scrubbed it spotless.

I poured warm water over Tommy's slippery, naked little body. He giggled, splashing water back at me. Last night, he'd slept in between Pria and me, holding onto my arm. I kept waking, thinking I'd dreamed him, then finding him curled up tight beside me. In the morning, the sunrise had exposed a dark sky, signalling an oncoming storm. I wasn't going to sail out in that. We'd stay another day. I was beginning to wish we could just *stay*. Life here on the island could be so damned simple. All the struggle and push to make money seemed unimportant now.

But we couldn't stay.

Tomorrow we'd leave—this afternoon if the storm came and blew over quickly.

The smell of bread piped through the house. Pria was making her own in the oven, to go with the soup.

"Hang on," said Jessie. She ran into Tommy's bedroom and returned with a plastic toy. His yacht. She sailed it in the water, Tommy grabbing for it.

I raised my eyes to Pria, confused. Tommy had that yacht with him when he vanished.

But Pria nodded, smiling as though she'd anticipated my question. "I found that. *You know where.* Knowing it was his favourite toy, I made sure we brought it along."

Returning her smile, I turned back to my son.

The situation I was in was insane. No man should be asked to deal with this. But right now, *to hell with it,* I was going to be happy. I had everything I wanted right here. Jessie seemed a little more relaxed in some ways, tickling Tommy's feet as she slipped his socks on, but even more tense in others. She'd glance from her mother to me and then turn her head away fast.

I dried and dressed Tommy by the fire, in the new clothes Pria had run out and bought for him when she'd first found him—everything with the tickets still on them.

Pria laid out the soup and bread on the table. Hungrily, I ate it all and had seconds. Tommy dipped his bread in his soup and ate that. I couldn't stop watching him. Every one of his little gestures and movements seemed a miracle.

"Oh, look," Pria crooned, as his eyes started fluttering downward. "I think our little man is tired out from his bath."

I laughed. "He's battling hard to stay awake, though. Typical Tommy."

Jessie left the table abruptly, heading out the door. The wind outside made the door slam hard.

"Damn," I said, indicating towards Tommy. "I think we're paying too much attention to a certain someone."

"She's being silly. Tommy's just a little boy, and she shouldn't be jealous of him. She needs to understand how things are right now."

"I'll go after her."

"No. Let her go and cool off."

"I guess you know your daughter best." Gathering my drooping son up, I took him into his room and tucked him into bed. I was amazed to see a large nightlight on the dresser beside Tommy's bed. It was exactly the same nightlight that Tommy used to have—the one that Phoebe destroyed. Pria must have run out and bought it the day she went to buy him the clothes. She'd thought of everything. Taking advantage of Tommy's sleep time, I headed out to chop wood in the shed. It'd be another chilly night tonight. Pria had returned to cleaning the house of dust and dead insects.

I noticed Jessie down on the beach. She was kneeling on the sand, making a sandcastle. That was exactly what kids her age should be doing. Instead of all their electronic games. I'd explore the island with her later. Try and get a relationship started.

Standing suddenly, she kicked her sandcastle down.

I decided to go walk down and ask if she'd like to make a tree house later. There was a big stack of wood in the shed. And trees with low, wide branches not far from the house.

Leaning the axe against the shed wall, I dusted my hands off and headed down to her.

When she caught sight of me, she began running away along the beach. I knew Pria would tell me to let her go, but I felt bad for the kid. It must be a huge and confusing change having me around—and now Tommy. I sprinted up to her, making an exaggerated puffing noise. "Hey, I'm old. You can't make me work this hard."

She stopped but didn't look at me. "I don't want to talk to you." Wind blew her hair over her small shoulders.

"Okay. Are you going to tell me why?" I stepped around to face her.

Immediately, she looked out to the sea. "I just want to get off this island. I don't want to be here anymore."

"Too boring? Or is it because of Tommy? Look, I know you're used to having your mum to yourself. And Tommy's getting in the middle of that."

She sucked her lips in. "Mum keeps saying he's ours. He's not *ours*. He's yours. And Phoebe's."

"That's true. But sometimes, families change. I know it's going to take time for you to get used to me. And to Tommy. He's been missing for a long time. It must be strange, him just appearing out of nowhere like this." I blew out a stream of cold air. "I thought maybe we could make a tree house later. Just you and me. Would you like that?"

She thought for a moment then shook her head.

"Okay, well, you're getting your wish about the island tomorrow. We'll be going home."

She tilted her head, screwing up her forehead as though she didn't believe me. "That's not what Mum says."

"Your mum wants to stay longer, that's true. But we can't."

"No, Mum told me this morning that we'll be here for months, so I'd better change my attitude."

"You must have heard wrong."

"That's what she said. And I'm not upset that you and Mum are spending time with Tommy, if that's what you think."

"You're not? I hoped you'd understand. I've only just got him back."

She stared at me with her upturned Pria-eyes. "You've had him all along."

"What do you mean by that?"

She moistened her lips nervously. "You and Mum kept him upstairs at our house. To save him from Phoebe. I thought it was a puppy Mum was keeping up there. But it wasn't."

"That's not what happened, Jessie."

She shot me an accusatory look, her voice rising. "Yes, it is. Why are you lying to me, Mr Basko? Why do all you adults lie to me?"

Stepping forward, I held her trembling arms. "He was only there at your house for a few hours. You've got it wrong."

"I heard him, *Luke*." Her voice suddenly sounded so damned mature. She was so like Pria. "He's been there all year. Sometimes, he'd throw things around. Mum would blame it on the dog going wild. But there never was a dog."

Panic started banging in my chest. Pria had casually mentioned a dog the night we left her house. But she'd never talked about a dog before that to me. "I was at your house lots. I never heard anything."

"When did you come? After *the dog* was asleep for the night? Because that's what Mum used to tell me. She'd tell me that Buster was a heavy sleeper. I'd hear him in the afternoons sometimes, when the house was all quiet and there was no TV on. But at night, I never did. And plus, Mum had new walls put on the playroom and a really thick door."

"She what? When?"

"I'm not sure. I missed the school bus one morning, and so I came back home. I couldn't find Mum. The door to the playroom was open, and I could see everything. Plus there was a TV and toys in there. I finally found her in her bathroom. Her clothes were all wet, and I thought maybe she'd been bathing the dog. She screamed at me. Told me to get back down to the bus stop and just wait for the next bus and told me it was my fault I was going to be really late."

Jessie backed away from me, pulling her arms free. "Mum tells me lies. You're telling me lies, too. And we're not leaving this island, are we? *Are we?*"

I heard Pria's voice, calling us from up the beach. "Jessie! Luke! Jessie!"

"Pria!" I called back. "Where's Tommy?"

Pria looked back up the sharp slope of the beach at the house.

Hell, she'd left him alone.

The house had no locks. And an open fire.

I tore along the beach. Pria just stared at me helplessly. I was out of breath by the time I reached the house. Flinging the door open, I raced in and entered Tommy's room.

He was still sleeping, his knees tucked up to his chest under the blanket.

Panting, I closed his bedroom door.

Pria stood in the frame of the front door. "He's fine, Luke."

"He's not fine. He can't be left alone."

Stepping inside, she closed the door behind her. "I just got worried. I couldn't see either you or Jessie."

A crushing pressure weighed on my mind. I studied her face, panting, searching for hints of what Jessie had just told me. She looked frightened of me suddenly.

"Luke?"

"Why weren't you worried before when you couldn't see Jessie? You were quite happy to let her go off around the island on her own."

"I don't know. I just—"

"Pria, it seems to me that you only got worried when you saw me gone, too. When you came down to the beach and saw me talking with your daughter. Do you want to tell me why?"

"What did Jessie say to you?" Her voice deadened.

"Is that what you're worried about?" I inhaled through teeth that were set tightly together, still breathless from the run up the steep hill.

"I'll tell you what she said. She told me that you were keeping Tommy in the playroom upstairs at your house. The whole time he's been missing."

She gaped incredulously, but her eyes gave away what I needed to know. Her face grew pale, high spots of colour in her cheeks.

"No. *No, no, no,*" I breathed.

"Luke, yes, I saved your little boy. Let me explain—"

My hands clenched repeatedly, the palms slick with sweat. "Tell me this. Was it you who took Tommy from the playground that day?"

Raising her face, she avoided me, gazing at the rafters as though there were some celestial light shining from up there. "I did the right thing."

I collapsed into the nearest chair, my fists on the table. "It was you. You all along."

Her mouth drew in, and she looked directly at me. "This doesn't change anything. I rescued him from her. And now you've got him back again."

"Do you have any fucking idea what you've done? Any idea at all?"

"But you've got him back—"

"You keep saying that. Like it's going to change anything." I swallowed back an intense desire to hit her. Shake her. Make her hurt. "The letters—was that you, too? No, don't bother. Of course it was you."

"If you just give me a chance to tell you why."

My voice darkened to a snarl. "Here's your chance."

She flinched. "Please. You'll know that I was only trying to do the best thing when you calm down. We had to do it this way. Everyone kept covering up for Phoebe. Her drinking. Her neglect of Tommy. She neglected you too, Luke. I dropped in to see her, the day she destroyed Tommy's things. I saw what she did. Her grandmother and Mrs Wick and Bernice were already there. I was terrified for Tommy. I wanted to take him, but Mrs Wick—evil witch that she is—shooed me away. I helped Nan take the toys away, in my car. She wanted to hide them in the toolshed. A few days later, Phoebe had forgotten everything. There was nothing to stop her from doing it again."

"That wasn't your call."

"Someone had to make the call."

"How did Tommy's blood get on the last letter?" I demanded. "What did you do to him?"

"You've seen for yourself that he's fine. He fell over and nicked his elbow. I collected a small amount of blood. No harm done."

"Don't tell me there's no harm done. You're insane. You gave Phoebe the third letter that night when she was sleepwalking, didn't you?"

"Yes. She was raving. Thought I was a wizard. Do you see, Luke? She's the crazy one."

A thought flashed through my head. "You watched our house. Your house is high enough on the hill to get a good angle from the top storey. You knew when Phoebe left the house at night. You knew when she was sleepwalking."

Her failure to answer told me that I was right.

"Hang on, it was *you* who suggested to me the name of those pills she was taking. I remember. Then Phoebe talked her psychiatrist into prescribing them, telling her she was desperate. And she *was* desperate. My wife was barely existing from day to day back then."

"That brand of sleeping medication is renowned for causing sleepwalking incidents. I didn't know it would cause her to sleepwalk, though. We just needed to disrupt her sleep patterns. People show their inner selves when they're exhausted. If that medication didn't work, there were others on my list. It's too easy for violent, neglectful mothers to get off on charges against them. We had to do something to show everyone the crazy inside Phoebe. Bring it out into the open."

"*Hell.* All that time, I was coming to you to try and release the stress, I was bloody telling you all about Phoebe, offloading on you. You used that information for your own purposes, didn't you?"

"We did what we had to do. You'd tell me about her state of mind, and I'd plan what to do next. We were a team. And we succeeded." Her mouth drew down and tightened. "But you took a long time to love me. I gave you so many chances to show your desire for me. It had to be you who made the first move. You took nine whole months. It was the last thing that needed to happen before we could start a life together. And it was beautiful when it happened. We did it, Luke. We made it."

Her smile vanished before the look that I gave her. Bloody thoughts churned through my mind. I wanted to kill her. "Stop saying *we*. There is no *we*. I didn't do any of this."

"You were there, all along. And you were the one who talked your wife into those pills. Take some responsibility. Be strong, like I've had to be."

"That's not what happened."

"It's exactly what happened. You can't pretend you didn't play a part in this. You've been coming around to see me since October last year. You know you have. We were a couple, in secret. Maybe not so secret. Bernice used to watch you coming in. You wouldn't have noticed her. All you wanted was to be with me, but you couldn't. You couldn't divorce your wife and leave her alone with Tommy. You were so terrified of what your wife would do to him, you had your mother move in. Your mother couldn't live there forever. So, we took Tommy away and kept him safe. And then you sailed him away to the island. You did all that. For us."

Hell. Hell. Hell.

Everything clicked through in my head, everything she'd said. I *had* been having an affair with this woman. The physical affair itself had only started a week or so ago, but no one knew that except Pria and me. Once this reached the media, they would blow it out of all proportion. And Tommy had been kept at the house I'd been visiting since he disappeared. I could hear the cries of people reading that juicy piece of news: *"How could he not know?"* they'd say. I'd look guilty as hell. I was the one who negotiated the sale for this island. *Me.* And she was right. I'd brought her, Jessie, and Tommy here. *Willingly.* When this went to court, I could end up in prison. It could easily go that way.

Pria stepped over to sit at the table. "Luke, everyone thinks Tommy's dead. Phoebe will go to jail on the strength of that. There's enough evidence against her. And I have more evidence prepared, if needed. She won't be able to hurt Tommy again. You're free to go on and live your life and raise your son. We can stay here. But if you raise the alarm, Phoebe will get Tommy back."

She touched her fingers to mine, her face strangely composed again.

I struggled against the recalibration inside my mind. The vision of Pria and me together against Phoebe had been cemented over the past few months. Phoebe the wicked, crazy one. Pria the warm, earthy, and sensible one.

I had my son back with me. Phoebe had never been the kind of wife and mother that my mother was. She never could be. There were days I'd spent at work terrified that I'd come home to find that Phoebe had done something terrible—either to herself or Tommy.

"Luke," Pria said softly. "We can have another baby, together. A little brother or sister for Jessie and Tommy. You told me that you wanted Phoebe to have another, and she refused. But I'd give that to you. It's only right, anyway. I was the first one to have a baby with you, not Phoebe."

A picture of Pria at age sixteen rushed through my head. Pria, after a tense month while she decided whether she'd keep the baby or not, meeting me at number 29 to tell me she'd lost it. Tears streaming down our faces (with joy) we'd downed a half a bottle of Southern Comfort (with lemonade).

"You remember, don't you," she said, "the baby we had and lost. You thought I was happy it was gone. I wasn't. You were happy, and I was devastated."

"That's why you were crying?"

"Of course."

"I didn't know."

"You didn't ask."

"You're going to have to forgive me."

"You abandoned me afterwards."

"I thought that was what you wanted."

"I wanted you. But you didn't want me, enough. You let me go without another thought."

"It was just a short time we were together. And we slept together just one time at a party, Pria. One time."

"So you thought you could just discard me? And run after Phoebe? I tried everything I could to keep you, but—"

She stopped short, her eyes darting away from me suddenly. I glimpsed the tremor in her jaw. It struck me as fear rather than trauma.

Had there ever really been a baby? The possibility had never occurred to me before. When her gaze shifted back to me, I sensed the truth.

Jesus. What was I thinking?

Was there even anything real inside Pria?

In a defensive gesture, she wrapped her arms around herself, hanging onto her shoulders. Her jacket sleeves rode up, exposing an ugly dark line on one of her wrists.

"What happened to your wrist?" I asked.

Her mouth went tight. "Just a bit of extra evidence."

"What?"

"I cut myself before we left my house and let a bit of blood run into the tub. I just thought that if we were going to be gone for a long time, it might be best if it looked like something happened to me . . . ."

"Why would you—?" Rage blistered through me when I realised the answer for myself. "You wanted to make it look like Phoebe did that to you. Like you were forced to leave Sydney to escape from her. Or maybe to even make it look like she killed you, before she was taken away to the psych ward. You never intended us ever leaving this island."

I jumped up from the table. "I'm taking my son and Jessie to the yacht."

Her face dropped. "You can't sail out. There's a storm brewing. Take some time to think, and you'll—"

Leaning over the table, I roared in her face. "No! I'm not taking time to think. And I'm not sailing out either. I'm going to radio for help, and the kids and I are going to sit tight. In the yacht. Until the police arrive."

"I won't let you abduct my daughter."

"And I won't leave her here with *you*. Not another minute."

I watched her, her face and jaw tightening and her eyes going dark. She stood.

Keeping my eyes on her, I threw some things into a backpack. Bottles of water and packets of food. Enough to last the kids a few hours. Wrapping Tommy in the blanket, I left the house.

"Jessie!" Wind blew in from the sea, my loud voice waking Tommy.

Behind me, Pria walked in a straight line towards us, her expression oddly poised.

51. PHOEBE

Thursday

THE POLICE TRANSFERRED OUR PARTY TO a large boat. Police and Rescue from Victoria joining the crew.

If it was cold at home, the air was arctic here, freezing our faces into blocks of ice until we could barely speak. Wind whipped the waves into high peaks, snatches of rain gusting in and then catching on a wall of air coming from another direction and vanishing again. The storm was making everyone shout.

Bernice's skin reddened, her eyes watering in the cold.

"I'm sorry," I started. "I shouldn't have asked you to—"

"Don't bother saying it." She plunged her hands in her pockets, bringing her shoulders up tight. "I want to be here. It's not for you—I didn't come here for your sake. But I want to see justice for little Tommy."

I sucked my lips in, nodding, the wind drying the tears on my cheeks to salt. "That's all I have left. Hey, it was you that night, wasn't it? At my mailbox, after I'd been sleepwalking. What were you doing there?" I shut my eyes for a brief second. "No accusations. I'm just curious."

"Watching you," she answered.

I frowned at her. "Why?"

"I'd seen you roaming the streets before. I guess it seemed exciting, you heading out in the small hours. At first I thought you were having an affair, like Luke. Later I realised you were sleepwalking. So I kept an eye on you."

"You did?"

"Yeah." She shrugged. "Wasn't like I had anything better to do."

The afternoon darkened, the storm intensifying. It seemed that night was closing in hours early. At least, we were going to get there a lot quicker than a yacht would. An hour, I was told.

It was the island we saw first. In the distance. Dark, sharp hills like giant waves. The view of the island matched the picture Pria had drawn.

My fingers closed tight on the boat's railing. God, were they all there? Luke, Pria, and Jessie? The island seemed hostile and vulnerable to the elements at the same time.

What had Pria called it? *Ab ovo.* Her new beginning with my husband.

Detective Gilroy spotted the yacht next, through his binoculars. He told us he'd seen it, then he said something I couldn't catch to Annabelle, glancing back at me with a tense expression.

As we drew closer I saw what he did.

The yacht listed on its side, water spilling in and out with the rock of the waves. One sail flapped uselessly.

The wind caught my cry, snatching it away.

My lungs felt raw as the police roped the yacht in.

Had Jessie been on there? Luke?

Luke was a question mark in my mind. I didn't know him anymore or whether I should care. *What had he done? What had he known? What was he responsible for?*

Police Rescue jumped on board, clad in wetsuits. They searched inside the cabin. And came out shaking their heads. *No one on board*, came the shout.

All of us scanned the sea on the way into shore.

Looking for survivors.

Or bodies.

We sailed onto the beach in two inflatable dinghies.

Immediately as I stepped onto the island, it seemed *hers*. Pria's. The island she'd drawn and dreamed about. *Her Ab ovo.*

There were footprints up and down the beach, vertically.

They'd made it. Either something had made them leave again, or the weather had destroyed the yacht and blown it away.

Bernice walked onto the beach. She tilted her head back, her eyes sweeping the scene before us. She made a low whistle. "Pria's island, hey? Who would have thought?"

Faint trails of smoke rose from between the thick, gnarled trees up on the ridge.

"You two stay here on the beach." Trent had a hand inside his jacket, on his gun holster. He glanced behind him at Annabelle.

She nodded at him.

The police rushed away.

Were they all up there, in that house? They would have seen us land on the beach.

I wanted something to do. Someone or something to look for. But this was the end of the line—that invisible thread I'd sensed that connected it all—and there was nothing for me to look for anymore. There was nothing to do but wait.

Bernice and I jumped from foot to foot, trying to keep our faces from the path of the biting wind. At least the sand wasn't blowing about and whipping us. It was damp and coarse and crunchy underfoot.

A basketball blew along the sand.

Jessie loved playing netball. I retrieved the ball. Her initials, JS, were written on the ball in black marker. Jessie-sized footprints were here everywhere.

Bernice crouched down to the sand. "It looks like they've got a little person with them." She swivelled her head back, squinting at me. "Tiny footprints."

I didn't believe her. I couldn't. I'd built a castle wall against thinking about that possibility. Armed the turrets. Dug a moat.

"You're not going to look?" she said. "I'm not saying it's—"

High above at the house, something was happening. Police were moving back. Giving room.

Detectives Gilroy and Yarris brought a woman out from the house. Pria. Her body rigid but calm.

Jessie's ball dropped from my hands. Without a word, without realising what I was doing, I was sprinting. Across the sand. I was on the stairs and charging all the way to the top.

The police didn't try to stop me. There was no danger here. Pria wasn't a woman with a knife or a gun. But she *was* dangerous. And I needed to know exactly what she'd done.

Avoiding my eyes, she stared past me, out to the sea. Her thick hair damp and back in a headband. Dressed in ordinary clothes, like the mothers you saw walking to pick up their children from the local schools. You wouldn't pick her out in a crowd or a video as a danger to anyone. Her clothing was also damp.

"Why?" I'd found my voice. The intensity of it fearful. I was capable of murder in this instant. *"Why?"*

Her eyes didn't shift to me, but her mouth turned down. "Someone had to rescue him." Her voice grey, ashes. So unlike the Pria that I knew.

"You stole him away from me. It was *you* that day at the playground."

"I saved Tommy from you. You didn't appreciate him—or Luke— the way you should have. You had everything. But it wasn't enough for you."

I recoiled, knowing what Pria had done but still shocked at my first glimpse of the scorched earth inside her head. The real Pria, the person she'd hidden so well.

"How could you do it, Pria? We were friends." My voice grew gravelly, stones lodging in my throat. "What did you do with him? Where'd you put him? Where is he?"

"Gone."

"Where's he gone?"

She pointed out to sea.

I twisted around at the thrashing waves then turned to face her again. "He's not out there. You tell me what you did with him."

"Luke took him. He took Tommy, and he went. I saved both of them, but he didn't care. He left me here."

Trent Gilroy nodded at me, his strange expression making me terrified. "Phoebe, we found nappies and little-boy clothing inside the house. And this." He produced a plastic object from inside his jacket.

A toy yacht.

Tommy's.

I cried out, my fingers trembling as I reached for it.

Pria watched me take the toy. "If you were trying to find Tommy, you should have come sooner. Luke took him and my daughter on that yacht. He should have known not to sail in that weather. Now I've lost all of them. Do you understand? I've lost my whole family."

Inside my chest, my heart jolted.

My castle walls came crumbling, smashing down. "Tommy?"

"We brought him here on the yacht," she told me in a matter-of-fact voice. "We fed him and bathed him and sat around the fire, like a real family."

Detective Yarris grabbed Pria's arm. "Tell us exactly what happened. Where's Luke and the children?"

Pria's eyes grew anguished and then dulled again just as fast. "It's too late. The yacht tipped, and I saw them fall out. They were way, way out. Is it my fault? Would anyone blame me? I don't know. I couldn't stop him from leaving. I tried to give them a better life here, but Luke didn't want that. Even Jessie turned against me."

"How long ago?" I screamed at her. "How long?"

For the first time, she looked directly at me. "About an hour before you came."

"Did they have life jackets on?" Annabelle asked desperately.

Pria hesitated, then shook her head.

"Everyone move out!" Trent bellowed.

One of the officers took hold of Pria, putting her in handcuffs. Annabelle spoke on the phone, calling for more boats.

For a moment, I was alone in my terror. Not knowing which way to head.

My jaw shook as I turned to face the ocean.

Bernice stood behind me.

"They were in the yacht, Bernice." I didn't recognise my own voice.

Bernice spun around, watching two of the police head for the boat. The others were organising themselves, shouting, running in opposite directions along the sand. I didn't know which way to head.

"Wait," Bernice said. "I don't know everything about yachts, but I did it as a job for a while. Seems the current's pushing left. Look, maybe they grabbed hold of something from the yacht and they've stayed afloat. We can try cutting straight across the island. Pointless following the police anyway."

I knew from the look in her eyes that she didn't believe that. They'd fallen out. They had no time to grab anything. For me to almost have Tommy and then lose him again in the same instant made me want to run to the topmost part of the island and throw myself from it. But I nodded. I needed to see this to the end. "Let's go."

"Pria." Bernice strode up to her, startling the officer holding her. "Is there a way directly across?"

She eyed Bernice coolly. "I haven't had time to explore. I've been busy making food and settling in. We had everything set up. Everything we could possibly need. Why are you even here?"

"Because Tommy could use another friend. Rather than an enemy like you." Bernice walked on past her.

I followed, stepping up alongside her.

"Please," Pria said, making us stop and look back. "I don't want to see Jessie. You tell the police. I don't want to see my daughter . . . *dead*."

I didn't answer. I had no sympathy. Not an ounce. If Jessie had drowned out there, my sympathy lay entirely with Jessie.

Bare rocks punctuated the hilly landscape, no trees daring to exist on the uppermost points of the island. Gasping and driven back by the wind, we climbed the slopes. Once we reached the tree line, we were protected from the storm, but the trees were dense, the ground soft and muddy in places. Rabbits scattered ahead of us through the scrub.

"Here!" I yelled. I glimpsed the ocean through the straggly bunches of native palm trees. The island had to be far longer than it was wide, as it had taken us only twenty minutes to get across.

We walked out onto an outcrop. The curve of the beach entirely composed of smooth, rounded rocks. A small cove. Hundreds of geese occupied the left end of the shore—all a pale brown with small beaks.

The waves in the cove were far calmer than they'd been on the other side of the island.

There was nothing in the water. No sign of bodies. They were either far out at sea or under the water. The nightmare drowning deaths I used to dream of Tommy were haunting me now, reaching up into my throat and taking my breath from me.

"They're not there." My head went faint.

"Phoebe. Don't stop. We keep going, okay?"

"They're not there," I repeated. "Do you see?"

"Just keep moving," she ordered. "We're here now." She sounded just like her mother, ordering Nan to go and see a doctor.

Her words brought me back.

I sprinted ahead of her, trying to shake off the nightmares. Those images had been tightly wrapped around me like a shawl, for months and months.

When I first saw the smoke, I thought it was mist.

But mist didn't curl upwards in a column.

I cut across the forest to the right, trying to get in a straight line with the smoke. Small rocky hills pushed into the trees here, making me climb again.

Bernice followed silently. She didn't have to push me on anymore.

I stood at the edge now, the beach below littered with dead palm fronds. I made my way down between the boulders, jumping the last few feet onto the sand.

The smoke ribboned upward from a small cave. Barely a cave at all. Shallow, but deep enough to keep a couple of wooden crates and old fishing rods and gear dry. There was no fire either. Just smoke in a pile of mostly damp palm fronds.

I imagined Pria smiling to herself right now.

She'd lied again. She *had* been to the other side of the island. And she'd done this.

Did she guess we were coming and she wanted to play one last trick? When I turned around, they were between me and the ocean.

Two children.

A girl with a small child on her hip, both of them bedraggled in wet underwear.

It was Jessie. And a boy with bleached-white hair and six months of growth I hadn't witnessed.

Tommy.

Tommy, alive and staring at me curiously.

A sobbing cry tore from deep inside me.

"Phoebe?" Jessie ran halfway to me, then she stopped still, nervous and uncertain as she held Tommy out to me.

I rushed to them, encircling both of them in my arms. Tommy's little face pressed against mine. I cried openly. I didn't want to scare him, but I couldn't stop myself. They were here, and I didn't understand why, but they were here. I kissed him, kissed Jessie, kissed Tommy again.

Tommy held out his arms to me. He was shivering. As was Jessie. Stripping my overcoat off, I pulled it around Jessie's shoulders. I shrugged off the jacket I wore underneath that, bundling Tommy in it and taking him from Jessie.

"How did you get here?" whispered Jessie, wrapping the oversize coat tightly around her.

"I finally found out what I should have known all along." I kissed her forehead, rubbing her arm. "Let's get you two out of the wind."

We headed into the cave, the weight of Tommy's body in my arms seeming strange as much as it was a remembered thing. He was bigger, his features slightly changed and matured. He'd lost the baby look, his legs losing their dimply knees. He was wearing a saturated disposable nappy. I removed it from him.

"I couldn't get the fire started." Jessie pointed at the crates. "There's matches and firestarters in there, but they're crumbly. I'm sorry. I had to take our clothes off. We got wet."

"Don't you be sorry." My voice shook. "Don't you *ever* be sorry."

"I had to go to the toilet, and I took Tommy with me. I couldn't leave him." She looked behind her fearfully. "Mum is—"

"I know," I told her. "Don't worry. The police are on the island. They're with your mum now."

I heard her panting quietly in relief then, and it broke my heart.

The fire was never going to start. Everything was too damp. It was a wonder she'd even got a spark out of the pile she'd made.

Tommy twisted his head to stare up at me, a hint of doubt in his brown eyes. Pria had had him for the last six months. I needed to give him time to know me again. And this time, I'd be different.

"Where's Luke," I asked Jessie in a gentle tone. "What happened?"

She drew her knees up to her chest, her eyes grown distant. "He took Tommy and me onto the yacht. To call for help on the radio. And . . . to get away from my mother. She tried to stop us, but Luke pushed her, and she fell. What we didn't know is that she'd already wrecked everything when we first got to the island. She never wanted us to leave. She'd even ripped the lifejackets on the dinghy. But Mr Basko said it was just a short trip to the yacht, and so he took us. When we got onto the yacht, we found out the rest of what Mum did."

I hugged her, brushing wet hair back from her face.

"She smashed the radio," Jessie told me. "And untied and cut the sails. The storm got a lot worse. Mr Basko said we had to go back to shore. It wasn't safe. There was an extra set of lifejackets in the yacht and he put them on us. He was about to put Tommy and me back on the dinghy. I was holding Tommy while he got it ready. Then the sail swung around and hit us. We all fell into the water."

"*No* . . ." I breathed. The visual was too much to bear. Pria hadn't been lying about seeing them all fall out of the yacht.

Jessie chewed her lip, her expression tense and afraid. "It was freezing. Mr Basko must have got knocked out by the sail, because he just floated away. I didn't see him again. The waves were *scary*. I pushed Tommy to the dinghy. I couldn't get him in. So I held him up as far as I could and shouted at him to crawl in. He did it. Then I climbed in. The yacht was filling with water, and I was worried that if it went down, it'd pull us down too. I found a knife on the dinghy, and I cut the rope. I tried to paddle the boat in, but I wasn't strong enough to lift the paddles. The ocean took us to the other side of the island. The waves dumped the dinghy onto the rocks. I jumped out with Tommy. The boat took off again. I got our life jackets off and brought Tommy up here. I wanted to take him back to the house, but I couldn't. *I couldn't.* Because Mum—" Her eyes shone wetly. "So I looked for somewhere to hide."

"You were brave, Jessie," I told her. "So very brave. What you did—"

I could barely comprehend it. I was holding Tommy in my arms, flesh-and-blood Tommy, not a *dream Tommy.* I'd almost lost him for a second time, only I hadn't known it. While we'd been sailing to the island, Jessie and Tommy had been fighting for their lives.

What had happened to Luke? If he was unconscious and out in an ocean in a wild storm, he couldn't survive it. I prayed he'd woken, that the police rescue boat would find him quickly. For Tommy. I didn't know yet if it was for me, too. My feelings towards Luke were numb, broken. And I hated him for bringing the children here.

I looked over my shoulder at the crunch of footsteps on the rocks and palm fronds.

Bernice wiped her wet eyes. I'd never seen her cry. But then, I'd shut her out of my life all these years. I hadn't seen it because I hadn't been there to see it.

Distant shouts carried on the wind.

The police were almost here.

52. PHOEBE

Thursday

PRIA STOOD ON THE BEACH, her clothing still damp, the wind whipping her hair every which way.

Two officers stood by her, waiting for the police boat that was coming to collect her. She didn't move an inch, as if she'd become a fixture of the island itself. I guessed the island had formed part of her over the past few months, when she'd been dreaming up her plan to take Tommy and Luke away from me, and then all the months after that when she was setting her traps. In her mind the island represented a new life, her end game.

I pulled the blanket that the police had given me around myself, heading across a sandy beach that had been scuffed by many feet. Tommy's tiny feet had touched this sand, too.

Everyone else was already on the boat that would take us back to the mainland. Luke was on there, too. They'd found him far, far out, his face blue. In his life jacket—*thank God for the life jacket*—fully conscious but exhausted by the intense cold and his failed attempts to swim back and find Tommy and Jessie in the water. He hadn't known they'd made it out. The rescuers had dried and wrapped him in a thermal blanket after they first found him. He'd been suffering cold exposure, but he'd recovered well. Luke had always been what my mother called an iceberg—in winter heading down for swims in the outdoor Olympic pool near Luna Park.

I had one last thing to say to Pria.

Pria bent her head slightly as I approached, her lips whitening as she pressed them hard into a thin line.

I stopped dead in front of her. "Did you want to kill me?" I said, keeping my voice steady. "When you cut the stairs, were you trying to kill me?"

The police officers glanced at each other, then lifted their chins and turned back to the ocean.

Pria didn't answer, not that I'd expected her to. I'd just needed to say it. We'd been friends since we were nine years old. My mind was still fighting against this new perception of her, all the things she'd kept hidden from me.

I hunched my shoulders against the icy wind. Pria didn't even seem to be feeling the cold, despite being soaked to the skin.

"I just remembered something," I told her. "That day at number 29 was the last time we ever played *The Moose*. It was your idea. You shuffled the names and handed them out. I was you and you were me. You made sure of that. You were me from that day on, weren't you? You never stopped playing the game."

"I wasn't playing a game."

"You took my son away from me, Pria. You kept him and left me in torment."

"I rescued him. And I rescued Luke. Luke should always have been with me. I loved him better than you."

"They didn't need rescuing." My voice lost its conviction.

In all truth, I couldn't say for sure what would have happened to Tommy had Pria not stolen him away. My rage back then had terrified even *me*. Despite the terrible things Pria did, I couldn't say for sure that she hadn't actually saved Tommy. And was she right about Luke? Her love wasn't a healthy kind of love, but in some twisted way, maybe she did love him more than I was capable of.

"I know why you're wet," I said. "You went in the water after they fell from the yacht, didn't you?"

She nodded vacantly. "The waves were too high. I got driven back. And then I couldn't see any of them. I didn't mean for any of them to die. They were supposed to come back on the dinghy."

Pain grew hard inside me. "They almost did die out there. I can't forgive any of the things you did. I never will."

I turned away from her then.

As I entered the yacht, I looked for Luke first, because I knew he had Tommy. He was sitting on a bench seat, a woollen blanket around his shoulders, facing away from the island and away from Pria, his head down, his arms around Tommy in that protective way that men held their children—the gentleness of their large bodies accentuating their masculinity.

Jessie stood with Bernice at the railing, looking out at Pria's *Ab ovo*. Walking up to Jessie from behind, I slipped my arms around her, wanting to protect her from the sight of her mother being left behind on the island, trying to urge her away. But when I caught the expression on her small, cold-pinched face, I saw something that I could only describe as *release*. The usual quick, nervous look was gone from Jessie's eyes. What I'd always thought was Jessie was not really Jessie.

I didn't know what she'd been through being Pria's daughter. And I didn't know why I hadn't noticed that things weren't right. In retrospect, there'd been signs. But I'd missed them all. I'd lived on the same street for almost the past three years, too caught up in my own life to see what was happening around me. Silently, I made a promise to Jessie that I'd be there for her now.

Jessie had been shy when the police had praised her for saving not only her own life, but Tommy's also. The boat and the relative warmth of the cave had prevented them from becoming hypothermic. I owed her everything.

Bernice, holding the boat's rails, glanced at me. The storm had died, the intensity of it showing on her face. Her skin was not the type to deal with extreme weather well. Her cheeks were dry and scaly, her lips almost blistered. We all had a touch of exposure, but Bernice had fared the worst. A few minutes ago, Detective Yarris told her it would be best for her to get out of the elements, but Bernice had refused. As I watched her now, she raised her face to the sky, letting the breeze stream past her. It seemed she'd become a vacuum, scooping up everything: the salty air, the restless ocean, Pria-on-the-island. She shot me a brief smile, and I smiled back, nodding. I was sure of one thing. The daughter that had left Mrs Wick's house last night was not the same daughter that would be returning today.

Trent Gilroy approached me somewhat sheepishly. In the rush to organise the flight here, he'd forgotten to call Nan. He put his phone on speaker and dialled. Nan answered, her voice strained thin with apprehension. She and Mrs Wick were together at Nan's house. Bernice crept across to listen.

I could imagine Nan and Mrs Wick huddled together in Nan's tiny living room, watching the news for updates. Apparently, so far, the media knew nothing except of my escape from Greensthorne and that the police had found Bernice and me breaking into Pria's house and had brought us into the station. He gave them a brief overview of what had happened with Bernice and me over the past few hours. And he told Nan we had Tommy.

Their cries and screams of disbelief and joy had fresh tears stinging my eyes.

When the conversation ended and he'd put his phone away again, Trent locked eyes with me, exhaling uneasily, as though he had a lot to say but couldn't find a beginning point.

"It's okay," I told him. "I've got Tommy back."

I understood he'd done what he had to do, with the information he had to go on. I didn't hold anything against him.

But right now, my focus wasn't on providing a salve for his conscience.

"I think Bernice might have something to tell you," I said carefully, meeting Bernice's eyes.

At first, her expression froze. But then she drew in an audible breath and gave a nod.

"There'll be lots to go over in the coming days," said Trent. "We'll do it all at the station, where we can get official statements."

"This isn't about Tommy," I told him. "It's about something that happened a long time ago. The after-effects of which gave me the wrong impression of Bernice. Because I didn't know what happened."

With a deep frown, Trent turned to Bernice.

I could see that it was taking all of Bernice's strength as she began. "It's about Luke's father. And house number 29 . . . ."

Excusing myself, I headed over to the other side of the boat, to where Luke was sitting. I wanted to give her the space to tell her story without me there listening. I'd been one of the people who'd added to her pain all these years.

I'd asked Jessie to come with me, but she wanted to stay where she was, watching the island. I could see the conflict on her face as she kept her eyes fixed on her mother. Perhaps, mixed with her love for her mother was a desperate desire to be certain that she was really getting away from her.

Luke was reluctant to give Tommy up when I reached for him. Partly, I guessed, because he'd fallen into the trap laid by the person who abducted Tommy, and now he wanted to be Tommy's human shield.

But I insisted, taking Tommy's tiny blanket-wrapped body into my arms.

"Boat," Tommy told me excitedly, pointing.

It was the first thing I'd heard him say.

"Yes," I cried, trying to steady my voice and failing badly. "This is a *big* boat."

"Phoebe . . ." Luke's eyes swept over Tommy and me. "I didn't know. I deserve how you feel about me. But I didn't know."

"Jessie told the police everything. Yes, you didn't know. But you didn't have to come *here*."

"I'll never forgive myself for that mistake."

Tommy held my face between his hands, taking my eyes away from Luke. This had been a typical Tommy gesture when he'd wanted someone's attention. It surprised me that he still did this. Somehow, I'd expected that all the things that used to be *Tommy* would be different now.

I kissed his warm cheek, inhaling the scent of his skin. I could feel the connection between Tommy and me—physical, visceral. He was the being that had once been inside me, part of my body, a heart beating under mine.

The wind careening into the boat made me uneasy. As though it could sweep Tommy from my arms and take him. There was far, far too much sea and sky. The clouds scudded too fast across the horizons.

"I'm taking Tommy inside," I told Luke.

He sighed, nodding, then bent low over his knees, his head in his hands. I could guess that the storm hadn't yet eroded in his mind.

I headed into the covered area of the boat. Seating myself on the bench seat, I held Tommy close against me, one hand stroking his newly flaxen head. From here, I had a filtered view of the island.

I vowed never to let Tommy out of my sight again—Jessie either, if I was allowed to keep her. Maybe I'd move to a country town where there weren't too many people.

And I'd watch Tommy out in the garden with his beloved caterpillars and snails. He'd spent a long time in Pria's trap, unable to see the insects and dig in the dirt and run his trucks over stones.

Nan would come to my new house, too. Getting her there would be like breaking in a wild horse, but once she'd settled into country life, she'd surely love it. Not that she'd ever admit it.

Luke wouldn't fit there. Not Luke with his big dreams and his big life. And I didn't even know whether Luke fit with *me* anymore. Did Luke and I make sense together?

Flynn wouldn't fit there in my country house either. Flynn was a traveller in life. He couldn't be held to one place too long. Back when we were a couple, it was understood that we were going to be free spirits. Adventurers. No children.

Six months ago, both of us had wilfully forgotten that. I remembered now what I'd told him that day over the phone, at the moment Tommy had gone missing. I'd told him *yes*. I'd planned to pack up Tommy and myself and go live with Flynn in London. It was a way out of the consuming depression and bleakness that had coloured my days.

But I couldn't figure now why I'd agreed to such a thing. (I guessed that I was still holding the phone when I was searching for Tommy down at the harbour, and I'd dropped it in the water without noticing. Flynn, once he'd heard in the news what had happened with Tommy, must have known I wasn't coming. He never did make contact again.)

I'd played such a terrible game, from Tommy's first kick in my belly, making myself believe I could be who I wasn't. Pretending and pretending and pretending until there was nothing left of me. And then pretending again with Flynn that we could pick up where we'd left off.

If I didn't know who Phoebe Basko was, I knew even less about Phoebe Vance.

None of that mattered now, though. Tommy was back, and he was going to expand into every empty space in my life.

The distance between the boat and the island grew too great to be able to see more than a faint image of Pria, until she disappeared completely from view.

53.   PHOEBE

Six months later

TOMMY PUFFED UP HIS CHEEKS AND blew out the three candles on his cake. Nan and Mrs Wick busied themselves giving out slices of cake to the guests.

Jessie and a friend from her new school collected slices of cake, then walked down the hall to Jessie's bedroom, giggling about ten-year-old girl things.

I paused after I snapped a photo of Tommy, glancing out the window beyond his laughing, cake-smeared face. Green hills rolled away to a small village, the air saturated with yellow summer sunshine.

I'd bought this new house after Luke and I had sold our house on Southern Sails Street. The house was located an hour north of Sydney, on the coast.

I'd returned to my Southern Sails house with Luke after that terrifying day at Pria's island. Both Luke and I had wanted Tommy to return to his own house and his own bedroom. Tommy's reaction had been shock and joy at seeing his home again. I couldn't give him back all the things I'd destroyed, but he still had some things, including his beloved train tracks.

But I'd known from the start that I couldn't stay there long: I didn't want to stay there. We put the house on the market after the first three months and it'd sold almost immediately, at auction.

After selling my house, I couldn't have stayed with Nan even if I'd wanted to. Her home, and all the rest of the terrace houses on Southern Sails Street had been demolished months ago. They were all gone now. All the people gone.

I was glad that house number 29 had been torn down, but a part of me also felt the terror of what might have happened if it had been demolished six months earlier. I would have never found the boat from the nightlight. Sass would have never made the connection that the boat wasn't from Tommy's nightlight. Sass wouldn't have rescued me from Greensthorne and she, Bernice and I wouldn't have shared the discoveries that led to Pria's island. If no one had found out about Pria's island in time, Luke could have drifted around in the cold winter ocean of the Bass Strait until he died of exposure. Jessie and Tommy would have been left alone and defenceless on the island—with an unstable woman who was capable of carrying out terrible things. I thought of what she'd done to the cats that she'd imagined hadn't loved her enough and I couldn't stop a shiver from travelling down my bare arms.

Pria was in jail now, awaiting trial. Every time I'd seen her face on the TV, her expression had been a mix of cold detachment and bewilderment. The court had given me custody of Jessie. Her father, Jake, had returned from New Zealand when he'd heard what happened, willing to take her, but Jessie didn't even know him. He'd left Pria when she was pregnant with Jessie. We learned then what we didn't know. That Pria had made Jake's life hell, alternately being spitefully jealous of every woman he spoke to and telling him he'd never be half the man that Luke was. Jake promised he'd be in Jessie's life now. I hadn't allowed him to take her away anywhere with him yet, though. He seemed nice, but I remained cautious.

Detectives Gilroy, Yarris and Haleemi hadn't made me come into the station to give my statements. They understood that I was suffering anxiety due to the hours I'd spent there being told I'd written the letters and then that I was under suspicion of harming Tommy. They came to Luke and me at our house. Detective Gilroy got down on the floor and played trains with Tommy. He'd never met him, of course, before the day we found him. He half let it slip to me that he'd thought Tommy was dead during the six months that he was gone. I didn't blame him for that. In my own mind, Tommy had been both dead and alive; a paradox that had almost destroyed me.

Nan didn't come with me to live at my new house, despite my urging. She'd said she couldn't leave Sydney. It'd been part of her for too long. Nan and Mrs Wick went into a retirement home together in North Sydney. They had been good friends as children, back in the 1940s. I'd sold my story of the search for Tommy to the media so that I could raise the money for Nan and Mrs Wick to go and live in a nice retirement home. A TV station paid me an enormous amount of money and the story made international headlines. The media had used me and so I figured it was a kind of justice to use *them* in return.

All of the elderly residents suffered when they had to leave their homes. But I think it was Bernice who suffered most of all. All of her carefully collected treasures were taken away from her. She had no money to put them into storage. I offered to pay, but she declined, saying I'd already done enough for her mother. She surprised everyone by taking off to travel the world as a yacht deckhand. Earlier today, Mrs Wick had shown me the latest photographs Bernice had sent her — pictures of sea and sky and exotic ports. Bernice said she would come back when her court case began.

Luke had refused to speak to his father since he'd learned about what he'd done to Bernice. Luke's father was going to plead *not guilty*, but I prayed that the truth would come out in the court room. Luke's mother was sticking firmly by her husband, and Luke was barely speaking to her either.

Luke was renting an apartment in the city these days. Still working hard at his real estate business, coming up to see Tommy every second weekend. I was still unable to reconcile my feelings for him. I still loved him, but I didn't know if I *liked* him. And worse, he'd kept secrets from me — about seeing Pria. Had he always kept secrets from me? When I thought back, to the days when he'd first turned up in London and how he'd swept me away so easily, I couldn't understand it. It almost seemed like he'd slipped past me, into my life. In the years afterwards, Luke had tried hard to shape me into the wife he wanted. Flynn had blinded me, too, in his own way. He'd sold me a picture of the incredible future we'd have together, then he'd pulled the rug from under me. I'd been stupid enough to buy that picture twice.

Luke was here today, standing awkwardly by himself, eating a piece of cake he was obviously not enjoying. Luke wasn't fond of cake. Especially not a children's cake with blue frosting and sugar frogs on it. (Tommy had asked for a cake that looked like frogs in a pond.)

Kate's twins skipped up to me, their eyes and cheeks bright with excitement and sugary party food. "Can we take Tommy outside to play?" Orianthe asked.

"Sure," I told her, glancing up to exchange smiles with Kate and Elliot.

Kate and I had made up a few days after I'd returned from Pria's island. She'd cried her eyes out and she'd been certain the friendship was over. But it would have been stupid of me to hold anything against her. I imagined I would have acted the same as she had, had I been in her position.

Sass gave me a sideways hug as she, Kate, Elliot and I watched the kids run outside, Orianthe and Otto pulling Tommy along. Sass had always been big on hugs, but she was especially grabby with Tommy and me these days, like she was scared she was going to lose us again.

Sass's phone buzzed then, and she went off to answer a call. The TV network that she worked for had recently asked if she'd run her own home renovation show for them. Up to now, she'd been one of the organisers of their shows, never in front of the camera. I could tell that this was the call where they were asking for her decision. I could hear the nervousness in her voice.

"Phoebe!" I turned to see Dr Leona Moran. "Sorry I'm running late. Oh damn, I missed the cake."

"We saved a piece for you." I smiled at her. She'd been making the drive from the city up to the Central Coast every second Saturday for six months now. On her own time. Unpaid.

She grabbed the plate from the table and took a bite of the cake. "Yummy. Did you make it?"

I nodded. "I'm not much good at making cakes, but I tried."

"It's lovely. Come and walk with me outside," she said. "I can only be here for a short time today. I've got to go to a family thing tonight."

I stepped away with her, through the glass bi-fold doors. Tommy, Orianthe and Otto were rolling on the grass. Luke walked outside with Elliot, glancing across at me.

"Tommy's getting so big" Leona said, flicking cake crumbs away from the side of her face.

"He got to three so fast," I said. "Too fast. I missed so much of his second year. One minute I had a little baby and now suddenly I've got a pre-schooler." I watched Tommy, doing all the things that had been denied to him in the months he was with Pria, locked away in a single room.

She studied my face almost too closely. "Phoebe, you know what we were talking about last time—"

"I know. I'm just not ready to talk about that stuff. Especially not today."

"Yes, of course. It's Tommy's birthday. It's just that I'll be going away on my annual leave tomorrow and I need to know you'll be okay. I'll be in Europe for a month."

"Enjoy yourself. Everything's good here."

She smiled as Tommy jumped like a frog down the slope and tumbled into a roll, Orianthe and Otto copying him. But then her expression pulled tight. "Phoebe, it feels to me that you're not okay."

I felt annoyed. "How am I not okay? I bought a fantastic house in a beautiful area. Jessie and Tommy are happy. Everything's great."

"Is it?"

I looked away. "Yes."

"I'm just . . . sensing something when we talk. You've been through an enormous set of upheaval and changes. I'll be honest and say that some things are worrying me. I can't put a finger on it. But I know. I just . . . *know*."

Putting a bright smile on my face, I took her empty plate. "Would you like a tea or coffee?"

For a moment, she looked startled, but then she closed her eyes, sighing and nodding. "Yes, I'd love a cup of tea."

I made my way inside to the kitchen to put the kettle on.

A knock came at the door and when I answered it, my neighbour Jocelyn was standing there with her young son. I'd invited them to the party today. She seemed a little out-of-breath. "Sorry, Phoebe, I got caught up. My sister's in a bit of trouble. She drove here from Sydney this morning." She lowered her voice. "Had to get away from her boyfriend in a hurry. I never liked him. She's going to be staying with me for a couple of months until she gets herself sorted. Hope it's okay that I brought Chrissie along with me today. I didn't want to leave her alone." She turned her head and looked over her shoulder at a girl who was standing near the end of my driveway. A girl who looked about nineteen—purple hair and Goth clothing.

A small well of panic bubbled inside me. No, it wasn't okay to bring a stranger to my house. But it was hard trying to explain that to people.

"Yes, of course," I told her, and showed them inside. "Tommy's out the back. I'll come out there in a second."

Sass and Kate were engaged in an excited conversation in the living room. I guessed that Sass had accepted her new television role. I wanted to go and congratulate her, but right now, there was something else I needed to do.

Stepping down the hall, I slipped inside the spare bedroom. The house had four bedrooms and this was the smallest. I was using it as an office. I closed the door behind me.

Up on the wall, I had a large Google Earth map of the town. I had every one of the two hundred and six houses marked, with a table of notes beside the map.

I opened one of the dozen thick folders on my desk. I made a new entry:

Chrissie—Jocelyn's sister (find out her last name and where she was living). Blonde hair, dyed purple. Blue eyes. She looks upset, but guarded.

I kept notes on everyone in town. I knew their names and where they went each day and what they did for a living, even if I'd never met them. From my yard, I could see everyone's houses and the local school. Everything like a grid, securely snapped into place.

I kept watch over everything. Kept count.

There were lots of ways to steal a person away. You could take them away physically. You could blind them with your love. You could bring them in from the desert and show them a glittering, breathless future. You could reshape them with cutting tools and scrapers and new layers, thinly bridging the gouges and filling in the cracks with fool's gold.

You slipped straight past me, Pria. You took my child and I didn't know it.

No one would ever get past me again. Not in any of the ways that it was possible to steal a person.

I would spend my days here, now, in this town where I could see everything.

Keeping watch.

ABOUT

THE GAME YOU PLAYED is Anni Taylor's debut thriller novel.
You can find her online at: **http://annitaylor.me**
Questions for book club discussion at the website above.

CREDITS

Tim Carter for his cover design.

My first readers, for their much appreciated time and effort in reading
the first draft and giving valuable feedback:
Brenda Telford, Katie Boettcher, Linda Gonzales, Kira Mattox,
Lena May and Carolyn Scott.

Cover and title page images used from:
Dreamstime.com, Unsplash.com, MoonGlowLilly, DemoncherryStock,
Rachel Bostwick.

NOTE

Is *Southern Sails Street* a real street?
No, it's fictional. The suburb that the characters of **THE GAME YOU
PLAYED** live in is never given a name in the book. But the fictional
suburb is loosely based on Millers Point, Sydney. All of the historical
facts are real—such as the terrace houses having been built by the
government's Maritime Services Board, the decades of the Bubonic
Plague, and one end of the massive Sydney Harbour Bridge having
been built in that location.
The Maritime terrace housing was taken over by government housing
in 1985. In recent years, the residents (many of whom have families that
had lived there for generations) did have to leave their homes (the land
being sold to developers). This has been happening for a while now,
and the details in the book about the timing (including one side of the
street being flattened before the other) are not accurate and are used for
dramatic purposes only.

34100844R00239

Made in the USA
Middletown, DE
08 August 2016